I JUST WANT ~~not~~ ~~Martha~~
HOW MUCH ~~I LOVE YOU,~~ . . .

but if anything happens to me, I want you to know that
I take the memories of you with me: Amanda coming
out to the workshed in Lockwood, Amanda seducing
me with Christmas—"

"Seducing? Lincoln Garner!"

"Amanda the day we cut down the Christmas tree near
the canal, Amanda shaving my beard and feeding me
those little meringue things . . ."

"Angel Gifts. Lincoln, I too look back, and yet I can't
bear to, now. We've got to look ahead."

"Yes. Yes, we will . . ."

He kissed her again. She seemed to unfurl like a flower
for him, her eyes opening to watch him, her body curving against his again. He would cherish and savor this
moment forever. . . .

Promises to Keep

Promises to Keep

BY

KAREN HARPER

A SIGNET BOOK

SIGNET
Published by the Penguin Group
Penguin Books USA Inc., 375 Hudson Street,
New York, New York 10014, U.S.A.
Penguin Books Ltd, 27 Wrights Lane,
London W8 5TZ, England
Penguin Books Australia Ltd, Ringwood,
Victoria, Australia
Penguin Books Canada Ltd, 10 Alcorn Avenue,
Toronto, Ontario, Canada M4V 3B2
Penguin Books (N.Z.) Ltd, 182–190 Wairau Road,
Auckland 10, New Zealand

Penguin Books Ltd, Registered Offices:
Harmondsworth, Middlesex, England

First published by Signet, an imprint of Dutton Signet,
a division of Penguin Books USA Inc.

First Printing, November, 1994
10 9 8 7 6 5 4 3 2 1

To my editor, Hilary Ross,
for her continued
support and encouragement

It Came upon the Midnight Clear

And ye, beneath life's crushing load,
Whose forms are bending low,
Who toil along the climbing way
With painful steps and slow,
Look now! for glad and golden hours
Come swiftly on the wing:
O rest beside the weary road,
And hear the angels sing.

—Nineteenth-century Christmas carol
by Edmund H. Sears

Chapter
One

❄

Amanda's Apricot Quick Bread

Soak 1 cup dried apricots for 30 minutes in warm water. Drain and cut in fourths.

Mix 1 cup sugar, 2 tablespoons butter, 1 egg.

Add ¼ cup water and ½ cup orange juice.

Sift 2 cups flour, 2 teaspoons baking powder, ¼ teaspoons baking soda, and 1 teaspoon salt.

Mix all of the above together, stirring in ½ cup walnuts (optional) and apricots.

Pour in greased loaf pan and let stand 20 minutes.

Bake in 350-degree oven for 1 hour. To be sure it is done in center, insert skewer or knife and have it come out clean.

Makes 1 loaf.

---

*Quick breads don't use yeast and, therefore, they take no time to rise. They are more cake-like than yeast bread.

November 21, 1866
Lockwood, Ohio

"I hope it snows like this the day before Christmas instead of just the day before Thanksgiving!"

Prudence Cuddy's shrill voice and sudden entrance to the parlor startled Amanda. Her nose bumped the kerosene lamp, tilted the globe, and tinkled the cut-glass pendants she had been blowing on. Ordinarily, she would dip them in vinegar water and air dry them so they shone, but she was taking shortcuts again today.

"I hadn't even noticed the snow," Amanda admitted with a sigh. She darted a glance toward the big bay window where Prudence peered out, then flicked her feather duster over the top of the upright piano and its glass domes enshrining wax flowers. "But it's too dark to dust well, even at three in the afternoon." Still, she gave the once-over to clustered bric-a-brac on the three-tiered corner whatnot hanging on the wall.

"And too dark for my last piano student to read his music without a lamp, so I'll be sure to give you something for the extra oil," Prudence said.

"Not necessary, Pru, though you're an angel to offer," Amanda replied, as she took a match from a small brass box, struck it, and lit the lamp.

"It's you who are the angel, Amanda," the younger woman protested, pulling her fringed shawl closer. "Without your taking us in, Eliza Tuttle and I could well be out *in* that snow."

"Nonsense," Amanda insisted and strode over to rest her hands on Pru's shoulders. "It has been a help and comfort to me—especially since Matt's the way he is—to have you both here. And I don't refer only to your contribution of room and board money. Despite our—our losses, Pru, I think you and I have a great deal to be thankful for tomorrow. Including the fact that President Lincoln, God rest his soul, saw fit to make Thanksgiving a legal holiday so we can all have an extra day of rest."

As an afterthought, Amanda hurried over to dust the gilt frames of paired etchings labeled *Abraham Lincoln, The Great Emancipator* and *General William Tecumseh Sherman, Ohio Union War Hero* hanging on either side of the marble mantelpiece.

"Rest? Not you," Pru said with a shake of her head. "You work yourself to the b—"

"I'm fine. You're the one who's got to hear 'The Farmer in the Dell' for the hundredth time to make your way in the world until your widow's pension comes through. But we shall both hope Tommy Keller does not have strawberry jam on his hands for his lesson today," she concluded and ran the duster up the ivory keys.

Ignoring the mahogany backs of the worn horsehair settee and paired armchairs awaiting her attentions, Amanda returned to the bay window alcove, where hanging ivy and banked ferns suggested a fashionable conservatory. This was as close as she could come to the grand one touted in *Godey's Lady's Magazine* for its salubrious effects on the family's health. Long ago, even before the war, Amanda Lockwood Wynne had given up pining over the hand-tinted prints of Paris gowns in *Godey's*. For safety and sanity's sake again today, she had chosen to forgo her hoopskirt in favor of several petticoats, and if Eliza Tuttle or Aunt Louise fussed at her for it, she'd just ignore them.

Both Prudence and Amanda were blonde, although Amanda had more color in her hair, complexion, and gown. As was stylish, both young women pulled back their long tresses from a central part into a net at the nape of the neck, but Amanda's lush abundance of honey-hued, flyaway strands softened the severity. Pru's black bombazine emphasized her fashionably fair skin; even Amanda's faded blue flannel day dress could not make her hearty complexion pale. Arched eyebrows and huge amber eyes in Amanda's oval face seemed as animated as her gestures and movements, while the petite Pru moved deliberately and delicately. Standing beside Amanda, Pru seemed fragile bric-a-brac set next to the sturdy parlor lamp.

In shared silence now, they gazed out across the spotless snow sifting onto grass and garden, etching the shingles of houses, catching in the ruts of the street that ran to the town square. Amanda perched her hands behind her waist and, as far as possible in her loosely laced corset, stretched muscles sore from bending, fetching—and wrestling Matt into bed last night.

"The snow *is* lovely," she admitted with a sigh. "Like little lace handkerchiefs covering all the littered leaves, the dirt and dust out there. How I wish those pure flakes could fall in here on the floors and furniture and that cook-stove pipe that needs reblacking till it's all shiny and new. Well—I'll see you at supper, so just enjoy Tommy's piano lesson," she added in a teasing voice as she started out.

"I just decided I'm putting the seven of them on Christmas carols, starting today with Tommy—in honor of the snow," Pru called after her. "So it won't be 'Farmer in the Dell' that will haunt you these next weeks, Amanda Wynne, but 'Silent Night' and 'Jingle Bells' dragged out like some funeral dirge . . ."

Pru's voice trailed off in her lame attempt at humor, but Amanda shot a smile back at her from the doorway. Trying to stay cheerful, she realized, even with the holidays coming—or *because* of the holidays coming—was the biggest burden of keeping up this big house and its patchwork family of occupants.

For one moment, Amanda's steps slowed and she stood, resting her warm forehead and nose against the cool, etched window glass on the front door. As the little cloud from her nostrils swelled, then shrank, she stared down the walk that now needed sweeping. Even though Pru and Eliza would lay the table, she had to pluck the turkey and roll out pie crusts for tomorrow. For "pin money"—actually, money for necessities now—she also baked quick breads, cakes, and cookies to sell in town; especially near the holidays, that demanded so much time.

For one moment, Amanda Lockwood Wynne felt her spirits spiral down and freeze like flakes on that wide, barren veranda outside. She regretted that she had no time to enjoy the first heavy snowfall of the year. In seasons past she would have darted out in it, or urged Father to have the sleigh hitched and its red leather harness strung with bells for Dapple and Dandy to jingle along the bustle of the canal basin. Once she would have loaded the family in for a dash through the town, calling to her friends, waving to her long-lost—thank goodness—beau, Mason Rutland.

But there was no matched team of bays, no bustle at the canal basin or in the fading town anymore. No Father, no family but for dear, doddering Aunt Louise, who thought they were all still living in the past anyway—and, of course, her husband, Matt. Amanda had even sold the sleigh before last year's dismal Christmas.

But, she told herself with a decisive nod as she rubbed her face marks off the window with a corner of her apron, things would definitely be better this year. They simply *must* be! For the others, but especially for Matt, she would create a perfect Thanksgiving and keep Christmas just the way it used to be. And then she'd hope and pray it brought Matt to his senses. How desperately she wanted things to be as they were before he went away, before he and everything between them changed. For, however much she had adored her family and treasured her past, Matt had been the love of her life; she was hoping the holidays would bring him back to her.

Lost in thought, she jumped when little Tommy Keller rang the front bell and grinned gap-toothed up at her, stomping his feet to come in.

The gently rocking ride of the rails soothed the tall, thin man into a sort of stupor. He curled up tighter, dreaming of his high, soft bed at home, of his wife's warm, silky limbs against his skin. He reached for her, but only fumbled to wrap his single worn blanket closer over his bent legs. When he slitted his eyes open, he saw snow streaming by the narrowly opened door of the empty railroad car where the six of them slept, waiting for whatever small town came next between Cleveland and Toledo.

Lincoln Garner slowly stretched his long legs. Each time he woke, he felt surprise that these vagabond refugees were the only human contacts he had left. Most Americans called them tramps or hobos, since some of the runaway farm boys in the ranks of the ex-soldiers tied their gear to a hoe—hoe boys. He admired that they held to tattered shreds of male pride by working for their food, rather than begging as bums did. Yet, even living with them, he never felt part of them.

Lincoln heard the *clackety-clack* beneath their feet begin to slow its relentless rattle. He nudged Freeman with his elbow to wake him and rose to peek out at the countryside.

"We somewhere good?" the wiry Negro roused himself to ask, then sneezed so loud and long he jolted everyone else awake.

"Just another little Lake Erie town," Lincoln announced with a shrug. "Looks like name of—Sandusky," he added as he squinted out into the blowing snow at a swinging depot sign. "Better get ready to ditch."

Devil take it, he thought as he gathered his meager possessions, but that air was sharp, however soft the snow looked. Reared in the deep South, he'd seen thick snow, especially up on Laurel Mountain outside of town, but never this early or falling so fast and furious.

"Hope folks got some good old family Christian charity in their hearts near the holidays," Ten Tom put in.

At the thought of holidays, hope, and family, Lincoln just snorted and shook his head as he stuffed his blanket and loose gear in his haversack.

Ten Tom's name was short for his nickname, Tennessee Tom, for on the rails few used or knew real names. This helter-skelter group included Lucky Lester, once a riverboat gambler out of Cincinnati—before he lost an arm at Vicksburg; Cuffs, short for Fisticuffs, a big, burly lout who too often got "likkered up" and began brawls at the smallest slight; and Lincoln's longest companions, St. Moses, who had been an itinerant preacher before seeing war close up turned him bitter; and Freeman, the only other southerner Lincoln had met for weeks, an ex-slave who had fought for the Union but had no roots either north or south.

Lincoln was known as Honest Abe or the President, for his first name, which had caused him problems from ribbing to ridicule ever since the day the so-called rail-splitter Abraham Lincoln had first run for national office. No one out here, not even Freeman and Moses, knew his last name or his true story, other than that he had left Mississippi because "Satan" Sherman burned his homestead like he had so many others.

When the train slowed enough, the men made a running jump off, then scrambled across the double set of tracks away from the depot, through a line of snow-shrouded firs. They located a ravine which cut the wind and some of the snow, found the remains of other tramps' campfires, and managed to scrounge enough kindling to get a good blaze going.

"Honest Abe, you a damn fool not to be wint'rin' down in your sunny South you fought for," Lester muttered, stretching his hand out toward the heat. "Real strange, your ridin' the rails up north in the wintertime, even if your place did get burnt out."

"Being pres-ee-dent," Ten Tom said with a snicker, "guess he can make a goodwill tour of the vic-tor-yus Union, even if he has to rise from the grave to do it!"

"Don't start again," Lincoln said, barely moving his lips. Despite his black beard and mustache, he was gaunt-faced and thinner than he'd ever been, and the cold seemed to stiffen him to stone. His belly ached with continual hunger, even when he got a good meal now and then for pushing a broom or chopping wood. He hurt and hungered all over, to his very soul, for lost dreams, lost people and places. And here, this stupid ass Ten Tom was on the rails partly to avoid going home to a woman and squalling kids he just plain didn't want—and at this time of year.

"Leave Honest Abe be, or else!" Freeman ordered, throwing an armful of wood on the fire with such force that sparks flew.

"I believe, my boy," Lester said, jumping back from the fiery shower, "that sort of remark from you would've been called uppity not so long ago. And we're the ones—but for that Johnny Reb friend of yours there you've taken to stickin' up for—who fought to get you that nickname you sport so—so freely!"

"Just 'cause the fightin's over don't mean the fightin's over," Cuffs put in, balling up both big hamhock fists.

"Leave it be, all of you!" Lincoln shouted. He shouldered past Cuffs and grabbed Lester by his arm, then shoved him back disgustedly and stalked away to clear his head. His voice and vehemence startled all of them, including himself. After what had happened at home, he'd vowed he would never hit a man again, and here he'd almost slugged a one-armed one.

"Let's not waste our strength bickering in this weather," Lincoln said more quietly when the men—even the testy Cuffs—shuffled back to their tasks of getting settled. "Besides, you all can find yourself another so-called Johnny Reb to take potshots at. I'm leaving the rails for a while, going to try to find a winter job, somewhere hereabouts, instead of just—traveling on."

"Running from somethin', you mean," Lester dared.

"We're *all* running from something," Lincoln muttered and grabbed up his things, despite how he'd first planned to go tomorrow after some coffee and hardtack and a good solid sleep by a fire.

He shook hands with Moses and Freeman, steeling himself to show no emotion, so all that he'd buried deep would not resurrect itself in a flare of fury. He nodded to the others, standing there slack-mouthed in surprise; then he shouldered his haversack and did not look back. Sandusky might be only two train tracks wide, but he wanted a place smaller than that to hide out and get his bearings for the first time in the three months he'd been on the run. He wanted a place one track wide, maybe even a town with no tracks, some rural burg where he could begin to build something again.

It was fast getting dark, and the snow slowed his steps. The new layers of blisters on his calloused heels where his last wool socks and stuffed newspaper had worn through hurt only as bad as the rest of him. Too soon, he felt weak and light-headed, and he stopped to scrabble in his haversack for his last bite of hardtack.

A barn where he could hunker down in the straw near the warmth of animal stalls, that was what he wanted, he thought as he chewed and forced himself to go on. A quiet, deserted place where no one would ask questions, where people were so backwoods they wouldn't recognize a deep South drawl, where no one would want to have a fancy Christmas to remind him of what he'd lost.

As he slogged on, his metal mess kit, match safe, and bayonet—for someone had stolen his sabre his first night on the rails—clinked like muffled, dissonant bells. He pulled his slouch hat down and the collar of his drab-hued, caped coat up. Hunching his shoulders, he turned away from the cut of the lake wind and set out on the road to somewhere.

Sarah Murry disembarked from the second-class passenger car of the Cleveland-to-Sandusky train, holding tightly to her five-year-old daughter Mandy's hand and to their single heavy carpetbag. She was hoping to catch a stagecoach or hire a hack to complete their journey to Lockwood, but it was beginning to look like they would need a sleigh. And it was getting dark for late afternoon. She straightened her Scotch shawl over her coat, adjusted the bonnet she'd never grown used to, and as the other passengers left the platform to be swallowed up in the snow, led Mandy inside to make inquiries of the stationmaster.

" 'Scuse me, sir, but I'm heading for Lockwood with my girl here and need to get me something to get there."

The white-haired gentleman adjusted his spectacles, tipped back his billed cap, and peered out of his cage at her and Mandy. Sarah was used to such scrutinies from her first nineteen years in slavery, but her child knew nothing of how even shades of skin, from beige to brown to black, could keep a slave in his proper place down south. The lighter the gal, the more likely she'd wait table or be a lady's maid in the big house; the darker the skin, the closer the cotton field or back door scullery, at least on Master White's plantation.

Now Mandy grinned up at the narrow-eyed man, who seemed to be so interested in their coal-dark skin, wide coffee-colored eyes, and curly hair. In the old days, many was the time Sarah had been scolded or smacked for staring back—acting impudent, Master White called it—for she was to drop her eyes and hang her head when his or the mistress's friends looked her over. Now she stared straight back.

"With this weather, won't be a thing available, 'til tomorrow," he informed them. "You just missed the daily stagecoach."

"Then I need a place here'bouts for the night."

"You from these parts?" he inquired, removing and wiping his spectacles with a big handkerchief.

"No, sir, or I'd have a place to stay the night. Just passing through to Lockwood, like I said."

Her own words "passing through" reminded her of the

other time she'd passed through here—with Mandy then too, though she'd been carrying her in her belly with hardly a swell. How she'd been chased by bounty hunters clear up into northern Ohio when she had thought she'd be safe just crossing the Ohio River—the River Jordan, they used to call it in whispers on the plantation. How she was shuttled along from place to place in danger and secrecy. And how, even though she had to flee this land until the war was won, she still thought of the country that bred her as home, scars on her back and her soul or not. But Father Abraham had freed the slaves with his blessed words, and the war had baptized them with blood—and this man's stare was really riling her right now.

"I'm afraid, ma'am, a room at the hotel will cost the likes of you too dear. And no real hope of finding some sort of boardinghouse now that's not full—with this sudden snow and—all the people trapped in town by it, I mean."

Sarah stood straight and tall, not flinching, though she did fuss a bit with her bonnet ribbons. "Then maybe the likes of us have to just sit up 'til tomorrow in the depot here—if a bit of heat from that stove's not already taken by folks *trapped* here." Still she did not look away; it was he who glanced nervously at the potbellied stove set on tiles in the middle of the wooden floor with several benches pulled near it but no one else in sight.

"Luck'ly," she went on, squeezing Mandy's hand as the girl began to squirm, "I done brought our own food 'til we reach our friend's house in Lockwood."

"Why, sure, that's fine," he said, and she felt gratified to see embarrassment stain his white, vein-webbed cheeks. "Lockwood's just a piece down the road. And when I go home for a spell, I'll see if the missus has some hot coffee to spare."

"No need," Sarah said more loftily than she intended, but she would not take charity laced with snobbish pride or pity. She plopped herself down on the bench and dug in the stuffed carpetbag for the last of the bread, cheese, and chicken she'd packed yesterday when they left Chatham, Ontario. At least this little stove beat all for belching out the heat, she thought. She only hoped they'd keep it going all night if no more trains came through.

"Mama, you said I could make an angel," Mandy said.

"What's that, honey child?"

"You know, in the snow, like at home!" Mandy pleaded and flapped her cape and hopped on her skinny legs to make her skirt balloon out.

Sarah smiled at the pride of her life but for the thousandth time wished the child looked like her lost love, Ben Blue, and not that Judas polecat Napoleon that Master had kept giving her to. But when she found Ben and he saw the child, he'd have to love her just like his own, wouldn't he?

"Oh, a snow angel," Sarah said. "You gonna get yourself all wet and cold. And I been telling you, this here country really our home now, not Canada no more."

"Then why don't that man," Mandy asked, not lowering her voice and pointing right at the watchful stationmaster, "like us?"

Sarah was surprised at the child's picking that up, however bright she showed herself with some book learning Sarah had gotten for them both. "Don't matter none," Sarah said. "*We* like us."

"And *I* like to make angels. I won't get wet or cold, Mama."

"All right, just one 'fore we eat, and we gonna have to visit the outhouse." Sarah toted the heavy carpetbag outside too, because it and the thirty-seven dollars stuck in her high-laced shoe were all they had in the world.

As she watched her daughter make an angel in a pretty patch of snow that the cinders from the trains had not stained, Sarah thought of the long road that had brought her to this spot. She saw again Ben's face; then the hopeful but burdened expressions and weary forms of those she'd loved, toiling in Natchez; and those, both black and white, who had helped her flee on that earlier railroad called "the Freedom Train" that ran "underground." And she saw again one particular white woman's kindly, concerned, then angry face, a lady who had hidden her and risked her own life the night the bounty hunters came looking for her with that slick-tongued lawyer.

"Yep, that's a mighty fine angel you done, Amanda Murry," Sarah told the girl as she brushed snow off her gray wool cape. As daylight fled, they stooped to admire the scraped place in the snow. "But then, it's good snow too, clean and bright, a'coming right down here on our new home, straight from heaven."

Amanda Wynne wiped off her floury hands when she heard the shouting outside. This apricot quick bread was not going to be done very quickly if she kept having interruptions. She glanced at Mother's sewing room clock that she'd moved down into the kitchen since she spent so much time here now; it was nearly five o'clock and almost dark. Perhaps that's why both Matt and Aunt Louise apparently had overslept, though this caterwauling could wake the dead. She grabbed her wool work shawl and the lit lantern and skidded out onto the walk to the carriage drive.

To her amazement—in this wind and snow—her elderly boarder, Eliza Tuttle, leaned shouting out her upstairs bedroom window.

"Whatever is it?" Amanda called up to her, as she ran farther from the house to see her and be seen.

"*That man* has been mocking me—pretending to serenade me beneath my window, and I'll not have it!" Eliza shouted down in her best schoolmistress voice.

Amanda knew immediately who "that man" was, for the bane of Mrs. Eliza Tuttle's sixty years was Captain Rufus Quinn. It amazed Amanda that Captain Quinn still came calling, however attractive Eliza was for her age, immaculately groomed and dressed, silver-haired and rosy-complexioned, with an ample bosom and grandmotherly appearance. Only one thing could make Eliza forget decorous demeanor, and that was Captain Quinn. He now peered around the door of the carriage house, which he had creaked open to wave at Amanda. To make things worse, the old man, as if he were taking curtain calls, stepped out from behind the swinging door and swept off his ragged captain's cap to Eliza with a dramatic flourish that sent her into new paroxysms.

His red flannel undershirt peeped from the sleeves of his worn double-breasted jacket, and his florid, once handsome face, seemed almost as colorful. His hair and beard were bushy white, and his belly hung out a bit over his wide belt. Once a dashing figure with the romantic calling of Great Lakes schooner captain, Rufus Quinn yet clung to the tatters of that bold aura—if with a slightly tipsy swagger.

"You know he's not to be lollygagging about the premises like some errant, overgrown schoolboy!" Eliza called down to Amanda. She closed the window with a bang, then scraped it open again. "And with his attentions to ardent spirits above all else, I'd not trust him in *my* carriage house, where his wretched cigars could send the place up in flames!"

"As my poor heart flames for you, even after all these years, my beautiful, ardent-spirited Eliza Marchmont!" Captain Quinn shouted.

"Poppycock! You know I referred to your love of spirits of the whiskey bottle, Rufus Quinn!"

The man's use of Eliza's maiden name, when she had been long ago wed and widowed, and her fierce prohibitionist stand set her off again. Amanda had so much to do before supper, she had a good notion just to walk back into the house and let them shout it out. But perhaps Eliza had a point about Captain Quinn's being in the carriage house with his cigars. Amanda held up a staying hand to silence the reluctant Juliet, hanging out her balcony—for *Romeo and Juliet* was Eliza's favorite Shakespearean play—and motioned Romeo Quinn to follow her into the carriage house. She hooked the lantern inside the door and faced him with her arms crossed over her chest.

"Now, Captain—"

"By thunder, such a fine figure of a woman, my Eliza, even with a few extra years clinging to her here and there," Captain Quinn said with a sigh. He rocked back on his heels against a stall and laced his fingers over his rotund middle, looking quite pleased with himself.

"Captain, you know how it riles her when you come calling—and in such public fashion."

"No other way to arouse her emotions, as she won't receive me, and we're hardly getting any younger. You just mention *that* to her tonight, my dear."

Amanda had never been good at scolding the old man, even when he needed it. And it had annoyed her that Eliza had insisted she would not sit at the table—especially in the house where she "paid perfectly good room and board"—if *that man* were invited in to dinner. Many a day Amanda had sneaked food to the town's most eccentric soul while he sat on the veranda or at the kitchen table. He did drink a bit too much, but he was not a bad sort. He was never a mean drunk—only a grandiose one—like now, when he reeked of liquor as sharp as cigar smoke. And who could blame him for his tendency to show up at mealtime when he had so little left but stories of his past, before the canal had silted up and trapped his ship in the basin.

"Captain, you know tomorrow is Thanksgiving," Amanda began again.

"I do and can only hope to share a bit of the bounty from the tables of my friends."

"But you know how disturbed Mrs. Tuttle gets when you have an invitation to partake at the same table."

"Always was skittish, like a coquette. Were you that way when Matt came courting, my dear? Ah, you should have seen that woman as a girl. Used to dip her pigtails in the inkwell at the rote school where she first took to all her fancy learning."

"Captain, our main table is rather full tomorrow, but if you would care to come a bit early and help me carve the turkey—I'm serving a small ham too—I would certainly give you a plate and some pie. And, before Christmas, I could try to put in a good word for you, to allow you to sit at our Christmas table. Matt would like another man there, I'm sure."

"How very kind. You know, I should never have given my affections to a coldhearted woman, but fools rush in where angels fear to tread. Turkey and ham, you say?"

"Yes. And I wondered if you'd be of a mind to help me with getting the manger scene out of the carriage house and putting it up next month for the Peace on Earth pageant, like you did when Father was alive. Then I could take that labor in exchange for other meals this winter—*if* you don't press your suit so blatantly with Mrs. Tuttle."

"Ah," he said, laying his finger beside his nose and giving a nod, "I take your point. A covert pact between us, my little Cupid."

"Captain Quinn, I am not volunteering to be a go-between for you to Mrs. Tuttle. Only to negotiate a truce for you at the dinner table, *if* I can."

"She doesn't deserve a man of my devoted nature anyway, you know. By thunder, never did. Never knew why she wed Hiram Tuttle when she could have had me. Just because, I reckon, I took a nip now and then, as seafaring men do—your father, too, you know, but he imported his spirits clear from Scotland. I don't suppose there's a tot of it left in his library drawer after all these years?"

Actually, there were several bottles—of Matt's—there that she had never touched, but she'd not tell Captain Quinn. As he rattled on, Amanda walked over to shove away one of the bales of hay which hid the life-size, skeletal manger scene against the back wall. The merest glimpse and touch of the hand-hewn, rough-wood beams brought back memories of pre-war days when Peace on Earth had evoked only thoughts of Christmas.

Ever since her parents, George and Emma Lockwood, had built this house with Grandfather Ebenezer's help, the family had presented the pageant for the town, with its first school-mistress, Eliza Marchmont Tuttle, reading the narrative. But the pageant had been held in abeyance, like so many things, during the hard war years. Now, with the neighbors' help, Amanda had decided to give it again, with its carol singing and the Christmas story. Perhaps Captain Quinn could be one of the three kings. And when Matt saw it, maybe he would recall their first holiday season together and his Christmas leave when they were so passionately happy . . .

For the first time in weeks, she knew she would cry. "I'll see you tomorrow at the back door—and no smoking in here . . ." she choked out, as she took the lantern and hurried past the old man.

Suddenly she could not bear one more moment of his dramatics that blew romantic love so out of proportion. Nor did she want to face Eliza right now, for since she—when she was still Miss Marchmont—had been Amanda's early teacher, the younger woman had trouble calling her by her first name or giving her suggestions, let alone orders like being kinder to Rufus.

Amanda tore into the house, plopped the lamp down by her unfinished bread, and ran up the back servants' stairs that she often used because they connected the second-floor hall and the kitchen. Sitting on the steps halfway up, she put her chin on her knees, wrapped her arms around her bent legs, and fought the urge to sob.

Why, she fumed, did she always have to tend to others? Didn't people know she had needs too? To be cared for. Protected. Yes, spoiled! Oh, not as in the old days when they had had servants and fine things and the town was flush with canal money. But support, attention, love—to have more help than Pru's shy concern or the church sewing circle's polite inquiries could give. To have Aunt Louise as a comfort and, above all, to have Matt back in her arms and her bed.

She sniffed hard and wiped her nose and eyes with the corner of her apron. Dinner would be late now, drat it.

Still fighting tears, she scuffed upstairs to wash her face before making certain that Aunt Louise was up and gowned for dinner. She opened the door to the second-floor hall and strained to hear Matt. Nothing. If only he would keep quiet until later—she was far enough behind now. Planning to wash her face in Aunt Louise's room so as not to disturb him, she knocked and went in. Except for being unbuttoned in back, Louise Lockwood sat dressed and bolt upright on the edge of her sewing chair, gazing out the window.

"So you've been watching the snow, Auntie," Amanda said and went over to the pitcher and basin to splash water on her face before her aunt saw her tears.

"I saw you out in it without bonnet or cloak. And with that—that big work apron on," her aunt said, pointing at it. "The maids can do that dashing about to tell folks outside to stop shouting."

Amanda welcomed the scolding, as she preferred vexation at her aunt to the self-pity that had almost swamped her composure just now. Her voice came muffled from behind the towel as she patted her face dry.

"You remember that we had to let the last maids go when the canal closed, Auntie."

"Of course, I remember. It was hard to keep all those Irish names straight anyway, as every one of them wanted to be called Mary some saint or other. But my point is, the neighbors don't have to know we let them go, and they will if you run about outside that way. The Lockwoods are the founding family of this town, and we've got to keep up standards for everyone's sake. I'm only lecturing you, dear girl, because you're motherless now—and to spare both of us your father's displeasure."

Amanda decided not to proceed into her usual litany of reality, but began instead to button her aunt up the back. She always wore old-fashioned gowns with hamhock sleeves and narrow skirts, quite the opposite of what was in vogue. It was just as well, since they had bought so few new Lockwood frocks since Amanda's wedding six years ago. Her father's older spinster sister, Louise Lockwood—Miss Louise to most of the town—had always lived with them. Sometimes it seemed that calendar and clock had stopped for Louise between Mother's and Father's deaths, before the family fortune with its foundation in stock, trading, and shipping profits drained away with the canal and Father's great mistake of keeping the railroads out of Lockwood.

One could talk about things in the past to Aunt Louise, but that was generally all. Even Matt's presence, especially now that he seldom spoke to them, often went unrecognized by Louise, although she used to think him "quite a nice young man, and clever too." Nor could Aunt Louise be convinced that the Great National Conflict had devoured many of the town's dearest sons and husbands. "Why ever would American boys need to fight each other?" she would ask. "They'd best be vigilant to fight the British, for we've had to beat the stuffings out of them twice already!"

"There you are, Auntie," Amanda said now and patted her back.

"Thank you, dear girl. I don't know what I'd do without you. Are my curls on straight and smooth?"

"Here, just a touch off," Amanda told her and straightened the dark-brown wig with center part and false curls that Louise still insisted on, however silver her real hair.

"You go to your room and fix yourself up for the cook's supper bell now," Aunt Louise said. "Just send one of the 'hail Marys' up for me when your father's back."

Amanda lit a lamp for her and then went out into the hall and downstairs. This time, as if to comfort herself with the solidity and constancy of the house, she descended the big central staircase with carved oak banister and faded floral carpet runner held in place by metal rods. In the front hallway she hung up her feather-trimmed bonnet, which had fallen off the hat tree, and straightened the umbrellas in the tall brass jar attached to the bench and full-length beveled mirror. The house always made her feel that she could control something in life—if she only kept things clean and tidy.

Lockwood House was a handsome, if faded, blend of styles and materials. New England arched dormer windows peered out from two third-floor attics through an Italianate mansard roof over a formal Federal front. Amanda's father and grandfather had just wanted a grand home that they liked—hang the proper unities of architecture! In the back attic were small servants' rooms accessible from the rear stairs and now used for storage of boarders' possessions; the front attic contained a clutter of Lockwood history and an extra, informal bedroom assembled from a hodgepodge of castoffs. It was here—and in the secret crawl space behind the upstairs linen closet—where Amanda had hidden her human charges during the days when she was the youngest female stationmaster on the Underground Railroad, sending escaped slaves north.

Outside, once pristine white paint peeled from Lockwood House like mottled skin. Even the sturdy, dark-green shutters needed scraping and healing. The L-shaped porch, which *Godey's Magazine* called a veranda, wrapped around the front and the west side, supported by ten delicate—now decaying—pillars with gingerbread decoration arched between them. Someday soon, when there was extra money or she could learn how, Amanda had long promised herself, everything would be repaired and renewed.

Inside the house, the richly decorated interior was kept much as it had been for two decades. Five bedchambers— three of them large—and two large closets lined the upstairs hall; the master bedroom had a small attached sitting room– sunporch, where Matt now slept. Downstairs, off a formal entryway and central hall, were four large, square rooms: overlooking the front lawn and Church Street were the formal parlor and library; behind them, the dining room and back parlor. The latter, where much daily living occurred, was filled higgledy-piggledy with everything from mending baskets to stereoscopic slides. At the end of the hall, the big kitchen opened onto the rear garden, with the old pump, a tiny chicken coop, and the outhouse before the line of trees and a wooded ravine that plunged down toward the canal basin.

Amanda was just ready to return to her breads and pies in the kitchen when she heard Matt's shout. Lifting her skirts, she turned and ran back upstairs. She should not have left him on his own so long; despite the early dark of the snowstorm, she should have looked in on him. But then, what if he had insisted on going out in it when she had so much to do here?

He shouted again as she dashed into their room. She fumbled for a match, turned up the lamp wick by feel, and lit it. "Matt, I'm coming! Just a moment."

As ever when she approached him, even when he was sitting downstairs in the library or the parlor, she held her breath, hoping, praying that he would turn to her and smile and speak civilly, rationally. Then the engulfing fears—his and hers—would go away.

"Matt, it's all right. It isn't the bad dream again, is it?" she crooned as she rushed to him.

She hated how she talked to him as to a child, the child they never had to make a nursery of this room. But she hated it more when she tucked him in at night and he sometimes called her "Mother." It made her feel that not only was he lost to her but she was surely lost to him as wife, helpmeet, and lover.

Now, lamplight caught his wide, distracted stare. It etched his classically handsome profile—like that marble bust in the library, the one of the ancient Greek orator Demosthenes that she had given him for their first Christmas together. Matt's cheeks were shadowed with late-day beard stubble; she didn't want him bearded, however much extra work it was for her to shave him each day. That would be as if he were hiding from her even more, as if some stranger went about in disguise in her husband's body. And his deep, ringing voice, which had always made her quake sensuously, now sounded hollow, as if the real Matt had fallen down a deep well.

"No, no noise! They're coming!" she heard him moan again, thrashing against his bonds.

"Matt, it's only me. It's Amanda. No noise, it's all right, my darling. No noise. Nice, soft, silent snow is falling, you'll see."

She unknotted the old velvet drapery ties that held him to the single bed, first feet, then arms. She had put him in here at night and for his naps after several spells had made him swing and kick at her in their big bed. He seemed to prefer the closeness of the little room.

Once freed, he lunged at her, crushed her down onto the bed, then climbed over and off her. As if she were not in the room now, he rose to urinate into his chamber pot in the corner. She scrambled off the bed and leaned back against the wall, her heart still pounding from his touch. He had not hurt her this time, but it stunned her how impersonal it had been, as if she could just be thrust aside.

Even now, when he was quiet and calm, she did not know him. He buttoned his pants—little things at least he knew—and went out of the room. She took his waistcoat and hurried after him, hoping he would sit in the kitchen with her until supper. At this moment he seemed totally undisturbed by what Dr. Mills had called his "battle nightmares." But she never quite knew what he would say or do, what might set him off, where he would wander if she didn't watch him. And most of all, she never knew anymore what he was thinking or feeling—the man who had been the most brilliant lawyer in Lockwood, her beloved husband, Lieutenant Matthew Andrew Wynne.

Chapter
Two

❄

Pioneer Pumpkin Cake

Cream ½ cup shortening and 1½ cups sugar.

Add 2 beaten egg yolks.

Sift Together 1½ cups flour, 1½ teaspoons baking powder, ½ teaspoon salt, and 1 teaspoon each cinnamon, cloves, and allspice.

Add 1 cup canned pumpkin (as for a pumpkin pie) and 1 teaspoon baking soda.

Beat everything together well with a spoon.

Pour batter into a greased and floured 8″ × 8″ baking pan.

Bake in 350-degree oven for 40 to 50 minutes.

Serve plain, iced, or with whipped cream.

※

"Drat, the gravy's got lumps even though I shook that thickening to kingdom come!" Amanda muttered, and stirred it harder with one hand while she ladled hot cranberry sauce into a dish with the other. She almost leapt from task to task to get the Thanksgiving meal on the table at two o'clock.

"This the sharpest carving knife you've got?" Captain Quinn asked, pointing the blade as if he were about to fight a duel.

"Yes, and we're not going out back to the whetstone in this cold, nor do I have time to bind up someone's wounds so be careful with that!" Amanda responded and bent back over the cast-iron cookstove.

Pru spooned the oyster dressing out of the big bird so that Captain Quinn could carve it on the central worktable. She would mash the potatoes and help dish out and carry food to the table, but Amanda was overseeing everything else. As the church bells on the town square tolled two o'clock, she knew they would be a bit late to—and with—the dinner.

Amanda had also invited Miss Vina Bowes, the schoolmistress who had succeeded Eliza, and Amanda's fellow member of the Lockwood Abolition Vigilance Committee before the war. Like Aunt Louise, Vina was a lifelong spinster. Now, at age forty, she was not likely ever to know the joys of wedlock, given the shortage of men brought about by the war. And so her "children" were her pupils, whom she strove to keep in their places with as much exacting discipline as she did each strand of hair and item of her clothing.

Eliza, who considered Vina her protégé, had laid the din-

ing room table for the six of them, then gone to sit with
Aunt Louise, Vina, and Matt in the parlor. The last time
Amanda had looked in on them, the women had been chattering, and Matt had been holding a law book, as he often
did, and staring avidly at the portraits of the martyred president and General Sherman, as if they were doing all the
talking.

Somehow, the joy of the day kept getting as lost as the potato masher that Amanda scrabbled for noisily through her
utensil drawer. She found it and smacked it on the big table
where she'd set a place for the captain. So the ham would
not get cold waiting for the turkey to be sliced, Amanda began to carve that herself, while Pru beat the potatoes.
Amanda had recently decided to have ham as well as turkey,
thinking that she could coast the rest of the week on it, but
now she was beginning to wish she'd just done the turkey.

"In the old days, used to always carve *at* table," the captain remarked, layering succulent slices of breast meat onto
the big Blue Willow platter—and putting ample pieces on
his own plate.

"As I tell Aunt Louise till the cows come home," Amanda
said, taking two muffin tins of yeast rolls out of the oven,
"this is *not* the old days. Still, that's the way Father and
Matt always did it too, and come Christmas—if we can get
you to the table—we'll carve there, Captain. This year, I
want to keep Christmas just the way we once did," she
added, blowing on fingers burned from popping the rolls out
into a napkin-covered basket. "I think it might help
Matt—to remember and get better."

"Then as soon as I'm done eating," the captain announced, "I'll be shoving off to get a good daylight gander
at the condition of that old manger in the carriage house.
Thanksgiving or not, we've got to plan for that special
Christmas. I'll show Eliza Tuttle I'm still a hard worker. Just
so she doesn't come waltzing out here while I'm partaking
of my meal and ruin everything!"

"If you keep your deck-of-the-ship captain's voice down,
she'll never discover you're here," Amanda said, hoping
he'd take the hint. "Unlike others of us," she added with a
sigh which matched that of the kettle heating water to warm
the chafing dishes, "Eliza Tuttle refuses to accept that the
kitchen might be a place for her in these different, difficult

times. Just because she was a prairie schoolteacher once and knows her books doesn't mean she can't learn a thing or two yet!"

"Then it's lucky I'm at home in the kitchen," Captain Quinn announced, "for I reckon I'd as good as starve otherwise when I win her over."

Pru's disbelieving gaze met Amanda's; Amanda only rolled her eyes. And out the two women went with the main course for the dining room table.

Sarah's confidence deflated as the little hack she'd hired bumped them closer to Lockwood on snowy, rutted country roads. They saw only one man walking the whole way, but the driver just hurried them past him. She'd had a good nerve to demand that they let the poor soul ride too, for she'd had to pay double for this so-called inter-city conveyance—and pay ahead. What did she know of a day called Thanksgiving that Mr. Lincoln had officially declared for the nation, which would cancel the holiday coach and make hacks twice the price? On Master White's plantation of Fair Oaks, you can bet people never paid a bit of attention to holidays valued in the North, and especially not one that Father Abraham liked.

"This here's Lockwood, ma'am!" the driver called to her.

Sarah poked her head through the split in the curtains that she'd been peeking through to cut the cold. Mandy had slept the whole way with her head in her mother's lap, but then Sarah could hardly expect this place to mean the same thing to the child it did to her.

"Where'd you say you wanted to be let down?" the man shouted.

"Lockwood House, not far from the town square!"

"But what street or what direction?" He slowed the vehicle along the square with its facade of wooden buildings facing each other across four streets and a big, snow-covered yard with a little gazebo in the middle.

"Don't know for certain," she called back to him. "I was only here at night before. We'll get out and find it. Can't be far, and if the family has the same last name as the town, folks are bound to know where to find them."

She climbed down and helped the drowsy Mandy to the street. At least the man clambered down to hand out her car-

petbag and touch his hand to his cap. He was obviously only
too happy to be returning home on this cold day. Feeling
fear nip at her for the first time, Sarah stood, watching the
black horse and hack disappear.

A bell in the tall church steeple just across the square
tolled half past two. The sound sent shivers up her spine.
She knew that bell. She had told the hours and half hours by
it during her two nights in the Lockwoods' attic and that secret place, before they spirited her even farther north. She
blinked back tears, for she felt the bell was a sign of welcome to her and Mandy.

"Where's all the people, Mama?"

"In warm houses, where we ought to be," she said and
lifted the carpetbag. "I think where we going is down that
street with the church over there, 'cause I recall the sound of
that sweet bell, yes I do."

Sarah stopped only to shift the carpetbag from hand to
hand as they walked on, scanning houses. Without even asking anyone, she would know that big white place when she
saw it. She had peeked at it from behind the sacks of grain
on the wagon when she'd been brought in. And, as she had
been led away in the dark down toward the river valley on
the last leg of her journey to Canada, she'd looked back at
a lone light like a beacon in the kitchen window. She just
had to know the house by day—sure, she did!

When she found it, she simply stared at how tattered and
worn it looked despite its rawboned strength. Six years ago
and in the dark it had seemed so grand to her, not a bit in
need of fixing up.

"This it, Mama, where the lady lives you done named me
for?"

"Done named you *after,* honey child. We gonna live and
work in America, we got to learn to talk good American,"
she said. Her heart was thundering. The shiny windows of
the place stared at them like giant eyes.

She marched Mandy along to the little side lane toward
the back yard. An old man with a white beard walked out
from behind the house and went into the carriage house, but
he did not see them. He looked pretty raggedy, but his round
form showed he'd been eating well—a better sign than the
peeling paint on the place. Sarah did not know who he could
be, because Miss Amanda Lockwood had said her father was

dead, and even if she was married by now, that man was far too old for her. She and Mandy went around to the back door, and she dropped her carpetbag and lifted her hand to knock.

"Why don't we go in the front, like at home—I mean back in Chatham, Mama?"

" 'Cause for right now, this the proper thing," Sarah insisted, rapping her knuckles on the wooden door. "We calling as friends, but we gonna ask for a job."

"Washing other folks' dishes like you done before?"

"Washing anything I need to wash to get us a place till I can find your daddy," Sarah said, but her usually clear voice sounded so small and the rattling knock so loud.

Nothing. She waited. As she lifted her hand to knock again, the door opened. Good Glory, Sarah thought, *she* stood there in the flesh, her deliverer that awful night she almost got took back to slavery.

"Ma'am—Miz Lockwood, it's been a real long time," she began as the woman's golden eyes got bigger, "but I hoped you might remember me. Sarah Murry, who you done helped six years ago to travel to Canada, and this here's my girl, name of Mandy."

"It's really Amanda, named after you," the girl blurted. "And don't cooking smell good in there!"

"Mandy!" Sarah said, but she and the lady just kept staring at each other.

"Sarah, of course!" the woman exclaimed. "From that dreadful night the bounty hunters dared set foot here in Lockwood. Whatever are you doing out in this snow? Come in, come in!"

Sarah and Mandy stepped inside a spacious kitchen with savory smells just hanging in the air so thick you could almost bite into them. Warmth from the open oven reached out to wrap them in a hug. The whole kitchen needed to be put to rights; evidently, that hired man had eaten here and left a mess of plates, even if they were slicked off down to the shine, Sarah thought. Might all this mean Miss Lockwood did not have a cook or a housegirl?

"Please, take your coats off. You're just in time to join us for dinner! And my name's Amanda Wynne now," Mrs. Wynne told them and bent to unbutton Mandy's cape. "What a big girl you are already! I've never had anyone named for me."

"For all you done—'specially that night—for me, and both of us, 'cause I was carrying Mandy then," Sarah said, but her tongue kept tripping over itself. She could not help but look at empty muffin pans and the waiting pies and pumpkin cake. Mingled spices and rich meat smells scraped way down into her belly and made her mouth water.

"Now you two just step over here to wash up—warm water in this copper wash-boiler—so we won't keep the others waiting in the dining room and your food gets cold. How perfect you came on Thanksgiving, Mrs. Murry—or may I call you Sarah?"

"Oh, yes, that'd be fine," she managed, but at the mention of others waiting and the dining room, she began to shake deep inside. However right it felt to be free, however determined she was to ask for a winter job here doing housework or kitchen work, it didn't seem quite right to be sweeping in like invited guests and sitting down at the main table with family and friends. But, when she tried to say that she and Mandy could just eat here like the hired man, the words would not come out. But the wash water felt so good, she wished she could swim in it. The towel was so fluffy, she could have slept on it. Exhaustion and hunger suddenly swamped her, but she felt alert and alive too as she tended to Mandy's hands and face. Finally, she found her voice again.

"I guess we look a fright after all our traveling. Fine with us to have a bit right here at this table."

"But I'm thrilled to have you as guests. I must tell you though, Sarah and Mandy, that my husband, Mr. Wynne, has not been well since the war, and doesn't say much. But don't think he wouldn't approve of your visit, for he was the one who first got me to helping needful folks flee north."

After that warm welcome, Sarah Murry would have faced even those bounty hunters or Master White's whip, iron collars, and hounds again for Mrs. Amanda Wynne. How could this white woman make one feel so to home, she marveled, when most others—even ones kindly enough—gave out with the stares and little half-hidden frowns and made you feel like you were taking handouts. And so, she stood, trembling, facing all those surprised white faces in the big house dining room while Amanda Wynne made introductions.

"Sarah and Mandy," she concluded, "we are happy to have you with us. These three empty chairs in the corners were looking kind of lonesome anyway." She bustled about, carting two of them toward the table to squeeze them in between her and the young lady, Mrs. Cuddy, who moved her things down. "Who knows, maybe there's even a third person yet to come!"

"Not Captain Quinn, I daresay," the pursy-mouth woman named Mrs. Tuttle put in, as everyone—except Mr. Wynne, who was looking at his plate—went back to their eating, even if they kept up their sideways staring.

Sarah perched rigidly on the edge of her chair, then helped Mrs. Wynne lift Mandy onto a pillowed seat next to her. "Imagine, Amanda," the prim-faced one named Miss Bowes said, "one of the fruits of our labors grown to embrace freedom right before our eyes!" Mrs. Wynne only nodded, because she was filling both their plates with food which Mrs. Cuddy passed down the table.

Sarah had never been served like this and not in such surroundings. All the pretty plates and shiny silver reminded her of the ones she'd washed for years after Master White's family ate. A picture jumped into her head: herself as a wide-eyed girl, daring to peer in a window at the big house dining room while the family sat at table, waited on by their slaves, just like Mrs. Wynne waited on her now. Then, suddenly, it was all just too much to bear.

Sarah's shoulders shook; sitting upright, with her hands clenched in her lap, she sobbed without a sound.

"Mama, what's the matter?" Mandy asked, her mouth already full of food.

Sarah only shook her head; to her dismay, tears flew off her lashes to splatter her plate and the linen tablecloth.

"Oh, dear," Mrs. Wynne said, putting her hand on Sarah's shoulder. "I should have realized how exhausted you were from your journey, but I was just so pleased to see you. Here, let's take these plates out into the kitchen to keep warm and then you can decide whether or not to rest first."

"I don't want to rest first," Mandy piped up. Sarah wanted to grab the girl down off that pillow perch and steer her out to the kitchen, but she felt frozen in place.

"Come along with your mother," Mrs. Wynne insisted and lifted both plates of food. "Sarah, I know you'll be fine after a little respite upstairs."

Sarah got to her feet in the deathly silence, nodded to the people, and went, holding Mandy's hand, down the short hall to the kitchen.

"I'm sorry, Sarah. That was very thoughtless of me to—"

"Don't you never go apologizing to me for nothing, Miz Wynne," Sarah choked out. "It's just that—it's such a change from the old days. But I reckon it's gonna be like that when all of us get to heaven—so much beauty and goodness and all poured right on us—and so glad to see the one give me my salvation . . ."

Sarah sobbed again, this time against Amanda Wynne's shoulder as the woman pulled her into her strong embrace.

When the people talking went away, Matt did too. Away from the mess tent. To the lighted officers' tent. Looking at the face he liked on the wall, the good man he thought he should know. In that gaunt, bearded face he could see reflected light.

He turned to the window. Outside, he heard a wagon and horse go by. Supplies. More troops coming closer. Quiet now, but soon, noise and colors. Battle blasts coming.

Get your guns, men. Stay in rank, and fire when ordered.

By the tree with hats, he stared at the scared soldier when he took his gun from among the others in the tall brass jar. That man did the same. Out the front door of the tent, armed, running low. Slippery snow but no blood yet.

The boys in blue laughing to be brave. We'll fight till we run, ha, ha!

Fan out and hide, men. Fire on command. Don't straggle or you'll lose the regiment.

Hard to tell friends' faces in battle. Snow. Smoke, Noise. Lost. Around trees, running. Sliding down toward the stream. Then up through trees, searching for the boys, running from Rebs. Wanting to run clear home to the warm, wise woman. Lost in trees, like to hide in a tree. Snow and cannon boom, boom, boom.

"Then we are decided," Amanda told Sarah as they sat in the last unused upstairs bedroom, to which she had led her two surprise guests after they had eaten in the kitchen. "This room will be yours, and you will help with cleaning and cooking in even trade for room and board this winter. And we will inquire and correspond with whomever we must to locate your lost husband. I can't tell you what a godsend you are to me, Sarah Murry. And I don't want you to thank me again, because *you* are helping *me*."

"But this here last room of yours is for boarders, when you say there's servants' rooms upstairs—"

"Why let this big one sit empty? Besides, you're a boarder as well as housekeeper-cook, and I can use another hand to keep an eye on Mr. Wynne ... Which reminds me, I'd best rescue the others from him. He very willingly takes afternoon naps. That's exactly what I hope you two will do, so we'll talk more later, especially about getting Mandy into school on Monday. And if you sleep right on through, I will see you for breakfast in the morning."

"I'll be down bright and early. I might have just watched most of the cooking back in Natchez while I was scrubbing up, but I know a thing or two, and I learn fast."

"I know you do, Sarah. Mandy too."

Amanda left them to get unpacked and settled. Such a shock to have the past come calling like that, and she could hardly afford to feed two extra mouths all winter. But Pru had said she would pay a bit more when her widow's pension came through after the new year. If only Matt's honor could be cleared and he could become eligible for a disability pension, it would solve all her financial woes. This winter, she intended to apply for it again, even if she did have to go through Mason Rutland to do it!

But Sarah's help around the house would be welcome. Best of all, Amanda thought, it would give her an opportunity to, as Vina Bowes had mentioned, see one of the lives she had touched so briefly blossom in freedom. It had always been important to Amanda that, once the slaves were freed, things be done to help them learn to live free. Under President Lincoln, Congress had established a Freedmen's Bureau to assist ex-slaves during Reconstruction in the South. But the new president, Andrew Johnson, was southern-born and had reorganized Lincoln's plan, letting the former Confederate States go more their own ways.

Worse, their defeat had not humbled the South nor taught

it a thing: she had read that the stubborn state of Mississippi, for example, had enacted a brutal "black code" to regulate the lives of ex-slaves so severely they might as well be back in bondage. How she'd like to get involved in fighting that, for what was abolition if it didn't lead to true freedom? But with her own problems here, she had not even written a letter of protest to Washington.

"Is Matt still in the parlor, Pru?" she called down over the banister.

"I saw him go in, but Eliza and Miss Louise must have thought I was with him after they saw Vina out," Pru admitted. "I was carrying dishes out to the kitchen and don't know where he could have gone."

They raced through the downstairs, then looked upstairs. "I wonder if he saw Captain Quinn and followed him," Amanda called down the hall to Pru.

Sarah's door opened. "Anything wrong, Miz Wynne?"

"Sorry we bothered you. My husband seems to have wandered off. He's done it before, so don't fret."

"So *you* don't fret, I'll help you look," she said and darted back inside.

Eliza opened her door down the hall. "What's going on?" she asked, then lowered her voice. "How long will those two be staying? The child might be noisy, and you know I'm a light sleeper. And why would Captain Quinn be in the carriage house after that ruckus yesterday?" she demanded, her voice rising, her arms folded over her ample breasts.

"Eliza, since you're blithering on about all that, evidently you did not overhear that we can't find Matt," Amanda said, running to her room for her wool pelisse, long gloves, and bonnet.

"Dear me," Eliza called after her, "I thought Pru was watching him! We'll find him, Amanda, just like we have before!"

By the time the women, all but Aunt Louise, assembled in the downstairs hall, Amanda had run to the carriage house and found it deserted. She had searched the basement while Pru and Eliza checked the attics.

"All right," Amanda said, trying to keep her growing panic reined in. "We know he has just come back before, but with the snow and cold, we've got to go looking. He's evidently not taken a coat or hat, though his umbrella's missing.

Pru, you search the surrounding streets with Sarah. I'll go down along the canal, as he's always had a few haunts there. And Eliza," she said as the others hurried out, "I'm going to ask you to do me a very great favor."

"Of course, Amanda."

"You know how Matt tends to follow bearded men. It's possible he followed Captain Quinn when he went home. Yes, I fed him in the kitchen because he was unwelcome at the table, Eliza. Now I'm asking you to walk uptown and make certain Matt's not with him. And please check the enclosed stairs up to Matt's old law office."

"Well, of course, I want to help . . ."

Amanda squeezed the older woman's gloved wrist. "The others don't even know which window is the captain's, to call to him without going up, and you do, so please don't argue. If Matt's not there, ask the captain to help search. If we don't find him soon, I'm going to spread the word and get the whole town out. Darkness is coming and he could freeze out there tonight. I should have been watching him better!"

"We all should have, dear Amanda. We'll find him." To Amanda's great relief, Eliza nodded and hurried out.

The canal basin and string of six locks that had once linked Lockwood to Lake Erie via the Monsey River lay unused now. The basin, looking like a lake, sported only seasonal rowboats; the locks were marshy during heavy rains and dry the rest of the time. A carding mill and a small steam sawmill remained along the once busy inland port, but the warehouses, shipyard, and taverns lay derelict in the ruin caused by the war's need of men and the rise of the railroads elsewhere.

Calling Matt's name repeatedly, Amanda ran along the once bustling towpath. She squinted to scan the basin where sleek lake schooners, some Lockwood-built, had cast off on their maiden voyages down the network of canals to the Ohio River and New Orleans or set out to New York City via the lake and Erie Canal. Many ships used to anchor here awaiting wagon loads of Ohio gold—corn and wheat— before sailing to the markets of Europe or rounding Cape Horn en route to the Orient.

The exotic treasures of these far-off places flowed back into the northern Ohio Firelands, this section of the Western

Reserve given to Connecticut settlers burned out during the American Revolution. In the 1840s and 1850s, this little ditch had brought the world to the wilderness. But where spars and sails once stood thick, Amanda now ran past only ghostly triangles of fir trees white with snow.

"Matt! Matt, are you out here?"

Nothing but the wail of wind and the echo of her voice. If it weren't a holiday, at least some workers would be here to help her. Should she look farther, get help from the neighbors, or go home to wait? She had learned the hard way that many things lost, however dear, never returned.

Keeping a sharp lookout for Matthew, Eliza Tuttle picked her way purposefully behind the brick town hall and along the back entrances of adjoining stores on the east side of the square: Loher's Barbershop and Dentistry was still open, but Benton's Dry Goods, the Family Oyster Saloon, and Roscoe's Clothing Emporium had gone bust in the crash of canal stock. Still, Mason Rutland, who had leased the row of stores to past proprietors, evidently felt he could trust Rufus Quinn to be caretaker here. The captain lived in a single room over the last store—of course, you might know, Eliza sniffed—the Cigar Store and Billiard Room.

She recalled that last summer Rufus had told her that when the leaves were on the trees, he could not see the canal locks from his room, but when "autumnal blasts undressed their limbs," he could glimpse again the scenes of his happiest days from his lofty crow's nest of a room. Amazing, she thought, that the blighter could be so poetic about the days of yore, considering how his slavery to the bottle must be pickling his once sharp brain.

She hesitated only a moment at the wretched thought of standing in this back alley, howling up to him as he had to her yesterday. But poor Amanda and Matthew needed her help. Such a tragedy to befall an intellectual, idealistic man like Matthew Wynne to come home from war *non compos mentis,* and with his honor tarnished too. Men might reclaim their place in society if they returned without an arm or a leg, but not without their wits or their reputation.

She sighed and shook her head to recall that Matthew had been her best student, even if the one in briefest attendance. A rural lad from the woods near Clear Creek whose father had not approved of "book learning," the boy had walked four miles each way to and from school in Lockwood. And that was in the worst winter months when his father couldn't make him work the fields. Many a book she'd loaned to young Matthew and thrilled to discuss the ideas therein with him. How proud she had been when he put himself through college by working as a law clerk in Oberlin before he came here to clerk for Mason Rutland.

Matthew had been the most promising public figure of Lockwood in years—since Amanda's father, really. Granted, Mason Rutland, Matthew's senior law partner, had become a well-to-do, influential man about the town and state. But people knew Matthew had left Mason in his dust—in the law courts *and* in courting the Lockwoods' only daughter.

Yes, Eliza understood full well why Matthew Wynne's hero was Abraham Lincoln, for they had both been poor, backwoods boys who pulled themselves out of poverty by their own bootstraps with quick wit and determination to protect people through the law. Matthew's sharp but homely sense of humor was another similarity. He had become an ardent abolitionist at Oberlin and, with the strong-willed Amanda, established a station of the Underground Railroad. So, like Mr. Lincoln, he had helped to free the slaves. And now, both of those fine, upstanding, self-made men were, through two tragedies of fate, gone.

Eliza picked up pieces of gravel and hurled them at the window that must surely be that of Rufus's cubbyhole. Amanda had talked her into accompanying her here to bring him a meal once last year when he had a fever, though Eliza had been convinced that, as usual, it was his rampant imbibing that ailed him. But she had not gone up the inside stairs to his room then, and she would not now—or ever! She could only thank her lucky stars that these stores were deserted so that no one would see her.

"Captain Quinn! Captain! Matthew Wynne's gone missing! Have you seen him?"

His face appeared in the window, looking every bit like that Santa Clause drawing the artist Thomas Nast had done for *Harper's Weekly* during the war. But she would nail his old hide to the wall if he tried to tease her about serenading him under his windows. She stood her ground stiffly as he scraped his window up.

"What's that? Matt missing? No, I've not see him, Mrs. Tuttle. But I'll be right down to help you look!"

"No need! I just—" she called out as the sash banged down "—wondered," she concluded to herself. She had a good notion to depart before he made it downstairs, but at least he had not mentioned a thing abut this turnabout in their positions, nor had he addressed her improperly. And, after all, she thought, as she walked around the end of the stores toward the square, his words weren't slurred, he had a good meal in him—and as vexatious as his histrionics were at times—if he just weren't smoking one of those horrid stogies, she wouldn't mind a companion for the search—in this emergency only.

She thought again of the sensitive little speech he had shared with her last summer. With a bit of rearranging, it could almost pass as something by that poor poet Shelley, who drowned young while sailing in a storm. With just a little—no, a great deal—of rearranging, Captain Rufus Quinn himself might be fashioned into something better than a blustering abuser of tobacco, the bottle, decorous speech, and civilized propriety.

"When the leaves are on the trees," she recited to herself, "I cannot see the river locks. When autumnal blasts undress their limbs, I glimpse again my happiest days . . ."

Yes, there was really rather something to that, she thought. But when Rufus ran out to join her in the search, she said, "I trust you have not been tippling again, Rufus Quinn, or I'd sooner look for poor Matthew alone! Come on, then. We're to check the stairs leading up to Rutland Suits-at-Law in case he's gone back there."

Lincoln Garner liked Lockwood the moment he saw it. He felt as if he had stepped into a Currier and Ives print of rural winter. It was quiet, with no railway tracks and few wheel or sleigh tracks in the snow. A central square balanced four major streets running past it, clearly marked by signs painted on buildings: Church, Main, Front, and River streets. Other tree- and house-lined streets neatly intersected those. The place pleased his eye and calmed his heart. It made him yearn for his home of Median, Mississippi, as it ought to be. And Lockwood was fringed by farmers' fields, where he'd

had a warm barn to sleep last night with only a horse snort-
ing and cattle snoring instead of the same from humankind.

No one was abroad, yet he'd have to approach someone
about a place to work and find a meal before he fell over in
his snowy tracks. And he'd definitely decided already that,
however backwoods this place looked, he dare not use his
real name—at least not his family name. As for his given
name, Lincoln, it just might put him in favor here in the
North.

Finally he spotted a man to ask for information, though a
strange-looking, hatless one, sprawled on his stomach under
a pine tree before a small frame house. When he squinted to
see better against the expanse of snow, he thought the man
held a rifle stretched out, sighted, and ready to shoot. Instinctively, Lincoln leaped behind a tree trunk, then got hold
of himself.

"It's a damned umbrella!" he whispered, peeking back
around the tree. Slowly, wondering if he'd found the town
eccentric or just a big boy out playing soldier, he approached
and hunkered down a ways from the man.

"Hey, there, fellow, you live hereabouts?"

The man said nothing, but crawled out and stood, without
brushing off the caked snow, holding his umbrella at ease.
Lincoln saw he was not a boy at all, but a man, perhaps in
his middle thirties. He stared straight at Lincoln, but there
was something strangely disturbed about his riveting gaze.

"I'm new in town and looking for any sort of work and a
place to stay. Your people got any odd jobs? My name's
Blake. Lincoln Blake."

"Lincoln," the man said clearly and shuffled closer. Lincoln could see now he was not dressed to be outside. He
must be some sort of town idiot. He'd actually stumbled on
someone in more dire straits than he.

"Lincoln," the man repeated. The voice was indeed that of
a full-grown man, strong and deeply resonant.

"Yes, Lincoln Blake," Lincoln said again, fingering his
beard. Suddenly he felt responsible for this man, when he
needed to be taking care of himself. "Do you have a home?"
he asked, pointing to the closest house. "Go home?"

"Lincoln, this way," the man said again, and shouldered
the umbrella as if he were standing at attention. He came
closer and took Lincoln's haversack from him, and hooked it

on his other shoulder, despite its weight. He plodded purposefully away, so Lincoln hurried after him.

"Going home?" Lincoln asked.

When the man smiled, Lincoln saw how handsome he
must have been—or was—when that furtive look left his
face. It seemed curious to think this about a man, but for one
moment, his face had seemed—almost angelic.

They cut between two houses and came out on another
street. The man led him toward the biggest house on the
block, a mansion that was a jumble of architectural styles. It
was a bit of pillared plantation house, a smattering of Vir-
ginia colonial, and a lot of New England transplanted to
Ohio, Lincoln thought. Wouldn't his classical-minded draft-
ing professors in Savannah have marveled to see it?

The man went right up on the wide covered veranda,
opened the front door and walked in. Lincoln hesitated,
knocked the snow off his soles on the bootscraper, then followed him in, quietly closing the door behind him. The man
turned right into a furniture-crowded parlor and stared at the
mantel—no, at a picture hanging beside it.

Lincoln walked closer. And there, gazing out at him,
Abraham Lincoln, pen in hand, stood ready to sign the
Emancipation Proclamation. On the other side of the hearth,
an etching of the man Lincoln Garner hated from the very
depths of his soul hung smugly in a gilded frame as if this
were a damned Union altar: General Sherman.

For one wild moment, he felt sick with repressed rage; he
fought to keep from yanking the portrait off the wall and
smashing it against the coal grate. Satan Sherman was an
Ohioan, so could fate had led him to the Sherman home?
But no, surely not. No doubt the black-bearded face—and
name—of the assassinated Union president was what this
confused man had brought him here to see.

His host didn't blink an eye, but Lincoln jolted when a
woman's voice behind him said, "Oh, Matt, thank God,
you're back!"

A tall woman in her late twenties, with butterscotch hair,
hurried toward the man, but she did not hug him or raise her
voice as Lincoln was expecting. Still, she wrung her hands
together while conflicting emotions flitted across her fine
features.

"Thank you, sir, if you had a part in bringing my husband

back home. Oh, Matt, have you been rolling in the snow?"
She brushed carefully at his hair and shoulders.

"He was hiding under a pine tree with his umbrella loaded
and ready, ma'am," Lincoln said. He could see the woman
blush, even in the wan light of the single lantern—or was
she just that flushed and dishelveled from running in search
of this poor soul? Lincoln studied her as she slowly reached
out to retrieve the umbrella from Matt's unresisting fingers.

She was slender but emanated a sturdiness of body and
spirit. He had always appreciated calm women, not ones
who fluttered and chattered. She looked fetching in her state
of dishabille, with much of her hair come loose in radiant
strands like golden ribbons the lantern light caught—an intimacy that was only a husband's right to see. And yet he
could not look away.

"An umbrella for a gun," she was saying. "He has bad
dreams about battle sometimes."

"Yes, ma'am. I guess we all do."

"Lincoln, safe now," Matt intoned and smiled at him
again.

The woman's head snapped around to really study her un-
invited guest for the first time. "Oh, I *do* see," she said.
"The beard and all. Matt has long admired Mr. Lincoln, you
see. But he seldom speaks so distinctly—anymore, and not
to strangers."

"My name is Lincoln Blake, so that misled him too."

"Yes, I guess it would. And please forgive me for not in-
troducing us properly. I am Mrs. Amanda Wynne, and this is
my husband, Matthew Wynne, who, as you can see, returned
from the war severely addled, as the town doctor puts it."

"I'm real sorry for you all."

"Thank you, but I have found being sorry does not one
whit of good, Mr. Blake. Please, won't you come out to the
kitchen with Matt and me and have a plate of food before
you head on? And where are you going, sir?"

"Actually, Miz Wynne, I'm here looking for work and a
place to put up for the winter."

"I'm afraid you've wandered into a rather bad area to find
work. We've become a backwater town since the canal
closed, I regret to say."

"Then I'll be heading on, as it's my policy not to eat without working."

'Oh, I do have some wood chopping and a few basic repairs that would last a few days—I didn't mean that," she
told him in a rush. "I just mean full day jobs are scarce as
hen's teeth around here. Oh, Pru, there you are. Matt's come
back on his own—with Mr. Blake's help. Can you tell the
others? Mr. Blake, I'd like you to meet Mrs. Prudence
Cuddy, one of my boarders."

"Pleased to make your acquaintance, Miz Cuddy," Lincoln said, noting that she was in mourning and remembering
at last to doff his hat. He silently cursed himself for living
too long with men on the rails. His mother would spin in her
grave if she thought he'd abandoned his manners, no matter
what he'd been through. He noted this Mrs. Cuddy hardly
hid her mistrust at his tattered appearance—and maybe at his
gray coat—as Mrs. Wynne had managed to do.

"I believe you are a southerner, Mr. Blake," the petite
woman said. "Amanda, he says 'Miz' just the way Sarah
does."

Lincoln stiffened. He'd met with this wary coldness before that came when northerners discovered he was a
southerner—and therefore, a Confederate, a Johnny Reb, the
enemy, even though the war was ended. He took his haversack from Matt. Besides, as placid as Mrs. Wynne remained,
he had the feeling he was making her very uncomfortable.

"Perhaps he is a southener and will tell us more about his
home sometime, Pru." She came to his defense just when he
was ready to walk out. "Every American's got to be from
somewhere. Please, Pru, can you walk uptown to rescue
Eliza before she is forced to speak at length to Captain
Quinn and never forgives me? I intend to feed Mr. Blake and
get Matt settled for the night. Right this way, Mr. Blake. I
hope you don't mind if I just set a place for you in the
kitchen. It's much warmer there, and I have so much to do
to make it presentable, so please don't judge my housekeep-
ing by the aftermath of our Thanksgiving meal."

So she could speak at length when it pleased her, he
noted. But it pleased him too, her blend of gentle command,
no-nonsense kindness, and feminine warmth. He stood for a
moment as she tugged her husband gently by his wrist so
that he would go with her down the long hall. Looking
around to admire the layout of the rooms in the first intact

house he'd been in for long months, Lincoln Garner followed her back toward the kitchen.

Lincoln felt strange, eating with Matt staring at him, but Mrs. Wynne was kind enough not to stare. She worked away at washing dishes, clinking china and pots, bustling about, making his heart yearn for his long-lost home with a woman's touch of domesticity. He tried to eat slowly, politely, but he kept shoveling down about the best ham, potatoes, gravy, and apricot bread he'd ever tasted. It scared him to realize how hollow he still felt.

She'd offered him turkey too, but this ham tasted of home to make his nostrils burn and his eyes prickle with unshed tears of memory. It was smokehouse-cured ham, though not studded with cloves or glazed with cane sugar the way he had favored once, but it was rich, hot, and wonderful. She plied him with huge hunks of both mincemeat pie and pumpkin cake with whipped sweet cream, though he could have devoured entire pies and cakes. He held the big china coffee cup between his hands to warm them as he tried to savor each strong swallow in his mouth, down his throat, and into his belly.

"I regret you're drinking the dregs of that, Mr. Blake."

"It's delicious. All of it's delicious, ma'am. I'll have to chop cords and cords of firewood to work off this feast."

She turned and smiled at him from her position over the steaming dishwater. Smiled at him with her eyes too, a sunlit amber hue even in the fairly dim light here. The effect made him downright dizzy.

"You may not have to chop all of it," she said, turning hastily back to her task when their eyes momentarily locked. "Fallen trees are thick out back, just above the canal basin, from a big windstorm that went through this autumn. And, Mr. Blake," she said more slowly, turning back to face him again with her hands dripping, "it is obvious to me that Matt likes you."

"Yes, ma'am, in his fashion, though it unsettles me if he thinks I'm Abe Lincoln back from the dead."

"I really don't think he reasons things out like that. But whatever is working the magic, I worry so that he does not get outside enough for good bodily exercise because I don't, I can't—I mean, as you witnessed tonight, he needs close watching. If it wouldn't be a bother to have him with you—though I suppose he could get in the way if you're working with an axe—"

"That would be fine, ma'am. I'll keep a good eye on him, and he won't bother me a bit."

"And if he does, just bring him right in to me. However, I am planning to take him uptown with me on an errand tomorrow to his old law office."

"He was a lawyer?"

"Yes," she said, drying her hands on the dish towel. He heard the catch in her voice; his throat went tight too. "This is not just wifely pride to tell you, sir, that Matthew Wynne was the best young lawyer in all of Huron County. He graduated from Oberlin College *magna cum laude* and won many a challenging case. I have not been able to work myself up to selling his library of law books and literary works, though I suppose he would prefer that I donate them to Oberlin. Well, enough of that. It's getting late and we shall show you to your room—in the chilly attic, I'm afraid. I hope you don't mind heights."

She smiled at her little jest as he rose from the table, then stooped to retrieve the big linen napkin that cascaded from his lap to the floor. He had turned to a barbarian, he thought. He'd forgotten it was there once he'd opened it.

"I'll be sure you have enough blankets," she went on, "but you may have to chip ice off your wash basin in the morning. And if you'll carry that hip tub and one bucket of hot water, I'll manage the other one for you."

Matt smiled when Lincoln swung his haversack back over Matt's shoulder for him to carry. Amanda led him and Matt up the front stairs with her bucket and lamp. Up the second flight of stairs to the level under the eaves of the big house, Lincoln Garner kept repeating in his mind something Amanda Wynne had said a minute ago. No, he was not afraid of heights, but he felt he trod the heights already. A good meal, a warm bed under a real roof, work awaiting him in the morning. And kindness from a Yank family who breached his mistrust and even hatred of northerners, which had festered in him so long.

"Extra blankets in here—the few left that didn't go to the troops," she told him, putting down her bucket and lamp and lifting the top of a humpbacked trunk. "Oh, sorry, the smell

of mothballs is a bit strong," she added and fanned her face
with her hand.

"Then moths won't get me either. Is this usually a servants' room, ma'am?"

He saw her smile go shallow and then stiff. "Actually, sir,
it was the place where other unfortunate southerners passing
through like yourself have spent the night. Only they were
folks who had to flee to escape their southern bondage."

Her voice for the first time was sharp-edged with defi-
ance, even anger. You might know, he thought, that he'd
been taken in by a flaming, maybe even vindictive, abolitionist. He should have realized earlier that this was not a
dream, not some heaven he had stumbled into. It was a Yank
home, and he, above all else, was still a Reb, the enemy,
even though he had never owned a slave in his life and had
refused to let his wife buy one. And after all, though he
would never dare tell this woman, he too was an unfortunate
southerner fleeing to escape bondage—or worse.

He faced her squarely, legs slightly spread, hands
clenched at his sides. "I thank you again for everything tonight, ma'am. If you all want me to leave at any time, including now, just say the word."

"My only word is good night, Mr. Blake. Come along,
Matt. Matt," she repeated a bit louder and lightly took her
husband's arm when he didn't budge.

Lincoln pointed toward the stairs; Matt went, now pulling
Mrs. Wynne along. On the top step, she turned back. She
looked a bit abashed. "Sleep well," she said and hurried
down.

But he did not sleep well that night, even as exhausted as
he felt. The hot bath and warm bed felt too good, too soft.
The floor was too steady, with no clacking roll of wheels on
track. But for the toll of church bells and erratic creak of
cold timber, it was too quiet, too safe. And it had been so
long since he had been sheltered in a house that smelled of
wood and dust—and family.

Resentment that the house stood at all, when so many
homes he had known did not, racked him. He'd reveled in
the so-called Thanksgiving meal, when many he knew went
hungry. He stared into ceiling shadows, seething with belly
bile so bitter he might never sleep again.

* * *

Once curled up in bed, Amanda took herself to task for blurting out to the stranger that she had harbored escaped slaves upstairs. Some townspeople knew it, and she was proud of it, but she admitted to herself that it was resentment of the man's southern background that had goaded her to bait him with it at the last minute. She had read reports in the *Abolitionist Gazette* of large bounties offered by slaveowners for the murder of Underground Railroad conductors. Perhaps some southerners could not forgive and were still out for revenge against those who had helped to rob them of their human "property." In a small town, one never feared to take strangers in, and yet . . .

As the church bells tolled midnight, she got up to tip and wedge a chair back under the knob of her door to the hall, then scurried back to bed.

It seemed the sheets had grown cold that fast; she pulled her feet up under her flannel nightgown and bunched the covers about her shoulders in the big bed. Through the open door to the sitting room, she heard Matt stir, moan, then his heavy breathing in slumber again. She should get up to be sure he hadn't wriggled his covers off, but when she approached him in the dark, it sometimes set him off, so she curled even tighter in a little ball and stayed put.

Why, she fumed, did she have to get "the female yearnings" tonight? Her lower belly fluttered, her breasts felt heavy, and her thighs tingled for Matt's touch when she was utterly exhausted in body and spirit after this day. She forced away remembrances of Matt's hands and mouth against her skin like wool against satin. Unless she could get him back, cured somehow, that was all gone now too.

Her mind drifted to the stranger again—Lincoln. What a name for a southerner, from Georgia, he had said, though he had been named for an ancestral home in Lincolnshire, England, generations back. He'd seemed such a unique blend of self-containment and raw need. It seemed a hunger that went deeper than appetite or ambition—she could tell by that glint in his clear blue eyes, even though his big beard and mustache hid the lower half of his face. Thank God, Matt trusted him, even if for crazy reasons. The man did not really look like the former president; Lincoln Blake's face was not so craggy nor bushy-eyebrowed, though his cheeks did have that chiseled look and lines showed he had suffered. Anyway, if things worked out, perhaps Matt would have someone else to watch over him for a little while besides her and the female boarders.

She flopped over and stared up at the ceiling. Lincoln Blake's narrow bed was just above. He might hear Matt when he shouted at night; he would know how bad things really were between them. But surely he would be moving on soon. She had no job to keep him more than a day or two, for it had been enough to take in Sarah and Mandy.

And to think, last night, even with Thanksgiving upon her, she had begun to wonder about Christmas gifts she would give. Dear Lord, she prayed, were the three new arrivals actually Christmas gifts You have delivered to my doorstep—my gold, frankincense, and myrrh? After all, her three visitors would have filled the dining table chairs for the first time in years, and the way Lincoln Blake devoured that ham made her feel she had been fated to fix it. Perhaps, after all, the Lord had not forgotten her and Matt despite their trials and had sent them some new friends to get them through this winter.

It gave her hope for facing Mason Rutland tomorrow. Even with the way he was—with the ruin of all that lay between them—perhaps the holiday spirit would touch his heart too and, for once, he would help her.

Chapter
Three

❄

Orange Christmas Cookies

Cream in big bowl, 1 cup soft butter, 2 cups sugar.

Add 2 eggs, 1 cup orange juice, and grated rind of one orange.

Add and stir in 1 cup of sour milk (add 1 tablespoon vinegar to 1 cup sweet milk).

Sift in 6 cups flour, 6 teaspoons baking powder, 1 teaspoon salt, 1 teaspoon baking soda. Beat, adding in a bit more flour if needed to make a stiff drop batter.

Drop by heaping tablespoon (or size desired) onto greased baking sheet.

Bake at 350 degrees for approximately 10 minutes. Do not let them get brown. Done when slightly firm to touch.

If frosting is desired, mix powdered sugar with a little cream and ½ teaspoon almond flavoring to right consistency to spread or dribble on each cookie. This is a light, fruity cookie which mixes well with other more heavy or ornate holiday varieties.

❄

When Amanda went downstairs to light the stove at seven the next morning, she found Mandy pretending to feed a piece of toast and jam to a cornhusk doll at the worktable and Sarah bustling about an immaculate kitchen. Coffee brewed and ham slices sizzled.

"Sarah!" was all she could manage at first. "What time did you get up to do all this?"

"Bright and early, like I said. Hope you don't mind if I took a peek at the pantry, Miz Wynne."

"No, of course not. It's your bailiwick now as well as mine. It's not too well stocked, but there are crocks and jars and drying vegetables in the basement and root cellar."

"I'm real good at stretching things, ma'am. I'm fixing to fry us some flapjacks we can have with this honey."

"Oh, I love those. We call them pancakes here. Which reminds me, I hope you'll call me Amanda like Eliza and Pru do—if we're to be friends, too."

"All right, since you put it that way, Miz Amanda."

"Not Miss Amanda. Up here, it's different from down South."

"Mm-mn, don't I know that, though I got to admit, after all this time, I sometimes wonder how things really going down there in Miz'sippi for folks I knew. Gonna ask that new hired hand of yours sometime."

"You've met Lincoln Blake?"

"Gave him some coffee when he come through this morning. Says he going to cut wood, and I told him breakfast be ready in a bit. He was real surprised to see a Negro woman in your kitchen, that's what I think. He don't say so, but I think he's from deep South Miz'sippi, 'cause he talk just like white folks in Natchez."

"He told me he's from east coast Georgia—Savannah."

"Mm-mn, guess I got ears," Sarah muttered as she flipped another pancake onto the growing stack of them under the steamed china dome.

With things in such able hands, Amanda went up to get Matt, sat him down at the table to his food, then wrapped herself in her paisley shawl and went out to fetch Lincoln Blake. She saw him appear from the trees behind the gardens, a bulging load of kindling-size wood in his arms.

"Good morning, Mr. Blake!" she called to him as he came closer to dump the wood on a knee-high pile.

"Morning, ma'am."

"By the way, if you see any good-looking pine trees about your height down there, please let me know, as we'll be needing a fresh-cut Christmas tree soon enough. Do you have Christmas trees in Savannah?"

"Unlike up here, things are in dire straits in the South these days," he said as if that answered her question. He propped one booted foot on the slanted wooden door of the root cellar.

She felt something powerful pulse between them again. It made her spine tingle and her stomach flutter. But he was the first Reb she had met in the flesh, so perhaps their unspoken animosity was to be expected. And really, what did it matter where he was from down there when he'd be moving on soon? If she were traveling south and staying in Savannah, she wasn't sure she'd be boasting about being a Yankee or from General Sherman's home state, after his victorious march through Georgia.

"Things are in bad shape here too, as you can see," she said to break the awkward silence while she picked at a piece of peeling paint beside the back door.

To her surprise he snorted. "The war wasn't fought right on your doorstep by a pack of vandals going through. No, the South won't be much for celebrating Christmas this year, Miz Wynne, nor me either. I'll cut whatever hearth and stove wood you all want, and I'm going to make a few inquiries in town about other odd jobs, but I'd like to be left clean out of Christmas."

She wanted to extend sympathy, but she could only glare back at him. He said "Christmas" as if it were a cussword, as if he could ruin all her hopes for it this year. His voice, his big, lanky body, and his face had gone as stiff as stone.

"Fine," she said. "Well, I didn't mean to make you stand out here when food's ready. Matt's eating, so won't you join him?"

He nodded tersely, scraped his feet, and pulled the door open farther than she held it indicating she should enter first. Matt looked up from his food and smiled to see Lincoln, as he never did to see her anymore. Amanda let them eat together while she set four places at the dining room table for herself and the three still upstairs. She kept her shawl on, for the wind and his words had chilled her to the bone. The man would have to go, and soon.

It broke Amanda's heart to see Matt so well dressed in what he had jokingly once called his "lawyer getup" of cutaway jacket over his fitted waistcoat, shirt with turned-down collar, and bow tie. She had even put his pocket watch on him, with its chain swagged from buttonhole to waistcoat pocket. She too had dressed carefully, with her newest steelspring crinoline, best serge gown in deep blue, and frogged fitted jacket. The feathers and ties of her brimmed bonnet flapped so hard she had to hold it on despite its hatpins through her hair. He let her take his arm as they strolled uptown against the wind.

The few people they saw waved or stopped them to remark on how well Matt looked, as if his usual haphazard attire was all that had gone wrong. As Matt stared at or nodded to them, Amanda could almost pretend things were normal once again. When she opened the door to the covered stairs to the second-story law office, he stepped inside eagerly, looking around the enclosed area. For one moment, she thrilled, for he seemed to be quite content. He even preceded her up the stairs without coaxing and appeared to read the words painted on the glass-topped door.

She knocked where it had once said in this same flowing gold script "Rutland and Wynne, Suits-at-Law," but now Mason's only name remained. His new young red-haired, law clerk opened the door for them, nodded to her, then studied Matt.

"Please come right in, Mr. and Mrs. Wynne, and Mr. Rutland will be with you directly."

The young man hung up their coats. To her disappointment, Matt seemed to show no further curiosity about the place, including his old office overlooking the back alley. The door to it stood ajar; his oak keyhole desk, conference table, and empty bookshelves sat in the darkness of drawn curtains. Would nothing lure or jolt him back to reality? she thought. Dr. Mills had said that bruised brains sometimes healed with time, that even the severest form of head-injury amnesia sometimes reversed itself. But if Matt's home, his office—and being with her—did nothing for him, dare she place so much hope in an emotional Christmas? So far, all he had really responded to was a tight-lipped, bitter Confederate who happened to share a name and a black beard with Abraham Lincoln!

As she agonized, Matt just played with his watch, clicking its engraved cover up and down. It made Amanda want to scream, but she silently tapped her foot under her skirts and waited.

And waited. Despite the promise of a prompt interview, they sat ignored for nearly a quarter hour, while Amanda's stomach twisted tighter. It was obvious to her that her former beau was not going to make this interview any easier than he had their other meetings since she had faced him in the parlor at home eight years ago to tell him she was rejecting his suit in favor of Matt's.

Anyway, she thought, trying to buck herself up, just as Captain Quinn said that Eliza had never deserved his devotion, Mason had not deserved hers either. He was her first spark, and she had fallen hard for him. But she eventually heard the rumors about his other light-o'-loves when he went back to Cleveland to visit his parents on weekends. Once, from a distance when she was picking blackberries, she had seen him walk out of the woods brushing off Nettie Groves's skirt, and even a sheltered sixteen-year-old like Miss Amanda Lockwood knew Nettie's fast reputation. Still, it took Amanda much heartache, self-censure, and confusion over Mason's golden-tongued excuses before she realized he was, as her father put it succinctly, "a bit of a rogue out to get his wild oats sown before he settles down."

But Mason Rutland's biggest miscalculation was asking

his shy, gangly junior law partner to squire his girl to the Independence Day picnic and patriotic concert. Amanda and Matt had fallen quickly in love, so it was her independence day from emotional ties to Mason too. Later, Mason married one Dorothy Spencer from Cleveland, and they had two young children, but whispers of his still sowing his oats floated about on the wind now and again.

At first, after Amanda rejected Mason, she and Matt had feared that Mason would dismiss him. Later, from the cold, callous way Mason treated him, they realized that might have been best. But Matt loved his work and helping people; if the war had not intervened, he would have begun his own practice. And Mason kept Matt on because he knew full well it was Matt who successfully argued two widely reported cases, Matt who would exhaust himself to find legal precedents and interview potential witnesses for any shred of evidence to clear his clients. It was Matt Wynne's growing reputation that was swelling their business in the final prewar days of the canal boom.

At last the wooden door to Mason's office opened, and he emerged, resplendently attired as usual, especially for a small-town lawyer. The idea of Mason Rutland with shirtsleeves rolled up was unthinkable. An auburn-haired, green-eyed man with the boyish good looks of eternal youth, he disguised the gap between his front teeth under a thick waxed mustache. But lately, as Mason approached the age of forty and continued to pursue the pleasures of life, his increasing girth, thickening jowls, and smile lines at mouth and eyes made him look almost mortal.

"Amanda—and Matt—how good to see you! Won't you please come in? Charles," he told his clerk, "here is this affidavit that must go out via telegram to New York City at once." The boy grabbed his coat and banged the door to leave the three of them alone.

As ever, Amanda noted, Mason's assessing stare slid over her, lingering on her bodice and midriff, either to appraise her form or to see if she were in a family way. She refused to acknowledge the look and lifted her brocade reticule like a shield, digging in it for her notes. Her nose wrinkled instinctively at the smell of stale cigar smoke. He did not try to shake hands with Matt, but indicated they should sit in the Windsor chairs facing his desk; across its vast, polished expanse, he sank into his deep button-tufted leather chair, which expelled a soft sigh.

"Mason, a new year is coming," she began, "and so I hope that in your capacity as Northern Ohio Pension Commissioner, you might be willing to listen again to reason about some sort of government disability pension for Matt. After all, he did help you build the firm, so I'm sure you will be magnanimous enough to help him—and me."

"Ah, who ever would have thought the last of the Lockwoods would need help?" he asked with a tight smile, leaning forward and steepling his fingers over his nose. "You are fully aware that business for the firm is hardly what it once was? Thanks, I might add, to your father's convincing the town council to 'keep those dirty, noisy railroads away, since the canals are the wave of the future'!"

"We aren't here to speak ill of the dead, Mason, but to help someone deserving who is still among the living. The point is that anyone can see Matt is disabled and broken in spirit. President Lincoln in his speech of—ah, here it is— March 4, 1865, his address at his second inaugural, clearly stated that the nation will 'care for him who has borne the battle and returned home broken in body or *broken in spirit*.'"

"I see you've become the family debater now, as well as everything else, Amanda. But you're out of your element with me. I must abide by the letter of the law. When Congress passed the Act of Levy Relief in April of that same year, it was made clear that families of those who deserted in battle were—"

"Matt did not desert! You cannot prove that!" she exploded before she realized her mistake. At her sudden shout, Matt jumped up and leapt at Mason's bookshelf and pounded on it to shudder the rows of volumes. Then he cleared the top shelf of its law books before wedging himself in the corner of the room with his eyes screwed so tightly shut he looked as if he were in bodily pain.

"Matt, Matt—it's all right. Come sit down," she urged, hurrying to him. After a few moments, fortunately, he obeyed. "Mason, I'm sorry," she said and knelt to retrieve the books.

"It only goes to show," Mason said, his voice a silky whisper that made her spine crawl as he came to stand over her so her head came to his hips, "that, despite his sorry state, he reacts guiltily to suggestions that he ran in battle."

She stood, but stepped back from him. "I believe you lawyers call that a *non sequitur*," she insisted, her voice low. "Obviously, he reacts to sudden loud voices or noises, and I should have known better."

"About a great many things," he whispered. "Besides, I find it difficult to credit your supposed financial need if you can hire a Negro kitchen girl from Canada. I believe I heard someone say you had met her before, so she knew right where to come for—more help."

Amanda gripped the books to her. She would not let Mason trap her into admitting *how* she had known Sarah, for it was he the bounty hunters had brought to her house that night looking for the girl—and the five-hundred-dollar reward for her. Some in town had guessed about Amanda's covert pre-war activities, and her closest friends knew what she did to hide "railroad passengers." But once Mason had taken his stand that the Fugitive Slave Law of 1850 must be followed to the letter to return escaped slaves to their owners—even in free Ohio, however immoral he privately admitted it was—she had lied more than once to him about harboring slaves.

So, steadying her voice, she said only, "As long as I've lived in Lockwood, it never ceases to amaze me how fast gossip travels—or how much faster it can be distorted." Fighting the urge to throw his books at him, she only dumped them on his desk and sat back down next to Matt. "Mason, I'd like to return to the business at hand, whether or not rumor has it that I have money to hire a housekeeper for my boardinghouse."

"Fine. For now," he said ominously.

"You know full well that Matt was discovered wandering out of his head, but with no apparent cuts or contusions, behind his regiment's lines after the Battle of Chickamauga," she began. "Yet it is obvious he had somehow suffered a blow to the head that gravely injured—traumatized, one book I read called it—his brain. None of this indicates that he deserted. I have numerous newspaper clippings and a letter from his commanding officer that say stragglers were often caught behind the ranks during the confusion, noise, and smoke of bat—"

"And I have two accounts from men who say he could have fled from cowardice, Amanda, quite probably before he was injured. It's always been made clear that no pensions nor stays in Soldiers' Homes are available to those who might have served dishonorably. And I think we both know the only fighting Matt has ever really favored has been in the courtroom. He detested all sorts of physical violence, and war was anathema to him."

"Yes, but he believed in the Union's cause enough to enlist right away—long before some others I could name."

"You're in no position to fling mud, Amanda. We both know Matt enlisted in his passionate fight against slavery, but I'm afraid when it came right down to the blood and guts of battle—excuse me for putting it so bluntly—he took the clever coward's way out."

"That's ludicrous and you know it. He was in previous battles and did not flee."

"And he hated it, he hated doing his duty. So he lost his nerve and patriotism when his fellow soldiers and his country really needed him."

"Mason, how can you, of all people, judge battle nerve or blood and guts when you spent the war behind a desk in the capital? Look, please," she said, gripping her hands in her lap to keep from raising them either to plead with this wretch or to pummel him, "you *knew* Matt. He was—is—an honorable man. I realize shocks in life can change men, but—"

"Yes, we do know that, don't we, Amanda? But you never gave me a second chance for a mistake I made once, did you?"

"As you said, let's not fling mud. And it was not a mistake you made *once,* I fear."

"So you do want to talk about the past? Amanda Lockwood, always so—so passionately intense, so idealistic. Shall I assume you would do anything you could to help Matt?"

She pressed her knees together and sat up straighter, afraid of what was coming next, but knowing how badly she needed this callous wretch's help. "And?" she said instead of the affirmative answer he obviously expected.

"Wouldn't you feel better if we spoke of it another time, perhaps more privately, without Matt?" he went on, leaning forward over his desk and lowering his voice again. "I have canceled a few morning appointments, but I do have others coming in and my clerk will be back soon."

"Tell me what you mean now, Mason. I cannot mislead you or sully myself to promise that I would ever consent to a more private meeting place with you."

He shrugged grandiosely. "*You* are the one who should have gone into battle, Amanda. Perhaps you will reconsider as time goes on. Now, since the pension or a place in the Soldiers' Home in Cleveland looks to be entirely out of the quest—"

"I don't want to send Matt away. If I had the pension to which Matt is justly entitled, I could better care for him myself here in Lockwood."

"But he's so volatile, probably dangerous to himself and others. You must see that. I really think I could help you in one way that would be best for Matt and free you up here—to live your own life as an attractive young woman should."

She stood. "I believe you are giving me no choice but to write my congressmen about the pension directly."

"Amanda, those are exactly the men who have seen fit to let me make the decisions for our county. I knew both Ohio senators when I served in Washington. But enough of this fencing. My suggestion is that you take Matt to Cleveland, perhaps after the holidays, if you deem it safe to keep him home that long, and see about having him admitted to the Northern Ohio Lunatic Asylum in nearby Newburgh. It would be for his own good to perhaps be cured there."

"What? Matthew Wynne is not a lunatic!" she cried before lowering her voice again.

"Look at him, Amanda. I know you're distraught about losing him, but I see it as your only reasonable option. It's unfair and unjust if you don't seek help for his damaged mental powers. For heaven's sake, he doesn't even react, no matter what I say to you. For his good *and yours,* you'd best take my advice."

"Matt's good? Mine? You obviously care for neither and just the opposite!" she cried, holding Matt's wrist, hoping he would not bolt.

"Think it over. It's a state asylum, so it won't cost much to keep him there. On the other hand, the one in Columbus is only for the indigent, if things get worse for you. Stop glaring, Amanda. I'm trying to help. I'd be willing to pull some strings to get him the good care there at the Cleveland Asylum where you could visit once in a—"

"My only real option is to never set foot near you again. Matt, come along. Matt—"

"If something should go awry with him, Amanda—say, he should hurt someone, you even—he could then be permanently committed without your permission, you know. My signature and one other is all it would take for me to come to the house—"

"Like you invaded our home with bounty hunters once," she muttered.

"Ah, now you've brought up your new servant girl again. You know, Amanda, I never could quite figure out where you stashed them, but I know they were there. Now, think about my offer, before things with Matt slip completely from your control."

He did not know it, but that last threat was her greatest fear. That Matt, their marriage, the house, her past, present, and future would be lost to her, whirled up and away in a hurricane of horrible events over which she had no control.

She hurried Matt home, furious at Mason, at the government, the war, even at poor Matt, heaven forgive her. At Eliza and Rufus, at Vina Bowes, after she'd fed them all yesterday—or at whoever had blabbed to Mason Rutland about Sarah's being a former acquaintance when everyone knew Amanda had never been down south or to Canada. She'd never forgive Mason for agreeing to issue a search warrant for her house to the bounty hunters so they could terrorize her that night; she knew he'd hoped she would beg him for his help with Matt away at war. And now she would never forgive him for this new betrayal.

The moment they were in the front door, Sarah was there with a tea tray in her hands. "Thought you two could use a warm-up with that chill out there. When I told your aunt, she said come up to her room for it," Sarah told them in a rush as Amanda unpinned her hat and coaxed Matt out of his coat.

"How thoughtful. Thank you," Amanda said, instead of screaming as she wanted. She only stabbed her hatpins through her bonnet, but she felt like running through Matt's library and clearing the shelves of books as he'd done at Mason's. She wanted to grab that umbrella Matt had thought was a gun and break windows, the chandelier in the dining room, mirrors, plates . . .

She managed to walk upstairs, holding Matt's hand, with Sarah right behind them. "Bad time, Miz—I mean, Amanda?" Sarah asked. "I was wondering if this lawyer you gone to see the same one that came—you know, that night."

"Yes, Sarah, it was," Amanda said as she opened the door to Aunt Louise's room for her. "But don't worry about it, because there's not one blessed thing the man can do about you now."

"Not even with that man from Miz'sippi in the house?" she whispered, putting her tray down on the table she had prepared. Aunt Louise sat, hands in her lap, smiling, awaiting her treat.

"Don't worry, Sarah, because Mr. Blake won't be staying long," Amanda said, suddenly wondering if it might have been Lincoln, out and about this morning looking for odd jobs, who had told someone who knew Mason about Sarah—and of Amanda's slip about hiding slaves upstairs.

Amanda urged Sarah to take tea with them, but she went back down, saying Mandy was playing in the snow outside. Amanda drank the tea and ate her own delicious orange-flavored cookies, but she hardly tasted a thing. She could not stand the silence, even though she was contributing to it. Finally, Aunt Louise said, "I rather like the new girl."

"Sarah. Good," Amanda answered and stood to look out the side window, leaning her shoulder there, feeling grateful for the chill air that emanated from it to cool her heated face.

"Not a drop of Irish blood in her," Aunt Louise was saying as Matt drank his tea and Amanda just nodded, hardly listening. Now how, she thought, could a man be admitted to a lunatic asylum, if he could sit and enjoy teatime? "The girl has a good, solid Old Testament name, not one of those saints whatever," Aunt Louise concluded.

Amanda was impressed that Sarah had made inroads into Louise Lockwood's usual prison of the past. But wouldn't an asylum, despite its name suggesting a haven away from harm, be a prison in itself? Could Matt ever be cured there?

Out the window she saw Lincoln emerge from the trees with
an axe in one hand—and a squirming Mandy under his other
arm!

"I'll be right back!" she told Matt and her aunt and ran
out into the hall. She headed toward the back stairs, rapping
on Eliza's door; she opened it with a book in her hand.

"Please, Eliza, keep an eye on Aunt Louise and Matt in
her room having tea, won't you? I've got to see to Mandy
outside."

"I hear her wailing. I told you the girl will be a prob—"

But Amanda was already thudding down the servants'
steps. When she got to the kitchen, Sarah was comforting
the sniffling child and Lincoln Blake was nowhere to be
seen.

"What happened?" Amanda demanded.

"Mr. Blake say she bothering him, getting in his way,"
Sarah said. "He yelled at her and scared her, and carted her
back up here like a sack of cotton, that's all."

"That's not all!" Amanda said. Grabbing her shawl, she
banged out the back door. Now, where had he gone so
quickly? And to think that last night she had wondered if he
might have been a gift from God to bring her help! More
like a plague of prejudice sent by Satan himself, however
many cords of wood he chopped!

She started out toward the trees, pulling her big, bouncing
skirts as close as she could. She had to slow down on the
slippery slope that, in better weather, was one of the well-
worn paths down to the canal basin.

She saw him farther down the path, axe over his shoulder,
staring up at a still-standing dead tree, grasping its trunk to
shake it as if he strangled its long throat. What a bully he
was to frighten and manhandle little Mandy like that. He
looked even taller and bigger than she had remembered, but
she did not stop.

"Mr. Blake! A word with you!"

His eyes widened, and his nostrils flared. He stared at her
so hard she felt more aware of herself than usual: her walk,
the ankles she must be flaunting, how her thighs brushed together through her long cotton drawers, the cold air that
came swirling up under her skirts as she picked her way
down the path, trying to avoid snagged skirts.

"I didn't know you all were back," he said. "Is something wrong with Matt?"

"Not with Matt. I won't have you frightening that child. Just because you can't abide her—that *is* it, isn't it? You don't even want to have her around you!"

"That's right. She's underfoot. And with this axe and falling trees ... But," he said, frowning now, "that's not what you mean, *is* it?"

"You've somehow managed to upset both Sarah and her child! Now I wonder why."

"I don't take taunting well, so spit it out, ma'am. Of course, you know *all* about me and my brutish bigotry because I'm from the South, is that it?"

"Exactly."

"Did every one of you pompous, pious northerners detest slavery enough to die for abolition? Well, did you?"

"Not quite everyone, of course. But how dare you call—"

"So I can't just assume every single Yankee wanted freedom for the slaves?"

"We are talking about you."

"Don't go judging me, lady, because you don't know me. I admit I'm not real pleased to be sleeping in your little shrine to abolition upstairs anymore than I am seeing Matt spend his time worshiping at the Union altar in your parlor. But that doesn't mean I was for slavery, even if the South's future depended on it. Never owned a slave, never would, and didn't go to war to save the institution. But never mind all that. If you're here to let me go from this job, that's your business, but don't go pinning the old darkie-hater, Simon Legree tag on me!"

"You've read *Uncle Tom's Cabin?*"

"It's a free country. Have you read *The Planter's Southern Bride,* where a southerner marries an abolitionist, which gives the other side?"

"I wouldn't read such prejudiced rubbish."

"There, you see. You know all about books you haven't read—and people you've never met."

"I *have* met you, and—"

"Look, Miz Wynne, I can't help it if Sarah thinks I talk like someone she hates down south, or I scared her girl just because I don't want her getting hurt. My own daughter," he got out before he looked down at his feet and his voice softened, "fell down an old well once, following me around—at just that age."

"I'm sorry. I didn't know."

"That's right, you didn't."

"Was she all right—your little girl?"

"That time."

"And now?"

"Did you come to tell me to move on, Miz Wynne? If so, that's your right, but I have a deal I'd like to make with you, if—that is—you're willing to bargain with a Johnny Reb from a slave state."

"I don't mean to judge, not so hastily, at least." Despite his doubtful, challenging look, she added, "What deal?"

At last he came up closer to her. She felt the nip of cold wind again when a moment ago she had felt she was burning up with embarrassment, shame, righteousness, anger, something . . .

"I take it that old shed is on Lockwood property, the one just down yonder," he said and nodded toward it.

"Yes. The old gardener's shed. I used to pretend it was my house when I was a girl—and I fell in the canal down there once when my father wasn't watching me. I'm sorry I accused you—"

"Strictly a business deal now is all I'm after," he interrupted, even as he thumped his axe into a tree to make her jump. With both hands free, he took off his gray caped coat as he spoke. "In addition to paying my weekly room and board, I'd like to rent that shed month by month from you, clean it out, use it for a carpentry workshop—if I can also use some of those old tools in that beat-up work chest. I was real pleased to see there's a little potbellied stove out there."

"I knew that, but not about the tools. We haven't had a gardener or odd jobs man in years."

She was amazed to see what he intended. She began to trip over her words and to shudder with the chill, even as, without asking her permission, he came yet closer and swirled his big rebel-colored coat around her, settling it over her shoulders, then stepping back.

"I'll pay you a dollar a month for use of the place and fix it up," he said, his eyes studying her, evidently to see if she would accept or stomp on his gentlemanly gesture. "In addition, I'll repair those rotting pillars that hold up your veranda, all ten of them. Now, what do you say?"

"You're a carpenter?"

"Of sorts. My father was. You're more full of questions than the little girl who says she's named for you."

She almost felt as if she were observing the two of them from afar, as if they had been painted on a china plate or etched for a print of two friends who'd gone out to cut a Christmas tree in the snowy woods. Her voice still trembled and had gone strangely rough. She did not sound like herself or feel like herself, but, thank heavens, her bitter anger had drained from her.

"Carpentry's a noble profession," she whispered. "You know, this time of year, the carpenter from Nazareth."

He looked away, his face tense again. She remembered that he hated Christmas. She both regretted and resented that, because, for one moment, his eyes had been warmer than his big, heavy cloak that smelled of crisp wind and wood and leather.

"Where are your father—daughter—wife?" she dared to ask.

"Gone in the war. What about the deal for the shed?"

"Yes, under one condition."

"Namely?"

"That you let Matt come with you sometimes. I know it might be as bad as having Mandy around, but it would be so good for him. And that you let me apologize for jumping to conclusions and feel free to use "the shrine" upstairs to sleep. I did not mean to insult you last night or today. But did you mention to anyone uptown today about Sarah being an old acquaintance of mine?"

"As you can tell, I'm a man who likes my privacy, Miz Wynne. So I'm not one to abuse that of others. And, for now, I'll accept your one condition that is really three of them, as long as you let me pay room and board too. Shall we shake on the deal?"

She extended her cold hand. Amazingly, for he wore no gloves, his big, calloused, rough hand felt so much warmer than hers. After they shook, she turned to precede him up the path. Only then did she, as cozy as she felt cuddled in his cape, realize she trembled even harder, perhaps from all that had happened this morning, or all that was yet to come.

* * *

"Mama, I think I might get sick," Mandy told Sarah in the middle of their bed in the middle of the night, and promptly did.

"Oh, honey child, poor baby!" Sarah scrambled to light their lamp, then rushed back to hold Mandy's head over the washbowl as she retched again.

"Mm-mn, too much of that Christmas cookie dough 'fore it's baked. Here, gonna put you wrapped up in this chair so's I can change the sheets. If you feel sick again, just you get your head over that bowl. Your little body not used to all that sweets, and I hope this 'keeping Christmas' stuff don't do you in!"

Actually, Sarah thought as she sponged off the soiled sheet, then pulled down the covers to yank it off the bed, she was also hoping this keeping Christmas stuff Amanda was putting so much stock in didn't do all of them in. It wasn't the work, no, but the feelings it loosed—the expectations, in all of them. For Sarah, it was like sitting down to the Thanksgiving table over and over again to see all the lovely things and good feelings to have and share. And sometimes, though it filled her with happiness and joy to belong, it scared her too—for Mandy, for herself, but especially for Amanda if her hopes for Mr. Wynne didn't come out all right.

Now, the wind was howling outside and it was cold in here, even with the woven rag rugs on the floor. She knew she could just have them sleep on the top sheet and pull the blankets up over them. But in this house where Amanda wanted things done proper, she'd just go down the hall to get another sheet and wash this one out tomorrow, even if it did dry stiff as a board on the back line.

She thought again of warm, sunny, breeze-billowing days near Natchez when she'd help Elvira hang sheets for the big house family and they would smell so good. But she thought of that day she was supposed to be hanging them when she had slipped away to meet Ben by the brook. She's come up missing and been called a lagger and been beaten by Master—no, she'd only think of him as Mister now—Mr. White, because he loved the power of the lash. But even that was not as bad as the time she'd been put in the collar for sassing Miss Lizzy and Mrs. White overheard her.

The collar, she remembered now, as she clasped her throat, was one of the worst "gentle" punishments used on slaves at Fair Oaks, for it shamed and ached, rather than pained. It was an iron chain with spikes and bells on it; when Amanda had carried on today about sleigh bells ringing from the necks of horses in the old days, she had thought of it then too. She gripped her neck to recall it.

For the curved spikes stuck out three whole feet above the head, like a cage, and it weighed over ten pounds. Wearing the collar, you couldn't sleep, couldn't stretch out, and had a sore neck and back for weeks, not to mention that everybody heard you coming and turned to stare every time you moved. They'd left it on her for nigh on ten days: she could not risk sneaking out to be with Ben during that eternity—and the horrible "necklace," as that demon Napoleon called it, didn't stop him from bothering her and laughing while he rode her hard, pressed against the stable wall.

But Sarah Murry knew she had that collar-cage to thank too. For in those ten days, she came to see her life for what it was. And afterwards decided, whatever they would do to her again, she was going to run. She talked Ben into it, convinced him it was worth the risk, even if he had to leave behind the sleek racehorses he loved to tend for Mr. White. She made Ben see he was as much a piece of horseflesh to him to trade or beat or sell as the great racing beasts.

But, fleeing, she'd lost Ben. When they were chased by hounds, he'd decoyed the bounty hunters away from her, then never returned as he had promised. She still had hopes that he'd escaped, because those same men had come here looking for her weeks later, after she'd even passed on up the Underground Railroad. And, right here in this house, she'd heard them say that they had to take back at least one of the escapees or Edward White would be furious. Though she never liked to think of it, they could have killed Ben Blue. But she was just sure he was alive and out there somewhere, looking for her too. But what would he say when he saw Mandy?

She startled from her reverie; her hands still clasped her throat, and her feet were nearly numb with chill. She shoved them into her wool mules and cocooned a blanket around herself. Mandy slept already, sitting in the rocking chair. Taking her lamp, Sarah went out and down the dark hall to the big, shelved linen closet to get another sheet. The hall boards creaked under her soft tread; shadows seemed to reach out for her, but here in this house she would never be afraid.

For it was this very closet that had saved her the night the bounty men came with that lawyer Amanda went to see but wouldn't say much about. The door moaned on its hinges as she opened it and put the lantern on the corner stand. Right back here, behind this shelf now stacked with lavender-scented sheets and towels, the wall slid away and a wide but shallow crawl space went back under the attic steps. She just had to peek back into it the other day when changing the beds, and she'd nearly jumped out of her skin when Mr. Wynne suddenly appeared behind her and peeked in it too. She'd had to fetch Amanda to keep him from crawling in, and so together, they'd closed it up and nailed it shut.

"Matt likes enclosed places, and I'm not sure why," Amanda had said. "But sometimes I'm sure it's part of the mystery of what happened to him on the battlefield the day he—he took sick."

Suddenly the door creaked behind her; Sarah spun around. It was Amanda in the flesh this time, as if all her thinking about her had called her.

"Sarah, I heard someone—are you all right? Sorry if I startled you."

"Didn't mean to wake you. Mandy took sick, so I thought I'd change the sheets."

"Is she all right? Let me help you."

"She's gonna be fine and even went back to sleep. Strange to be standing here at night, the same month we was here back six years ago, Amanda."

"That it is. You were my last passenger through this station and the one I almost lost."

"That would have lost everything for you. I heard later it could've meant half a year in jail and a one-thousand dollar fine plus that much for ev'ry slave you been caught hiding."

"You know, Sarah, I suppose you don't want it," Amanda told her with a shake of her head, "but I still have the poster they showed me with your description and bounty listed."

"Maybe I should keep it for Mandy, so she understands someday—you know, how things really was then. Amanda, I got hid and then hustled away so fast that night I never told you 'bout how I woke up earlier—upstairs, you know—and couldn't even remember where I was at first. I'd been running so long, passed on all those weeks, so anxious about Ben gone missing."

"We'll find him now that we've got some leads on where to write."

"I hope so, and that we get your man back too. But when I woke that night, and looked around upstairs, 'fore I heard you arguing with those men at the front door, and then they went riding off to fetch that lawyer—when I could think where I was, I wondered if I might have died and gone to heaven. Those white curtains in the attic windows looked like lighted angel wings in the dark with the moon out. But when you come running up the stairs and hid me in case they came back and then they did—I know right then that the delivering angel in my life was you!"

"If only I could find a delivering angel for me and Matt! I haven't told anyone, but I'm afraid I might have to put him in a—a lunatic asylum, to give him a chance to get well, if keeping Christmas doesn't get him back! Oh, Sarah, I didn't want to face it, so I didn't want to tell anyone, but . . ."

Women's voices invaded Lincoln's exhausted sleep after a hard day of manual labor outside. His mother calling him to dinner? Lindy crying when she broke her leg in the well? Melanie sobbing when cholera took their only child and he was away at war and not there to comfort her? That other voice both kind and quarrelsome, tart and sweet like those delicious orange-flavored cookies she gave him today. Gentle feminine whispers, sensual sounds, calling to him, enticing him . . .

He moaned and stretched, but his stockinged feet popped out the end of the too short bed. That woke him; he stopped breathing to concentrate on the sounds. Yes, women's voices—at the attic door? It must be after midnight, and he'd never heard a voice other nights.

Despite the chill, he rose and shuffled toward the stairs. As dark as it was, his eyes seemed accustomed to it. Strangely, the voices—he knew them to be Amanda's strong one and Sarah's melodious tones now—seemed to emanate from under the stairs. He saw a crack of light between two

steps. What were they doing in the linen closet this time of
night?

He felt his way several stairs down and sat, pulling the
nightshirt borrowed from Matt around his knees. The women
were talking of the time bounty hunters and someone named
Mason Rutland—evidently Matt's law partner—had come to
the house with a writ, demanding to search it for slaves.
How the hunters had turned the place topsy-turvy but had
not found Sarah hidden in some crawl space. And this same
lawyer had evidently refused Matt a pension and advised
putting Matt in a mental institution in Cleveland. Worse, he
had threatened to commit him there if she did not.

Lincoln clenched his fists against his shinbones. He knew
he shouldn't eavesdrop; only last week he'd told Amanda he
respected the privacy of others. And yet her voice, just like
the woman herself, compelled him. He did not want to listen, but he did. He did not want to admire Amanda Wynne
for her fortitude and sacrifice, but he did, even though she
was as prejudiced and pigheaded as some of those she detested, even though she thought she had it hard in this house
and town and could not begin to fathom the hell of a town
without houses.

He did not want his life on the run to become entangled
with hers, or Sarah's, or the child who looked at him with
those huge, dark eyes that screamed she needed a father in
her life. And Matt—what a tragedy played out. Most of all,
Lincoln knew, he could not afford to want to help Matt and
Amanda, but he did. Like the Christmas holidays the stubborn women insisted on preparing for, everything here
sucked him right in when he wanted no damn part of it!

He was ready to make his way back to bed when he heard
his name and froze. "He's hiding something, I suppose,"
Amanda went on, "but I guess every man who's been to war
has enemies he's killed—things he'd like to forget. But even
if he does talk just like that devil of a slaver you ran from,
Sarah, or if he's hiding things, we've got to give him the
benefit of the doubt until we know he did something *really*
wrong."

At that, even though his teeth had begun to chatter, he felt
warm and radiant. For the first time since he had heard that
Melanie was dead too, he experienced a jolt of yearning to
touch a woman—but to give as well as take in return. He'd

never share that need with anyone. Amanda was forever forbidden fruit, even if she put poor Matt away.

Besides, there was something that Lincoln Garner, alias Lincoln Blake, *had* done really wrong, that he could only hope Amanda Lockwood Wynne—none of them here—would ever know. His choice was either to live as a fugitive or else risk death to reclaim his place, his past. Wrapping his arms around himself, he hurried back to bed.

❄ ❄ ❄ ❄ ❄

Chapter
Four

✳

Soft Oatmeal Cookies

Cook raisins in 1 cup water for 2 minutes. Drain and cool.

Cream 1 cup butter, 1 cup sugar, 2 eggs, 1 teaspoon vanilla.

Mix 2½ cups flour, 1 teaspoon baking soda, 2 cups rolled oats (quick-cooking).

Add raisins and 1 cup walnuts (nuts optional).

Roll between floured hands individual pieces of dough in heaping-tablespoon size.

Bake on greased cookie sheet at 350 degrees for approximately 10 minutes. These keep well in closed containers and travel well, for picnics or through the post.

※

"I think I got it by heart now," Sarah told Amanda as they bent their heads together over the letter. "I'll try to read it one last time."

She lifted the precious letter to get good window light in the library. The regular *whack-whack* of Lincoln Blake's axe outside sounded so slow next to the banging of her heart. Her hands shook a bit, and not only because she'd needed considerable help to choose the words and write them down. She trembled that, even if this letter somehow reached her man, he would not want her.

"Wish Mandy was here," she told Amanda, " 'cause with her new schooling, she gonna be a fine reader."

"You are too, and we shall work on it soon," Amanda assured her. "Go ahead. I think we've got it just right now."

Sarah began in a strong but halting voice:

Reverend Alexander Carlson
Cherry Street Methodist Church
Toledo, Ohio

Dear Sir. I am searching for my husband, Ben Blue. I think he came north in the flight of slaves before the war. Maybe he passed your way in the winter of '60. Maybe to Windsor, Canada instead of Chatham. I used to live in Chatham. Ben Blue, from Natchez, Mississippi, is 5 feet and 10 inches tall, stocky and broad-shouldered, with light Negro complexion. He has a scar on his right cheek and R brand on his left hand. He is a strong, fine-looking man, and

mighty good with horses. He might have traveled alone after he lost touch with his wife, Sarah Murry. That is me. I
live now with Mrs. Matthew Wynne on Church Street in
Lockwood, Ohio. Thank you most kindly for any news to
help me find him. I am in your debt.

Sarah Murry

"Good," Amanda told her with a decisive nod. "But I still
think you should have mentioned Mandy, as that would
bring him running too. Now what's that long face for? We'll
find him, whatever it takes!"

"I don't like to talk much 'bout the old days," Sarah said,
laying the letter down and smoothing its edges on the shiny
tabletop. She could not meet Amanda's stare. She nearly
burst to unburden herself about her and Ben—and the man
she feared was really Mandy's father.

"I understand, Sarah. Painful memories. But maybe, like
with a nightmare, if you share it with someone, it won't ever
seem so awful again," Amanda suggested, placing her hand
on Sarah's next to the letter.

"Then I'll tell you," Sarah declared, but she only bit her
lower lip and stared out the window.

"Sarah, I'm sure whatever this deep sadness, you were not
the cause."

"Sometimes if things bad enough, don't matter who or
what the cause," Sarah insisted, but she sniffed and sat up
straighter. "See, on Fair Oak Plantation, Mr. White—the
owner—he done treated his racehorses better'n anything."

"Certainly better than the slaves he kept lower than ani-
mals," Amanda put in, her voice instantly hard and angry.

"More'n his own wife and family, too. And he had him a
rider, a jockey boy, he call him, wore bright silk shirts in the
races. Used that one for a house servant too, keeping his
coats and hats brushed off and like such, not much work, really. Master—I mean, Mr. White—done spoiled that jockey
Napoleon like his horses. He'd rather take a whip to the
slaves than his horses."

She hesitated a moment, staring down at Amanda's white
hand that tightened over her dark one. Sarah pulled hers
slowly back, crossed her arms over her breasts, and stuck
her hands under her armpits. She listened for one more moment to that *whack-whack* of the axe outside.

"Well," she went on, "for some reason not known to no one but the good Lord above, that rotten Napoleon done took a fancy to me, when there was sure others around who'd give their eyeteeth—the rest of themselves too—for a roll in the hay with him, 'scuse me just spitting it out that way. Napoleon had himself nice clothes, even a pocket watch with a shiny chain, shirt studs—and a real cocky way 'bout hisself some gals liked, but not me."

"But what about Ben Blue?" Amanda asked, when Sarah didn't go on.

"Ben, he begun as stable boy and rose real fast, taking care of the racehorses, even helping with their breeding. Good glory, that man could talk to them big beasts, and they'd listen and get real gentle-like. Wished he'd told them to throw that polecat Napoleon on the track and give him a good kick in the head too!"

"But Ben was—a very talented man to win over horses—and your heart."

"Yes, the best man I ever saw. He loved me for me. But that Napoleon wanted me so he could control my spirit—like those racing fillies, he said once. Weren't for my looks nor my willingness, no sir. And 'cause I wanted Ben, who was under him in the plantation pecking order. But I was strong in love with the stable groom and Napoleon knowed—knew—it. Mr. White give me to him anytime he wanted me, anything to keep his jockey boy happy. I guess sometimes Napoleon took me to tame me and sometimes to keep Ben in his place, like maybe Napoleon thought he was master over us slaves, but there only one of them and that the white one."

"Sarah, I'm so sorry about all this. But now that you and Ben are both free and have Mandy . . ."

Amanda's voice trailed off when Sarah hunched her shoulders, got up, and walked to the window. The blows of the axe sounded loud again. Sarah wondered if Amanda had guessed her deepest fear, but, even when this perfect time came to share it, she could not. Besides, she had already told Amanda that Ben was Mandy's daddy, and she knew Amanda had a trusting heart.

"Ben and me wasn't really married," she said, afraid Amanda would see through her earlier lie. "Not wed proper, not even like slave folks done back there, jumping over a broom. You know, maybe he not even really my husband on the plantation or off, 'cause we only promised each other we was wed and *always* would be. Still, when I find him, we gonna do it up real proper!"

"Of course, you will. Besides, with the terrible times you've been through, no moral-minded person could blame you for exchanging your own vows. And no one is going to call Mandy a child born out of wedlock if I can help it. Now, I'm going to mail this letter on the way to my meeting and, if it doesn't find him, we'll send ones till we do!"

Sarah nodded and smiled, though her face felt stiff. She hugged herself harder as she felt the chill draft off the window and turned to look out. Lincoln Blake, whom she had secretly renamed "Miz'sippi Master," had Mr. Matt piling pieces of wood, just like a slave. Sarah still didn't like and didn't trust the southerner for his treatment of Mandy and his lie to Amanda about where he came from, though, of course, she told herself now, she too had lied to the fine woman who had taken her in. As Amanda bustled out, Sarah still watched poor Mr. Matt replacing pieces of wood that rolled off, in repetitive, pointless motions.

That's the way she felt sometimes when she got real low, she thought, like what was the use of doing daily things over and over. Then only Mandy saved her, though the child was the proof of her pain. Now she had a friend in Amanda, but even she thought her worry was that Mandy was not made in wedlock instead of that her daddy was a man she and Ben both hated. And all of life went on around her—even this fancy Christmas being planned—until she could find Ben and convince him that Mandy was the child of their united love if not their loins.

When Amanda and Pru left the house for the sewing circle meeting at the Methodist parsonage, carrying the big picnic basket full of oatmeal cookies held between them, Lincoln was working on the porch pillars again. The man never ceased to amaze Amanda. He had several odd jobs going and more lined up about town, the winter wood piles had grown to pyramids, he had repaired the old gardener's shed, and he was on the sixth of ten pillars. Matt sat on the front steps now, unopened law book in one hand and piece of wood in the other, just watching Lincoln, who kept up a steady stream of talk to him about what he was doing. Perhaps she'd have to find a way to convince Lincoln to stay all winter.

"You're making fine progress, Mr. Blake!" she called out, tugging back on her basket handle to halt Pru.

"Just in time, or the weight of snow could cave in the veranda roof," he called down to her. She'd used the rickety ladder twice a year to wash second-story windows, but she saw he'd repaired it too.

"I appreciate it, and how Matt's helping," she went on. "He seems to like to listen to you, at least. Now, don't forget Sarah has hot cider and oatmeal cookies for you two inside."

"Not likely I'd forget some of your mighty delicious baking when it's offered, Miz Wynne," he said.

She was startled at how that little compliment, even brusquely spoken, made her knees go weak as she and Pru set out against the wind, their skirts, coats, and bonnets billowing and blowing.

"Everyone's going to be so happy to see you at the meeting today," Pru told her. "You haven't been since Matt came home."

"How could I? He never sat for me as he does for Lincoln Blake. Besides, during the war when we were the Soldiers' Aid Society, I could see the effort, but I always was as terrible at darning and stitching as you are good at it, Pru. I don't know what I'd do if you didn't help me with the mending."

"Mama always thought it was a skill ladies should have, and she was determined that I be a lady. As if it were some mortal sin, she admitted on her deathbed that she had ripped out my perfectly good napkin hems time after time and made me redo them just to teach me humility, fortitude, and obedience."

"That sounds like her. As for your learning obedience, no wonder she was furious when you eloped with a canal boat captain."

"I can still see her to this day, livid, right through that milk-white complexion," Pru admitted with a shake of her head. "That was how she first discovered I'd been out with Sam, you know—sun color on my wrists and hands when they should have been like snow. Out walking with him, I had taken my gloves off so we could hold hands," she whispered, "bare skin to skin. She said I looked like a field hand, but I stood up for me and Sam. Oh, Amanda, how I wish I still had that pre-war gumption, and I don't even have Mama to fear anymore. If I were only strong again—like you—I'd take my gloves off and go after that stubborn Ned Milburn and convince him I could love a one-armed man—that he is a whole man to me!"

Amanda nodded as they slowed their steps near the post office on the town square. Before she went in to post Sarah's letter, she squeezed Pru's arm. She wanted to encourage her friend in her unrequited love for the young man who lived next door on Church Street, yet she felt drained after Matt's nightmare last night and her comforting Sarah this morning. How she would like to help Pru, Sarah, even Eliza find their loves, but losing her own, even though he was still among them, had worn her down.

As for Pru's predicament, they had both known Ned Milburn since grammar school. Two years after Pru had lost Sam, Ned had returned home without his right arm, lost to infection and amputation in a surgeon's bloody tent after Gettysburg. Yet he joked ruefully about still being his father's right hand to keep the family home going here. The Milburns' hardware store had closed in the canal slump, so his father, Edward Senior, commuted to work in a store in Cleveland and came home only on weekends to the house that had been saved by Ned's disability pension of nineteen dollars a month. Ned talked kindly to Pru, his green eyes lit to see her, but he had never come calling and had admitted bitterly to his sister Sally that he'd never court anyone he couldn't put his arms around.

"I didn't mean to carry on so, Amanda, not with the way Matt is," Pru said as Amanda emerged from the post office and they headed for the parsonage. "Sometimes, I think for you it's even worse than if Matt had—like Sam—not come back."

"A terrible thought, but, yes, it is," Amanda admitted. "I am so grateful he's returned and—has the chance to get better. But it is like he dies over and over each time he enters the room or turns to look at me—and he just isn't there anymore. Each time I wake and recall about him, it's like I lose him anew. Remember that line from the poem *Maud Muller* by Whittier that we liked in *Godey's*? 'Then she took up her burdens of life again,/ Saying only, "It might have been!" ' "

Pru nodded with a sniffle. "We're not alone in that, Prudence Cuddy," Amanda went on, trying to keep her voice from snagging. "There are widows and orphans and sad sisters country-wide, and we've just got to help each other and keep going!"

Holding their laden basket between them, they did.

As conversation in the sewing circle continued, it was harder than ever for Amanda to keep up a cheerful front. This was the yearly meeting where charitable contributions were packed in willow baskets to be donated to the town poor; even compared to the war years, the high number of baskets was sobering. And deep down, she feared that she too could come to be among the town poor, for even with two boarders and the baked goods she sold, she was barely keeping things together.

Today, jam and preserves, a jar of watermelon pickles, a small slab of bacon, a loaf of bread, even a bar of soap were put into forty-four baskets for delivery. To each, Amanda added a paper packet with a dozen of her soft oatmeal cookies. They were sturdy and stored well, though she knew the recipients would probably devour them at once, not store them in crocks in a chilly pantry, as she had been doing for months so she could sell them with other Christmas baked goods.

Twenty-two women belonged to this sewing circle, including her neighbors Delia and Sally Milburn, Ned's mother and sister; the parson's wife, Faith Mannerly; the mayor's wife, Effie Roscoe, and her married daughter, Pauline Keller; and Mason Rutland's wife, Dorothy, called Dottie. Eliza Tuttle belonged too, though she had gone to the schoolhouse today to help prompt the children for their Christmas program recitations, and they had brought her contribution of pencils with gum rubbers on the tips.

"Amanda, what *is* the real story," plump Effie Roscoe asked, "about those new visitors of yours? Imagine a Reb in Lockwood! He looks so grim and gaunt, though Will has hired him to rebuild some livery stalls. Will says the man doesn't want to talk about the war, so what do you know of where he fought? And is the girl a servant or a boarder—the woman, not her child, I mean? Is she from down south or up north?"

"Both, as she was from Mississippi, but has lately lived in Canada," Amanda said, choosing to answer only the most innocuous of the spate of questions.

"Where in Christendom is her husband?" the elegant-looking Dottie Rutland piped up. She was always dressed to the nines, even when the rest of them wore day dresses. But she went on before Amanda could give any explanation, "You know, ladies, they say a great many of them—the colored—were only wed by leaping over a broom, and even if they did have a man of the cloth there, he only made them vow till death *or distance* do us part!"

Amanda bit back a sharp retort about Mason Rutland living exactly by those words—faithfulness only until distance intervened, while just this morning, Sarah had confided to her that she and Ben has promised each other fidelity for *always*. But Amanda said only, "Considering the cruel fact that southern states refused even to let their Negroes congregate in a worship service of their own, I don't doubt the slaves had to do things their own way, and more power to them."

"Just let's not get into that hornet's nest of any talk about southern Reconstruction again," Delia Milburn said with a shake of her silver head as she tied a red-ribboned sprig of holly on the top of each calico-covered basket. "The South deserves to suffer for all they've done to the slaves and our boys in blue like my Ned, and that's that!"

"Besides, Amanda hasn't said a word about the odd jobs man," Sally Milburn put in. "So, did he say what battles he was in? I declare, if Ned hears he was at Gettysburg, he'll fight him one-handed."

"Now let's all just remember that Christmas is coming!" Pru sang out with a shaky little smile. "Ned has lost a great deal, and I greatly sympathize with him, so I hope he isn't vexed by Mr. Blake's living in our attic. However, the former Rebel is a gentleman, and I will tell Ned so myself if I get the chance. Besides, I assure you all, Amanda says Mr. Blake has lost a great deal too."

"I hope they all have, every last Reb rascal of them!" Dottie cried. "Why, the war was all their fault. Everyone who is anyone agrees on that. Mason read me from the *New*

York Times just last week that southerners are impudent even in defeat and should be made to suffer to really bring them to their knees."

"And," Pauline Kelly added importantly, "Eliza Tuttle told me that Ralph Waldo Emerson said the same. And Father thinks southerners will be even more insolent and insufferable and keep causing trouble if we feed them for free, like the government is now, sending down all that food to distribution centers because they are supposedly poor and hungry!"

Momentarily, they stopped their busy hands from loading baskets of food and looked uneasily at each other.

"Hard words in the face of Christmas charity," Amanda said quietly in the awkward silence. "But yes, I've felt that too, that the South deserves to pay for the war."

"Then it's they, not *you,* Amanda," Effie said, "who should be taking in people like that hired girl. They made them slaves, let them care for their freedom now, not us."

Amanda stood, shoving back her chair from the table. "The point is, thank God the slaves are free now, and we should all help them go anywhere they want so they can *earn* their way and receive equal opportunities for things like schooling and jobs. And that is what Sarah Murry is doing—earning her way, no matter how much is owed her. I haven't just 'taken her in.' And even if we blame the South—hate southerners in general—when you meet one in person—like Mr. Blake—one who has lost things and suffered too—you begin to think things over . . ."

"Don't tell me you, of all people, have gone soft on southern slaveholders!" Faith Mannerly hissed.

"Never! But, as Pru said, it's almost Christmas. Speaking of which, ladies, I am hoping you and your families will join us next Saturday evening for the renewal of the Peace on Earth pageant, at seven. Perhaps there we can put aside the bitter past."

"Will *he* be there, the Rebel?" Effie asked. "I just don't know about a Peace on Earth pageant with one of those warmongers in attendance."

"He wants no part of it, so surely you can see your way clear to come—for old times' sake, at least."

She excused herself and stepped outside into the cold to get her breath and keep herself from launching into a worse tirade against them, one in which she really would have to include herself. It terrified her how much she too still wanted revenge against the Rebels when she should feel forgiveness. She had bridled her tongue because she could not bear to endanger the success of the Christmas pageant. The holidays must be warm and wonderful this year, so Matt would have a chance to be touched, comforted, and healed.

She blinked back tears, praying that everything coming apart around her could be as—as rebuilt as those porch pillars, to keep the world's roof from falling in.

As she watched Rufus Quinn, Ned Milburn, and a few other men work to prop up the manger in the lot between the Lockwood and Milburn houses, Amanda, ashamed at her feelings of vengeance toward the former Rebels, decided to wage a military campaign of her own to help the one of them that she could. Carefully she laid plans to capture Lincoln Blake with Christmas.

Surely, she thought, she could breach his defenses toward it, give him a good holiday, and therefore clear her conscience. Her strategy was to involve him in Christmas preparations and to get him to attend and enjoy the pageant—even if some of Lockwood's citizens walked out— and thereby induce him to enjoy further blessings of the day itself. Besides, then he would help Matt enjoy Christmas this year too. She had to admit it would make her feel immensely better to have a guest in her house who was an ally and not an enemy—at least about Christmas.

Amanda made her first sally to snare Lincoln one afternoon before supper, when she wanted to bring the holiday decorations down from the attic. With Matt at her side, she knocked at the door. She was certain she had heard Lincoln go upstairs to await supper; surely he would get a bit in the spirit if he helped her and Matt cart boxes downstairs and then was at the table when others opened and unpacked them. She knocked again. Was he going to ignore them, or had he slipped downstairs already? She would just have to try again after dinner.

But as she turned away, Matt opened the attic door and went up the stairs. "Lincoln?" he called. "Lincoln— Christmas!"

She clasped her hands together. So Matt did have some

awareness of Christmas! Her plans—all of them—just had to work. She hurried after Matt, calling, "Mr. Blake? Are you up here?"

He wasn't, and since she was, she decided to carry down one box. But first she joined Matt at the window overlooking the side yard where the men had erected the manger, a one-dimensional set of beams, propped up in back with boards to make the silhouette of a triangular roof and two walls.

"We're going to have a lovely Christmas, Matt!" she said and laid her head briefly on his shoulder. Her heart thrilled when he turned to her and blessed her with a fleeting smile before looking back outside.

She walked into the dim reaches of the front attic and found the big hatbox she was looking for. "Come on down to supper, Matt," she said as she headed for the steps, but he still looked out the window. Holding the box by its cord, she lingered, studying from afar the familiar corner of the attic that Lincoln Blake now inhabited.

The bed was made in tidy, military style—corners tucked tightly up and—hardly warm or cozy. She shook her head to see he had hung his gray Confederate uniform jacket with buff lapels, bright buttons, and a sash of red silk net on the old dress dummy on the other side of his bed. It appeared he was a major, if the insignia was the same for the Confederates as for the Federals; he had outranked Matt! Tiptoeing carefully closer, she touched the lapel and fingered one button: each had a raised letter E on it. E for what? she wondered, but she'd dare not ask him later or he'd know she'd been snooping.

On the old trunk he had pulled next to the bed for a nightstand sat a few items, aligned in a row: a small, worn Bible, a comb, and a gold piece of jewelry. She shuffled closer to stare down at it. A double locket, the frame edged in tarnished gold filigree lay open to tiny, oval, tintype faces of a pretty dark-haired woman and a winsome young girl, by resemblance mother and daughter. A shiny dark lock of hair curled out from under each picture, a vibrant memento of all that was lost.

Amanda jumped a foot when Lincoln's voice rang out. "What is it? I had to go out back."

"I—we just came up, hoping you would help us carry some boxes down. We knocked. I didn't mean—"

"To spy on me? I guess it is your house, but this is mine." He strode closer, swept up the locket, and snapped it closed in his big hand.

Matt came over. "Cut wood for Christmas—outside. In the snow."

For a moment, Lincoln and Amanda did not react, despite the triumphant logic of the comment. Lincoln's icy blue eyes glittered at her from beneath dark, frowning brows. She felt pinned like a butterfly to cotton under glass.

"I did not mean to spy, really," she said. "I just needed some boxes and thought you would help me carry them." She saw his jaw set hard; tears burned her eyes. "I am sorry, Mr. Blake," she whispered. "About everything."

"Lincoln?" Matt put in.

"It's all right, Matt," Lincoln assured him, and laid a hand on his shoulder. "It's just that—" he said to her, his voice a whisper now too, "it is all I have left."

"You have memories," Amanda said. "Can't they be happy at Christmas, instead of sad? That's what I'm holding to with Matt—memories and hope."

"Hope?" he began, his voice bitter, then just shook his head. "Matt, it's time for supper," he said, obviously unwilling to discuss himself further. "Now, what is it you all wanted carried down?" he asked her. Even when he looked away at last, she felt his stare still impaled her.

"A few things over there—Christmas decorations."

He shook his head again. "*You* are one stubborn, fool-hardy, but brave woman, Miz Wynne. And since Matt calls me Lincoln, don't you think you should too?"

That move surprised her; she had invaded his territory, yet he was being conciliatory. Ordinarily she would have re-fused his request. It was not the done thing, such casual fa-miliarity with a recent acquaintance of the opposite sex, but none of this was the done thing anymore. A few moments ago, as angry as he'd been, she had felt intimate with him. And, after all, wasn't victory hers, since he was going to carry things downstairs, which he knew were for cursed Christmas?

"All right, Lincoln. And, of course, you may call me Amanda."

"Then may I negotiate one more thing in this truce?" he asked, surprising her by revealing that he too saw them as adversaries. Before she could answer, he touched her elbow. That mere brief brush of his fingers jolted her as if she had hit her crazy bone and couldn't feel a thing—and yet she felt lightning surge through her arm clear to her stomach and head.

"What?" she mouthed.

"You all won't say one more blasted word about Christmas to me."

She frowned. "If you insist."

"Here, let's get this stuff downstairs," he said and bent to lift one box into Matt's arms while he took the other two. It was, she thought a pyrrhic victory; she had won the battle but lost the war. Still, she was not giving up this easily.

And so, four days later, on a sunny but brisk mid-afternoon a week before Christmas—the very night of the pageant that Lincoln had managed so far to ignore—Amanda ventured forth on another mission to the enemy's citadel, this time Lincoln's work shed. Because she wanted to win this skirmish, her weapon was a packet of the big, soft oatmeal cookies that she had seen he loved.

For even though Eliza had invited him and Mandy had tried to wheedle, he had refused to attend the grammar school Christmas program earlier that week. Singing by the grades, recitations, popcorn and oranges—no bribe or plea had budged him. And he had taken himself out of the house the entire evening while Pru's seven students gave their holiday piano recital amidst parents, apple cake, and cranberry punch. He also had made it inordinately clear that he would not attend the Peace on Earth pageant, even when Amanda asked him simply to come down to keep an eye on Matt, even when he learned that most of the town would be there, many of whom were now his employers.

Today, the manger and its scenery were completed and Matt was taking his afternoon rest upstairs, so Amanda thought this her best time and tactic. She pulled her wool pelisse closer over her steel-gray work dress and held on to saplings to keep from slipping on the downward path behind the house. Pleased that the curl of smoke from the stovepipe protruding from the slanted roof showed he was there, she also observed that he had cleared a small, neat area around the shed where the brush had been so overgrown.

As she walked by the single window, she glimpsed him inside, his profile to her, hunched over, planing curls of wood from some item on his makeshift workbench. She was at first tempted just to watch him, but she didn't want to be accused of spying again if he glanced out at her. She really did like to observe him, though: he was a hard worker, always purposeful, pushing himself, even in the coldest weather. A lean, angular grace animated his movements, a muscular stretch governed his long limbs, as if she could see strong sinew and sturdy bone even under that gray caped coat he always wore.

As now, even inside, he had tied one of Matt's old scarves around his neck and chin to try to cover his ears under his hat. That scarf bothered her, just the way the beard did. One made him look like a bandit; the other reminded her of those other brigands, Confederate generals like Longstreet and Stonewall Jackson whom she'd seen depicted in *Harper's Weekly*. Perhaps she could strike a bargain with Lincoln: if he would shave that big beard, she would store the picture of General Sherman that he'd admitted he hated for the winter. How she would have liked to have Lincoln clean-shaven like Matt, to really see his face. She had heard it was a point of honor with Confederate officers that they kept their beards, so it would be a real victory to see it gone to the postwar styles of long side whiskers or mustache. More determined than ever, she knocked on the closed door.

He opened it, obviously startled to see her. He yanked the scarf down and doffed his hat. "Is everything all right?"

"I brought you something to eat. Besides, I haven't seen what you did with this place inside."

He stood back and gestured her in. She stepped past him, her skirts brushing heavily against his long legs. Unlike the cozy, casual clutter of items in her house, absolutely every tool and piece of wood here in this spartan setting had a proper place.

"It's cold, so I'll have to close the door," he said and thumped it shut. And then she saw what he had been working on.

"Oh, a child's sled!" she exclaimed and ran her gloved

hand over the sweep of boards. "I had one something like this once."

"The runners on it might have been yours. I found them all rusted and bent under a pile of barrel staves in the carriage house. Henry Hanks straightened and cleaned them at his blacksmith shop in trade for some work. He gave me some red paint too."

She stood amazed, her hands with the paper packet of cookies pressed to her breasts. He was obviously proud of his work. Tears stung her eyes and speckled her lashes. "A child's sled—for . . . ?"

"For the girl," he said gruffly. "Mandy."

"Oh, Lincoln, how kind of you! It will mean so much to her! It will really make her Christm— See, I almost said it!"

He shook his head, but didn't smile, and held up both hands as if to ward off her rush of gratitude. "It's not going to be from me, but from Santa Claus. I regret mightily that I scared her that day, but—you know why."

"Yes. And Sarah will be so pleased!"

"I know she doesn't like me, but as I said, it's a secret."

"But—"

"I always thought that a gift is really a gift if the giver doesn't get the glory. But this hasn't changed our agreement that I'm not part of the festivities. I'll surely enjoy the food, but not the rest. And," he concluded, emphasizing each word, "you will have to leave it at that, Amanda Wynne."

"Oh, here," she said and extended the cookies to him. Let him think she was flying the white flag of surrender, because she had not yet begun to fight. "I guess I should have just left them on your doorstep here, so you don't think I was after the glory," she added and rolled her eyes.

He looked as if he'd like to smile at her teasing, but his lips just stiffened. He tossed the sack once in his hands, evidently certain of what was there. "I'd know they were from you—everything you bake tastes of your care and concern for things. Thank you, but you'd best go on back now."

"I suppose so. I have a lot to do to prepare for tonight. And, despite your crusty exterior, I have seen that the spirit of the times has caught you too, and I wouldn't be a bit surprised if you just happened to wander by the pageant tonight," she said and risked a wide smile.

Although he had moved several steps away to put his

hand to the door latch, he did not open the door. He just looked at her and she at him from the yawning distance of three feet. Her smile trembled and faded. Slanted, late-afternoon sunlight swirled through the small windowpane to glitter snowflakes of sawdust and motes drifting between them. The sweet wood smell sifted into her head and made her want to sneeze, but she did not. Somehow, she stood bedazzled and enchanted. The heat from the potbellied stove wafted out to wrap them in a deep warmth. But most of all, his sky-blue eyes heated her, held her rooted momentarily, eternally in memory, to this sunstruck spot.

He sucked in a sudden breath and pulled the door open for her; the cold outside slapped her to reality as she went out and trudged back to the house.

That evening from his attic window, Lincoln Garner gazed down at the half-moon-shaped crowd of Lockwood citizens milling around the manger scene. He was certain they could not see him, for their lanterns and torches must glint off the windows of the house. This vantage point must be the same heavenly view the angels had, "bending on hovering wing," as the song they sang below put it.

He had meant to go out to the shed to hammer and saw away at something to block the sounds of the soaring, sweet Christmas carols, but he stood as if nailed to the floor. Lockwood mothers adjusted bulky burlap-bag costumes over the coats of little shepherd boys, while others herded real sheep and cows just outside the wooden structure. Captain Quinn and two other older men, decked out in old velvet and brocade curtains, preened like peacocks. Kingly costumes, no less, when women he knew at home would give anything for a scrap of good dress material. Amanda ordered shepherds and kings alike to get out of the way to await their cues to approach the manger.

Now, Lincoln felt doubly guilty he hadn't helped Rufus Quinn with the setup this week; he'd intentionally made himself scarce. But especially when he saw the one-armed veteran from next door struggling to help, he hated himself for not lending them his two skilled hands. From this vantage point, he could see they had made a botch of it, just propped it up instead of digging postholes for the major support pieces.

But he was glad he had fought getting involved in their—in *her*—Christmas joy. He was terrified that if he gave in and took part, helped them with their fancy frivolities, the dam of his control would break. Then he'd recall everything he had pent up there, and cry and rage for it all again. No matter what, he had to harden his heart toward that woman and her Christmas.

Yet, between the carols, children's laughter floated up to Lincoln, laughter like he remembered amidst family gatherings with the eggnog tarted up by a good jolt of his father's favorite bourbon. He saw again, hanging on the front door of the sturdy house he'd built, the wreath of Spanish moss, studded with gilded pinecones and nuts; he saw swags of holly, smelled sharp-scented pine, recalled again Melanie's smiling face tilted up to his for a kiss under the mistletoe while Lindy giggled as she snuggled her face in the silky coat of her new puppy.

As winged angels took their places beneath him and shepherd boys tended their sheep, Lincoln Garner stood, arms up, pressed along the frame of the narrow attic window, fists clenched atop his head. Shoulders heaving, he sobbed silently and stared down—and back—at Christmas.

It came upon the midnight clear, That glorious song of old,
From angels bending near the earth, To touch their harps
    of gold:
"Peace on the earth, good will to men, From heaven's all-
    gracious King,";
The world in solemn stillness lay, To hear the angels sing.

The familiar song floated up to him, then Eliza Tuttle's voice rang out, "Glory to God in the highest, and on earth peace, good will toward men. And it came to pass . . ."

The pageant unfolded, watched by townspeople as if all Bethlehem had come out to see the sight. Joseph walked beside Mary, riding a rather cantankerous mule, which Rufus said had once served on the canal towpaths and had "more than once made an ass of himself." The shepherd boys came and knelt, the kings came calling, proud and pompous. Angels hovered in sheets with wings of wire covered by dimity that Lincoln had been stepping over all week in the back parlor when he went in to get a glimpse of the daily newspaper. They sang, strumming cardboard harps, while one played a real trumpet in an old army call to battle.

It was then that he saw two things happen which Amanda surely must not have planned. Matt rose from his seat and marched up before the angel with the trumpet. Lincoln wasn't sure from his vantage point, but it looked as if Matt snapped a sharp military salute to the baby Jesus. Matt then stood, at ease, among the angels, something Amanda evidently decided to let go, as she didn't budge from her position off to the side. At least Matt wasn't cowering or running, but that was probably because all week Amanda had insisted he hear the trumpet and sit in on the singing so he would not bolt.

But the other thing Lincoln saw worried him more. That "ass of a mule" was butting the big side post, one of the two which held up the flat silhouette of the manger. Perhaps the beast didn't like the sheep or cows or the music or Mrs. Tuttle's voice, but he banged it again, like a bull. The whole thing shuddered, then toppled forward, keeping its formation and just missing the assembled cast within and the audience without. Sheep scattered; people jumped. Two torches flared and sputtered out in the snow, fortunately missing the straw strewn about.

"Crazy Christmas!" Lincoln muttered. Now he'd have to run down to help, she'd know he'd been watching—and this was all her fault!

Not even stopping to grab his coat, he thudded down the attic stairs. After the stunned silence outside, he could hear the rumble of the crowd now, a few shrieks. He was halfway down the big front staircase to go out the front door when Matt came pounding up toward him, fear contorting his face.

"Matt, it's all right!" he called to him, but he ran right past. "Matt!"

Torn now, he turned to follow Matt upstairs. To his amazement, the frenzied man rushed to the big linen closet next to the open attic stairs and darted in, leaving the door open. Lincoln followed him. Matt yanked sheets off the shelf at the back, then tried to wedge himself on the shelf.

"Matt, it's Lincoln. It's all right. You don't have to hide."

"Matt?" he heard Amanda's terrified voice downstairs. "Matt?"

"He's up here!" Lincoln called as he pried Matt off the

shelf. Matt swung at him, catching him just above the left eye, so he pinned his arms to his sides.

"Oh, thank heavens you found him. I didn't know what he'd do when that thing fell!" Amanda said as she stood breathless in the dim doorway. "Matt, it's all right. It isn't a battle—no cannon, no guns."

Matt stopped struggling in Lincoln's arms. He stood, head down, gasping for breath. Amanda reach up to touch his shoulders. "No one will hurt you, Matt. It's all right now. He must have been trying to get in that little crawl space we boarded up." She crooned as if to herself, "It's all right, my Matt."

Matt reached for her from his elbows down, for Lincoln still held his upper arms. Matt grasped Amanda's hands, then tried to hug her, so Lincoln slowly released him. But Matt reached for Lincoln too, hauling him into a hard embrace not only in the man's arms but pressed face-to-face up against Amanda.

She gasped and stiffened at first, but Matt held on harder. Tipping her head into Lincoln's shoulder, she stood still. Lincoln could feel Matt's heavy breathing and Amanda's trembling. Her breasts rose and fell against him; his right hand was trapped in the deep folds of her skirt.

"You worked so hard for that—and then an accident," Lincoln said softly. Again, he felt the bruise of guilt, worse than the swelling coming over his eye; he should have helped the men shore up the old manger scene.

"It—it can't be an omen, a sign from heaven about this Christmas and Matt," she said. "I won't let it!"

"No, of course it isn't."

He wanted to comfort her desperately, though something good had come from this: her husband held her—as Lincoln had surmised he never did anymore. But Lincoln wanted to put out his arms, now stiff at his side, and really hold her too. He breathed in unison with her, felt her warmth, but smelled the cold outside air caught in her lavender-scented hair where her bonnet had tumbled loose. Suddenly, every muscle in his body, every bone, ached with yearning so intense he felt he could dissolve in anguish.

"I'll take care of Matt," he said at last. "You'd best see to things outside."

Slowly, they both stepped back, disengaging Matt's grasp.

Lincoln stared into Amanda's eyes in the dusk of the closet which had once sheltered other runaways.

"Thank God, no one was hurt," she said.

He nodded, but a little voice in his head warned, But so many have been hurt already, and there's still no way to stop the pain.

❄ ❄ ❄ ❄ ❄

Chapter
Five

Heavenly Meringues

(ALSO CALLED *ANGEL WINGS* OR *ANGEL GIFTS*)

Beat 2 egg whites until stiff.
Add gradually while beating, ¾ cup sugar, ⅛ teaspoon
  salt, ⅛ teaspoon cream tartar, 1 teaspoon vanilla.
Line baking sheets with paper sacks cut open.
Drop in peaks like angel wings or single peak.
Hide chocolate chips, nuts, or candies inside each.
Bake on paper at 300 degrees for about 25 minutes. Can
  get slightly browned to set, but not too brown.

Alternate version: Do not hide things inside, but fold 6
ounces chocolate bits and ¼ cup chopped nuts into batter
before baking.

❄

"It's time to cut our Christmas tree!" Amanda announced to everyone in the parlor on the afternoon of December 24. "Anyone who doesn't mind the cold, bundle up and let's go!"

Sarah looked doubtful, but Pru and Eliza quickly set aside the backgammon game that Aunt Louise had been watching, and Eliza volunteered to stay behind with the old woman. Mandy abandoned her cornhusk doll to jump up and down. Matt nodded so sagely that Amanda dared to hope he understood and would continue to become more involved in Christmas, even after the disaster of the pageant. Lincoln, who had just slipped in to take the newspaper upstairs with him after everyone else had read it, refused to look at her and headed for the door. He had not let her get near him earlier today to tend the black eye Matt had given him, either.

But now she smiled smugly; she had timed this salvo exactly to hit him broadside. This was her last-ditch tactic to involve him in holiday preparations before tomorrow.

"Mr. Blake," she called after his retreat, "since you want no part of you-know-what things, I hope we may stop on our way and borrow your axe and saw from the shed."

He spun back, frowning at her. "Which one of you all knows how to use them safely to cut down a tree?" he demanded. "If you're not careful, it can fall *on* you!"

"You could come too!" Mandy cried, as Amanda saw both him and Sarah grimace.

"No, Mister Blake don't want to come out with the likes

of us to get no tree, honey child," Sarah put in pointedly, and gave Lincoln a sharp stare, though he still looked only at Amanda.

To everyone's surprise and Amanda's great joy, he intoned, "I see I'll have to come along so we don't lose any limbs besides those lowest on the tree." He looked as if he'd just been invited to a funeral.

Those who were going out scattered to fetch coats, hats, gloves, and scarves. Amanda scented victory. She only hoped Lincoln didn't think she had used Mandy to make him capitulate. Perhaps it had been Sarah's challenge that had convinced him, or the fact that he was even more protective of Matt after the pageant. Strange, but ever since that night when Matt had clung to both of them in the closet, she had begun almost to think of Matt as her son and not her husband. He still called her "Mother" some nights when she put him to bed. And if she was like a mother to him now, and Lincoln watched over him like a father, then . . .

"Any of you all object to letting Miz Wynne have the final say on the tree to avoid pointless arguments?" Lincoln asked, as he stood there bundled up, glaring at her to let her know he was hardly talking about just picking a Christmas tree.

"I thank you all for the vote of confidence," Amanda told him as she herded the revelers out the door.

Amanda noticed that the new snow was tramped down quite heavily toward the outhouse and the path to Lincoln's shed, but then the tracks stopped, and they crunched down new pathways. Even on this untrod path, however twisting or downhill, tree limbs pointed like signposts. If Matt did not get better, how Amanda wished the agonizing choices that lay ahead of her could be so clearly mapped out. As Matt hurried to the edge of the canal, she ran to pull him back from the thin, brittle ice, just before Lincoln reached him. One moment she was sure Matt was better, the next she knew she'd have to get special medical help for him. But she would never follow Mason Rutland's callous, cruel advice to put him in the lunatic asylum!

"Here's a good tree! Look at this one! How 'bout this? Ooh, is this a tall one!" came the cries as the search party fanned out to look for a good pine along the old towpath and up the hill.

"It has to be well shaped and just under six feet with a straight trunk all the way up!" Amanda shouted, though the chill air burned far down into her lungs. "And have branches spaced so we can light candles without burning them!"

"Any other royal decrees, your majesty?" Lincoln muttered just behind her.

She turned to face him. "If you had wings, I'd send you south to bring back some mistletoe. We always used to import it from down there for Christmas in the old days, as I don't think it grows up here. But then," she added hastily, looking away from his intent stare, "there's no real need for it this year."

"And, besides, you've been thinking lately I don't have wings, but horns and a forked tail."

"That's not true." She turned to face him again. Two sharp blue eyes, one partly obscured by a puffy, darkened lid, studied her from just above the brown scarf. "I believe," she said, deciding to be gracious in her victory of his capitulating to Christmas, "in answer to your original question about any other decrees I might have—well, with you along to help us today—except for Matt's getting better, I have all one woman could ask for this Christmas."

She could not see his mouth, but his cheeks lifted and the corners of his eyes crinkled. Her insides felt as if she were lurching and careening down this hill on a sled, while trees whooshed by and thin canal ice threatened. But it was worth the thrilling ride.

Though Lincoln set up the tree in the corner of the parlor, he did not return to help or even watch them decorate it, the banister, mantels, or front door. He refused to attend the evening church service with them, so Amanda prayed even harder for him as well as Matt. After they all trooped back noisily into the house, not even the smell of popcorn and cinnamon punch could lure him downstairs. But Amanda's spirits soared that Matt joined in the festivities.

Both Mandy's and Matt's gaze widened as they decorated the branches with tiny tin soldiers, crocheted angels with starched wings, painted wooden ornaments, lace whimsies, red ribbon bows, and various hard-baked cookies. Popcorn and cranberry strings looped up and up, and a shiny tin star on top lifted eyes and hearts. The candles in their tole holders went on last, but would not be lighted until tomorrow morning at the gift exchange. Amanda knew that others in town lit candles on Christmas Eve, but this was the way her family had done things, so nothing must change.

Afterwards, Aunt Louise kept telling the fidgety Mandy disjointed stories that began, "Now, when I was a girl . . ." or "In the old days . . ." Pru drifted in and out of the parlor until Amanda followed her across the hall to realize she was watching Ned across the spare lot, sweeping snow slowly off his walk with that one arm. Amanda tiptoed away. Slowly, chattering about tomorrow, everyone went off to bed. After Amanda put Matt and then Aunt Louise in bed, she wandered back downstairs to complete her tasks.

She stoked the cookstove again, adjusted the dampers, then let the oven begin to cool. She whipped egg whites and sugar until she could form peaks of meringue. In each she would secrete a surprise: a chocolate drop, cinnamon candy, a piece of hoarhound, citron, walnuts. When Amanda was growing up, even jewelry like earbobs, a ring, or a tiny brooch had been hidden within—until Aunt Louise broke a tooth and Father ordered the cook to stick to edible treats. Like her mother before her, Amanda called these cookies Heavenly Meringues or, sometimes, Angel Gifts, for their prizes and the look of their upswept, winglike peaks. Now she dropped them on paper sheets, put them in the cooling oven, and left them to set for a while.

Exhausted, she took off her apron and plopped down on the horsehair chair in the parlor. It felt more slippery than usual when she wore this brown plaid taffeta gown. In the light of the single table lantern, she stared at the tree. Though yet unlit, it seemed to shimmer; it wafted out the clean, sharp scent of forest. Once or twice, as she sat there, trying to soothe herself to sleepiness, she thought of things to do and got up. She checked on her meringues; twice she bent down to rearrange the gifts she had put under the tree, purchased with the hard-won profits from her baking. Whatever would Mother think about her daughter being "In trade"?

Her mind slid back to other Christmases, when everyone was together and it seemed that nothing could change that:

elaborate meals with friends dropping by, sleigh rides, expensive gifts imported via ship from the East Coast and England. She got up again to be certain her old porcelain-headed doll she was giving Mandy still sat upright. Its face was white, of course, but Sarah had said she wouldn't mind, for her cornhusk doll was all yellow.

Amanda's thoughts drifted to that precious, passionate Christmas furlough of Matt's that they had shared before he returned to his destruction. Could it have been only four years ago? It seemed forever. Then, they had sat in the dusky light here—over on the settee—talking, planning, sharing, kissing and fondling. At that memory, the treacherous feelings she called her "woman's yearning" slid back over her like a luring tide, to lap at her thighs and flow through her belly under her taut corset and stiff taffeta.

She startled at the form that suddenly loomed black against the tree's gray-green silhouette.

"Oh! Lincoln!"

He turned. "Amanda? I didn't see you sitting there."

"You brought Mandy's sled. It's lovely, all bright red."

She could not quite be sure in this light, but she thought he stared at her lips, as if to read the words there.

"Yes. And I trimmed it in brown, the only other paint I had. I wanted to leave it here—with a note from Santa."

He slid the sled under the tree. Paper crinkled and she realized he had more things. "A sack of chestnuts I hope you all enjoy," he explained. "I got them in trade uptown. Don't roast them, though, unless you all drill a little hole in each first or they're likely to explode."

"That's very thoughtful of you. But all we—I—wanted was for you to join us tomorrow and enjoy the day. Whatever we've all been through, I think we could and should do that," she added as she rose to turn up the wick of the lamp to give them more light.

"*We?*" he said, his voice so bitter that she jumped. "Should *we?*"

"I didn't mean—"

"I'm sorry. You've been very kind to me, especially under the circumstances. If I could give you more than chestnuts and helping with Matt—whom I like for his own sake, honestly—I would."

"Then there is one more little thing."

His narrowed eyes glittered in the reflected lamplight. "Which is?"

"I was wondering if you wouldn't like to cut—shave—that long beard."

"I'm used to it. It keeps me warm outside," he said and bent down to fiddle with the sled again.

"But you always wear that scarf—and besides," she blurted like a child who could not wait to share a secret, "I made you some earmuffs and I have a bigger scarf for you, and I can't even tell what you look like. Then too, it makes you look like you're hiding."

His head jerked around. "Meaning?"

"Meaning nothing other than that."

"I had thought of shaving it," he admitted, standing and stroking his chin. "But what about Matt losing his Mr. Lincoln?"

"I've prepared him for it, by showing him one of our pictures of a younger, beardless Lincoln. If you're willing—and I'd be glad to help, as I've shaved Matt's off and shave him every day—I'd even take down the parlor etching of President Lincoln for the winter—and Sherman's too. I mean, the war *is* over."

Her voice trailed off. He seemed not to be listening, staring beyond her, lost in thought, still fingering his beard.

"I really think," she added, "it isn't good for Matt to keep staring so strangely at those pictures or at you either. I just know he's going to continue to improve now."

"The thing is," he said, not moving from his stance by the tree, "you thought you had prepared Matt for the angel's trumpet at the pageant too—"

"But it was the scenery falling that set him off, and that scared everyone. I know we can do this—forgive the 'we' again. But he needs to be weaned away from his belief that you are Mr. Lincoln and just come to see you as a friend."

"And to remember you're his wife."

"Yes. He has to stop having these—these nightmares spells, or I'm afraid—that—to tell you the truth, some people think he should be admitted to a lunatic asylum to get help. But I won't have it! He has never done anything extremely dangerous or threatening, not really—just kind of momentarily wild."

"Like hitting me. Has he ever hit you?"

"In the middle of the night, once or twice, when he had a spell. We don't—he can't hit me at night now." He nodded. She felt her cheeks flame, realizing what she had admitted to him.

"I'm telling myself," he said, "that you've talked me into too much already. But I'm game about the shave. When could we do it?"

"Now?" she asked, unbelieving that he had capitulated. "There's still hot water in the kitchen, and I could get Matt's strop and straight razor right now."

"But," he said, stepping toward her at last, "could a staunch Rebel trust a passionate Yankee not to cut his throat?"

His voice had taken on a raspy quality, deep and disturbing, like she had never heard from him before. It was part mocking, part menacing, yet she was not afraid of him. Her voice too came out softer than she had intended.

"She would be willing even to soothe that rough throat with some of the cinnamon punch that you forfeited earlier tonight."

"At least tomorrow, if no one recognizes me," he said, heading for the kitchen, "folks will leave me out of things."

In the kitchen, they felt suddenly awkward again and went from chattering about the weather to discussing his suggestion that he paint Mandy's new doll's face brown. She agreed it was a good idea; he had some paint left from the trim on the sled. Then their conversation slid to silence.

From the cooling oven, she removed her meringues and offered him one, then another. It always made her feel warm inside to have someone really appreciate her baking as he did, for unlike the rest of the meal—which, fortunately, Sarah was learning to take over—baking was her art. She popped one in her mouth too and reveled in the rush of sensation: sweet meringue, then chocolate with the slightest tang of bitterness.

As if she were creating a new concoction, she beat the soft soap and water to a lather in a soup bowl with Matt's best boar bristle brush while Lincoln steamed his face under a hot towel. To position himself, he tipped back in a kitchen chair, leaning it against the table. With her big sewing scissors, she trimmed the beard as short as she could. But, after she layered on the lather, they decided she did not have a good angle to get at his cheeks, chin, or throat.

"How's this, then?" he asked, pulling the chair out and sitting down on the seat. He sprawled out his crossed legs and tipped his head onto a rolled towel on the back of the chair.

"Oh, yes, good," she said as she tied an old tablecloth around his neck, careful not to touch him. She pulled it down over his broad shoulders and threw it over his knees, but didn't smooth it over him as she would have with Matt. She stepped behind him, careful not to push herself so close that his head was cradled against her. How strange it felt to put her arms around his head like this, as if she were going to hug him from behind or kiss his cheek or nibble his ear. He was so near that she could see each separate dark eyelash and feel his breath on the sensitive skin of her inner wrists.

"Matt's beard was never this thick, but here goes," she said jauntily, but her snagged voice betrayed her nerves.

"*Now* you tell me."

"Don't talk, or I'm not responsible for damage."

"This isn't the way you rid the world of Scrooges who don't like Christmas, is it?"

"*Shh,* I said."

"Or like what Delilah did to Sampson in the Bible when she took his strength by cutting his hair? I'm going to keep some scraps of it just to be sure."

"Would you stop talking?"

He cleared his throat and swallowed; stretched back like that, his throat displayed his Adam's apple. They breathed in counterpoint and then in unison. She worked steadily, scraping away the thick, dark bush of beard. The lather was so slick against his taut skin when she bared each new stretch. A slant of cheek emerged, a square chin. A thinly chiseled upper lip and a much fuller lower one with a sensual curve in it. A handsome face, when she had been so foolish to imagine Abraham Lincoln's craggy visage hidden here. Lincoln Blake, she decided, though she'd not say so, like the past president, had a face of character.

For Lincoln, it was a revealing act too, almost as if he were stripping his clothes off. He should never have let her talk him into this, but perhaps it would be a better disguise for him than if he'd kept it; after all, he'd had a beard, though a trimmed one, when everything exploded at home.

But all that seemed so far away from this intimacy of her hands sliding over his face—even though she held a straight razor. In the relaxing, lingering luxury of it all, he closed his eyes, concentrating on her sweet lavender scent, on her closeness. He could feel her warmth; he reveled in her occasionally bumping the top of his head against her belly before she jumped back. He could tell it was going to happen each time her taffeta rustled. How long it had been since he had lain with his head in a woman's lap.

Amanda began to tremble deep inside. The tremors feathered up and out to her fingers, so the razor nicked his chin.

"Ouch! I've had sabre wounds kinder than that."

"Sorry, but it's not even bleeding."

"It will."

He was right. She bent before him to dab at the blood while he watched her through slitted lids. From this angle, she thought, black eye or not, his appearance was even more imposing—no Adonis, but downright disturbingly masculine, even though the new skin she had uncovered was snow white in contrast to his good color above it. He looked a bit more aristocratic now, even arrogant, but what would she expect from a southerner? Perhaps she had been crazy to do this, for the trembling in her continued to build, quaking her body as if she were cold, when she felt quite the opposite. Deep down, did she still detest him, was that why? This felt so much like her woman's yearning that she quickly moved back behind his chair as if she'd been burned.

"Not too much more now," she said, bending back to work.

"I hope we haven't made a mistake with this."

"What? Oh, about Matt, you mean."

"Yes, but it feels so good it's worth the risk."

Worth the risk, he repeated his own words to himself as she wiped away more lather and beard. He knew her hands were unsteady, but it could be from lifting the razor for so long, reaching around him, touching him without touching him. Yes, that too was what she had done—touched him deeply, even when they didn't touch. He wanted to mistrust and even hate her. At least to resent her for all she had in this house and town, though she thought she was struggling.

Right now, *he* was struggling to keep his composure, for his loins clenched and his hands ached to touch her skin without this sharp edge between them. He was very grateful, of all things, that this tablecloth she'd draped over him hid his body's betrayal of his man's needs.

"Here's a mirror," she said suddenly and produced one, tilting it at him. "Maybe you can wipe off the rest of the lather while I get some bay rum to soothe your skin."

"Anything with alcohol doesn't soothe, but braces and tightens," he said and got to his feet to tug his jacket down before peering at himself closely.

"I should know that from watching Rufus Quinn's effect on my favorite temperance advocate, Eliza Tuttle!" Amanda said, for Lincoln had also observed the exotic courtship shenanigans of the elderly pair.

Lincoln smiled at her jest, but his face felt so taut he put his hand out to massage it. She darted away to search a shelf; he shifted back behind her chair. He assessed the face he had not seen for so long. So much had happened, so much changed and lost.

"Looks fine," he said. "I do thank you."

"As I said, I prefer it on you," she said, with a shaky smile from clear across the kitchen, "so it's your gift to me. Merry Christmas, Lincoln, even if that is still a bad word, and this is the only holiday celebration you will join in."

"Merry Christmas, Amanda," he managed, though his tongue suddenly felt as stiff and as sore as his skin. Just for old time's sake, he stooped to gather up a big piece of the cut beard. Then, before he could say more or stay longer, he took the entire bottle of bay rum from her extended hand, and just kept going, all the way to the attic.

A mantle of heavy, soft snow fell on Christmas to cleanse everything anew—coal soot, tracks, slush. It seemed dusky out all day, but not cold. Still, after breakfast, Amanda built the traditional yuletide fire on the hearth, right on the coal grate, and everyone—except Lincoln, who had gone back up to his room after an early breakfast—stood about as she lit the candles on the tree.

Mandy's and Matt's wide eyes reflected the lights as if they glowed within. He smiled, perhaps at some distant thought or plan; it was that same look she had learned to recognize when she'd watched him in court, the look that said he was clever, in control—and had something up his sleeve to win. Amanda thrilled that Matt seemed to be more attentive, more rationally talkative than usual. She had worked and prayed so hard for this; surely, he would begin to heal now, a Christmas miracle indeed!

Meanwhile, Eliza fussed nearby with the bucket of water and sponges on sticks, prepared in case there was a mishap with the flames, while Pru kept glancing out the front window. Aunt Louise smiled and rubbed her birdlike hands together as if she were gloating over a sack of pirate's gold instead of the little pile of wrapped gifts on her lap blanket.

"All right, everyone sit down to open presents!" Amanda said, and, feeling like Santa Claus herself, whipped off the sheet hiding Mandy's sled—with a brown-faced porcelain doll sitting next to it with her wide-eyed look of perpetual surprise.

"Mine? Those are mine, Mama?" the child cried and jumped and shrieked while Sarah nodded and cried in joy. Amanda only hoped that the child's anonymous benefactor, sequestered in his cold room in the attic, could hear her and know the ecstasy he'd brought.

Other gifts exchanged hands and hearts in a tumble: Sarah gave new velvet neck ribbons to display old brooches: Eliza gave books—even one to Matt, who carried it about as if he would open and declaim from it. Amanda presented calico balls of dried lavender to scent drawers of unmentionables and small bags called "strawberries," filled with emery powder to keep sewing needles sharp and clean. She gave Matt a new muffler and pencils and paper, which he also carried about importantly but seemed not to want to use, even when Mandy helpfully showed him how. Amanda had a new paisley dressing jacket for him too, which had cost her a pretty penny, but she would give him that later in privacy. But when she saw what Sarah extended toward her, her eyes prickled with unshed tears again.

"Oh, Sarah! How did you know how much I love these?" Amanda asked as she accepted a ribboned stack of *Godey's Lady's Magazine.*

"Got the new one uptown, and found some back ones for you too. Good for me to practice reading in, I reckon. Heard you gave them up even 'fore the war, but I knew times are gonna be better now," Sarah said as Amanda hugged her.

"You know, if I hadn't been a small-town girl—if I had lived somewhere elegant like Boston or New York City—I would have been a lady editor, just like this Mrs. Hale. And not because of the Paris fashions here, but because of the things for the good of the mind and body. Speaking of which, Eliza, I see there is one more book from you under the tree."

"Yes," she said, as she tugged down her best fitted, frogged dress jacket. "Since you saw fit to ask Captain Quinn to sit at the table this afternoon, I thought the man must have something or other, not to feel left out, though I've warned you what encouraging him about overeating— just like drinking—can do to one of his weak, wavering disposition."

"How very thoughtful of you, Eliza!" Amanda said, fighting to conceal a triumphant grin. Yesterday, just when the stubborn woman had launched into another tirade to refuse the captain a place at the same table, Amanda had dosed her with her own medicine: a Shakespeare quotation, one of the few Amanda happened to recall. " 'Methinks the lady doth protest too much' about the captain," she had pronounced archly to Eliza. Despite Eliza's sputtering and a narrow glare over her spectacles, that had done the trick to get Captain Quinn invited to dinner.

"All right now, everyone," Amanda announced in the lull, "Miss Mandy Murry has agreed to grace us with her recitation piece from the grammar school program the other night."

" 'specially," Sarah added, "since she forgot the second part then 'cause she never done the like before, and not 'cause she can't do memory work."

"All right, Mandy," Eliza said, asserting her schoolmistress presence again, "stand up straight and sing it out."

"I didn't ever sing it, Mrs. Tuttle," the child protested.

"That means declaim—speak—in a loud, clear voice, my girl."

Amanda watched Eliza glow as if Mandy were her student. The child clasped her new doll in her hands and stood straight—and still, for once. Despite initial protests about keeping Sarah and Mandy here, Eliza had come around,

Amanda thought. Now if she could only find some way to patch up the bad feelings between Sarah and Lincoln! If they were all going to get through this winter together here, people at least had to be civil.

Mandy said in her loudest, shrillest voice: "Christmas comes but once a year, and when it comes it brings good cheer. Christmas comes but once a year, but lasts a lifetime. Thank you."

Everyone applauded; Mandy grinned and bowed, then was back to playing with her doll and begging to go out to test her sled. "This afternoon, 'fore we fix dinner, for certain," Sarah promised.

Pru, who had remained quiet, said, "I've been saving a piece of reciting myself, but with words I've embroidered for you on a sampler, Amanda. For all you do for me—for all of us."

People—including Matt—applauded again. Eliza, who had been Pru's schoolteacher too, indicating she should stand. As if she were still a child, Pru hastened to obey, turning the framed sampler she'd done to face her little audience. It was simply yet elegantly embroidered, with a sliced loaf of bread, a plate of cookies, and a cake set in a green frame of trailing ivy. Pru cleared her throat and recited the scripted words: "Little acts of kindness, little words of love make our earthly Eden like our heaven above."

Amanda stood and hugged her. "And," Pru said, "I'm offering both Sarah and Mandy piano lessons while they're with us—if they want them."

So much joy, Amanda thought, even in trying times. And such simple treasures born of time and caring meant the most.

When the candles burned down low where they could catch the branches, she went around snuffing them out, her mind already jumping ahead to preparing dinner. The sound of distant sleigh bells outside sent her spinning back again to memories of other Christmases. She hurried to the front door to see who was going so grandly by.

The old Lockwood harness of sleigh bells jingled merrily as she pulled the door open, for she had hung it there amidst greenery, now that the family sleigh and matched pair were no more. Sarah and Mandy came to stand beside her. "I love these bells," Amanda told them and bounced the string of them.

"Not me," Sarah admitted with a shudder that obviously went deeper than the cold. "Reminds me of once when I had them put on me for punishment."

"Were you bad then, Mama, and didn't you get anything for Christmas?" Mandy asked, but further conversation was forgotten as a sleek sleigh with two adults and two children snuggled in buffalo lap robes went by.

Amanda recognized the Mason Rutland family immediately, but it was too late to retreat without being seen. Mason's dapple-gray trotting cracks, which also made excellent racers, pranced by and Dottie "hallooed." Mason merely craned his neck to look. Caught, Amanda waved, turned immediately and started back in. But Sarah still stared after them.

"Mm-mn, those are fine horses, ones like your daddy used to tend, honey child," she told Mandy as Amanda stepped back onto the veranda. "You all run in now, 'fore you catch your death of cold, and we'll go out later so you can give Miz Wynne that surprise for her." She gave Mandy a little nudge back inside.

"What's the matter, Sarah?" Amanda asked as they lingered in the crisp air. As different as their pasts were, it amazed Amanda how she could sense when something was amiss with Sarah, and she had seen it work both ways.

"You done so much for Mandy—that sled and doll, no matter if the note says Santy Claus! Can't thank you enough, with all the burdens you got."

"The doll is my gift to her, but the sled's from someone else."

"Who else could be Santy Claus 'round here?"

"I promised I wouldn't tell."

"Good glory, Miz Tuttle done that?"

"I didn't say who."

"And who else but you be kind enough to think of turning that doll's face dark like hers?"

Suddenly, Amanda could not stop herself. After all, if Lincoln had not come down to breakfast a bit sleepy and smelling of bay rum on his breath as well as his face, he would have had the sense to clean his hands. Amidst the flurry of excitement over his beardless face—and, thankfully, Matt had taken it so well as to give Amanda increased hope for his continued adjustment—Lincoln had obviously not thought to erase the evidence, and she hadn't said she wouldn't point at least to that.

"I suppose Santa was whoever forgot to clean under fingernails for brown face and sled paint." Amanda dropped the comment like a cannon ball on Sarah's foot as she hurried back inside.

Sarah caught up with her in the hall. "You not telling me that? Not that *he* done that for my Mandy?"

"I didn't tell you a thing, Sarah Murry. Santa has his secrets and Christmas is Christmas, with its own miracles, and I'm hoping for a big one for Matt."

She left Sarah muttering in the hall as she went back in the parlor.

Eliza knew she sat stiff as a board at dinner, but she couldn't help it. At least, she thought, Amanda had not been so presumptuous as to seat Rufus next to her, but it was actually worse that he sat right across, where their eyes met all the time. He was on his best behavior, even if his foot wandered the width of the table to touch her ankle once and she almost tossed the tureen of gravy into the air. But it was, hopefully, evidently, unintended, as he had not even been looking her way at the time.

Other than the fact that Eliza saw Sarah staring most rudely down the length of the table at Mr. Blake's dirty fingernails, which were quite appalling, it was a lovely meal for more than the food. The child was squirming to get outside, but everyone else chatted. Mr. Blake and Rufus became quite chummy as they spoke of shipbuilding and the construction of the locks.

"I can tell, sir, you are a builder of sorts," Rufus declared, "but a landlubber too."

"I must plead guilty on both counts, Captain. The nearest I ever got to traversing big water was building a pontoon bridge over the Middle River in Savannah."

"During the war?" Amanda asked. "It must have been a unique experience to be stationed in one's hometown."

"The war was, no doubt, ma'am, a unique experience for everyone, no matter where he was stationed," he said.

At that, everyone looked at Matthew, then back to their

eating. "Lincoln builds porches and houses," Matthew announced in the sudden silence.

Eliza saw Amanda gasp at that clever revelation; Rufus dinged a spoon on his plate; even Miss Louise regarded Matthew for once. He did not speak again, but it was more than he had said in months, and something he had obviously recalled and remembered from experience and conversation. Eliza noted that Amanda's eyes welled up with tears and she bit her lip. The poor dear was so hopeful, so certain that these holidays would heal Matthew, and perhaps she was right to believe that his wounded brain could recover.

After the meal, while Eliza sat with Aunt Louise and Matthew, Rufus came into the parlor and stood in the door, hat in hand. "I was going to head on out, but Amanda said you had something to say," he said warily.

"Actually, I have something for you. I have found I cannot quite forget that impromptu poem of yours about looking out over the old canal basin, because it recalls to me Shelly's poems. So," she said and bent down for the last gift under the tree, "I thought you should read some of his works."

Rufus looked stunned. "Just on loan, you mean?" he asked. "That way, after I read it, I could bring it back, discuss it with you, like you say Matt used to talk books with you."

"Yes, I suppose that would be fine. But I would expect you to ponder these works, not race through them. And," she added pointedly, "to read them in a sober state of mind."

He nodded, looking entirely more sober to her than he had in months—years. Their fingers brushed as he extended the book to him.

"I knew you liked Shakespeare," he said, his usually deep voice squeaky, "but I didn't know about this Shelley fellow. Maybe there's something in that *Sh* sound to their name that puts the poet's heart in them."

"You know, I never looked at it that way," she said, instead of telling him it was the most lackbrained idea she had ever heard. Because it was Christmas. Because Amanda had been right that "the lady doth protest too much." Because once, way back before he began to romance sailing ships instead of her, Rufus had stolen her poet's heart, though she would never, never let him know.

"I'll be going then," he said. "Told some folks I'd go caroling with them tonight. Don't suppose you'd like to come, Mrs. Tuttle."

"Pru is going to play the piano for us later, and she'd be disappointed if I weren't here," she said. But the truth was, she was instantly disappointed that she had turned him down.

"Did you hear that girl follow my lead on 'Deck the Hall' and 'Marching through Georgia'?" Pru asked Amanda. "She has the ear for the music, even though she doesn't know fingering or scales! If she can just sit still long enough, who knows to what heights she can climb on the keys?"

Amanda smiled at Pru's exuberance. It was, indeed, a day for revelations. Here Pru had been moping ever since dinner, wandering into the dark, chilly library to glance over at the Milburns', where Ned swept the walk again—as Lincoln and Matt were doing theirs now—then drifting back in, looking entirely too woebegone for Christmas.

"Pru, while Mandy and Sarah go out—they're going to try the sled, then surprise me with some Christmas angels in the new snow—why don't you take some hot spiced cider out to the men, Ned too. It's cold out there, and they need something."

"Oh, I suppose. All right, if you come with me."

"I've done enough to get Matt and Lincoln in new scarves and earmuffs. It's your turn to care for them."

"Amanda, I don't know about including Ned, unless he walks over. You know how he is," she said, wringing her hands.

"Bosh! I know how you are, Prudence Cuddy, and I think it's time for a New Year's resolution already. You stood up to your mother years ago for the man you wanted, but you won't stand up to the new man you want."

"Stand up to him!"

"I mean, put yourself in his path, encourage him—quite correctly—if that's what it takes."

"Amanda! You can't tell me you got that fast idea out of *Godey*'s!"

"I got it out of my own gumption. Now, please, do the Christian, neighborly thing, Pru, and offer Ned some cider. And if you get the chance, ask him and his family over for your Christmas concert tonight too."

* * *

Amanda became more and more excited as the day went on. Matt showed no inclination to take his usual nap, so she let him stay up. He and Lincoln had moved inside; they had all gone way up to the front second-story windows earlier to gaze down on Mandy's artwork of angel scrapings in the snow, special ones, with straw hair, pine-bough-lined skirts, bittersweet berry mouths, and wings of fluttering birds. Evidently in exchange for the hot drink, Ned had brought over blueberry juniper and dried sumac for the birds and spread them on the angels' wings. And he and his family had accepted Pru's invitation for this evening. Now, if only Rufus would come back somehow for Eliza, Amanda thought, it would be a miraculous day indeed.

In the early evening, when carolers came to the door with glowing lanterns, Amanda saw Rufus Quinn among them. Lincoln had disappeared upstairs again, but everyone else went out onto the veranda to listen. Aunt Louise smiled and clapped her hands; Sarah and Mandy were all eyes; Eliza sent a brisk, approving nod Rufus's way. Amanda stood with her arm in Matt's, while the carolers sang, "God bless the master of the house and bless the mistress too, and all the little children that round the table go . . ." Only then, in this lovely, long day, did a twinge of regret pain her that there were no children here besides Mandy.

Then it was time for the mistress of the house to step forward with the plates of cookies she'd had waiting all day in the hall. After eating and chatting, everyone joined the carolers in the slow, soaring "Silent Night." Pru squeezed Amanda's arm as the Milburn family walked over to join the festivities, while the sounds and sights and smells of Christmas simmered in all their hearts.

Matt heard the slow, sad song. Saw lanterns and the campfire inside the house through the window. Hummed along with words he knew: " 'Silent night . . . We're tenting tonight on the old camp ground. Give us a song to cheer our weary hearts with songs of home and friends we love so dear. Many are the hearts that are weary tonight, waiting for the war to cease . . .' "

He slipped inside to warm himself by the fire for the of-

ficers. Rolling a piece of paper to take some fire to the boys.
Flames. Lighting signal candles in the trees so they would
see, lighting campfires for all of them away from home at
Christmas. Be warm. Not afraid. Christmas in the South instead of at home. Enemies. Memories.

Candles flared, lit new campfires. " 'Tenting tonight. Silent night. Tenting tonight.' "

"Matt! Matt! The tree's on fire! Get back! Help me! Help,
everyone! Fire!"

The woman screaming, Amanda. War is hard and hot
work, boys. Can't a woman understand? Sentinel fires on the
enemy's lines!

Men around him. Running, shouting. "Put it out! Get
more water from the kitchen! The rug! Stamp it out! Tear
down the drapes! Here! Hurry!"

He ran. Ran screaming into Lincoln's arms, before he held
him tight.

Late that night, when the others thought she was in bed,
long after Matt was safely secured in his room, Amanda
stood at the parlor door. But for smoke and soot, it had not
gone beyond this room, though it could have engulfed everything. She should be grateful but she felt only—empty.
Drapes burned, the rug, one chair, the tree, of course. Blackened ceiling and walls. A smoky smell that sank into the pit
of one's stomach. But more than that had gone up in flames:
it was the conflagration of her hopes and dreams for Matt at
Christmas, for believing he was not really dangerous to others.

She tightened her flannel wrapper over her nightgown and
tucked her loose hair in its neckline to keep warm. She
should have put stockings on too. Someone had broken a
window in the chaos of carolers rushing in, the throwing of
the water. Lincoln had patched the broken pane with boards,
but the night crept in. She sniffed back tears.

"Amanda."

"Lincoln. I didn't know you were still up. I'm not—
decent."

"It's dark. I won't look. I just thought I'd see if the patch
job on the window was holding." He walked past her to feel
around the edges of the board. He seemed to be completely

dressed, but it occurred to her that it might be too cold way upstairs for nightclothes.

"I'm sorry," he whispered when she said nothing but still stood sentinel in the dim doorway. "I know how much you all cherished this room—the past. And Christmas."

"I learned something you should take to heart too, Lincoln Blake. You can't go back to the past, even on Christmas, not with people gone or changed. I was so hoping it would help heal Matt. But it only proved what I feared but have been ignoring—denying."

"That he can be dangerous?"

"Yes! Even when he's not startled. Worse, it will be all over town with the carolers. I can hear it now—Matthew Wynne may have been a town leader once, but he's a lunatic now—a dangerous firebug! Lincoln, they are good, kind people, but they are people! That bastard Mason Rutland will have Matt committed in a moment—indefinitely, and I can't let that happen! I didn't want to take him to Cleveland—not even to see the place, but now . . ."

"The lunatic asylum?"

She nodded, squeezing her eyes shut, turning her head and leaning her forehead against the doorjamb as he came closer. "I can't bear the idea of committing him. But what if he strikes someone, burns something again, only worse?"

"I was thinking he could take that razor from you when you shave him," he added.

"I'm wrong to keep him away from the asylum, if it could help him. I'm afraid I'd better at least take him for a visit before others step in and seize things from my hands."

In a monotone, she explained to him about Mason Rutland—all of it. She had no idea why she bared her soul to him, but it just fell out of her. When she stopped speaking, he said only, "Don't blame yourself."

"I blame Mason! Others have been disappointed in love before and not made a lifelong quest of subtle, sadistic revenge! Others have been eclipsed by a partner in business brighter or better than they and not lain in wait like some poisonous spider to snare that person! But you know Matt's not really harmful—not hatefully so, don't you?"

"Not spitefully, of course I do."

"If I decide to visit Cleveland, to take Matt along for an

interview, would you go along to help me—keep him happy? I'd pay our way on the train."

"Yes," he said so vehemently that she focused her teary, aching eyes on him at last. He had come quite close. She hugged herself harder; she should go back upstairs, but her feet seemed fastened to the still wet floor.

He reached out slowly to rest his hands lightly on her shoulders. As spent as she was, lightning coursed through her. But when she just stared dazedly at him, his big hands tightened their hold. And then, somehow, she was held hard in his arms.

Her hands pressed to the powerful muscles of his back. She wanted to burrow inside him, hide there from all the fear and fury. No wonder Matt in his terror liked to hide in safe, close places.

As she pressed her face into his shoulder, she realized he wore his Confederate uniform. Because it was warmer? Because he was still, at heart, a Rebel? It didn't matter, none of it, not now, as he held her tight and let her cling to him, his mouth pressed into her loose hair so she could feel his ragged breath in her ear.

And then he set her sharply back. "You'd best go on up," he said.

"Yes." She stepped away as if awakening from a dream. But with her foot on the first stair, she said, "If it's too cold in the attic, we could fix you a pallet in the kitchen. And thank you today for helping put out the fire."

He just shook his head at that, and she hurried up the stairs.

Chapter
Six

❄

Louise Lockwood's
Apple Cake

Prepare a tube pan (or regular one) by greasing and flouring.

Sift dry ingredients of 2¼ cups flour, 1 teaspoon cinnamon, 1 teaspoon baking soda, ¼ teaspoon salt.

Beat 3 eggs in a large bowl.

Add 2 cups granulated sugar and 1½ cups vegetable oil and beat until light.

Add sifted ingredients, stirring them in well (batter will be stiff).

Fold in 3 cups pared, chopped apples and 2 teaspoons vanilla, as well as 1 cup walnuts, if desired.

Bake for up to 1 hour and 15 minutes in 350-degree oven, checking for doneness after one hour by inserting knife in center. If it comes out clean, the cake is done.

This is a good winter cake if you have apples stored in your pantry or root cellar. Excellent for church socials when most fruit is off-season.

If you wish, make a glaze to dribble on top by combining 1 cup packed brown sugar, ¼ cup milk, and ½ cup of margarine. Combine these in a saucepan and, stirring, let boil 2 to 3 minutes. Beat to desired thickness and pour over cake. However, it is a wonderfully moist cake without the icing and travels well by wagon or train.

"Those big icicles dripping already," Sarah told Lincoln, setting his plate of breakfast eggs and toast before him. When he only nodded, Sarah added, "Gonna be warm for a mid-January day." It wasn't even seven o'clock yet and still dark out. But early hours never stopped Lincoln Blake, she'd noticed that. And that he looked real dressed up for once, because he was escorting Amanda and Mr. Matt to Cleveland on the train today.

When Lincoln began to eat without a word, she said, "Gonna be hard for us southerners, whether we from your Georgia or my Miz'sippi to get used to these Ohio winters, and this one not even got its feet under it yet."

Lincoln stopped his fork's plunge toward his plate. "Are you still trying to prove I'm from Mississippi, so you can show I'm some sort of liar, Sarah?"

"No, sir," she said, putting down her spatula and wiping her palms on her apron. "I'm trying to tell you if you say you from Savannah, that's fine with me, 'cause in Miz'sippi nobody knows how to make sleds, so you gotta be from somewheres else."

"I believe we have a mutual friend who's been talking out of school," he said and went back to eating.

"She didn't say it was you. I been fixing to tell you I saw it on your hands—the brown paint."

"And discovered my guilt."

"Discovered you got a heart buried inside you and for more than helping Mr. Matt. And that maybe I been wrong about you. I been thinking," she said and plopped herself down on the other side of the table with her hands clasped in her lap. "Here I been so all-fired angry at you 'cause the way you talk sounds like my—the man who owned the plantation I was on."

"I understand."

"No, you don't, 'cause you ain't been where I been! But, see what I was doing was what I was hating you for doing—or not doing. I *mean,* I was hating you, thinking you was Miz'sippi white, and thinking you hated me and Mandy for being freed Miz'sippi black."

"Sarah, even if I were Mississippi white, it doesn't follow that I would hate you and Mandy. I didn't mean to scare her that time, but she could have gotten hurt."

"Amanda told me that, but I didn't believe her at first. Imagine, not trusting her. Well, now," she said and got to her feet to try to keep Amanda and Mr. Matt's eggs hot since they were really dragging their feet this morning, "I admire you for not taking no credit for kindly things you didn't do, but me and Mandy sure do thank someone who been Santy Claus to her."

She busied herself toasting more bread when she heard the others coming, but she caught a sideways glimpse of that fine-looking face of Lincoln Blake's Amanda had uncovered for him. He kept right on eating, looking at his food, but she saw a stiff little smile just sitting on the corners of his mouth.

With Matt between them, Amanda and Lincoln walked uptown to catch the coach to Sandusky, where they would get the train. Amanda's stomach churned; she felt they walked to an execution, but this had to be done. She had intentionally not brought Matt's things. In case the asylum people said they wanted to keep Matt today, she'd have a reason to bring him back home again—at least for a while. But if there was any chance he could be helped by doctors at the asylum, she had to take it.

Besides, several Lockwood citizens, including Mason Rutland, had made pointed inquiries about whether she was seeking "outside" help for Matt's "destructive and incendiary tendencies," and she could not risk having others step in to try to put him away permanently—even if they thought they were doing it for the common good. And it was a real fear now that Matt might inadvertently hurt someone. In desperation, despite Mason's warnings, she had written letters to her congressmen and a prominent lawyer Matt had known in Cleveland, who was now a pension attorney. He had responded, but he only presented her with more brick walls to bang her head against—and how did she know the man was not a crony of Mason's anyway?

As they waited outside the stagecoach office for the coach to appear from the livery stable, Julius Ross, Lockwood's postmaster, approached them. "Morning, Amanda, gentlemen," he said and tipped his hat in his usual sprightly fashion. "Just wanted to let you know a letter just came in on the Toledo stage for that hired girl of yours. Do you want to take it to her?"

"Oh, good! Lincoln, maybe some news for Sarah about locating her husband! No, Mr. Ross, I'm leaving town for the day and she deserves to get that letter soon. Can you send your boy up with it, please?"

"Sure enough. You mean this is *the day* for your trip?" he asked. He looked from Matt, who nodded to him, to Lincoln, who didn't budge or blink an eye, back to her. "Have a pleasant journey," he said, tipped his hat, and hurried on.

"A pleasant journey, my foot," Amanda whispered. "Word's all over town where we're going. And I wish I could be with Sarah today of all days, whether that letter brings good news or bad."

"Amanda, you can't be everyone's protector," Lincoln said.

"Yes, but if you knew the things she'd been through! And now to have to search for her lost husband and just hope he'll come back to her . . ." she said, but her voice drifted off. She bit her lip and put her arm through Matt's as the coach rolled toward them down the street.

"Amanda, I know this is going to surprise you," Lincoln told her as they sat in the depot in Sandusky, "but there's a quick errand I have to run."

"What? Here? The train's coming in twenty minutes!"

"I know, but I have an idea that might help Sarah find this Ben Blue you've just been telling me about. And as long as I'm here, so close . . ."

"Close to what? Lincoln, don't leave us right now. Were you going to send a telegram?"

"Of sorts. Trust me on this, and I'll explain when I get back. Matt, you stay with Amanda and take good care of her. All right, Matt?"

"Take care of Amanda," Matt said and looked out the window again.

"Lincoln . . ."

"Fifteen minutes. I'll be back." He headed out the door.

It touched him how she had wanted him to stay, but then, she was relying on him to help with Matt, that was all. He would explain this sudden inspiration to her later: who knew but that this Ben Blue didn't ride the rails too or maybe had fought in Freeman's colored regiment. Amanda said they were trying to trace Sarah's husband through the old Underground Railroad, but this other underground railroad of hobos, tramps, and life's losers might turn him up too.

Besides, Sarah's words to him just this morning—I discovered you got a heart buried inside you and for more than helping Mr. Matt—kept haunting him. It was true, but the frightening thing was, his heart went out not only for Matt, or Mandy, or even Sarah. No, the worst thing was, his heart had gone out—and more than that—to Amanda.

He hurried across the tracks and strode for the familiar line of pines that hid the ravine. The tramps on the rails had a very efficient system of passing news, one that probably rivaled what the Lockwood postmaster could do. Devil take it, he thought, but he'd get his boots and trouser legs all muddy and slushy here when he wanted to look respectable to accompany Amanda on her doleful duty today.

"Hello!" he called to the four men—all strangers—seated around a campfire in the same place he'd left his own comrades behind nearly two months ago. They looked for a moment as if they might bolt, but his wave and smile evidently steadied them. He walked close enough to see that they had hardtack biscuits and a tin of thin, greasy soup set in the ashes; he thought again how blessed he was to be eating at Amanda's table this winter. She had packed a picnic basket of food that these men would probably kill for—though he hadn't meant to even think of that.

"I used to ride the rails, but I've got a winter job," he explained to them. "I went by the name the President or Honest Abe. I'd really appreciate it if you all could pass something on to a Negro tramp called Freeman—"

"Oh, him," one man said. "Not many darkies on the rails, 'specially not ones fought for the Union. Not seen him for weeks, though. What's the word?"

"I need to talk to him to see if he could help me find another ex-slave who's turned up missing. Name of Ben Blue. Husband of—of a friend of mine."

"Yeah?" another man said. Their tired, dirty faces seemed to blur together for him into one face, one past, one nightmare in his life. He hadn't realized how glad he was that it was over—even if perhaps for just a while.

"So where can Freeman find you?" the first man asked.

"I'm in the little town of Lockwood, not far from here, doing house repairs and such with the name of Blake—Lincoln Blake. Or if he sends word somehow, I'll meet him here, pay for his coach ride, or whatever."

"Real generous. Times gotta be good for you."

He had no reply to that, so he thanked them and trusted them and climbed from the ravine. Amanda stood with Matt in the window of the depot, watching for him as he hurried back across the tracks. Both of their faces lit to see him. Strange, how merely walking toward them as they peered from the window took him back again, made him feel as if he were coming home to his waiting family. Yet he didn't picture Melanie this time, nor the excited Lindy with her; he saw only Amanda and Matt. He walked even faster and forgot to scrape his boots, so he tracked mud across the wooden floor.

"Oh, I'm so glad you're back, Lincoln! I think I hear the train. You went down to say hello to your old fellows, is that it?" she asked as she gathered up their things and Lincoln took the basket of food from her.

"I went down to see if they could ask a friend of mine—an ex-slave—to contact me. It's a long shot, but he might know something of Sarah's Ben Blue, or at least someplace else to look."

"We will hope that Sarah had good news in that letter from Toledo," she said, "but I thank you, and Sarah will too. Though I suppose Santa Claus doesn't want her to know this either."

"Just so we don't get her hopes too high. And," he raised

his voice as they went out on the platform, and both kept a good hold on Matt as the steam engine huffed closer, "Sarah and I began to mend fences this morning anyway."

"Did you?" she shouted back. "Then that's a sign that today will be a good day. And I didn't know you have a friend who is an ex-slave, but there's so much about your past I don't know."

Fortunately, Lincoln thought, that leading comment was interrupted by the increased noise and their need to board. Matt hesitated, then mounted the wooden conductor's steps and the wrought iron ones; Amanda gathered her skirts and climbed into the second-class passenger carriage. Lincoln hesitated at first, even as Matt had, but for different reasons. How strange it seemed to board with the conductor watching instead of sprinting for the moving car, head low, haversack flopping. He tried to shove all that down deep inside him, but Amanda didn't forget her last comment about his past.

"What was it like to be with those men out there again?" she asked when they were settled in facing black leather seats. "What was it like all those months on the move?" As they watched the winter scenery go by, with the icy expanse of Lake Erie on their left, he found he really wanted to tell her. He spoke until the train stopped at Vermilion and then headed on toward Lorain.

"And you hadn't known this Freeman friend of yours down south?" she asked.

"No. Amanda, just like Sarah, I think you have a rather too narrow view of southern whites. We did not all own plantations and slaves. I didn't."

"So you said the second day you were with us, or I don't believe I would have kept you on, Lincoln."

"You don't know how it was, that's all I'm saying."

"But I want to know—to understand, even to sympathize—I really do."

"It's going to take something stronger than sympathy or even government Reconstruction to get the North and South back together, Amanda. But go ahead, ask me a question about what it was really like—just one or we'll miss getting off in Cleveland."

"All right, just one, and then I'll feed you and Matt some sandwiches and apple cake. My stomach always gets queasy on a train, and watching you two eat will be quite enough.

Lincoln, what really happened to your wife and daughter in the war?"

He wasn't expecting that, but he said, "Cholera," not looking at her now. Snow-shrouded fields and fences flew by. "We lost Lindy first and then my wife, Melanie, died of it too. The truth is," he said sitting up straighter and frowning at her now, "after your hero Sherman's march through the South 'relieved' us of our homes and livelihoods, all our livestock, railroads, next to everything, people did die, Amanda. I know you all sing that song Pru pounds out, 'Marching through Georgia,' and think Sherman spared lives and 'only' hit at us through property loss, but that's not true. Take everything away from the populace, including food and clean wells, and their health goes too, disease comes in, there are no doctors. Amanda, you aren't going to be sick? You've gone white as paste."

She shook her head. Matt leaned forward, turning to them from his perpetual gaze out the window. "It's just I never thought of Sherman's march that way," she whispered, twisting her handkerchief in her hands. "A lot of Ohio boys were with him, and they tell it so differently. And it's ironic that you lost two you loved to cholera. I had two older brothers, taken in the cholera epidemic of '37, the year I was born. They were Father's hope and pride, and there I was, a newborn girl, and unaffected by their illness or their loss. So, I guess, I became everything to my parents. Once I knew of the family tragedy, I always tried to make their loss up to them. Sorry, I didn't mean to get off on myself."

He wanted to hold her hand; his rush of hatred had ebbed already. "And I was away in the army when Lindy died," he whispered. "I hope Melanie forgave me for that. In a letter, she said she didn't, but her sister said she forgave me on her deathbed. Still, with a fever, you know," he said, looking down at his hands gripped in his lap, "people probably just say things."

"On their deathbed, don't you think they'd tell the truth, knowing they were going to meet their Maker soon?" she asked, leaning toward him across their almost touching knees. "I'm sure she forgave you!"

"Amanda, always the comforter. But I've had some quarrels with our Maker more than once," he admitted, his voice bitter.

"I too, lately, even when I try to just accept. But I'm relying on Him—and those doctors—to help Matt. And on you too, Lincoln, for Matt and I are very grateful you are here to help us. So, we'd best keep up our strength for everything. I'll just get some ham sandwiches and apple cake out for you two and eat myself after we get off this train."

He watched her capable, graceful hands as she unpacked the food. It was crazy to think of food as spiritual medicine, but more than once he had seen Amanda use it that way. Strange, but it soothed him now, calmed him, filled him like love once had. His fears that Melanie had hated him at the end—war duty or not—faded.

Instead of agonizing about that, he studied Amanda. He admired the way she tended to him and Matt when they needed something, how she kept up conversation, even though she'd admitted the swaying motion of the cars that soothed him always made her slightly sick. He observed her again as she closed her eyes to steady herself; the late-morning light made a halo around her fine profile and head. Later, as the train halted at another small depot for passengers to board and disembark, he saw her gold-brown eyes spark as she reread to him the letter from the Cleveland pension attorney that both gave her hope and denied her help.

"So," she concluded, "here's the latest dilemma. 'A Union Army soldier must suffer *permanent* bodily injury as a direct consequence of military service' to be eligible for the eight to thirty dollars per month. And 'said veteran must prove that his disability left him unable to perform *manual* labor.' You see, Lincoln, neither of those things exactly fits Matt, but then how do they fit someone like Ned Milburn either?—and he's eligible. Drat this government, but Matt might fall through the cracks even if I can clear his reputation. With that pension money I could hire on someone to really watch him when I can't. I could be certain that, even if my boarders leave, even with selling my baked goods, I would be able to afford to keep our home. But perhaps, as I said, I've got to put my hopes in these doctors at the asylum."

"That's good to a point, but remember what happened when you put too much hope in Christmas."

"Yes," she said with a sigh, as the train jerked and huffed into motion. He watched as she crossed her arms over her stomach and closed her eyes against the relentless swaying again. "Yes, I know."

From the big, busy Cleveland depot, they took the Newburgh hack to head east to the rural town where the asylum was located. A Mrs. Bigler, a Newburgh farmer's wife who said she did mending for the asylum staff from time to time, was the fourth passenger. After initial light conversation, Amanda seized the opportunity to discover all she could about the asylum.

"Do the patients seem content there, Mrs. Bigler?"

" 'Content' is a strange word for it, I suppose," she said, squinting out the window. "I see some lunatics out on the grounds once in a while who obviously don't have a care in the world. And they're probably called inmates, Mrs. Wynne. You sure what we say won't bother your husband?" she asked in a stage whisper, with a quick glance at Matt.

"No, and I would really appreciate your candor."

"Say, look at the size of those houses, would you!" the woman cried, pressing her nose to the blurry isinglass window. "Some call it 'millionaire's row' here, you know. There's a lot of money from retired ship's captains and captains of industry in Cleveland. Love to see the insides of those places, I would. Imagine having more money than a body could spend! Got rich on the war, a lot of them. Hear they're looking for summer or retirement homes away from downtown Cleveland now, in some quiet little hamlets. Wish they'd come out to Newburgh, as I'd rather mend their fine linen any day. Imagine that—a place that big and they're looking for little rural houses of some sort!"

"But the asylum," Amanda prompted, looking at the distorted view of mansion after mansion through the window. "Do you think the doctors there are good?"

"Sometimes late with paying their mending bills, I'll tell you that. But I'd say if you want to know about things inside the big white house—just wait 'til you see that place—you should do what I do and go up the back staircase and peek in the wards yourself. Now I only go up there to have the mending handed out and my friend Hannah gets staff laundry the same time, but I suppose you could learn a lot that way, I can tell you."

"What have *you* learned that way?" Lincoln asked her, evidently noting Amanda's growing frustration with the talkative but apparently inattentive woman. And, though he didn't know it, Amanda thought, she felt growing annoyance that the woman simpered like a schoolgirl whenever Lincoln looked her way or addressed her.

"Oh, it's a good enough place, a sort of refuge for the lost," Mrs. Bigler said with a sigh. "It will help your husband, I'm sure it will, dearie." Though she patted Amanda's hand, she rolled her eyes at Lincoln and looked back out the window.

They dropped Mrs. Bigler off first. When the three of them disembarked from the hack and Lincoln paid the driver to wait for them, Amanda stared up at the imposing, pillared facade. "I don't know what a lunatic asylum is supposed to look like, but I didn't expect Queen Victoria's palace," she said. As they climbed the shallow steps under a lofty portico, she asked Lincoln, "What did you make of what that woman said?"

"I make of it that's she's not happy with anything real in her life, so let's forget about her and decide for ourselves." He put his hand to the big brass knocker and banged it down.

The Northern Ohio Lunatic Asylum had opened its broad doors twelve years before. Three stories tall, with a many-windowed front and huge wings, it commanded a parklike setting, which would, no doubt, be lovely in temperate weather. Today, the glare of snow, white paint, and glass hurt the eyes. And a Christmas wreath that had obviously been left to molder right on the door dropped its brittle needles all over the entry to be ground under their feet.

"I wonder how we'd find the back staircase Mrs. Bigler mentioned," Amanda muttered. She thrust her gloved hands in her muff while they waited.

"Let's just see what we learn from a frontal assault," Lincoln said. "And, remember, I will be glad to stay with you or with Matt if you want to speak to them alone."

"You're a friend of the family now. And I'd really like another opinion I trust, so I hope you will be able to sit in. Oh, for heaven's sake, where are these people? I wrote them we were coming and they said they would be prepared . . ."

The big door swung open to a wide central hall with many

narrow doors closed upon it. A tall, thin, graying man greeted them with a welcoming smile. "Mrs. Wynne and husband Matthew is it?" he asked, then responded with handshakes all around as Amanda introduced Lincoln. "I'm the overseer, Clinton Owens, with whom you corresponded, so won't you step right into my office?"

It scared Amanda more than anything else that Matt did so eagerly, before Lincoln could even take her elbow to escort her in.

"So you see, Mrs. Wynne and Mr. Blake, we use what we term the tried and true Moral Treatment Methods of mental medicine here," Mr. Owens plunged on in a one-sided discourse that had already run a quarter hour. Two doctors had taken Matt to an adjourning room to "interview him." Amanda could tell that Mr. Owens was doing his best to assure her that this was the place for Matt. "Good diet, fresh air," he was saying. "You've seen the beautiful grounds."

"Are the patients exercised daily on these grounds?" she asked.

"Whenever feasible with whatever inmates it is possible to supervise, ma'am. Although, of course, we must await the diagnosis of the doctors, from all you've said and my brief observation of your husband, it appears to me he suffers from dementia caused by a head injury and perhaps aggravated by battle stress. Such a blow puts a sort of dent in the brain, you see—changes its surface, so to speak. So our treatment here must strive to erase these distortions, and the longer the illness is allowed to progress, the less flexible the brain's surface. That's why—depending on my learned colleagues' opinions, of course—it might be best if you leave Mr. Wynne with us today—"

"I'm not prepared to do that. But this treatment for dementia consists of exactly what? I have had to tie my husband in his bed at night, but I don't want him restrained during the day."

"Only as necessary, I assure you. No chains or whatever dire thing your wifely worries are conjuring up. And he'd be in a ward with others who have dementia, not with the suicidals—he hasn't ever shown those tendencies, has he?"

"Absolutely not. As I said, he just has these battle nightmares and seems seldom in touch with . . ."

The door opened, and the two doctors came in with Matt. Amanda and Lincoln stood. Matt looked calm, very calm, even a bit dazed. "What—what did you learn, sirs?" she asked.

The doctors seated Matt between Amanda and Lincoln again and themselves in chairs facing their visitors. "Sometimes your husband seems sentient and sometimes not—ah, that means, aware of what is really going on around him," Dr. Glassburn, the older man told her, tapping his pen on his bony knee.

"That is precisely what I was telling Mr. Owens and could have explained to you, doctor."

"But the point is, ma'am, we must make our own scientific observations. Now, the good news is, we have hopes we can shock him from this unfortunate state."

"Shock him?" Amanda said as Lincoln shifted in his seat. "With—what?"

"Medically approved techniques that we can employ include spinning him in a chair to fill up the spaces in his brain caused by the blow, a cold shower, or a sudden noise to startle his senses back to reason."

"No, he flies into a frenzy at loud noises. That would not work."

The two doctors exchanged glances, before the younger, red-haired Dr. Milton leaned forward and said, "We understand your concern, but you are hardly able to judge—"

"He's my husband, doctors! I have tended him day and night since he came back from battle like this over three years ago!"

"Of course, and admirably so. But since the noises which have set him off have been accidents with no restraints of his reactions, you have had no control over his behavior, nor could you work toward a cure for him."

"And you would? How much attention would my husband receive each day?"

"It would vary, of course."

"And how often would I be able to visit him?"

"Let me answer that for my illustrious colleagues," Mr. Owens interjected from behind his desk. "Our extensive experience has taught us that we really need an initial three- to six-month commitment from the family, and then their support—perhaps from a distance—after."

"Meaning?" Lincoln spoke for the first time since the doctors returned.

"We don't forbid relatives' visits, but they are discouraged for a while," Dr. Glassburn said. "The point is, you see, we must gain control over the mentally disturbed person until there is a beneficial change. And having the distractions of outsiders, even well-meaning family, reminders of the past . . ." Dr. Glassburn let his voice trail off as he shrugged.

Amanda felt hollow inside. Hollow, but even sicker than she had on the train with its swaying, forward rush. Anger ebbed, fear faded; defeat began to nibble at her. They were confirming that her elaborate plans for Christmas—all her hopes to coax Matt back by the best of the past—were pure foolhardiness, as evidently they had been. The love and care she had poured into him since he'd been home—was it all for naught?

"Sirs," Amanda said, her voice trembling as she reached out to take Matt's hand, "what is your success rate with such cases?"

"Each case is individual, I'm sure you understand that," Dr. Milton said, his voice so soothing.

"Then in Matt's case," Lincoln cut in, "how long do you think you would need for him to show marked improvement?"

"I believe we could better answer all these pointed questions after we spend a bit more time with him today, to do a few simple tests to see his reactions to things. Most of our previous examination was a physical one to ascertain there was no bodily cause."

Amanda gritted her teeth. She had told them there was absolutely no sign of a blow and had never been since the day he was sent back home. Still, she thought, perhaps she needed to, as they put it, keep control. But three to six months, just abandoning him here to—to strangers?

"I see," she said and cleared her throat. "Another examination. All right. But I must tell you I cannot bear the idea of your 'shocking' him, as you say—doing to him exactly what causes his pain."

"But you must know that to set a broken leg causes pain, Mrs. Wynne," Dr. Glassburn pronounced with a wise wag of his gray head. "Medicine is not always pleasant, but it is necessary for cure."

"Cure—if only I could hope for that, then yes, it would be worth it," she admitted. "Would you mind if Mr. Blake and I step out in the hall to confer while you are with my husband?"

"Of course not. And if you'd like some coffee or tea, we could provide it."

Amanda and Lincoln strolled the hall slowly at first, then quickened their steps to pace it. "I guess it's necessary, but there's something here I don't like, something under the surface I just *feel*," she told him.

"There's *everything* here I don't like, but your options are not good either. If Matt could at least be brought back more, maybe he could recall what happened in battle and clear his own name, so he could be eligible for regular veteran benefits."

"Yes, if only he could clear his own name before them all. Oh, Lincoln, you should have seen him in court when he would plead his cases! His words were so convincing, his demeanor so confident, it said to judge or jury alike, 'My client is guiltless, and here is why.' And he left no stone unturned to obtain evidence and witnesses."

She realized then that she had taken Lincoln's arm and he'd pressed it to his ribs. Surprised, she tugged it back, but it was her own realization which had startled her more. "That's it," she said. "That's what Matt would want us to do to decide."

"What?"

"Gather evidence and listen carefully to witnesses, beginning with the first one we met, Mrs. Bigler. Surely, we can find the back staircase off this hall."

"Amanda, you can't just go wandering in a place like this."

"Why not? Mr. Owen said earlier we couldn't, but why not? I'll be careful. Could he be hiding something? If I'm discovered, I'll say I was just stepping out for a breath of fresh air and couldn't find the back door—got lost or something, or wanted a higher view of the grounds. You can keep an eye out for them, in case they come to summon us."

"I'm not leaving you alone. Come on, then."

They listened at doors like robbers, then tried two at the

far end of the hall. Locked. The third one opened onto the staircase, and they hurried up it to the first landing with a window overlooking the courtyard. "This big place is built like a hollow square," she observed in a whisper. "At least they have benches outside, so that's a good sign that the inmates are not just locked up."

The next landing had a door marked "2ND." It was bolted closed, but Lincoln shot the bolt, cracked it, and peered into the hall. "It's a women's ward," he whispered. "I see inmates wandering way down the hall, but no doctors or matrons, I guess."

"Let me just peek into a room or two. If someone challenges me, I'll say I'm a friend of the mending woman. I won't be a minute."

"That's exactly how long you have, or I'll come after you!"

Her heart thumping, she glided down the hall past two closed, grated doors to the first open one. Within, a woman lay in a low, cagelike bed, so narrow in height that she surely could not even turn over. Slats covered the sides and top, making it look as if she were ready to be grilled on a gridiron. She moaned in low, gasping sobs, and the room reeked of her filth. Amanda backed out, pressing her reticule to her nose and stifling her own sob.

But the room across the hall snared her. The single window was boarded up, and within sat at least seven women in strange, hulking chairs shoved into the corners. Amanda gasped and stopped, with her hands pressed to the sides of the door frame as if to prop herself up. Whereas the other woman had suffered in silence, these cried or cursed the moment they saw her, yet she remained, frozen, in the entrance, gaping, while the dim light threw her shadow on the dirty floor.

Leather belts strapped some to chairs; in addition, strange restraining coats wrapped and bound others' arms close to their sides. "Help me, help me, Mother!" one woman screeched. Suddenly, from the hall, other women in various stages of undress pressed in behind Amanda, shoving her into the room. Some had their hair braided, others wore it wild; several wore bizarre muffled gloves, from which they could not pull their hands free. Yet someone clawed at her, scratching her throat, pulling her hair loose and her bonnet awry.

Amanda pushed her way out, turned, and ran. She tore past Lincoln, who evidently had seen them swarm toward the room and was starting down the hall after her. She yanked the door open, fell to her knees in the corner of the landing, and retched, right on the wooden floor. It was what she had fought to keep from doing on the careening train, but now this massive place—the whole world—seemed to lurch out of control.

Lincoln shot the bolt behind them, then was instantly on his knees beside her, holding her forehead and supporting her shoulders while she heaved again. She did not even feel embarrassed as he helped her, saw her like this. The shock and shame of it diminished everything else.

He dabbed her face with his handkerchief. She almost sat sideways in his lap where they knelt together. She clasped his upper arm so hard he winced.

"Lincoln, it's hellish here! The downstairs may look quiet and calm, but they must be overcrowded with these poor souls. They tie them down, cage them. They not only confine but punish them! We have to get Matt away from them! I'll never sign those papers, no matter what!"

"All right. We'll get him, if you're sure. But maybe you were in a women's ward for hopeless cases," he said as he helped her stand. "Amanda, this shock has changed you. Maybe that shock treatment would change Matt."

She clasped his lapels. "It *can't* work for him. Surely only love can bring him back, not this—degradation, this danger!"

"Yes, all right. Let's go."

Her legs were shaking as they went downstairs; she leaned on Lincoln's arm. "Are you going to tell them what you've seen?" he asked. She shook her head as she wiped perspiration from her face, then stuffed his handkerchief in her reticule. She stood on her own now, brushing at her mussed and dusty skirts.

"We should have seen what they were hiding without having to look," she said. "Now I see through their cleverly worded statements, their need to keep family away, as if we were the cause of the affliction! Lincoln, I'll get that pension some way and hire doctors and a caring overseer for Matt, even if he—he never gets well. I'll keep him away from Lockwood people if I must, if they won't help, no matter what they say!"

"I'll help you. While I can, I'll help."

"You do help me and Matt too. But I know you can't do it forever. You have a life of your own to pick up again."

She saw his determined expression wilt; almost imperceptibly he frowned and shook his head. But she could not ask why now, because they had to save Matt. For the first time in her life she felt she might actually faint, but fury stoked her strength. She straightened her bonnet and jacket, and they went back into Mr. Owens's office.

"Ah, there you are," he said, glancing up from some papers. "I looked for you in the hall, but realized you must have stepped out for some air. The good news is, that with your minimal family income, we shall only charge you five dollars a month for Mr. Wynne's excellent care, and the citizens of Ohio will, of course, assume the rest of the cost for care in this state institution. Now, the doctors have reported they believe they can work with your husband, though they may need a quiet waiting period for him before they begin the actual treatments. Is—is anything wrong?"

"Where is my husband?"

"In the next room, taking a little nap. I believe you said he often does so in the afternoons. Now, if you'll just sign here and here, and either bring or send his effects when you can, then—"

"I am going to wake my husband and take him home, sir. I have decided this is no place for him."

"Mrs. Wynne, you must realize that your excitable, changeable, and demanding nature may be actually doing him some harm. It is most irregular that you would bring him to us and then so erratically change your mind."

"Will you commit me to your so-called care also? This is not a place for cure but custody. And you are overcrowded, I have learned."

"Who has been talking to you without my authorization? Yes, we're a bit full right now, but—"

"Is my husband in this next room?" she asked and strode to the door. She knew her voice was trembling. Clinton Owens darted up from behind his desk and tried to block her way. Lincoln leaped at him and thrust him aside. In the small room with a table, three chairs, and a bed, Matt lay asleep, just as the man had said.

"There, you see?" Mr. Owens said. "Just let me ring for the doctors again if you have qualms."

"Matt. Matt, wake up. We're going home," she said and shook his shoulder as if the man had not spoken. Lincoln took Matt's coat and hat from the hat tree in the room and, keeping an eye on Mr. Owens, came over to the bed.

"Matt! What's the matter with him?" she demanded of the man. "He always wakes right up, sometimes very fast."

"Because that is only one of the problems he faces at home," the man said, "I believe the doctors administered some opium."

"What? Without telling me? How could they interview him if he was drugged? Lincoln, he's dead to the world."

"Here, take his things," Lincoln ordered and stooped to pull Matt to a sitting position. He bent and heaved him over his shoulder.

"I really cannot allow this," Mr. Owen insisted. Seeing his chance to ring for help without Lincoln's stopping him, he dashed out and pulled a bed cord. They heard it ring, muffled but frenzied. Lincoln carried Matt toward the door while she ran behind, gathering their coats in her arms too.

"Now, just one moment!" Mr. Owen cried and tried to bar their way. To Amanda's amazement, with only one arm free, Lincoln banged the man back into the door, then pushed him away from it. She yanked it open and they fled, even as footsteps pursued them down the hall.

Outside, when the cold air smacked her, Amanda realized for the first time that tears glazed her cheeks. Still clutching their coats to her, she ran down the broad stairs and shouted for their hack, then ran toward it, gesturing wildly. Slowly the driver waved back at her, then finally snapped the reins and brought the vehicle to them.

"Madam, you simply cannot come to us like this, ask our help, and then abduct an ill, demented man," Dr. Glassburn said and took her arm. She shook him off and opened the door of the hack. Lincoln rolled Matt inside, then shoved the doctor back.

"It is you," Amanda declared, "who abduct ill people! And if you cause any repercussions from this, you will hear what I saw upstairs—when you read it in the newspapers!"

Lincoln, half pushed, half lifted her in after Matt, who slept curled on the narrow hack floor like a sodden drunk. Lincoln slammed the door and got in the other side, propping his feet on the opposite seat to avoid Matt.

"Driver, on!" Lincoln shouted as they jerked away, down the winding lane set amid bare-branched trees in stark snow. Amanda leaned over Matt, holding his hand, chafing his wrists. Then she looked up at Lincoln and squeezed his hand with her other one.

"It was a nightmare. Thank you—again," she said.

He nodded, brushed the tears from her left cheek with his thumb, then pulled his hand back as if he'd been burned. But all the way back to the Cleveland depot, they stayed that way, like marble statues in the cold: Amanda caught in the narrow space between the two of them, holding to them both.

Chapter Seven

❇

Holiday Leftover Cranberry-Orange Nut Bread

Sift together 2 cups flour, 1½ teaspoons baking powder, ½ teaspoon baking soda, 1 cup granulated sugar

Beat 1 egg

Add grated rind and juice of one orange

Melt 2 tablespoons shortening in enough boiling water to make ¾ cup

Mix moist ingredients together, then add and mix with dry ones

Add 1 cup raw, chopped cranberries and 1 cup chopped nuts

Bake at 325 degrees for 1 hour, inserting sharp knife in center to test for doneness.

Amanda got out of bed more than once that night to be certain Matt was all right. The opium those wretched doctors had given him had worn off, though he still slumbered soundly, tied in his bed. She jumped as she heard the floor creak overhead: just the cold house or was Lincoln pacing as she had, anguished over the twists and turns of the day?

Shivering, she got back in bed and finally submerged herself in fitful sleep. Or did she get up to look in on Matt yet again, to tiptoe into his dim room and bend close to see him in the narrow bed? But a woman lay there, tied hand and foot, trapped, unable to turn either way. And she bent close to see it was—herself!

Slats like prison bars held her there, while doctors came to probe and poke at her. And every one of them had Mason Rutland's laughing, leering face.

Then she was running, running down dim halls of doors, chased by people with no arms, with mouths crying, "Help me! Help me!"

Everything whirled around, spun out of control. She heard a train bearing down on her, roaring along the tracks. Hair and gown streaming behind her, she ran the endless hall toward the open door. People chased her, their voices huffing, chugging, their cries trying to crush her.

A man stood at the door in silhouette, in shadow, arms outstretched, eyes deep and wide as a well. Would she fall in? Was it Matt? Would he hurt her, burn her?

She thudded hard into the man's arms and held to him breathlessly. The roaring, the shrieking stopped. He felt so solid, but not safe. Still, she clung, burying her face in his gray-caped shoulder, feeling herself flow into him, the powerful, alluring body, the face, even the deepest core of him.

At first, he stood as cold as marble. Then he lifted her in his stone-hard arms and carried her away into warm, blowing darkness. She kicked at first, she fought, but then she held tight. He strode on and on; his mouth came down hard on hers to devour her sanity, her very soul.

And then, together, were they flying? Warm, waiting clouds swirled all around as he crushed her to him again. She no longer wanted this to end, but as they soared in the rush of wind, she forced open her eyes to see his face.

Not Matt! Thank God, not Mason!

Lincoln Blake.

"Oh!"

She sat up in a bed thrashed to waves of sheets wrapped around her. A dream, just a dream, she tried to comfort herself as she saw only the dim, familiar room. Her nightgown twisted tight between her waist and breasts. She was flushed and perspiring; the slap of cold air sobered her. Face in hands, elbows on bent knees, she sat, trembling, her heart thudding louder than the booms of the church chimes at four o'clock. The fantasy had been so real—so awful at first and then, so—so dangerous but desirable.

As she rearranged her nightgown and bedclothes, she knew she would not sleep again this night, perhaps did not want to, so she could remember, think, and plan. She burrowed into her nest of covers.

What had it meant, the end of that dream? The earlier nightmare part of it, of course, she understood. But not only to flee *to* him but flee *with* him, afraid only at first, then willing—wanting. That terrified her.

"Oh, no," she moaned to herself and curled into a little ball, fighting those treacherous female yearnings that haunted her at night. And this time it wasn't vague longings. Yes, she'd take Matt back here in a moment, but Matt—though he slept in the next room, the next bed—was gone. For the first time she allowed herself to face the possibility that the Matt she loved was *never* coming back. And that the man she desired, at least in the dream, was here, so near.

But no one, she told herself, must ever know of her inner longings. It was so wrong to lean on Lincoln as she had, because it only made things worse. He was from a different world, one which had recently been the enemy camp. He was still hostile and secretive sometimes. She knew little but his name, his state, and the story of how he lost his family.

It was only, she tried to tell herself, that she was so used to having a protective man in her life; that was the reason she had dreamed of running to Lincoln. First she had tried to be everything to Father; then she'd tried to please Mason, before she saw the traitor as he really was; then Matt, shy but strong, had been the center of her being. But these last years, she had become the head of the household and had taken many burdens on herself. She had promises to keep to herself and others. She had been worn down so she went overboard in relying on Lincoln's help. Surely that was all. But never again—especially not with a man who was a stranger, an outsider—would she allow someone else to control her life.

She must be careful to show Lincoln no special favors and to keep herself, let alone him, in line. Still, she realized, he had done nothing untoward, nothing a gentleman and a friend would not do, no matter how she caught him staring at her sometimes with that same ravenous look as when he'd sat down to that first meal she'd given him.

Men! she cursed silently. Yet however much pain a man caused, however well a woman might do on her own, she often needed and longed for a man. Pru did, and Eliza too, Amanda suspected. Sarah had done marvels on her own with Mandy, but was grieving about the Toledo minister's recent letter telling her that no one of Ben Blue's description had passed through on that route of the Underground Railroad.

Amanda had already ascertained through friends that Ben had not passed through on the Oberlin route, and those, along with Lockwood, were the only three lines north she knew. So, for some reason, Sarah's man had evidently never made it to Canada at all. Had he chosen to stay—or been forced to stay—in America during the war? Or, worst of all, could he be dead?

Amanda hated to do it, but she might now have to petition the government for another reason besides Matt's problems. If Lincoln's friend Freeman had fought for the Union, perhaps Ben Blue had too, and there would be some government record of him. He, at least, might be eligible for financial help if he had been wounded.

She flopped over and punched her feather pillow into submission. Why, as Eliza had quoted from Shakespeare a few days ago, did the course of true love never run smooth? Matt was as lost as Ben Blue, Ned Milburn too proud to court Pru. Rufus wanted Eliza, but didn't know what to do. And Lincoln, as for you . . .

Oh, drat, she thought. She was starting to think in rhymes, starting to go crazy. Maybe it was her own form of dementia that made her long for things—for a man, for a life—she could not have.

Treacherous tears tracked down her cheeks and plopped on her pillow. Wishing she could just hide forever, she pulled the covers up over her head.

Early the next morning, Amanda stood before the mantel in the back parlor with those who lived in Lockwood House—all but Matt, who was still in bed—seated around her. Her eyes burned from lack of sleep and from crying; she feared she looked a fright, but she had to go on and this had to be done. She gripped her hands tightly before her.

"I've called you together on rather sudden notice," she told them, clearing her throat, "for a sort of family meeting. I do think of us as family in a way."

"I should hope so," Aunt Louise said and popped another piece of cranberry-orange bread into her mouth from the plate on the table beside her. "Your father will be the first to tell you that it is family that matters above all else, even more than making one's way in the world, but I see he's not home yet."

Eliza shook her head at that, and Pru bit her lower lip. Sarah just rolled her eyes, but Mandy blurted out, "But he's dead. I helped Miz Wynne put a real nice Christmas wreath on his grave in the burying ground and made him a snow angel, too!"

"Now, Mandy," Sarah said, shushing her with a piece of bread, "you just let Miz Wynne do the talking right now."

"And he never did like children talking out of turn!" Aunt Louise insisted and shook a bony finger at Mandy.

Lincoln, bless him, Amanda thought, didn't blink an eye at Aunt Louise's carryings-on any more than he did at

Matt's. She knew she had to proceed, but she was finding it hard to form her words, even as much as she had rehearsed all this during the long hours of early morning, waiting for the light to come.

She explained in more detail what had happened at the asylum. "And that is why I could not leave him there," she said. "I can only hope and pray you will all understand. So, I must tell you I intend to hire some part-time help to be certain that Matt does not harm the house again—or any of you—but I realize you must think of your own safety first. If you believe it now unwise to board here, Eliza and Pru, I understand, but I hope you will choose to stay."

"All I can say is we will have to keep a better eye on him," Pru said, smoothing her skirt over her crinoline. "And I intend to contribute a bit more so that you can bring someone in to help and free yourself up from tending him, Amanda."

"Pru, I am grateful, but you pay plenty already."

"Perhaps I do since the new widow's pension came through, but you know you let me off practically scot-free for months when I couldn't afford the board. Besides, Matt would accept only a pittance from us when he won our law case with his brilliant tactic of calling in all those character witnesses for Sam so we could keep the canal boat, and I consider it fair exchange for that."

"But the boat is gone—"

"A lot of things," Eliza put in, "are gone now, Amanda, and we all must come to accept that truth and make the best of a new future. I believe this last Christmas illustrated that. I know it's a lesson I've been slowly learning, if with reluctance. Actually, I too have a bit of money put by, which can help to hire in someone to help with Matthew—now that Mr. Blake has taken on other building jobs about town which will take him away from the house more, and I am sure," she went on, emphasizing each word as she looked from Lincoln to Amanda with her best pinned-to-the-wall stare, "we all approve of his working elsewhere all he can."

"But," Lincoln said, his eyes only on Amanda, "I still intend to take Matt with me—when I can watch him and he can't get injured."

"All of you—I can't thank you enough," Amanda said, sinking weak-kneed into the chair by the mantel. "But the other thing is that some folks in town may try to force me to put Matt away at the asylum, perhaps permanently. Since the fire in the parlor, I understand their concerns. But if I can assure them that besides all of us, Matt has an official watchman, so to speak—"

"Who?" Eliza asked. "Do you have someone particular in mind?"

"I thought I'd ask Rufus," Amanda said and turned to face Eliza squarely. They stared at each other a moment without blinking or flinching. For once, Amanda did not even care if she got one of Eliza Tuttle's scoldings or even if the older woman stormed out to live elsewhere.

"Rufus Quinn?" Eliza demanded. "Good gracious, I don't know about that. I can foresee some problems there, and I do not refer to myself." Her mouth looked puckered as a prune again. "What if he loses himself to the influence of ardent spirits again? It's one thing if he hurts himself, but what if he lets Matthew wander off? Just because Captain Quinn seems to have turned over a bit of a new leaf lately doesn't mean he's a fit guardian for Matthew—or that Lockwood citizens are going to have their concerns assuaged by your hiring him, of all people, on!"

"I trust him and Matt likes him," Amanda countered. "I believe it would give Captain Quinn purpose in his life—other than bothering you, of course, Eliza."

"He's—as I said, he's been slightly better behaved lately," she said, and no more, so that Amanda knew she had temporarily won again.

"Then that's settled," Amanda announced. "Fortunately, people can change, and change their minds about others too." Her gaze slammed into Lincoln's steady stare. She realized she had been looking at everyone but him. "But," she went on, glancing away again, "I thought I'd best bring it up to all of you, because it means Rufus would take an occasional meal here. Sarah," she said and turned to face her, seated with Mandy on the big ottoman, "I know that would be another mouth to feed sometimes."

"Anything to help you out, Amanda. It's your house and your victuals. 'Sides, Mandy and me like the captain, don't we, honey child?" Mandy nodded, bouncing her ribboned braids.

"I—again, I thank you all. I am so grateful for your support, financial and moral." Her voice broke, so she cleared her throat again. "And the good thing is, with someone to watch Matt more, I will have more time to bake goods to sell to make more money. Now, enjoy the bread and tea while I go wake Matt, as we have an errand to run."

She was halfway up the stairs when she heard Lincoln's footsteps behind her and turned back. As he came closer, she stared at his broad shoulders. When he stopped, she stood two stairs higher; how strange it seemed to be staring down on him. He looked solemn as his eyes went over her and seemed to darken.

"Are you all right?" he asked, frowning. "I can tell you haven't slept."

"Can you? I mean, can you tell about me? I wasn't wondering if you can sleep—after yesterday and all."

"Amanda, is something suddenly wrong—between us?"

"Not at all. I told you I was grateful for all your help, and I meant it."

"You aren't taking Matt to see that lawyer uptown?"

"Mason Rutland? I should say not. We're going to call on Captain Quinn."

"If you want, I can go along, or take Matt with me for a while," he said and slid his hand up the banister toward hers. She glanced down at his big hand so close, his strong, calloused fingers almost touching hers. But they heard someone tread on the stairs, and both turned.

It was Eliza. "I'll be glad to accompany Amanda uptown; I have errands to do," she told Lincoln as she climbed the stairs. Amanda wondered how long she had been standing below and listening. "I am sure you have tasks awaiting you outside the house, Mr. Blake, such a busy, ambitious man as you."

"Is that a command or a compliment?" he asked, not budging as she approached them.

"Eliza," Amanda interrupted, "as perhaps you chanced to overhear, I'm calling on the captain and knew you wouldn't want to go, so—"

"Not to that bachelor crow's nest of his, of course, but we can call up to him, and he'll come down. I'll be ready in a trice, as soon as you rouse Matthew," she said with a nod and a stiff smile as she walked around Amanda and Lincoln.

"I believe I will take you up on your offer to keep Matt,

just until we get back," Amanda told Lincoln and turned to hurry up the stairs. Then, still annoyed at Eliza as well as herself, she looked back and whispered to him, "Eliza and I have not had time for a talk lately, and I think one is sorely needed."

He nodded. She could feel his eyes following her up the stairs. Suddenly, she became aware of the movements of her legs, her thighs, and her bottom, even under her voluminous skirts. The nape of her neck burned. She almost felt he had the power to pull her back down to him with invisible strings; she wanted to hurry to his arms as she had in the dream. But she kept going up the steps, not letting herself look back again.

"I did a lot of thinking last night, Eliza," Amanda admitted as the two of them headed uptown into a stiff northwest wind. She was going to take Eliza on about her brusque comments to Lincoln, but she planned to work up to that. "Obviously, I've been agonizing about keeping Matt at home, but also about Lockwood."

"You're worried how people will react to his living at home after the fire."

"Yes, but I think that problem could solve itself if we could find a way to revive the town, to funnel money and activity here."

"You sound just like your father with his big canal plans."

"No, that era is over. An old-fashioned Christmas is one thing, but an old-fashioned town just won't do."

"You're not going to invest in Mr. Blake's growing rebuilding and repair business, are you?" Eliza asked, holding on to her hat despite the fact that it was studded with hatpins to keep it secure. "You said you and Matthew are as poor as church mice."

"We are, despite how some folks are sure the 'last of the Lockwoods' must have a fortune buried somewhere down by the canal. No, I'm talking about possibly suggesting to the town council that they consider advertising Lockwood in the Cleveland newspaper as a haven for summer homes— getaway cottages, so to speak. I hear rich men there are looking for little rural places for escape or even retirement from the city."

"To Lockwood? But without the canal, we're not even on the lake for summer sailing now."

"But perhaps that will appeal to them, as they live on the lake most of the year. Such new visitors and investments could revive some of the stores like Milburns'."

"So you're long-term matchmaking for Prudence and Ned again?"

"Only since I've had to give up on you and Rufus, of course," Amanda said. Though she was expecting a tirade at that, Eliza only tut-tutted and even looked a bit sheepish. Amanda always ended up liking her, even when she didn't want to.

But when they turned the corner to the town square, Eliza stopped Amanda with a gloved hand on her elbow. "My dear girl, speaking of matchmaking, I must apologize for disapproving of Lincoln Blake spending time with you. I just do not want *you* to be hurt again."

"Hurt again?"

"To put it rather bluntly—though I realize it is no concern of mine, I daresay I might speak reasonably for your aunt who cannot do so anymore—I believe, Amanda, you are coming to rely on Mr. Blake's advice and his apparent helpful nature a bit too much lately. And in the—the rather fervent, admiring way he regards you, I can tell he is coming to care for you—as you do for him. After years of studying human nature through books and keeping an eagle eye on students, I can read between the lines, you know."

"Nonsense!" Amanda declared, but she felt heat suffuse her cheeks and hoped the stiff breeze polishing them would cover her embarrassment. She heaved a sigh that seemed to deflate her. "You're right, Eliza," she admitted. "I've been thinking about it too, and I shall be careful. And he will be heading on soon, in spring or summer, back to a life of his own down south. I'm certain of it."

"Did he say so?"

"He seldom offers anything about himself, but I can sense he has some duty at home in Savannah that calls him. He has spoken in a most heartfelt manner against Sherman's destruction of his state, so no doubt he longs to return with a little capital whenever he can and help to rebuild it."

She hesitated as she realized she was surmising all sorts of things she didn't know. "Eliza, he lost his wife and child in the war, when it's usually the women who face that grief. I just feel sorry for him, that's all. Don't look now," she added, immensely relieved for the change of topic, "but here comes the next-to-last person on earth after Mason Rutland that I feel up to chatting with."

However grateful Amanda was to have Eliza's stare dissect someone else, she had a good mind to march away before she had to face Dottie Rutland. But they were caught now.

"Hello, Dottie," they chorused.

"Hello, ladies. Don't you just wish we had a decent emporium or at least a dry goods store here these days?" Dottie said, as if she had overheard their conversation about rebuilding Lockwood. "I get all my gowns from New York through Cleveland shops, of course, and I'm going to be taking the children to spend several weeks there with Mason's people beginning tomorrow, but not to be able even to find a suitable gift to take . . ."

"The crosses one must bear," Eliza commiserated, straight-faced. "Is Mason going too?" she inquired when Amanda did not respond at all.

"No, the lucky man is going south, would you believe it, to a big Kentucky thoroughbred auction. I envy him, getting out of this raw weather and this stodgy little place," Dottie said with a roll of her green eyes and a dramatic sigh that shuddered the ribbons and feathers of her bonnet. "Amanda, dear, I hear you at least escaped to Cleveland yesterday, though not for pleasure, I take it," she added and reached over to pat her arm.

"That's right."

"Oh, well, anyway, I hear the war left those big, beautiful Lexington mansions pretty much untouched, so I'm sure Mason will tell us all about it when he returns, especially since that special Confederate visitor of yours seems so closemouthed about the supposedly ruined South. Mason says the Kentucky show is just a big horse auction for men only with breeding stock for his trotting cracks and he might even get into racers, but I'm sure there will be parties and soirees too," she added forlornly.

"No doubt," Amanda said, but omitted any comment on Mason's telling his wife the auction was for "men only." He had told her that about a sailing regatta on Lake Erie once, and she had later heard that ladies with blowing skirts were flaunted on every yachtman's arm the moment they came ashore.

"Here," Dottie went on, fumbling in her beaded and fringed reticule. "Look at this. It's last year's program for the auction, with a drawing of a pillared plantation house. Mason's going to take me down there next summer, he's promised—and without the children, a sort of second wedding trip. Here, take it if you'd like to peruse it—and dream about it—the Kentucky Bluegrass area, I mean. Nice to get caught up with you, and I'll see you later, then . . ." she said with a flutter of kid-gloved hand.

"Gracious," Eliza muttered, "you'd think her good taste in clothing would sink beneath her skin somehow. What an ill-timed ill wind, and I don't mean this icy breeze."

Amanda had almost thrown the little printed booklet back at Dottie as she swept away, but Eliza's comment bolstered her. She just shook her head and took Eliza's arm. "At least we're rid of Mason for a while. I was afraid he'd be after me about keeping Matt the moment he heard. That rat can have his breeding stock for trotting cracks or racers!"

But as they went on their way down the square toward Rufus's room, even as Eliza chatted on about how she would have straightened Dorothy Rutland out in quick order if she'd had her as a student, Amanda remembered Sarah's remark as the Rutlands had glided by in their sleigh on Christmas Day. Sarah had told Mandy how much her daddy would have loved those horses. And if Lockwood's town council could perhaps be talked into making inquiries and taking an advertisement in a Cleveland paper to lure outsiders here, why couldn't she take an advertisement in this magazine at this year's gathering of horse lovers to lure someone else here?

"Eliza, I've got an idea," she said, as she opened the booklet and skimmed the lists of blooded mares for sale, the small boxed or large-print announcements for jockeys and farms and stud fees. "I'm going to place a sort of bet over at the telegraph office. Come on, for a moment. Rufus will wait."

"You're not serious? Throwing what little you have away on a horse-racing wager?" Eliza demanded as Amanda propelled her across the square toward the black words on the glass window, WESTERN UNION TELEGRAPH.

"Not exactly a wager," Amanda explained, excitement ringing in her voice. "It says advertisements here cost three dollars and must be in for this year's book by next week. Here's the very address. I'm going to place a wild bet that just maybe Sarah's husband, Ben Blue, will show up in Lexington to 'talk to the horses,' as Sarah puts it."

"What?"

"Come on. If I have to give up matchmaking for you and Pru, I'll just have to take a chance on finding Sarah's love. Besides, you can take a respite out of this wind while I go over and talk to Rufus, since you will not set foot on the stairs to his lair."

"You know, Amanda," Eliza said as they bent together to cut across the windy square, "although Matthew was my brightest student, you were always the one with the quick mouth and more ideas than one could shake a stick at!"

Still perusing the rustling pages of the booklet, Amanda said, "You'd be the one to know, Eliza Tuttle. Any veteran of your schoolroom can remember that stick well enough!"

But Eliza chose not to wait in the telegraph office when Amanda set out to speak to Rufus. Not that she was going up to his room above the billiard parlor, but it didn't hurt to be along to impress upon him the import of the task, if he agreed to become Matthew's companion. Besides, two weeks ago, she and Rufus had spent a lovely hour in the back parlor at Lockwood House discussing the Shelley poems from the book she had given him for Christmas. And she kept hearing in her head that other little poem they had somehow composed together about glimpsing again one's happiest days.

For, despite a sound marriage to an important man in town, Eliza Marchmont Tuttle had to admit that her happiest days had been those of her youth, with family love surrounding her—and those brief, heady, halcyon days with Rufus before he'd gone to the lakes and she'd gone away to the Normal School to learn to be a teacher. After that, however much she loved her students, her secret sadness over never having her own children seemed to sour some of her joy in life.

Even with the wind freezing her face as it buffeted her and Amanda across the square, Eliza's memory of one particular spring day warmed her. She felt almost sixteen again. Her thick blond braids were her pride, and that rapscallion Rufus, at the desk behind her, had stuck one in the ink pot again. And, though Mama said it was more important than anything to act like a lady, she lay in wait behind a tree down by the river after school to make him pay.

Yes, there he came now, big-shouldered, sandy-haired, and handsome, scuffing his way along, hands thrust in his pockets, straw hat atilt at a rakish angle, whistling some sea chantey. It seemed appropriate to her that his heathen family lived outside of town, along the Monsey River, named for the lately departed savage tribe, in those years before the river was dammed to help form the canal basin. Even then Rufus was drawn by the sea, for he sailed little homemade ships on the river, one he'd even jokingly named the *Eliza May* after her.

Today his punishment would be what she would later learn to call poetic justice. She planned to speckle his shirt with ink from the same bottle he'd dipped the tip of her braid in. Now, she rechecked the stopper; she made certain the pen, which would be her weapon, could be plunged swiftly in, then flicked at the shirt before she fled. The only danger was that she knew she could never outrun him, and so she would have to act while he had his shirt off for his daily swim in the river, which his friend Jonah had mentioned to her.

And therein lay her daring, for Jonah Fencer had said the two of them swam every day "in the buck," as he put it. Even then she had to laugh at boys being so stupid they mixed up "in the buff" with "buck naked," as though, she thought, they swam with some big male deer. But the point was, Jonah Fencer was kept home to help his daddy plow today and Rufus was all alone.

Looking back over the forty-odd years since that day, the widowed Eliza now mused how sad it was in life that little hostile acts seemed to attract members of the opposite sex. Had she initially cared for Rufus when he first teased her and blackened her blonde hair? Had she fanned the flames of his lifelong fancy for her by snubbing and scolding him over the years? Had one-armed Ned Milburn doubled Pru's

ardor when he refused to court her? Had Ben Blue's being
lost to Sarah Murry through slavery and separation made her
even more determined to find him? And had Amanda's
earlier firebrand feelings against the South backfired somehow to draw her dangerously close to a former Confederate
she would once have snubbed as her foe?

All Eliza knew was that on that golden day long ago, she
and Rufus Quinn fell in love. Yes, fell in love for all time,
even though he was seduced by the sea and she wed another
man. And then came all those gray years without him, when
their disappointments and differences made him call her a
prissy, stuck-in-the-mud prude and her think he was a swaggering braggart and a drunken sot.

Those years all fell away now, and she saw not Amanda
climbing the steps while she waited for her in the dim entryway, but a young Rufus swimming in the apple-green
Monsey River. She heard not Amanda's rapping on Rufus's
door but the splash and swish of water and her own breathing as she crept closer to his discarded clothes.

On that long ago day, keeping low, she came around the
bramble bushes and crouched to unstopper the bottle of ink.
She dipped the pen in, stuck out her arm, and speckled the
shirt. Biting her lower lip to keep from laughing, she
restoppered the bottle and turned to flee.

"Hey! Hey, you!" came the shout from the river.

Seen but not caught. She ducked low and began to run.

"Liza, hey, Liza!"

But he was in the river, wasn't he, and didn't have a stitch
on? How had he recognized her? Surely he would not dare
to come roaring out after her even if he saw her. She considered standing at a distance and giving him a brazen shout
before she departed.

But she had misjudged. She darted a frenzied glance back
as she flew up the bank and took the path toward town at a
hard run that immediately winded and cramped her. A blur
of bare limbs behind her, Rufus dared to chase her with only
his shirt held before him like Adam's fig leaf!

The backward glance was disastrous. She caught her toe
on a tree root and tumbled. She scrambled up, ran again, but
he grabbed her arm and swung her back around a
tree.

"Rufus! Don't!" she protested and squeezed both eyes

shut. But before she did, she saw so much skin, muscle, long limbs, chest hair, all light brown and gleaming wet and so close up. He had her now, but she'd let him toss her in the river, douse her with the ink—no, she'd dropped that back there somewhere—anything but look at him.

"Don't what?" he'd asked, his voice both lazy and breathless as he put his hands bold as you please on her waist and pressed against her. "Chase you for ruining this shirt?"

"You deserved it," she argued, feeling like a dunce, arguing with her eyes tight shut. "Now let me go, and you go get dressed before someone spots us."

He dared to laugh, deep and sure, a man's laugh, not a boy's. "We've already spotted us, your hair, my shirt. No, you're gonna have to pay a forfeit now or someone just might tell your mother what you done, Liza."

"Eliza," she insisted, but her voice broke. It sent a shudder clear through her to hear he might tell her mama—or at least something was making her quake deep inside.

"Guess I can have a pet name for a girl who comes out looking for me, knowing she'd find me this way. You did, didn't you?"

"None of your beeswax!"

"Aren't you going to open your eyes, Liza? But that's fine and dandy with me if you don't, 'cause they say that's the best way to do it."

"Do wh—" she managed before his nose bumped her cheek and his mouth took hers for the very first—and last—really wonderful kiss in her life.

Her eyes flew open; fortunately she saw only his closed eyes, forehead, and freckled nose. The two of them seemed to breathe in unison, though faster and faster. He held her by both hands at her tiny waist and stroked upward, with his thumbs just grazing the underside swell of her breasts through the taut calico. She guessed he had his shirt jammed between them, for something was there, pressing hard against her skirt. All of a sudden, she just kissed him back.

Her hands lifted to his shoulders. He moved his mouth, kind of shaping it to fit hers, to coax hers to soften and slant and open, And though the river flowed, and sunlight streamed down, and every proper lesson in deportment her mother had ever taught her went by the wayside as she kissed a buck naked man, she still cherished that moment. It changed her life. Even when she pulled away and turned back to look at him once, as if to memorize that strong, young body and the moment forever, even when she ran away down the lane and down the years . . .

"Eliza, I said Captain Quinn has one thing to ask of you," Amanda's voice jerked her back to the present. Eliza looked up the dim staircase where Amanda stood talking with Rufus, that same Rufus.

"Ask of m-me?" she stammered. "What?"

"That you're not gonna fuss if I'm with Matt in the upstairs hall at Lockwood house, off and on," Rufus said down at her, and it seemed for one moment if a challenge still glittered in his eyes.

"Of course I won't fuss. Why should I?"

"By thunder, it's your God-given nature, Eliza," he said, though his voice was quiet. She could feel his eyes hot on her.

"And I hope it will be your nature to do a responsible job with Matthew," she insisted, but she still trembled with thoughts of long-gone soft breezes and the sudden hope of more to come. "Rufus," she called up the steps, her voice so gentle it surprised even her, "I'm certain you will do a fine job. Matthew has always been partial to you, even when he has not been himself these last years, you know."

Rufus descended several steps and leaned down, evidently to see her better. He wore pants patched on one knee, and this time a shirt speckled with something that was not ink.

"Now, that's real good to hear, 'cause there are some I have always liked and maybe not showed it proper over the years when I ain't—haven't—been quite myself."

She managed a little nod, with tears in her eyes and a smile on her lips.

"Let's go outside, Matt," Lincoln said, opening the door of the small stove in his work shed to be sure the fire had burned down. After Lincoln had finished a whatnot shelf for the mayor's wife, Effie Roscoe, "they" had been working on a wooden Valentine for Matt to give Amanda. Lincoln gathered up the axe, some twine, and the rest of Amanda's fruit bread to take along.

"Will Roscoe told me there are fish to catch under the canal ice," he told Matt as they set out and closed the door behind them.

"Will Roscoe," Matt repeated, as he often did people's names.

"Do you remember him, Matt? He told me you were one hell of a great lawyer, and folks would crowd into court just to hear you defend your client."

Lincoln had never told Amanda, but he tried to bring things up to jog Matt's memory, and sometimes the strangest, apparently unconnected, things came out. "Take care of Amanda," Matt would often say, although he seemed to have no awareness of what that could and should mean.

"Remember Will Roscoe and fish to catch," Matt said, as they went carefully down the slippery path toward the canal basin.

"That's right. When I was a boy, I used to fish down in Mississippi, outside my hometown of Median, with my father. Right before the Appalachian foothills began, a real pretty place, huge elms and live oaks on crests, something like the ones above the river here. I've told everyone here I'm from Savannah, Matt, but I'm telling you the truth, because I know you'll keep my secrets—lawyer's privileged information, we'll call it. Besides, a friend's a friend."

Matt met his eyes and nodded as if he understood. Sometimes it seemed to Lincoln that the real Matt must be just on the other side of a thick glass window, watching and waiting for the right moment to break through. It was strange, Lincoln thought, how he'd unburdened himself to Matt about so many things that he'd told no one else. And despite Matt's sad state, it seemed to him sometimes that Matt *did* understand, as if they could really be friends, or as if Matt were the brother he had never had. He'd had two close friends in his life, one in boyhood, one in his college days, but they never really needed him like Matt did.

That tormented Lincoln, because he admired and desired Matt's wife. But he vowed never to let her know, never to touch her as he ached to do—for all their sakes. Besides, the truth was, if he had it in his power, he would will Matt sane and whole for Amanda and then be on his way. That meant he loved her, would sacrifice for her—and Matt too—didn't it?

Lincoln sighed and gazed skyward as if for help and

strength to sort it all out. "You know, Matt," he said, and pointed up the hill a ways, "this is about where we cut the Christmas tree."

Matt nodded and blessed Lincoln with that pure, bright smile of his. "Christmas," he said.

Lincoln broke off a thick, low limb of another tree, and knotted twine around it. "Yes, and who knows what next Christmas will bring . . ." he muttered. His voice drifted off with his thoughts again. He had been so bitter and melancholy at Christmas. Sarah hadn't been speaking to him then, Mandy brought back painful memories, and Amanda's stubborn insistence on the past—

"All right, Matt," he said to halt his own wayward thoughts, "before we break a hole in the ice, let's find some grub worms in a log. That's what Will said to do when the ground's frozen. Come on."

Matt followed him as always and even picked out the grubs when Lincoln's axe turned some up. But when it cut into a hollow core of the fallen tree trunk, splitting it open, Matt tried to kneel, then lie down inside it.

"No, Matt, no. Come on. Fishing."

For one moment Lincoln though Matt would shove him off. That furtive look haunted his face again, but he finally rose, looked around skittishly as if expecting something, then let Lincoln lead him away. They shuffled out about ten feet onto the frozen canal basin, and Lincoln chopped a hole in the ice, baited the bent nail from his pocket, and let the twine dangle from the stick they propped across the hole. The wind was cold, but they turned their backs to it and ate the bread, bursting with cranberries but tasting too of the last of the succulent Christmas oranges.

"Do you think Amanda and Sarah will be proud of us if we take some perch or pickerel home for supper, Matt? They're supposed to be hiding under this ice for us to snag—the fish, not the women."

"Fish and women, come out!" Matt intoned, his deep voice echoing across the vast expanse of ice.

Lincoln laughed, then sobered. Such ringing tones, such authority in that voice, and for nothing anymore.

"You know, Matt, I'd give anything to take the old Matthew Wynne back with me to Median. I could use a brilliant lawyer there. You see,"—when the line pulled, he hauled a flopping fish up onto the ice— "if I go back there—when I do—I'm going to have to have a trial."

"A trial," Matt said, and deftly strung the fish through the gills on a stick as if he suddenly recalled all he'd ever known.

"Yes. I did something I haven't told anyone about. The charges would be very serious. I beat someone—murder charges, Matt, a capital offense case. Though I'm not guilty, I'm sure they've been looking for me, hoping to make an example of me, the government Reconstruction men down there. You know—Major Garner of the Confederate Engineering Corps, who helped defend Savannah, the one who came home and told them they were doing things wrong, and then . . ." He looked away, his voice shaken and bitter. "Meanwhile, Median's in ruins, and I want to go back to help rebuild it, Matt, not just repair run-down houses here in Lockwood."

"In Lockwood."

"But I can't, Matt," he went on, jerking at the twine, "or I could go to prison, or whatever they do to scapegoats in the damned so-called Reconstruction South. The Federals have let the innocents die, so what would they do to me? But I just know that if you could be the clever lawyer like they all say you were before you got hurt, you could help take care of things for me back in Median."

"Take good care of Amanda."

"Yes, that too, if only you could. If at least one of us could!"

Lincoln turned away and, head down, hunched over their hole in the ice. Amanda was never the type of woman to be pitied, yet Matt could not care for her, probably ever again. But neither could Lincoln care for her and be the man he must be. One's honor—what was responsible and right in this world—meant a great deal, even in defeat. The war had taught him that, even when he'd lost everything, even when he was sick of hiding, sick of lies, sick of being tempted to do that which would hurt those he cared for deeply.

A sharp sound yanked him out of his agonizing. Too late, he turned to see Matt hacking the ice with the axe. Lincoln stood unsteadily and moved slowly toward him across the slick surface. "Matt, stop it! Don't cut the ice. You'll fall in! Matt!"

He continued to chop the ice around him, though he must have seen what he did. He went in, thrashing, shouting, flailing, thrusting the axe like a bayonet so Lincoln dared not grab for him at first. When the axe skidded away on the ice, Lincoln lay on his stomach to drag him out, though he almost went in too, and they were both soon soaked with the icy water from Matt's frenzied splashing.

Had Matt actually tried to drown himself here? Just yesterday Amanda had assured the doctors that he was not suicidal. Why had he snapped when everything was so calm? And for one moment, God forgive him, Lincoln knew he had hesitated, thinking it might be what Matt really wanted and meant to do.

Forgetting the fish, they slipped and staggered up to the house. The wind cut like a sabre blade now, and they were both shaking so hard they could barely walk. Sarah saw them coming, and by the time they were at the back door Amanda came to help.

"Thin ice—catching fish," Lincoln said through chattering teeth, promising himself he'd tell her what really happened later.

"Catching fish? You'll catch your death of cold!" she cried. "Get out of those clothes at once, both of you!"

Damn, Lincoln Garner thought, shaking so hard he couldn't undo one coat button, but the thinning ice of his composure around her was going to break too. She ordered him about as if he were her prisoner of war, a child—or husband—someone she had every right to control, just like Matt.

But the jolt of anger that crackled through him turned again to need. Despite his honorable intentions, he wanted to grab her and shake her, hold her tenderly, *anything* to touch her. He told himself it was only because he was so stunned by the cold and his body's uncontrolled quivering that he did not protest when Amanda's hands unbuttoned his shirt while Sarah stripped off Matt's sodden coat.

So he had come to this, he thought. Half-drowned, defeated, torn, needy—a fugitive holed up like a chased fox. But, ah, he would remember this moment always when he left, whatever befell, for Amanda was touching him.

Chapter
Eight

❄

Emma Lockwood's Raisin-Filled Cookies

FILLING:

Grind 15 ounces of raisins in meat grinder.

Combine in heavy saucepan, raisins, 2 cups sugar, 2 tablespoons flour, 1 cup hot water. Cook over medium heat, stirring until mixture thickens. Set aside to cool.

COOKIE DOUGH:

Mix in large bowl, in this order, blending in each addition: 2 cups vegetable shortening, 2 cups sugar, 1 teaspoon salt, 2 eggs, 1 teaspoon vanilla, 1 cup milk, 3 teaspoons baking powder, 2 teaspoons baking soda, 7 cups flour.

Add a bit more flour if dough is not stiff enough to roll out easily.

Roll out dough to about ¼-inch thickness and cut into pairs of shapes. Place one shape of each pair on an ungreased cookie sheet. Put one heaping teaspoon of filling in the center of each shape. Top with the matching shape. Seal edges by gently pressing together.

Bake 8 to 10 minutes, depending on oven. Before removing from oven, touch cookies to see if they are firm. Do not let them become brown.

❄

When Amanda and Sarah had Lincoln and Matt stripped down to their long wool underwear, they flapped open table-cloths and draped them around their shoulders, holding them while the men managed to shed those last sodden garments under their makeshift tents. The heat from the cookstove's open firebox and oven had made their clothes steam; the smell of wet wool vied with that of half-baked bread.

"We've got to get both of you into bed with dry clothes, and pour some hot tea down you," Amanda said. She marched Matt out of the kitchen, with Lincoln right behind, while Sarah remained in the kitchen to prepare things.

"Where's the fish?" Matt asked through chattering teeth. "I'm going b-b-ack."

"You have to go to bed to get warm, Matt," she insisted, steering him toward the stairs.

"And I have to go to t-t-trial!" he added.

At that, she saw Lincoln hurried to catch up with them. "I'll help you get him in bed," he said. "Never mind his rambling. The whole thing was my fault."

They said no more up the stairs and down the hall. Under the circumstances, Amanda thought, why did she hesitate to open their bedroom door and have Lincoln help her put Matt in? He knew they did not share a marital bed. But even in this emergency, it seemed so strange to have him enter here, to invade her inner sanctum. Now there would be no refuge for her in the house where he had not been, though thoughts of him followed her everywhere already.

She pulled out a dry nightshirt for Matt and helped him

into it, then led them both into the sunroom. "Here, Matt, please lie down. I'll bring you some tea and raisin cookies."

Amanda regretted that Lincoln observed such childish bribes and had to help her tie and tuck Matt in. At least Matt did not call her "Mother" this time. She tried to avoid Lincoln's eyes, but at last she looked him full in the face. His hair was still wet, like polished ebony, slick to his head and making his ears appear to stick out despite the quick toweling she'd given both men's heads. He looked pale, almost bluish, and his big, lanky body shook. Promising Matt she would be right back, she led Lincoln from the sunroom into the bedroom. Passing her dressing table mirror, she caught a glimpse of herself there—serious, shaken, but steadfast in what she must do.

She spun around to face Lincoln. "I can't put you up in that cold attic now, even though you've refused the kitchen pallet before."

"I can't bed down in the kitchen with daily goings-on of you all there," he said through chattering teeth.

"I can sleep with Pru tonight. I'm going to put you in—in my bed here." She turned to yank the worn blue counterpane down.

"No, Amanda. There's no need—"

"There is! You're both severely chilled, and I can tend the two of you better this way. Just until you warm up, then, as that attic is absolutely off limits when you're like this. Please, let's not argue about this, Lincoln."

He leaned his knees against the side of the mattress. Holding the red-checkered tablecloth around his shoulders like a mammoth shawl, he nodded. Swiftly, she peeled the bedclothes back and smoothed the bottom sheet.

The bed smelled like her lavender dusting powder, and she thought he might refuse it for that. But his nose was running; he was sniffing already. She stood on tiptoe to get him one of Matt's handkerchiefs from the top drawer of the highboy.

"I'll run up to the attic and fetch a dry nightshirt for you, if you don't mind my being in your things up there."

"Desperate times need desperate remedies," he muttered and sank limply on the edge of the bed away from her. A huge sneeze, then another exploded from him. She turned and ran upstairs, thankful, when the cold air smacked her, that she had not been so thoughtless as to send him up here. On top of the trunk beside his bed lay the closed locket of his wife and daughter. On the top of his short, folded pile of garments she found the nightshirt. She ran back down and gave it to him where he still sat on the side of the bed.

"I'll be right back to get that bed warm," she told him.

He looked around at her. Despite his sorry state, his blue eyes lit and widened. She stood for an endless moment feeling as frozen as he looked, absolutely adrift in the clear pools of his intense, assessing stare. Then what she'd said hit her.

"With hot bricks, like for a sleigh ride . . ." she choked out.

"Good," he said through stiff lips. "I'd like that."

Late that night, Lincoln woke to sense Amanda's presence before he slitted open his heavy eyelids and saw her white silhouette at the side of the bed, hovering close. The room was dim with a distant lantern on the tall bureau across the way. She jumped when he spoke.

"For a minute, I thought I'd died and gone to heaven."

"Better than the other place," she said, pulling her beige shawl closer over her white flannel wrapper. "I was just taking a last look at both of you before I went to bed. I can bring you something hot to eat or drink, tea or some of those raisin-filled cookies you like. You know, my mother always said raisins were good for you in the winter when you couldn't get fresh fruit, and if you don't have raisins, drink apple cider vinegar, water, and honey." Her voice trailed off. He realized she felt as nervous and awkward as he.

"I'm not hungry right now. I guess," he said and could not keep from a luxurious stretch in the deep, soft bed until his feet bumped the wrapped, still-warm brick, "I've slept straight through since that big supper. How's Matt?"

"Sleeping the sleep of the dead—oh, I shouldn't have put it like that. He's coughing, but doesn't wake."

He had told her earlier that Matt had chopped through the ice when he should have watched him every minute, and it had really rattled her. Still, though he had caused this mess, once again she had cared for him—comforted him—and he felt a hot rush to do the same for her. He risked reaching out to take her hand. He got, instead, her wrist and curled his fingers and thumb around it: she was slender but strong, even there. His gentle grip pulled her down on the edge of the bed, where her weight bounced him. He could tell he had startled her, but she did not pull back or jump up.

"Amanda, stay a minute. I want to thank you for everything you've done—for me, of course, but for Matt too, since he's not able to thank you himself."

"There's nothing to thank me for. Matt's my concern 'till death us do part.' But for what you mean to Matt—and me—yes, you're very welcome. How do you feel right now?"

He dared not tell her his heart, but he knew she meant only how did his body feel. Touching the warm, smooth skin of her wrist, he almost teased her about how he felt his pulse pound. "I get cold, then hot," he admitted. "I feel so sapped, the only thing that wakes me is that coughing."

"Matt's or yours?" she asked as she tugged her hand away and placed it on his brow, brushing his hair back as she did.

That slight caress made his eyes fill with tears. She blurred before him. He could smell the sweet scent of her, however swollen his nose felt. It made his nostrils tingle as if he would sneeze—it made all of him tingle, however achy and floaty his head felt.

When Matt coughed in the next room, she removed her hand, as if reluctantly. "You're both feverish. I may have to send for the doctor in the morning."

"Again, I regret I didn't watch him better on the ice."

"Then you'll please do as you are told and take some Weaver's Salt Rheum that you refused after supper. Lincoln, I've got to dose both of you before it gets worse. And Mandy has donated some licorice you can suck on to keep that cough soothed."

He had never been a good patient; he detested being sick—weak. Now he took the medicine from the spoon she produced, then gladly sucked on the licorice to kill the taste.

"They say," she added, "that the licorice will also help you sleep. If you need anything, or if you think Matt does, please just call out my name, and I'll be here. I'm leaving your hall door and Pru's open, at least partly."

Her voice hesitated a bit on that, as if she and Pru—or maybe the watchdog Eliza—had exchanged words over this whole arrangement. He wanted to tell her she could have her bed back, but he felt so warm here, and his dreams had been so sweet about her, as if it were a magical bed, as if he'd had a feverish fantasy already. Perhaps Amanda Lockwood Wynne was the woman of his dreams and he could have her in his sleep, at least.

"Now, rest well and get better," she said. She stood with a little, awkward wave and went out, carrying a lamp.

"Good night, Amanda," he whispered into the single soft pillow.

Lincoln Garner slept that night, awakened only by his coughing or Matt's. As dizzy as he felt, as chilled as it was outside his cocoon of covers, twice he went in to be certain that Matt was all right. Amanda appeared once when he was there.

"I heard him coughing," she whispered. "Is he all right?"

In her white wrapper, edged by moonlight, with her hair down, she looked like an ethereal sprite. "Yes," he whispered back. "At least, he's quiet now."

"But you're cold again," she said and took his hand to hurry him back to bed. He could not help it, but he lifted his arms to encircle her, not for support or warmth as she might have thought when she let him do it. When she tried to push him down on the bed, still standing, he held to her, leaning on her, his face buried in her radiant hair that the pale moonlight poured through.

"Amanda," he said her name in one long breath.

She stood in his embrace, trembling barely perceptibly, nothing like what racked him. Then she melted from her stiff stance. Her arms clasped him close too; he could feel her body pressed to his. Her soft breasts molded flat to his chest, her full hips wedged against his angular ones. Suddenly dizzy to the depths, he only propped himself against her thighs and knees—when he wanted to sweep her into his arms and run away with her or tumble her wildly into the bed. But all that was impossible, here and now. Impossible always. She turned her face against his throat, pressed her lips to his thudding pulse there and held on tight.

Matt coughed. Still they stood that way, holding to each other and to this moment. The church chimes rang half past four. He felt unsteady again and wavered on his feet. And then she stepped back, and he let her go. In the dim light from the windows and the doors, he saw gilded tears track down her cheeks to wet her lips.

"When I am well," he said, lifting his hand to his spinning head, "I'll have to go—before—before I really want to. At home I have promises to keep."

She shook her head wildly in denial, then nodded once. She helped him into the bed, pulled the covers up, and fled with the soft scuff of wool slippers. That night, in the magical bed, as feverish delirium racked him, he tried to conjure her up. He tried to dream her back, to have her here, in his arms. But she had flown away, and as soon as he was well, for all their sakes, he must go too.

As Eliza had read the opening lines from the Charles Dickens novel *A Tale of Two Cities* to them one long winter evening in the back parlor, " 'It was the best of times, it was the worst of times.' " The last week of January and the first three of February were definitely the worst for Amanda, and she could only pray that the best would follow.

Unfortunately, Matt and Lincoln caught deep chest colds from the icy water. Both were wretched patients, if for different reasons: Matt was restless and kept insisting that he was going back outside; Lincoln returned to being testy and taciturn. His touch-me-not demeanor made it clear that she'd best not ask him if he regretted what he'd done or said.

After two doctor's visits, when, at last, Amanda was finished nursing the two of them, she came down with much the same chills and cough. She could only be grateful that Sarah cooked, cared for Aunt Louise, and, with Pru and even Eliza's help, kept house. In bed, she finally read her Christmas *Godey's* magazines and, with Sarah's permission, penned a letter of inquiry about Ben Blue to the nation's War Department. But time hung heavy on her hands.

The second week in February, a big blizzard blanketed northeast Ohio, howling off the lake and burying them so deep in drifted snow that it was two days before they could dig their way to the chicken coop to save what sitting hens hadn't gone stiff on their nests. Rufus had been helping with Matt the evening the storm hit and thought he'd wait to leave until the snow let up, so he was stuck in with them too. Now he and Lincoln both had pallets in the front parlor, which they had been slowly rebuilding after the Christmas

Eve fire. Unfortunately the whole first floor still smelled faintly of smoke to remind them of the calamity.

With Rufus actually living in the house with them for a week, the perilous balance of personalities changed again. More than once Amanda thought she must be living in an asylum, given Matt's and Aunt Louise's actions and comments. Now she had Rufus and Eliza alternately bickering and cooing. Mandy's pent-up energy amazed and sometimes annoyed them all, and, however fine the child's blossoming piano talent, she drove them to distraction as she endlessly pounded out piano pieces like "Row Your Boat" and "The Farmer in the Dell."

Pru turned petulant, pining for Ned but now cut off from him by piles of snow as well as his own pride. Worse, before the blizzard she had slipped on the veranda and broken her left wrist, and so she couldn't play the piano for two months or more—and that was the only real outlet for her frustrated feelings. Amanda knew how worried Pru was that, when the itchy, newfangled plaster of Paris cast came off, her bone would not be set straight enough that she could ever play well again.

Sarah's edginess over not finding Ben Blue—and Amanda's own secret tenuous situation of feeling trapped between Lincoln and Matt—made them short with each other. Sometimes Amanda thought that despite the awesome beauty outside, sealing them all in here together, everyone was tense, and even little things made her want to scream.

"This weather the only thing made me really miss Miz'sippi," Sarah said one evening at supper.

"You can count your lucky stars," Eliza told her, shaking a finger as if beginning a lecture, "you don't live there anymore, no matter what the temperature here. I recently read that Mississippi still has the most stringent black codes of any of the former Rebel states."

"Gotta admit I don't know what 'stringent' means, Miz Tuttle," Sarah said, taking another helping of hot squash. "But black codes—Amanda done told me all that."

" 'Stringent' means harsh and severe," Eliza explained.

"Then," Mandy put in, "this here is a stringent storm we got."

"All that aside," Amanda said quickly, to head off Eliza's correcting the child's grammar again, "Mississippi has little to be proud of lately. Forgive me for talking politics at the table, Lincoln, but we all know that Jefferson Davis, who helped start the war, was from there, and it was one of the first states to secede."

Lincoln's fork dinged hard on his plate. "I'm sure that explains why we all ought to castigate—that means 'scold'— Sarah for longing for southern weather compared to this howling mess outside!" He flung his napkin down beside his plate and stood while everyone gawked, silent now.

"I'm going," he added, looking a bit sheepish at his outburst, "to make sure this lovely snow doesn't block the front door, if you all will excuse me." He turned and stalked off.

"Pass the meat platter, please," Rufus said, and Mandy almost dropped it as she hastened to comply. Once again Amanda had to steel herself to keep from a simple, soul-sustaining scream.

The increased cold and isolation caused new problems that Amanda scrambled to deal with, even as she recovered from her own illness. She worried that they were devouring both the food stores and Lincoln's once lofty woodpiles just outside the back door. Wind seeped through walls and roared down chimneys, so she devised a series of hooks and hung the summer straw matting from the veranda floor against the outside walls—anything to keep out icy blasts. Lincoln nailed wood wrapped with cloth to the bottoms of doors, stuffed cotton batting around windowsills, and insisted that they keep keys in locks to halt draughts when no one ever locked doors in town.

Kitchen crises multiplied too. Blasts of cold air down the stovepipe made a mockery of time-tested baking schedules. Liquids froze in the pantry and had to be kept closer to the cookstove. Wet plates froze together, so dishes had to be wiped bone dry after washing. China cups cracked the instant that hot liquids touched them, so they had to be slowly warmed first. The sugar supply was depleted, so they had to switch to honey, then molasses (which was as slow as its proverbial self in January), then sorghum.

But there were happy moments among the sad and sad ones too. Before they ran out of tea, Amanda taught Mandy and Sarah how to drink it properly. "My mother and Aunt Louise taught me that you first cool it before drinking by pouring it from your cup into your saucer. See, that's why saucers are so deep. And you can rightly drink the tea from the saucer if you wish."

"Like a cat with cream," Mandy observed.

"Well, not exactly, as I don't want to see you lapping it!" The three of them shared a laugh. "But here's the fancy part. I've seen very elegant people—well, like Mrs. Rutland, for instance," she admitted, though the tea turned bitter in her mouth, "drink it like this. See, you lift your little fingers as the saucer is raised to the lips."

Mandy mimicked her, but Sarah snorted. "Then I'm just gonna stay old Sarah Murry and not be a bit elegant, if I got to be like her," she said and drank her tea with nary a lift of fingers.

"I don't know what I'd do without you two to bring me back to solid earth sometimes," Amanda said, savoring the very last of hers.

But on February 14, even as they began to dig out, the worst of times came back with a bang.

"Amanda," Pru called up the stairs to her that morning while Lincoln, Rufus, and Matt manned shovels and brooms to finally dig them out, "the postmaster's boy just brought two letters!"

Amanda wanted to run downstairs, but she was helping Aunt Louise and her progress was slow. As they descended the front stairs, she was annoyed to see that Pru had darted back to the door and stuck her head out. She was no doubt watching Ned struggling with their walks next door, though the other three men had yelled over that they'd be able to help him soon.

"Pru, you're letting that air in! Let me see the letters. What are the postmarks?"

Sarah came running from the kitchen, her hands white with flour as Pru gave Amanda the letters. Though operating one-handed with her broken wrist, Pru took over Aunt Louise's guidance as they all went toward the back parlor.

"Oh, no," Amanda said, "this one has a return address from Rutland Suits-at-Law uptown. But this one—Sarah, it's to me but from the War Department in Washington!"

"Good glory, maybe they done found Ben!" Sarah cried

and clapped her hands together so flour flew. "It's to you, Amanda. Go on and open it. Read it to me!"

While Pru settled Aunt Louise in her window chair, Amanda tore open the envelope. Sarah hung on her shoulders as she tilted the letter to the morning light and read, " 'Dear Madam. Our records of colored Union companies show that one Ben Blue enlisted at the Union camp outside Chattanooga . . .' "

Sarah shrieked so loud, they all jumped, and Aunt Louise lifted her hands to cover her ears. " '. . . and did serve with honor in the Fourteenth Colored Infantry, the Army of the Cumberland, under General George H. Thomas.' "

"Oh, Amanda! 'Served with honor.' Mandy," she cried and hugged the girl when she came running in, "your daddy done served with honor when he fought the Rebs for our freedom, yours and mine! But after we got sep'rated in Miz'sippi, how'd he ever get to Chatty—where was that now?"

"Chattanooga. It's in Tennessee—but there's more. 'However he was wounded in the Union victory of the Battle of Nashville, December, 1864, was sent back behind the lines for medical attention, and—and has not been heard from thereafter, even to make claims for pay. He—he is presumed . . .' Well," Amanda said, slapping the letter down, "they don't know a thing about what happens to soldiers who wander off in the thick of battle. Matt proves that."

"Let me see that letter," Sarah said and snatched it from her hands. " 'Dead,' it says here. 'Presumed dead.' "

"So 'presumed' doesn't mean he really is," Amanda insisted.

"Why else he gone missing for more 'nigh on three years and not tried to track me down like I doin' him?" Sarah shouted.

"Mama, is my daddy really dead? Where's Tennessee?"

"Sarah," Amanda said, trying to calm Mandy with a heavy hand on her shoulder, "he could have just wandered off like Matt did and he'll find you yet, but doesn't know where to look. We'll keep trying."

"You don't know, don't know a thing about it! Can't you see things are not all fine and dandy in this world, not for the likes of me? And I just know my Ben's not like Mr. Matt, not out of his head somewheres, I know it. He's not dead either, 'cause I would feel that! All your fancy ideas ain't gonna find him, 'cause he just don't want look for me, that's all . . ." she said as her voice trailed off into sobs and she pressed the letter to her face.

"Mama, is my daddy dead or not?" Mandy said, beginning to cry too.

Sarah reached out blindly and pulled the girl hard against her. "Maybe to us he is, honey child," came muted against the paper.

"Sarah, don't give up hope, please, because—"

" 'Cause he can be out somewheres like Mr. Matt?" Sarah said, yanking the paper down, her voice shrill. "So's he can serve with honor in a fine vict'ry fighting for us all, and then just disappear off the face of the earth? I don't want you searching for him no more, Amanda, no more, 'cause I can't bear it, can't . . ."

She shoved Amanda's hands away. But Eliza came in then and, at Amanda's nod, with Pru's help, took Sarah and Mandy upstairs. Amanda sank onto the ottoman and just stared at the other letter she still held while Aunt Louise finally looked back out the window. Then, biting her lower lip, Amanda tore her other letter open.

In it was what she had been dreading and more, and in Mason's handwriting. At least it began with one piece of good news. Her suggestion to the town council, of which he was a member, had been taken up at their last meeting, and he had been appointed to advertise Lockwood as a haven of rural respite in the Cleveland newspaper—and to correspond with specific well-to-do contacts he had in his home city. And then the rest.

"Upon inquiring about another haven—to wit, the Northern Ohio Lunatic Asylum—to see if I could expedite Matt's admittance after your visit there, to assure the safety of Lockwood citizens and its buildings—"

"You bastard," she hissed before reading on.

"And upon my return from a business trip south, I learned to my dismay that plans had not been made for Matt's future admittance, but quite the opposite. Upon my inquiries on your behalf in correspondence with the asylum, I received an epistle suggesting that you created quite a scene the day of Matt's interview. After your similar display in my office, Amanda, I feel I must fully agree with the doctors that you may be an unstable influence—perhaps a partial cause—of Matt's continued dementia. I must advise you to reconsider the ramifications of not admitting Matt of your own accord or something must be pursued for the common good here in Lockwood."

There was more, but she crumpled the letter loudly in her lap and bent over her hands. She shuddered once again, then sat still. She felt as trapped as the blizzard had made them.

"My dear girl, what is it?" Aunt Louise inquired and stood unsteadily to come to her. Quickly, Amanda rose to go to her and seated her again, leaning over her chair.

"Bad news about Matt, Auntie. That dratted Mason Rutland has never forgiven either of us and is determined to punish us."

Her aunt patted her hand. "Is that the letter where he said he's marrying someone else?" she asked. "Now that you and your father have told him off about his wandering eye, you mustn't fret. You'll be better off without him over the years. Perhaps you'll find someone else, or go on without a husband, as I have. I suppose I'm one to talk, with my spinster-hood and all that, but I've observed life, I'll tell you that, and no one man is worth all the agony we women go through for them. Besides, I really don't think there is one great love in a woman's life," she concluded breathlessly and leaned back in her chair to turn her head to look out the window again.

Amanda dropped the letter to the floor and stood with her hands on her aunt's shoulders. The old woman had not given such a lengthy speech in years, and never one so comforting, however off the mark it was, as usual. Now, as if exhausted by her impassioned little speech, the old woman sat quiet once again.

Amanda knelt beside her chair and rested her forehead against her aunt's puffy-sleeved shoulder. The scraping of shovels went on outside; sharp cold still drifted off the win-dowpanes. She had to find a way to stop Mason Rutland, but for this moment she would hold to the strength that came from the love of another woman, older and once wiser. Yes, somehow, she thought, trying to buck herself up, she must go on, just like her Aunt Louise, the blizzards of life not-withstanding.

Amanda heaved a huge sigh. Over her long years, Aunt

Louise had only one man constant in her life whom she
deeply admired and loved—Amanda's father, Louise's older
brother, George. Amanda knew whom she was always looking out the window to see; she waited for her brother to
come home and smile to see her and include her in his plans
and hopes and dreams ...

Aunt Louise shifted away from her, slumped in the chair.
"Auntie, let me walk you back up to bed if you're sleepy,"
Amanda said. "You'll hurt your neck that way. Auntie?"

But Louise Lockwood had gone beyond that window to be
with those who'd gone before.

The shock of suddenly losing Aunt Louise weighed on
Amanda. The cemetery ground was frozen so hard that they
could only put her in a friend's vault and bury her next to
Amanda's parents come the first good thaw. Alone in the
parlor, Amanda bid a tearful farewell to the old woman,
dressed in her best bombazine mourning gown, the one
she'd worn for the death of George Lockwood. Amanda
straightened her aunt's old-fashioned curls for the last time
and knew she'd never see the likes of her again. If she cried
more than she wanted to, perhaps more than she should, it
was for other things lost too.

With people still digging out from the blizzard, Amanda
sent the obituary to the *Lockwood Legend* but put off the
memorial service until later. Still, some came calling, including the Millburns, which pleased Pru no end. Though the
formal mourning period would not be extensive for an aunt,
Amanda and Matt wore black; she thought it suited them
both. Perhaps the death of one of Lockwood's remaining pioneers kept Mason Rutland temporarily at bay, for she heard
nothing more about sending Matt away. Perhaps, she
thought, he was giving her until the weather broke—or she
did.

One late-February day, as Amanda cleaned out her aunt's
room, which she intended to move Lincoln into, Sarah came
in behind her and cleared her throat. Amanda turned to stare
at her friend in the thin winter sun. Sarah had not let
Amanda comfort her since the last letter came, and they had
been pretty much walking around each other.

"Is everything all right downstairs, Sarah?"

" 'Cept that I been meaning to tell you something for nigh on a couple weeks now."

Amanda turned on her knees from going through old gowns in a hump-backed trunk. "You're not going to leave?"

"Oh, no, not 'less you want me to."

"Of course I don't. It's just that we haven't been—as much help to each other as we used to be, since that last letter came about Ben."

"That's what I need to tell you. I want to apologize for the way I flew off the handle that day—at you, when you done nothing but tried to help me always. I didn't mean to say nothing bad 'bout Mr. Matt that day, either. And I'm not saying this 'cause of the things you been through. I had no right to talk back nor argue."

Slowly Amanda rose to her feet. "I accept your apology, but you have every right to talk back or argue. That's one of the things Ben fought for, so that you and Mandy can be free in all things, including to argue with your enemies or friends if you must."

Sarah smiled and nodded. "But not free to be unkind to the best friend I ever had in God's creation, bar none. Still, wasn't that something that my Ben fought with honor and helped win a vict'ry?"

"It was indeed. Even if you never see him again, Sarah, you will always have that."

Pressing her lips together, she nodded. "Well, gotta get back down before them raisin pies burn. Oh, and it's a good thing those men got a deep path dug to the privy now, 'cause we are clean out of corn shucks in the house, and I was starting to think we might actually have to use the pages of those precious *Godey's* magazines of yours!" She laughed—the first time in weeks—her teeth and eyes starbright in her face as she headed out into the hall and back downstairs.

And Amanda heard her say, "Even if he not want me no more, he fought with honor, helped win a vict'ry . . . fought with honor, helped win a vict'ry . . ."

"So should we all," Amanda said aloud to the silent room and turned back to her task.

But amidst the worst of times, there were the best of times, too. The memorial service was deeply moving, and most of the town turned out, as if none of them still held grudges against the Lockwoods for the crash of the canals and the rise of the railroads elsewhere. And Amanda found comfort in the long winter evenings, when everyone in the house gathered in the back parlor like one big family. They listened to Eliza read from a Longfellow poem or a Dickens novel. They drank heated applejack and played chess, whist, checkers, conundrums, or acted at charades, where Eliza drove them all "batty," as Aunt Louise would have said, by forever doing Shakespeare quotes that no one else knew.

More often than not, Lincoln and Rufus would join them. Sometimes they would carve clothespins or work on new rolling pins for Sarah and Amanda or talk about how canal locks or clipper ships were built. When Rufus was there, Eliza sometimes seemed more like a schoolgirl than a retired schoolmistress. Amanda had to stifle a laugh one night when she overheard Rufus tell Eliza at the front door, "How about a quick snuggle to keep me warm all the way home, Eliza?"

There had been a moment of prolonged silence before the door opened and shut, and Amanda wondered if Eliza had relented. And one other time she overheard Rufus tell Eliza as she walked him to the door, "Why, you're leading a man on this way is enough to make a Christian cuss. Thunderation, Eliza, don't you know what years of unrequited longing can do to an able-bodied man?"

Amanda did not sleep well that night, not for thoughts of Rufus and Eliza, but because Lincoln had been so painfully careful around her ever since their nighttime "snuggle." And he was definitely back to being an able-bodied man. He seemed as healthy as a horse and had many jobs about town, more and more large ones. He was gone a great deal, and she found herself listening for his footsteps out in back, his voice to Sarah in the kitchen when he came home, a quick glimpse of him as he went out to his work shed. Unless they were with the others, it seemed he was avoiding her, and she resented that, however much she knew that it was best. But longing to be with him built inside of her like steam trapped in a pot, just waiting to blow its lid. Still, just to have the chance to see him daily made these days the good times too.

One afternoon late in February, Amanda was kneeling in the deeply bowed bay window of the front parlor amid ferns she had salvaged from the winter blasts by keeping them in a corner of the kitchen. Hoping for milder weather, she was going to put them back in this little makeshift conservatory and was hurrying to finish before Pru's next piano student arrived. Actually, Pru wasn't even back yet from taking a pie next door to the Milburns'. That must be her coming in the front door now, Amanda thought, as she clipped more dead fronds with a flourish.

She smiled when she heard Ned's voice in the hall. So he had been kind enough to walk Pru home! But she startled as they came into the parlor, their voices intense, passionate.

"I think you're foolish to fret over the fact that your wrist may be stiff when that cast comes off, Prudence," Ned said. Amanda cleared her throat, but they did not hear her. She knelt to rise. "At least, your injury will leave you with a wrist and arm!"

"I make my livelihood by teaching and playing, that's all I meant, Ned. But I think you're right to scold me. I quite admire you more than I would if you had two arms, you know. After all, you do everything manly so well—care for your house and family, harness and ride horses, shovel snow."

"Not quite everything," he said, his voice hard again.

"What can't you do?" she asked. "Show me. I don't believe it!"

Amanda knew she must make herself known, hidden here in the recessed jungle of her ferns. She felt embarrassed to be caught like this, and yet her pride in Pru's reclaiming her gumption made her feel reckless too. She almost cheered when she heard Ned say, "Tarnation, just this, you impossible woman!"

There was a *whoomph,* a little thud, a muffled squeal as Ned Milburn evidently put his one arm around Pru Cuddy and kissed her hard. Amanda moved farther back, pressing her hands to her mouth. The kiss and caress must have gone on and on, until she—if not Pru—was literally saved by the bell.

The doorbell rang, and Amanda heard the two of them jump apart.

"Ah, but you deserved that," Ned mumbled.

"I know I desired that," Pru countered, sounding breathless. "Now that's my next student at the door, so I'll have to send you off until later . . ."

"Yes, just until later, my Prudence," he said and bent to kiss her hand quite gallantly, Amanda thought as she peeked out at last. When Ned hurried out the back way and Pru, smoothing her hair and skirt, went to the front door, Amanda tiptoed out and into the back parlor.

After that, especially when the late-February thaw began, it seemed to Amanda that she just overheard everything lately, or read it in letters or newspapers. She was a mere observer of others in love, of those who really lived life while it quite passed her by. The very next day, as she dusted in the back parlor at mid-morning, she even overheard Lincoln's voice, whispering in the hall and hardly talking to her. As a matter of fact, it was very obvious to her now that he had been avoiding her, however closely they had lived these last winter months.

"Go on in, Matt. Give this to Amanda," she heard him say.

"Take care of Amanda."

"Yes, go on."

Amanda turned as Matt came in the room with something held in both hands. She heard Lincoln's steps go back toward the kitchen, his muted voice mingle with Sarah's there, and then the back door close. Matt stood holding his treasure—it appeared to be a carved red wooden heart.

"Is that for me, Matt?" she asked and laid her feather duster down.

"For Amanda," Matt said and extended it to her.

"Oh, Matt, a pretty wooden Valentine—and a note," she said and took the carved wooden heart in her hands. It was delicately done, with a double beveled edge and had a painted wooden sabre thrust through it instead of the usual Cupid's arrow. The heart was painted the same color as Mandy's sled had been. And the note said, "Dear Amanda. Sorry this is late, but with illnesses, the blizzard, and your aunt dying on Valentine's Day, better late than never. Love, M A T T."

Matt's name was scrawled as if Lincoln had actually put his hand over Matt's for the signature.

"Better late than never—Love," she read those final words again. But it was too late for her and Matt, certainly too late for her and Lincoln. And yet he had done this for her, realizing she would know it was not only from Matt but also from him.

"Matt, thank you," she said with tears in her eyes that splattered off her lashes when she blinked. "Thank you, thank you!"

She hugged him while he stood stolidly in her embrace. Apparently glad to escape the attention, he sat and watched out the window with her until Rufus came to walk him uptown. And then it seemed the moment Matt turned away from the window, she glimpsed Lincoln outside, coming up from the ravine with an armload of wood, for he was slowly restocking their low supply. Many household tasks awaited her, too; she needed to get her body as busy as was her mind. But still she sat, like Aunt Louise had in this chair, at this very window, the day she died—Valentine's Day, as the note said, the note she still held in her hands because Lincoln, not Matt, had written it to her.

Smacking her hands on her knees, she rose and went to the kitchen. She donned her winter wool pelisse and buttoned it up, added a scarf, bonnet, and gloves. At the last moment, she sat on the bench by the back door to pull on the single pair of old India rubber overshoes that she and Sarah traded off and on, depending on who was going out in the slush. She told Sarah she would be back soon and ignored her knowing lift of eyebrows that asked a hundred questions but gave only one silent warning. Following the path down to the garden shed, Amanda went to find Lincoln.

She saw through the window that he was inside, bent over some task. He looked up and saw her; his face registered joy, then alarm. The door opened before she could touch it.

"Are you all right?"

"Not really. May I come in?"

"If you think it's wise."

"I only came," she said and swept by him into the warm little space that smelled so sweetly of wood and so tartly of paint, "to thank you for the Valentine." To her dismay, he closed the door and returned to his task, not looking at her.

"I meant it to you from Matt," he said, his voice taut and controlled.

"What people mean is not what happens sometimes. Lincoln, I know you've been avoiding me—"

He slapped down the board in his hand and spun to face

her. "All right, just let me say things right out then. I regret what happened between us the night I was in your bed. Damn it, you know what I mean. I wasn't all that feverish not to know what I was doing—or what I wanted. And it wasn't just nursing and your sweet baking or goodwill that I wanted or want now, Amanda."

"I—I know."

"Then what in heaven's name are you doing out here, where I might be tempted again? There have, I recall, been periods of time when you have given me a wide berth. But what's the point of all this? You're welcome for my part in the Valentine. As I said, I meant it to be from Matt."

"Like Mandy's sled and black-faced doll were from Santa?" she demanded, her voice rising. "And when she and Sarah tried to respond, you couldn't admit that you have a good heart that people respond to?"

Leaning back against his work shelf, he crossed his booted feet at the ankles and his arms over his chest. He frowned hard at her. She stood her ground, glaring at him. And then, it seemed, something simply yanked them together.

His long arms swooped for her, and she flew into them. His hand came across the back of her waist, smashing her to him full length. Her full skirts bobbed back, her hat brim hit his forehead and fell askew. She clung to him as if balanced on the very edge of the earth.

His mouth crushed hers, but she met him fully. Her arms at first pressed to his hard chest, then lifted to link around his neck. She clasped his strong neck as he tilted and moved his head to kiss her deeper. She pushed her fingers through his thick, crisp hair. He almost lifted her from her feet.

And then, when she thought he might break her in two, he gentled to set her back down. Her feet were pressed between his, her knees leaned between his legs for support as the shed spun around them. He cradled her with one arm, while, with his other hand, he stroked her hair, her face; his thumb gently outlined, then caressed, her brows, nose, cheeks, her trembling lips, even the edge of her teeth as she breathed with her mouth slightly open.

Soon she too was exploring his face, touching the angular slant of his bones, the chiseled nostrils, the slightly cleft chin, and then his mouth with its full lower lip. He nipped at her fingers and she jumped. When he began to kiss her again, she responded.

He shifted his hips hard into her and moaned deep in his throat, almost a sound of animal pain, then stood them both upright and sighed, shaking his head once as if coming back to reality.

"Right now," he said, his voice raspy, "we think this makes things better, but it will only get worse. I don't know about you, but I want more and more." Holding her elbows to steady her, he set her back and turned away to lean stiff-armed on his workbench. "And what about Matt?" he muttered.

She felt as if he had hit her in the stomach. She knew he was right. But how could the feelings she had for him be wrong? Oh, how had this ever happened?

"I know," she finally managed. "You're right, and not just about betraying Matt. We would betray ourselves too. But I want to be with you every moment—to know everything about you—"

"Amanda, you don't know me at all—not really—and you shouldn't trust me."

"How can you say that—after everything we've been through together?" She was getting angry that he refused to look at her, especially when he just snorted and shook his head.

"Amanda, I had a whole other life before, one you can't share, one I have to return to if I'm ever going to live with myself again."

"You could stay in Lockwood. People trust you here. Look how many clients you've gotten in such a short time, and you an outsider . . ."

"A Johnny Reb, you mean," he accused, turning to face her at last.

"But if folks accept you knowing that, then they really think you and your work are to be trusted!"

"I can't stay in Lockwood doing repairs, even eventually rebuilding a house or two—maybe building new places if this plan to draw wealthy outsiders goes through. It's not just that I'm running from you—from us—believe me. I can't stay, Amanda, not while the South and my hometown lie in ruins. It would be like—like you deserting Matt, no matter how much you might entertain the idea in your deepest self sometimes."

"I will never desert him, and I don't mean to forsake him—even though he's not Matt, in a way not here, anymore." She pulled her bonnet up by its string and retied it, trying to smooth her hair. "This whole thing—us—is impossible. But I wish you didn't have to go. When?"

"This summer, when I get a bit more money saved. Unless regaining my good sense or mending my tattered moral fiber makes me go sooner. I should go right now, before something like this happens again. And Amanda," he added, his voice urgent, as he seized her upper arms and held her, almost dangling, before him, "the problem is, I want something like this—more—to happen all the time. Those pompous, self-serving bastards—Mason Rutland, the pension office—who say Matt lost his honor on the field of battle and so deserves nothing more—don't make me lose what's left of my honor. Help me to stay here a little longer, Amanda!"

She shook herself free of his desperate grip. "Yes, because I—I care deeply for you as my friend and Matt's too," she said. And, though it had best be left unsaid, because she loved him. Loved him and always would and not only as Matt's friend or hers. But at least she could give him this separation, this assurance—this belated Christmas gift—that he could stay until he was ready to go.

Something powerful flooded her from the depths of her weakness. She knew now, somehow, she must and would keep from throwing herself into his arms again. That knowledge both soothed and frightened her.

"I didn't mean to tempt fate out here," she said. "I will let this remain your man's retreat. I know you're busy—well, I am too. And I think we'd better stop thanking each other for things we do. I guess it only makes us feel beholden to each other, when what we've done for each other is a fair and square trade. We'll just remember that Matt is our only common link."

"Amanda, I never meant to hurt you."

"I'll be fine, and as you have always clearly pointed out, we are from different worlds, even if the government has managed to patch the country back together. So, I'll see you at supper later, with the others."

She didn't even sound like herself, she thought, as she shook out her mussed pelisse and went to the door to open it before he could do his gentlemanly duty. How poignant, the pretty picture, almost like a vision, that flitted through her brain right then, before she stepped outside: she saw herself riding on a horse with him toward a little cottage on a snow-swept hill somewhere. The first time she blinked, the scene disappeared.

She dared not look back. She banged the door and hurried up the slippery path.

Chapter
Nine

❄️

Caramel Pie

(ONE OF LINCOLN'S FAVORITES)

Boil 2 cups firmly packed brown sugar and 1 cup water for 5 minutes. Cool this mixture.

Add to mixture 2 drops maple flavoring, 2 well-beaten eggs, ¼ teaspoon salt, ½ teaspoon baking soda.

Pour into one 9″ unbaked pie shell.

Bake at 350 degrees until set. Check for this by inserting knife in center. When it comes out clean, the pie is done.

Top with unsweetened whipped cream and nut halves.

"Come on, Mandy, stop fussing with that doll, or we gonna be late," Sarah said as she bustled into their bedroom. "I'm gonna help Miz Wynne tote those cakes and pies up to the church bake sale 'fore the festivities really get started. You come along too, even if your school class don't sing 'til later."

"I got to fix up Lizzy for her first Fourth of July, Mama," Mandy replied pertly, without so much as a glance from her task. "You said our first Independence Day is real special."

"Well, it is, honey child. But I think you better just tie that little American flag to Lizzy's hand, 'cause it not gonna stick there on its own."

Sarah checked her appearance in the bureau mirror, wishing Mandy had not named the doll Lizzy. Miss Lizzy White, Mr. White's youngest, had been the bane of Sarah's existence in the bad old days. Sometimes Sarah fancied she could still hear the girl's shrill voice demanding: "Fetch me my dollie, kitchen gal ... I'm going to tell my daddy right now you been sassing me."

Good glory, Sarah thought, it was a blessing those days were over, though she had to admit she let her own flesh and blood come pretty close to sassing her sometimes. Still, Mandy was all she had of real family. She was starting to think she would never see Ben again. Maybe it was for the best, because if he came back and saw how Mandy's face, color, and form favored that preening polecat Napoleon, she might lose him for sure, and Mandy would blame her for it.

Sarah tied her old bonnet, newly trimmed with blue and

red ribbons, on her full head of hair and bent to tie Mandy's on. Bonnets were proper, though she still hated them. Reminded her of Natchez. Too much bother. Why, what did it matter if the sun turned brown skin a darker color, especially on a day gonna be as hot as this one?

"Come on, Mandy. Right now!" she said and marched her toward the door. But at the very minute she opened it, Sarah heard Miss Pru at Amanda's door call in to her, clear as you please, "Amanda, you won't believe it, but there's a Negro man downstairs from out of town, who says he got a message to come here!"

Sarah gasped and loosed Mandy's hand. "Stay here. Stay right here!" she ordered and ran out into the hall so fast she skidded on the polished wood before she regained her balance and hurried on.

"Mama, who is it?" Mandy's voice came muted as if from miles away. "You just said I had to come now!"

"Mandy, stay here with Pru," she heard Amanda say, but nothing sank in but Pru's words: *a Negro man downstairs . . . from out of town . . . got a message . . . to come here.*

She heard Amanda coming behind her, calling her name, but she did not look or turn back. Hand on the banister, she bounded down the stairs, then stopped just below the landing, leaning low, squinting at the man who waited with his back to her. He stood looking out the open front door as if he hated being in the house. His clothes were as dusty as his haversack at his feet. He was the right height, but could her Ben have lost so much weight? Still, war did all sorts of things to men, and hers had been wounded in his great victory. Nearly seven years apart, but how perfect Ben would come looking for her on this day celebrating freedom!

Her heart thudded so loud it drowned all other thoughts. She could not call his name, could not make a sound. She barely heard Amanda's words as she stopped beside her on the stairs.

"Sarah—is it him?" she whispered. When Sarah did not answer, did not budge, Amanda called down, "Hello there!"

The man turned, even as Sarah finally managed in a croak, "Ben?"

But he was a wiry stranger, lighter than her Ben, thinner, older, and not so good-looking by half. Her knees went weak as grass, and she sat right where she was in a whoosh of skirts.

"Sarah?" Amanda said again.

She could only shake her head.

Sarah stayed where she was while Amanda descended and spoke with the man. He said his name was Freeman, that he was a friend of Lincoln's. Lincoln was staying here, wasn't he? Folks lining up for the parade on the edge of town had said so.

Sarah's interest quickened again. This Negro had fought for the Union too; perhaps he would know of Ben. But right now Amanda was giving him her familiar welcome, full of smiles, talk, and food.

"I'm afraid you just missed Lincoln, as he's gone uptown to help set up the speakers' platform. Why don't you sit down to a breakfast while we pack our baskets—oh, I have some caramel pie I'd love for you to try too—and we'll walk up to talk to him. It's so lovely to have a guest with us on this special day."

As she steered the nervous-looking man back toward the kitchen, Amanda looked up at Sarah and gave her a pointed nod. "Lincoln will learn more," she mouthed.

Sarah nodded and stood, feeling not so deflated, even a little hopeful again. That's what anyone should feel on a day like this with a country that let everyone celebrate freedom—at least a little hopeful for the future.

Seeing Sarah was so shaken, Amanda took over, packing pies and cakes in baskets while Sarah quickly scrambled eggs and sliced bread for Freeman's toast. Evidently stunned, Sarah wasn't offering one word now. Freeman ate everything set before him almost before it hit the table.

"Fine food, ma'am, sure 'nough, fine food," he said between mouthfuls.

Amanda found herself remembering last Thanksgiving, when Sarah, Mandy, and then Lincoln had been deposited on her doorstep like early Christmas gifts. How long ago that seemed, and yet so near to her heart. She knew and feared that Lincoln would be pushing on soon; each day, each moment near him she treasured. Soon she might lose Matt too, for Mason Rutland had arranged for him to begin a year in the asylum on August 1—and if she did not deliver him there, "the law" would come for him. But today, Amanda told herself as she hefted a basket, she must not think of all that. Today, she would be with Matt and Lincoln—all her little family—and then store it as another cherished memory for hard times to come.

"Here, ma'am, let me help," Freeman said, and took two baskets, while she and Sarah carted one apiece.

Uptown, all across the square, Lockwood citizens prepared for the box social, group games, the parade, and the mock War between the States encampment. Amanda nodded and waves to friends and acquaintances alike. Most of the men proudly sported their blue Union uniforms, though Amanda had thought it best, under the circumstances, that Matt not wear his. She was glad in the grand array of patriotic colors that she had worn her best blue muslin dress with red and white ribbons on her bonnet. Over by the draped foundation stone of the monument that would later be unveiled as a memorial to Lockwood's fallen in battle, town leaders, including Mason Rutland, stood and talked. In the center of activities, Lincoln, though busy nailing bunting to the speakers' platform with Rufus, Matt, and Henry Hanks, turned to see them coming as if Amanda had called out his name.

He gave Rufus his hammer and strode to meet them. "That him without the beard, ma'am?" Freeman asked, and Amanda nodded with a smile. Lincoln was bareheaded and jacketless as the heat pressed in already; his shirtsleeves were rolled up to show brown, muscular forearms.

"Freeman, my friend, you got my message!" he called, and Freeman put one basket down to pump Lincoln's hand.

"I sure 'nough picked the right day to come calling!" Freeman told him, grinning. "Your landlady here done fed me up real good."

Lincoln winked at Amanda; her insides tilted as if she were sixteen again. "And you've met Sarah," Lincoln said. "I don't know how much of my message you got, but she's looking for a lost husband, who fought in the war around Chattanooga. And I thought you'd enlisted in Tennessee somewhere, so by chance you might have known him."

"Well now, that's right, I enlisted to help out right after those Rebs whipped the Yankees at Chickamauga in '64, 'cause that scared me stiff the Rebs might win. Now, what was your man's name, ma'am?" Freeman asked.

"Ben Blue," Sarah said, her voice growing stronger and prouder amid the hubbub of shouts around them. Mandy stopped her skipping and waving of Lizzie's flag to stand stock still and listen. " 'Course he was supposed to go by the plantation owner's name, White," Sarah explained, "but he out and out refused and took his favorite color—blue, like the wide, open sky. About your height, Ben is, but stockier. A man who loved to work with horses, and they always took a fancy to him. From Natchez. He fled north, and must have stopped to enlist in Tenn . . ."

Amanda meant to pay close attention, but Sarah's voice faded for her. Lincoln's eyes had darted to hers again when Freeman had mentioned Chickamauga, for that was Matt's last, fateful battle.

"Sorry, ma'am," Freeman said, shaking his head. "There was lots of us contrabands—that's slaves fleeing on the roads, some a who come in to fight. We'd hang 'round the camps 'fore we enlisted. I'm right sorry I didn't know your Ben Blue."

Rufus, with Matt in tow, approached, and Lincoln made more introductions. Matt nodded and repeated everyone's name as it was given. Amanda assumed Freeman was studying Matt so hard because he realized something was wrong with him but couldn't quite tell what.

"Miz Wynne," Freeman said, "I know you gonna think this real strange like. I mean, since you all thought I should know Mr. Blue and I didn't. But your husband here—can't tell you how he reminds me of a man by the same name I know fought in the Battle of Chickamauga. Only he had a beard and wasn't—well, like this—but that deep voice . . ."

Amanda almost tripped over a basket on the ground as she stepped closer to Freeman. "My husband was hurt in that battle. Could you have known him there just before?"

"Reckon so," Freeman said, snatching off his hat again and turning it in his hands as he still squinted hard at Matt. "Sure 'nough, he *is* the Lieutenant Wynne I knew. And even think I know how he got to be so—funny in the head."

At that, Amanda's head spun; Lincoln took her arm to steady her. For this stranger not to know Sarah's man, she thought, but to know Matt—it was a miracle.

"Let's sit down over here," Lincoln said. "Sarah, can you take care of those baskets?"

He walked them to the platform and sat Amanda on the steps. Everything seemed to blur around her: people hurrying toward the start of the parade; children running by, pushing hoops with sticks. The bunting lifted in the warm breeze, and leaves on the catalpa trees rustled. Matt sat at her feet and leaned happily back on his elbows, while Lincoln put one foot on the bottom step and bent closer, arms crossed over his thigh. Everyone watched Freeman. Amanda held her breath, wanting but not daring to hear something that would help her save Matt from the asylum, as she had long been hoping and praying.

Freeman explained to them how word passed quickly among the fleeing contrabands about which Union soldiers or officers could be relied on for a handout of food. And one particular man in the encampment in Tennessee not only collected and passed out rations to them, but gave good advice about being free, about getting jobs, and even about fighting for the cause of freedom.

"Yes, Matt wrote me he did that," Amanda said. "He told the Negro men to fight and the women to flee north until it was all over."

"That's right," Freeman agreed, nodding hard. "Could talk to a whole crowd of us at once, 'cause his voice would ring out so. Real convincing, Lieutenant Wynne was."

"Yes," Amanda said with a nod, as tears trickled from her eyes. Despite the building heat of late morning, her arms were all gooseflesh. She reached down to put a hand on Matt's shoulder as he gazed, unconcerned, across the busy scene.

"So told him I'd enlist," Freeman went on, "and spent a whole morning with him once 'fore the troops finally marched out to battle. He had dysentery then real bad—land, half the boys in blue did—that's what they called themselves."

"Yes, I know."

"Go ahead, Freeman," Lincoln prompted.

"But it was new to Lieutenant Wynne, see, so the camp surgeon dosed him real heavy for it right 'fore the march to Chickamauga, camphor pills and opium pills, he told me.

See, I belonged to a doctor once, and know lots about dosings and all."

"But opium pills?" Amanda cried. "Lincoln, you know how he gets with opium pills! He could have slept through the entire battle if he took those! Maybe he wasn't even in that battle!" Seeing that she was disturbing Matt, she lowered her voice. Both she and Lincoln kept Matt calm with hands on his shoulders.

"No, ma'am," Freeman said, "he in it all right. 'Cause 'fore I enlisted, I tried to see him again. Got told he turned real funny during the early fighting, dizzy, dead on his feet like. And—and—you sure you want to hear all this, Mrs. Wynne, my saying it right in front of him, and all?"

"It's all right, Freeman."

"The drummer boy in his regiment—one later got hisself kilt with a stray shot—he told me Lieutenant Wynne got real sick and exhausted. You know, dead on his feet from his dosing. Heard tell he crawled in a hollow tree trunk during battle, and his unit got way ahead of him. Then in retreat, a horse tripped over that tree, maybe fell right on it. Still, somehow he got out and went wandering, and without a mark on him, even though he was kind of funny in the head."

"That's it!" Lincoln said.

"That's it!" Matt repeated.

"It explains Matt's wanting to hide," Lincoln said. "He even tried to crawl in a hollow tree the day we fell through the ice. That new dysentery medicine drugged him. He was knocked out by it, and hid, then—"

"Yes, then," Amanda said, nodding. "It wasn't his fault. *They* did it to him with those opium pills, then dared to say he fled as a coward. Now, if I can only prove it before he is taken away!"

When Matt turned, frowning, to look at her, she wondered if he understood any of this. But, as ever, his eyes were blank; he was responding only to her tone and level of voice. She rose and looked around, amazed not to hear the sounds and see the sights of battle that she had been imagining.

And there stood Mason Rutland, just across the green, charming a little group of avid young ladies. Amanda wanted to run right over to the wretch and scream in his face that he and his cronies were wrong about Matt. He hadn't fled of his own accord; he had not shirked his duty nor tarnished his honor. But she knew she must lay the groundwork for Matt's salvation without Mason's knowledge, so he could not try to stop her.

And so, when Mason extricated himself from his admirers and came over with some men to mount the steps to begin the program, she was only too glad to step aside for him to pass. His eyes as always, dipped insultingly to her bodice. She wished Aunt Louise's brooch that she wore there would grow big enough to shield her and its pin could become a sabre to pierce him right through.

"I see, peacetime or not," Mason said quietly as the other dignitaries climbed the steps ahead of him, "you're still in the same old business, Amanda."

"Such as?" she countered, when she knew better than to antagonize a skunk.

"Taking in mongrel strays," he muttered so no one else could hear. "I saw your ad in the Kentucky Horse Auction book Dottie chattered to you about. Looking for another ex-slave to take in and get to work for you for free?"

He cleared his throat as Sarah came up behind her with Mandy; Amanda was certain they heard. She fought the urge to slap him or shove him down the steps, however impressive the rotter looked in his good-as-new uniform with its shiny brass buttons and his major's stripes. She knew it was a petty thing, but she'd always wished that Matt had outranked him, especially since Mason had spent his time behind a desk when Matt was as good as dying in the heat of battle.

"I can't believe you'd dare," Mason said, as if he'd read her mind to strike him. But when he added, "sir," with an insulting tone, she realized he was addressing someone behind her.

Amanda spun to see that Lincoln had donned his Confederate gray jacket with buff facings that had hung so long in the attic. She had seen him in the jacket only on Christmas Eve in dim light. He looked resplendent in it now. She had had no idea that he had brought it uptown with him today. And though he had no sabre, when she would have loaned him Matt's, he wore a red sash diagonally across his chest. His hat was cocked at an almost jaunty angle to make her think not only how handsome he was but still so brave. It hit her then—although on the enemy side, Lincoln had been a major like Mason.

The two men eyed each other before Lincoln spoke. "It seemed to be a day for pride in uniforms, so yes, I dared."

"A builder like you. I should have known," Mason countered. "Engineering Corps, I see. A clever, wily bunch, but you had to turn tail in the end, like all the rest."

"Come on, Matt, Amanda," Lincoln said. "Let's go enjoy the lovely day and the nice people."

Mason sputtered something in reply, but no one looked back. They were only halfway across the green when from the platform Mason's voice boomed out to introduce Mayor Roscoe, then the two men with him Amanda did not know. They turned out to be the first two Clevelanders who had bought lots for summer homes in Lockwood, a Samuel Wainwright and one Josiah Baldwin. You might know, she thought, the idea had been hers and there was Mason, soaking up the glory. But she was glad if Lockwood could be helped by the influx of new blood and money.

She began to walk again, but Lincoln stood his ground, so Matt did too. She turned back to see Lincoln listening to Mr. Wainwright's words of praise for Lockwood. Mason had introduced the man as newly retired from the army, who had been serving in the "fallen South."

"What is it?" she asked Lincoln. "You don't know him?"

He shook his head. "It's just a day for seeing resemblances, that's all. Let's get in the shade."

She was still trembling with fury at Mason as they walked away, but if Lincoln noticed he did not let on. She felt foolish that she had wondered what the little raised letter E's on his silver buttons meant, whereas Mason had known right away. Engineering Corps—whatever they did in the war. The way Lincoln had hesitated getting on a train, it obviously meant something beyond driving a locomotive. She realized again how very little she might know about Lincoln Blake of Savannah.

Like Mason, others gaped at Major Lincoln Blake's Confederate gray at first. A few pointed; Amanda heard one muffled "Boo!" But for months people had known Lincoln was a Johnny Reb and what a hard worker he was too. Perhaps their Yankee free-enterprising spirits and their gratitude to have peace made them both accept and even admire him.

If only, Amanda thought, that blasted Mason could let by-gones be just that.

Sitting on blankets at the edge of the square, Amanda and her friends watched the parade pass by. She sat between Matt and Lincoln; next was Freeman, then Sarah and Mandy next to Eliza and Rufus. The extravaganza began with flags, trumpets, and drums; in two lines, sixteen able-bodied veterans, whose banner read "The Grand Army of the Republic" marched by to wild applause. Then, to mingled cheers and boos, the temperance ladies, shouting, "Take the pledge, take the pledge!" Eliza belonged to their ranks, but she had chosen Rufus's company today, so she waved her handkerchief in salute.

Various small glee clubs that would later give a patriotic concert from the tiny gazebo stepped smartly by, holding their name banners aloft. Next, the four Lockwoodians who owned two-wheeled velocipedes rode them by, but Amanda could see why people called the contraptions boneshakers. It seemed one must have wonderful balance on the wood seat and circular foot pedals to handle the bouncing machine across the ruts in the street.

And then—you might know—like a cat with nine lives, Mason Rutland rode by with an American flag. Mounted high on one of the fine new Kentucky thoroughbreds that he had brought back to breed, he looked every bit the leader, the triumphant conqueror. Amanda could just have spit.

"That man gonna get what he richly deserves some day, you mark my words!" Sarah said, and boldly turned her back on him. But Mason rode on.

Then came the decorated wagons, so those marching ahead would not have to go through the horses' droppings: the New National Grange, "Patrons of Husbandry" with their pitchforks in a salute, and an "Anti-Johnsonites Say Defeat President Johnson" wagon, although this was not an election year. The Lockwood House contingent of spectators stood and clapped and whooped when Ned drove a wagon by with Pru pounding out "Battle Hymn of the Republic" on the tinny old oyster saloon piano there.

Following the parade, the gentlemen of the town bid on their ladies' box lunches to raise money for a Methodist church organ. Matt, with Lincoln's help calling out the prices, bought Amanda's—and bought Sarah's for Freeman, who shyly shared it with Sarah and Mandy as if they were a little family. Rufus made a big show of purchasing Eliza's; Ned got Pru's. But when Mason Rutland paid an exorbitant amount for his wife's, the fun of the day began to pale again for Amanda. She had to write another letter to Washington, this time with Freeman's statement written out and witnessed. She had to do it tonight!

After a crowded mass picnic on the green, people wandered from amusement to amusement. They listened to the singing, including the two songs by Mandy's class. "Bully! First rate! Hurrah!" filled the air. People shouted louder after each rendition of each new song, as more ginger beer and root beer was drunk, more fragrant pale orange muskmelons from Lockwood's sandy soil devoured, more baked goods eaten, more handkerchiefs wiped across brows.

"This caramel pie of yours is wonderful!" Lincoln told her once with his mouth full. "As much as I love southern pecan pie, I've never tasted better!"

In the shade of her ruffled umbrella, Amanda knew it could not be the sun that made her blush at his praise.

Despite the heat, youngsters ran in the three-legged and sack races. Penny-candy prizes were valued and flaunted as if they were pure gold. Ladies took turns at the bakery booth, then some, though not Amanda, wandered to look at Dottie Rutland's newfangled stereoscopic view of Pompeii, a once bustling city that had been buried by a volcano. At least, Amanda tried to buck herself up, Lockwood would no longer be buried by the loss of the canals and the coming of the rails.

At last, at two, came the awaited unveiling of the limestone foundation for the war obelisk to be built, when donated funds allowed its completion. It would eventually bear the names of Lockwood's brave fallen in the war. Ripped and torn regimental flags were hoisted; guns banged a salute after the mayor and others spoke again. As the drapery was drawn aside—unfortunately, by Mason Rutland—veterans, including Lincoln, stood at attention and saluted. Matt did too, to crumble Amanda's last resolve to see the day through without a tear.

* * *

Like the Independence Day parade, the hours and events of July marched faster and faster past Amanda in a blur. She tried to make time go slowly, to savor the short conversations she had with Lincoln, the lengthy ones they all shared at the dinner table, the moments she could be with Matt.

She haunted Julius Ross at the post office for a reply to her letters to her congressmen in Washington, to the man at the War Department who had responded quickly about Ben Blue, to the national pension office, even to President Johnson himself. She had sent copies of Freeman's explanation and recounted Matt's entire case. She asked that the stain on Matt's honor be expunged and that his rightful pension be forthcoming so she could get permanent resident help to be sure he was no danger to others or himself.

But there was no reply. If one did not come in time, she would just have to get Matt out of the asylum once he was there, and she knew how much harder that would be.

Amanda planned a picnic for Matt and his friends on the last Sunday in July: it was Matt's thirty-second birthday and just two days before he must go away. It was not only a celebration of Matt's life but—she feared—a farewell to him and Lincoln. Lincoln admitted he must be on his way soon—always soon, though he said he wasn't certain when.

On Sunday after church, the men carried baskets of food and crocks of lemonade down the path to the old canal basin—Rufus, Ned, Lincoln, and Matt, for Freeman had gone back on the rails long ago, telling her how to contact him if he needed to testify. Eliza, Sarah and Mandy, Pru, and Amanda, twirled their shade umbrellas and toted the tablecloths, napkins, and desserts.

How memories clung to Amanda today, as they had all month. The first time Matt had escorted her out was nine years ago this July, first to the Independence Day gathering and later to a picnic like this, chaperoned by Father and Aunt Louise. Both times, how they had talked and laughed. After the picnic, they had strolled home ahead of their elders, holding hands and making plans and promises. It had been the beginning of their lives together, and now, she feared, it might be the end for them and all Matt had once been. Separation and the asylum loomed over them like a dark shadow, chilling her to the bone despite the heat of the day.

She thought of losing Lincoln too, especially when they

passed his work shed. She recalled their two times alone there and the day she'd confronted him down on this very path in the snow. She had accused him of being bigoted toward Sarah and Mandy, whom he had won over as he had her. This very red-and-white-checkered tablecloth that she carried over her arm was the one she had wrapped around Lincoln after he fell in the canal, the one he wore the evening she put him in her bed. All these memories, these feelings for Matt and Lincoln too—where had those precious moments gone?

But she had steeled herself to keep up a good front today. The chatter over food helped, though she sensed that much of it was forced. Rufus bantered with Eliza; Ned and Pru kept touching hands. Amanda spoke and nodded, laughed and dished out more food, hardly tasting any of it herself. Not the fried chicken, nor her favorite potato salad which Sarah had learned to make so well, not the birthday cake she had made for Matt nor the caramel pie she had made because Lincoln had praised it once. In a binge of baking, she had made Matt's once favorite lemon meringue pie too, but he had not touched his piece of it nor seemed aware that the birthday cake was for him. She must face up to the truth, she told herself, that the Matt she knew and loved was long gone already.

Later, Rufus showed Matt and Mandy how to fly a kite made from an old piece of sheet. Remembering the girl's penchant for snow angels, Rufus had put a head with curly black hair and a halo at the top of it and drawn in wings on the two side corners. As Amanda watched the angel soar, Ned Milburn broke in on her musings.

"If you'll excuse me, Amanda, Prudence and I will take a little stroll. I love it here when it's so peaceful on a Sunday."

"Despite the two mills still going, it's even peaceful here on weekdays," she said with a sigh. "As for me, I miss the bustle, the old days, but you just can't go back again."

"No, that's right," Ned said. "Got to keep going ahead in this new day and age, no matter what. We'll see you later, then," he added and gave Amanda a surreptitious nod.

She watched them go, hand in hand, Ned's empty sleeve pinned to his shirt. He had told Amanda in strictest confidence that he intended to ask for that hand of Pru's he held today. Amanda had been thrilled; yet it made things that much harder to think of another leaving her soon. At least Pru would make a marvelous neighbor.

When Lincoln got up and stretched and went to watch Rufus's antics with the kite, Eliza and Amanda sat, putting away the last remnants of the feast. "I intend to give you some talk time alone with him today," Eliza announced matter-of-factly.

"With Lincoln? That's a change from your watching us like a hawk this winter."

"You've both been very brave. And," she said with a sigh as she turned to look at Rufus cavorting with Mandy and Matt while Sarah and Lincoln watched, "I know what it is to have abiding regrets and feel deep loss when one's alone. I know what it is to think a single rapturous moment is going to have to last a lifetime, when one is wed elsewhere. You see, Amanda, I never stopped loving Rufus, even the years I loved my husband . . ."

Amanda reached out to squeeze her hand on top of the pickle jar. "But, of course, the way I saw it then, Rufus went to sea, went away, deserted me," Eliza added. "I hope you don't blame Lincoln for jumping ship right now. Rebel he might have been, Amanda, but a man of honor. Perhaps they all were, all those Confederates, and that's why they kept fighting, even when it was a long-lost cause. I believe that, if Lincoln's intentions were less than honorable, he would stay after Matt's gone. I can read what he's thinking, that he wants to stay to comfort you but knows that he cannot because then it would be impossible for him and you—to—to . . ."

Amanda nodded and looked down in her lap through a blur of tears she had vowed to keep at bay. "Yes," was all she could add. She bit her lower lip, then loosed Eliza's hand to go back to putting things away. "Eliza," she said with a sniff, "you've been to me what Aunt Louise could not, and I thank you for that. But what about you and Rufus now?"

"I believe he's downright afraid to ask me to really share a life with him. Afraid he'll slip back to drinking and disappoint me, afraid I'll say no—"

"What would you say?"

"Even after everything, I'm not sure."

"Maybe he senses that you're not ready. As rowdy and

rude as he has seemed to be about it sometimes, Eliza, perhaps he really knows your heart."

"For so long I've told myself to listen to my head and not my heart," she said, pursing her lips. "I wage continual war within myself about that." She turned to smile wanly at Amanda. "Now why don't you just leave Matt's watching to Rufus and Rufus's watching to me and take a little walk down the towpath?" She leaned on her hands, then rolled to her knees to rise. Amanda jumped to help her stand, then did exactly as her favorite teacher had instructed.

Amanda had managed to compose herself when Lincoln came to join her for a walk, as Eliza had suggested he would. The stubborn woman had never stopped controlling "her classroom" even if she seemed not to manage her own life sometimes.

"Let's go down to the old locks," Lincoln said without any greeting or explanation. She took his arm, and they strolled the curving canal path that led past the locks and along the river.

"Have you seen the locks close up before?" she asked.

"You know how it is with builders and engineers. I designed and built houses before the war and pontoon bridges and earthworks during, but anything like this fascinates me. I've studied the whole locking system here, the wicket bar that opened and closed the doors, the stone base, the wooden floors and sides, the hinges. Some of the lock gates and levers are still painted red, but it's disappearing with time, even in the eight months I've been here."

"They used to call that Indian red," she said, aware that they were filling the air with inconsequentials to avoid what mattered today. "Lincoln, you should have seen the activities, the excitement down here once in the canal's heyday!"

"I can imagine." He turned to look at her for the first time. They stopped walking at the head of the deep, empty lock. Suddenly afraid of the hunger in his eyes, she broke their gaze and stared down into the lock. Nodding cattails, tangled morning glories, even seedlings had taken root in the marshy silt.

"The time has come for me to leave Lockwood, Amanda. I have things I must do elsewhere. I—I had planned to earn more money before I go, but it is time."

When she looked again into his intense blue eyes but said nothing, she thought he might seize her. But he walked away, slowly, along the cut-block edge of the lock, around the end with the rotting gate, across to the other side. He stared at her over the gap before he spoke again.

"I must push on, even though I'm leaving you at a terrible time. I am so sorry about the way things have worked out for Matt, so sorry about it all."

"I know you are. You have been wonderful for him."

"He's helped me. I feel I've had a friend. And you . . ." his voice faded, and he lifted his hands as he struggled helplessly.

She closed her umbrella and went to stand in the shade of the catalpa tree on the other side of the towpath, even though that put more distance between them. What she wanted to do was run to his embrace, but she must keep control.

"Amanda," he said and came back around the lock, stopping four feet from her in the shade, "I've got to say some things. If it bothers you or makes things worse, I'm sorry." He swept off his hat. "You have rebuilt my life for me, not only in giving me a place to stay, a family for a while, your concern—you even gave me Christmas. I can't thank you enough."

"As we've said before, we have helped each other. My favorite Confederate engineer has rebuilt some of my town, the pillars of my house, my parlor, and much, much more, even closer to home. I hope we may correspond upon occasion as you return home to help with rebuilding there. That is what you intend, I take it?" she said, amazed at her polite, controlled tone.

"Yes. I—yes. My home is gone, but I can give you an address of a friend there. Amanda, I knew I couldn't bear to say good-bye to you and Matt either, so let's just remember this beautiful day, and others like it."

He held his hat tightly in his hands before him. Shadows darted across his face; he looked racked by pain, a pain she felt too as it leapt between them. And then, like the last time in his work shed, it seemed some force simply pulled them into each other's arms.

She pressed her chin into his shoulder and kept her eyes tightly closed, savoring his strength, for she had spent hers on those last calm, sane words and steps away from him. He smelled of the warm wind, of the bay rum he splashed on after he shaved. When she turned her cheek against his cotton shirt, she could hear his heart beat, feel his pulse and skin beneath the softness of the fabric. It was a hard, commanding embrace, yet beseeching too—one, she knew, she would feel forever from afar.

Lincoln too felt stunned. Why had he leapt at her now, when he had kept himself on such a tight rein these past months, willing himself not to touch her, not to gaze overlong, or tease her, or begin an argument of the sort that had once fueled their forbidden feelings. Not to linger in the upstairs hall when she passed so that he could smell her lavender scent, not to listen for the ring of her voice, the tread of her quick step so he could pretend she was looking for him. Not to savor her cooking on his tongue and mouth that longed to kiss her. Not to love her and desire her as he did now, God forgive him.

Wanting to kiss her, wanting to just pick her up and carry her away with him, he set her away, then stepped back. "I didn't mean for that to happen," he said.

She bit her lower lip and nodded.

For one moment, staring at her as if he could memorize her beautiful face, her fragile expression that looked as if it could shatter, he almost blurted out the truth about himself. His real name, hometown, state. His sad past, his fearful future. But it might be best for her never to know.

And he wanted her to remember him this way, not as he was when he came, not as a fugitive or accused murderer. He wanted her to remember him as an honorable man, one who cared deeply for her and for Matt. One who wanted only the best for her when she faced the worst, even as he did.

It can't end like this, he kept thinking. Not with all we have come to mean to each other, all the beauty that could be between us. But instead, he said only, "Let's go back."

"Remember, we decided you can't go back," she whispered, but she opened her umbrella and walked up the old path at his side.

Even from there, they could hear Mandy's excited squeals

and see the white angel kite soaring in the sky overhead as if it had been watching them.

Lincoln Garner's stockinged feet hit the bedchamber floor that night after the church chimes rang three. He had not slept at all. He didn't want to flee like a thief, but he hoped the letter and the gift would help her to forgive him. He left them on his pillow as he smoothed the covers on the big bed that had once been Louise Lockwood's. Hurriedly, he pulled the rest of his clothes on. He was taking nothing with him other than what he'd earned fair and square; and, he thought, most of the money he'd saved would have to go for paying a lawyer if he decided to go through with a trial. But he was heading for Savannah first, hoping to see friends and find a job there.

He had stuffed everything he owned in the same haversack with which he'd come, but he was leaving with so much more. The strength and desire, at least, to fight for his future. And a love to last a lifetime, even if he never saw Amanda Lockwood Wynne again.

He carried his boots down the hall, past the attic door, remembering the time he had sat on the steps there, listening to Amanda comfort Sarah in the linen closet. He recalled the time he came up those stairs to find her and Matt wanting him to help carry down boxes of Christmas decorations. How many more Decembers would Amanda mount the stairs to fetch those things? Would Matt ever return from the asylum to go with her again?

He passed the closet where Matt had hugged them both the night of the Christmas pageant, and went down the front stairs into the silent hall. He had replaced the burned woodwork and floor in the parlor for her with castoffs from his other projects about town; he hesitated outside the door of the silent room, remembering the first time he saw her there, while Matt stared at the etching of President Lincoln and Sherman's portrait glared at him. The fury he used to feel at Sherman and the war—at life for its losses—was muted now, but he feared it would flame again when he went home.

He fancied he could smell, even now in the dead of night, some of Amanda's baking, which always said welcome and love. He sniffed the air, then almost sneezed; he put his shoes under one arm and jammed a stiff finger under his nose to stop the impulse. He had oiled the brass door handle, so it turned silently. On the veranda, he sat down to pull on his boots. Only last week they had sat out here late, listening to the creaking of crickets he heard now, enjoying the night breeze—all of them, this hodgepodge family Amanda had built here that made Lockwood House what it really was, far sturdier than wood and stone. Sitting here, they had counted falling stars and made wishes on them. He dared not hope that his might come true, so he might return again someday, at least write her or send her something for Christmas sometime, over the years.

He shouldered his sack and set out at a good pace, refusing to look back again. He had packed away the whole little town inside him anyway—Matt; Sarah and Eliza, whom he had eventually won over; Mandy, of course, who had both made him miss his own child and helped to heal his wounds; the townspeople, who had hired him on and praised his work; and Amanda. He wanted to stay to help her face losing Matt, but he could not risk what would become of their hard-fought battle to stay true to themselves if he comforted her after Matt was gone. At least Rufus and Eliza had agreed to go to Newburgh with her to admit Matt to the asylum there.

Near dawn, when Lincoln got to Sandusky, because Amanda had changed his life so completely, he did something else he would not—could not—have done eight months ago. Lincoln Garner took the train instead of letting the train take him.

Stunned, even though she had known that this moment had to come, Amanda stared at the letter and the wrapped box on Lincoln's pillow. Sarah said he had not been down early to go out; he had not appeared for breakfast. And then Amanda had known and run upstairs and knocked only once on the door before she entered.

She walked slowly to the bed and touched the pillow, then took the letter and the tiny package. Her knees shook, but she did not sink on the bed; she walked to the front window, to lean her shoulder there and let the sweet late-July air calm her. But it did not.

She sat in Aunt Louise's old chair and tore the envelope open.

Dear Amanda,

Forgive me for leaving this way, but I believe it is best. What could we—even the three of us—have said at parting? I could not tell Matt to "Take care of Amanda" now, for soon you will be without him for a spell. I pray he will come back to you, healed. I know you hate the asylum but, as he is not improving here, perhaps there is a chance there.

I must tell you what you mean to me—a deep, abiding admiration that was born on Christmas Eve and has been growing since. So deep that I can leave you, yet be possessed by you forever.

When I draw in a breath of sweet, warm July breeze or December's chill wind, when I taste something wonderful or see something brave or beautiful, I will thank God that He let me know you. And wherever I go, I will always carry Christmas in my heart. Consider this a late holiday gift I did not give you then or one to last a lifetime—

Lincoln

P.S. And the mistletoe was imported from the South, just as you said your family used to do. Good things can come from the South, Amanda. Think of me then, over the years, if you stand under its leaf with anyone else . . .

She stared out the window, clasping the little box in her hand until its corners pressed into her flesh. Mistletoe—he'd probably sent for it through his friends who rode the rails— the kissing plant. Her first impulse was to run to the livery stables, get a horse, ride to the depot at Sandusky in case he still was there. But she knew several trains would have been through by the time she got there. And she knew, too, he had to go home.

Quickly she tore the brown paper from the box, pulled the lid off. Where she was expecting sprigs of mistletoe, Lincoln's double-faced locket fell into her lap and snapped open. The faces and tresses were gone from it. And in their place was framed, on one side, a lock of his black beard that she had shaved for him on Christmas Eve, and, on the other, one small, waxy sprig of mistletoe.

Chapter
Ten

✳

Summer Squash Bread

(BEN BLUE'S FAVORITE)

Prepare 2 loaf pans, 9″ × 5″ × 3″, by lightly greasing and flouring.

Shred 2 cups finely chopped or grated squash, preferably zucchini. Use as much green rind as possible for attractive appearance of bread.

Chop ½ to 1 cup walnuts.

Mix in bowl, 1 cup oil, 2 cups sugar, 3 eggs.

Mix in separate bowl, 3 cups unsifted flour, ¼ teaspoon baking powder, 1 teaspoon baking soda, 1 teaspoon salt, 1 teaspoon cinnamon.

Stir dry mixture into moist mixture.

Add grated squash, nuts, and ½ to ¾ cups raisins (optional). Mix all together and divide into pans.

Bake at 350 degrees for 40 or so minutes. Test with toothpick to see it comes out clean before removing from oven.

Cool before tipping bread out of pans.

"Mm-mn, still hot as the hinges of Hades out here," Sarah muttered to herself. On this last day of July, the sinking sun bore down as she bent to cut cooking herbs in the backyard garden. A desperate Amanda had taken Matt to the parsonage to speak with their minister and his wife in a last attempt to keep Mason Rutland from his "kindness" of calling in his carriage tomorrow to take them to the lunatic asylum. None of Amanda's letters to the government had been answered yet, and she had nowhere else to turn.

"Curse that fancy lawyer for all he done!" Sarah said and spit on the soil, then ground it with her foot. She could not bear to have the last hours of the Wynne family's life tick away while she did nothing, so she kept to Amanda's tasks after supper, even though she knew morning was the best time to cut herbs. Now, she thought, that stubborn old sun was fixing to set on Amanda and Matt's last day together, maybe forever. She had to squint into it to see when Mandy came running down the side lane, swinging her doll by one arm.

"Lizzy's face color chipped off, Mama, and she got a big white spot right here," the child said, pointing to her own forehead, then displaying the doll. "If only Mr. Blake was still here 'cause he told me he knew where Santy Claus got his paint."

"Did he now? He knew, all right."

"He wasn't really Santy, was he, and gone away now till next Christmas? I think Captain Quinn is really Santy, 'cause of his white beard and big belly, and I told Mrs. Tuttle, but she said no."

"Well, not Mr. Blake or Captain Quinn is, really," Sarah said, pressing her hand to her sore back as she stretched. "But they's kind of Santy's helpers. You know, like even Almighty God got his angel helpers going here and there with his messages, gifts, and such like. And I just bet if we'd get Miz Wynne to look out in that work shed, there might be some paint there."

"Heard her tell Mrs. Tuttle she didn't want nothing touched out there and she put a lock on the door. And heard her say Lincoln Blake give her that gold locket 'fore he left, and she said it was the best Christmas gift she ever got, so maybe he *is* Santy!"

"Honey child, how you do carry on . . ." Sarah said before her voice trailed off. A man had come down the side lane, but the sun blazed crimson behind him so that he was only form and shadow. A slouch hat hid his head. He was Captain Quinn's height, but much more wiry. For a moment she wondered if Lincoln's friend, Freeman, had come back looking for him, but no. For Amanda's sake, she dared to hope it could be Lincoln Blake, but Sarah knew better. Her heart began to thud like horses' hooves.

"The mistress of the house not here right now," she called to the man, but her voice shook. "Can I help you, mister?"

"This the Lockwood place?" he asked, shuffling closer.

Sarah clasped the tray; it spilled herbs. Though the sun burned into her eyes, she stood staring. She clutched Mandy's shoulder so hard the girl winced and pulled away.

"Mama . . ."

"You looking for Miz Wynne?" Sarah managed to croak out.

"Sure am. Ma'am, are you . . ." he said and walked closer, throwing a long shadow that crept clear up Sarah's skirts, "you who I think? Miz Wynne's friend from Natchez looking for her husband? The one told 'bout in the Kentucky horse show booklet? See, I wasn't at that show, but the man I work for, he done showed it to me and read me the words printed there. It been long years, but you Sarah Murry?"

"Ben? Good glory, Ben! Ben, you came!"

She had told herself a thousand times she would not just run to him if he should ever show up here. She must be dreaming, of course, again. But she dropped the tray, she jumped past Mandy. She ran into the red sun with arms outstretched, and when he opened his, she hit into him hard.

"Sarah! Sarah, girl, thought you might be dead!"

"I been trying to find you for so long . . ."

They hugged until Sarah could hardly breathe. He pulled her off her feet and swung her around. And then she thought of Mandy, who could either bind them or break them. But she couldn't bear to let go of him, her Ben Blue. He was here, safe, alive, hers for right now. He was real.

"Mama?"

Ben set her down. Sarah swiped at her tears and sucked in a big breath.

"Why, this here fine-looking girl yours, Sarah?" Ben pulled off his hat and bent slightly forward to study the child.

"Is this my daddy, Mama?"

"Can't be, young'un," Ben answered when Sarah hesitated. "Sarah—"

"Please, come on in the house. I work for Miz Wynne, who's a friend of mine, and helped me—and Mandy here, when I was growing her like a seed in my belly. She hid us till we could flee north to Canada right after I lost you, Ben. Come on in and let me feed you, and we can talk, talk about it all," she added as she shooed him toward the back door.

Sarah waited for Mandy to protest that Ben Blue was indeed her father, that her mama had told her so. Or to cry or ask a hundred questions. But Mandy looked struck to silence. Sarah seized her arm and pulled her inside. Wide-eyed, Ben Blue followed.

Sarah fed him up real good, the way she knew Amanda would if she were here. Through mouthful after mouthful, he explained things to her. How he'd lured the bounty hunters away from her so far that he couldn't return for three days and when he did she was gone. He told about how, after he was wounded at the Battle of Nashville so late in the war, he went back to tending horses at the farmhouse where the folks had cared for his wounds. And when the war was really over, how he drifted to Kentucky to work a big breeding plantation for a real good salary.

After dessert, he still ate nearly a loaf of the fresh-baked garden squash bread, then kept nibbling on it, all the time looking from her to Mandy as Sarah told him her side of things: their years in Canada and how Amanda came to hire her, about the letters she and Amanda had sent places to track him down, and how proud she was to learn he had fought brave and victorious in the war. Even about Mr. Matt being taken away tomorrow by that same devil Mason Rutland, who had come with bounty hunters here to take her back into bondage just the way he was going to Mr. Matt.

"Would you believe it, Ben? Mr. White promising five hundred dollars for my return in that escaped slave poster, when you know a kitchen gal not worth that kind of reward money!"

"You worth it to Napoleon, and *he* worth it to Edward White," Ben said, his voice bitter. His wide hazel eyes narrowed at Mandy again to make Sarah wish she hadn't brought that up.

Then, thank the Lord, Pru came in with Ned and, after introductions, volunteered to take Mandy out in the yard between the houses to play croquet with them. The girl went willingly, but with a half-puzzled, half-hurt glance back that made Sarah realize she had to settle things between her and Ben real soon. The distant *click, click* of wooden croquet mallets on balls floated to them where they still sat at the table, awkward and quiet now.

"Ben, when Amanda Wynne come back, even though she got herself a mountain of worry, she gonna carry on about giving us a right proper wedding. I tried more'n once to tell her what was really fretting me about Mandy and what you'd think when you saw her, but I couldn't get it out."

He heaved a big sigh. "So she thinks that young'un mine and she expecting me to do the right thing. I can't stay here, then, Sarah, not till you and me settle things. On my way in I took a good look 'round, 'specially at the livery stable uptown. The owner real surprised how the horses quieted 'round me, so maybe I can hire on there. He say there a rich lawyer in town breeding racers, some he got in Kentucky."

"That's Mason Rutland, the man I been telling you about!" She shook her head and put her face in her hands.

"Then I gonna settle up with him, somewhere, somehow!" He reached out gently to pull her hands down. "I don't blame you for having that snake's child, Sarah," he said, his tone kindly, despite how his words crushed her hopes. "And I can't blame you for loving her 'bove all else."

"But no one who not seen Napoleon gonna know she not yours, Ben, I don't care how dark her skin and yours real light! She took after her mama, that's all."

"Sure, that's right. But I'd know and see the bastard in her form and face. Don't you, Sarah? Like to have kilt that snake in the grass and don't want to spend the rest of my days seeing him in her, however sweet she be."

"It's not her fault—and not mine, you say. I been so afraid you wouldn't want me when you saw me again—and her."

"I didn't say that. It's all too sudden, Sarah. I just need a little time, a few days, a week maybe to decide. I came, didn't I? I wouldn't of done that, if I didn't care deep as the Mississippi River for you still."

"I 'spose you got to go talk things over with those livery horses," Sarah said, joshing him as she swiped tears from her cheeks. Despite all the agony of their earlier days together, they had always teased, laughed, and enjoyed each other. Now, Ben Blue gave her a thin smile and shook his head with a little snort, just like a horse.

"If you ain't always had the strongest backbone in tough times—and the best backside too, girl—of anyone I knowed. Not got a bad front to you neither, and eyes like stars, a smile bright as the moon—"

"I know, and a mouth as big as the whole sky, you fancy talker. How many women you done buttered up since I seen you last, Ben Blue?"

"Oh, Sarah, Sarah," he said and shook his head again. "I just need a little time to think, that's all, a few days, and I can't stay in this big house to do that thinking."

"But you won't just up and leave town without telling me?" she said, remembering how devastated Amanda had been when Lincoln took off. She clutched at his hands. "Not after all I been through to find you!"

The front screen door banged and Sarah heard Amanda's voice. It carried down the hall, telling Matt to come in, then calling for her and Eliza.

Sarah ran toward the front of the house, with Ben following. But Amanda had already turned around and marched right back out without Matt, who stood, looking confused, at the bottom of the stairs. Sarah gasped: outside in dimming light, Mason Rutland sat on his big parade horse, ridden right up on the lawn to the edge of the veranda. Amanda faced him alone.

As Sarah hurried out, she heard Mrs. Tuttle come downstairs and try to hold Matt back from going out, but he followed Amanda too. They all looked up at Mason Rutland—Amanda, Matt, her and Ben, while Pru, Ned, his sister Sally, and Mandy came around from the side yard. If people noticed Ben was here, no one said a thing. But even with all those friends around her, Sarah began to shake inside at Mason's strident, demanding words, as years ago when he had come with the bounty hunters for her.

Amanda was furious that Mason had dared to follow her and Matt down the street from the parsonage, calling out to them orders about tomorrow. She wasn't certain, but when she had asked to see the Reverend Mannerly privately, he might actually have told Mason to come by. Was there no one outside this house she could trust?

"Mason!" Amanda shouted, interrupting his demands about her having Matt ready tomorrow morning early. "I have decided to take the train tomorrow instead of relying on your so generous care to deliver me and Matt. I would dread the ride going *and* returning with you. And quite frankly, you are not welcome here either, now or in the future!" she concluded, pointing to demand that he leave.

"Remember now," Mason replied, "what happened to Matt last time you raised your voice to me, Amanda." He shook a finger at her as if to counteract her pointing. "As I recall, the poor, simple soul flew into one of his dangerous, demented rages."

"I'm the one in a rage now, Mason. You've won, you've ruined and punished your younger partner because he was always smarter and better than you. He cared about people instead of their fees. I knew it, the town knew it, and I don't care who knows it now."

He frowned down at her. "Evidently. But I'll not allow defamation of my character with your lies and slanders. Meanwhile, I see you've taken in another—ah, refugee from somewhere, points south." He pointed behind her.

Amanda turned and gasped. "Sarah? Is it Ben?"

"Sure is," the man said, before Sarah could answer. He strode to the railing of the veranda and wrapped an arm around one of Lincoln's repaired pillars to reach out to pet the black thoroughbred that Mason rode. "Now, ain't that one beautiful animal," Ben crooned.

That annoyed Amanda, but she realized how Sarah had said he loved horses. Amanda noted that Sarah looked as if she could spit nails herself, at Mason *and* Ben.

"At least someone here," Mason said, "seems to have a bit of horse sense." He laughed at his own joke when no one else did, and patted his horse's arched neck. The big beast willingly nuzzled and snorted against Ben's hand as if he held an apple there. Then Amanda saw he did have a piece of her squash bread, which he fed to Mason's mount.

As if she had not clearly ordered Mason to leave, Ben lithely vaulted over the railing. He scratched the horse's neck and patted his flanks. The animal lowered its head while Ben murmured something in its ear!

Hadn't Sarah told this man, Amanda fumed silently, that Mason had aided and abetted those foulmouthed, vandalizing bounty hunters to terrorize her? The wretch had tried to imply then, as he had in his office earlier this year, that he would be willing "to protect her" when Matt was away. Is this what she had to look forward to without Matt here and with Lincoln gone? She'd shoot Mason before she'd ever let him near her house again, and Sarah's Ben Blue had better learn that right now!

"This man and his horse are not welcome here, Mr. Blue," she said.

"You know, boy," Mason said to Ben with a grin, as if she hadn't spoken, "you have an excellent way with Storm here, though I'm afraid not with Mrs. Wynne, fractious filly that she is. I've got four other thoroughbreds you might like to meet."

"Looking for a job too 'round these parts for a spell."

"No!" Amanda shouted, losing her battle to be kind to Ben for Sarah's sake. "Mason, get off my property. Ben, if you insist on fawning over this man's horses, do it somewhere else and not in front of Sarah, Matt, and me, all of whom he'd just as soon trample!"

Ben looked abashed; his eyes, just like the horse's, rolled white, as Mason yanked its reins to wheel away.

"Make certain that lunatic of yours goes where he belongs tomorrow, Amanda!" he ordered. "And stop acting like one yourself, or—"

The horse circled, whinnied, reared, then bucked. Mason shouted and grabbed for the reins. The animal jumped and bucked again as Mason tried to cling to its neck to stay in the saddle. In a blur of black motion in the thickening dusk, Mason flew up, off, and took a rolling tumble under the frenzied horse's hoofs in the middle of the street.

Pru screamed; Sarah shrieked; Amanda gasped and pressed her hands to her mouth. She grabbed Matt to keep him from running. Ned came up on the veranda to put his arm around Matt's shoulders. Amanda heard a shrill whistle. Had that come from Ben Blue? In the street just beyond the Lockwood lot line, the big black horse stopped and stood directly over the writhing, screaming man as if to guard him from all comers.

Amanda, Pru, and Ben ran toward the street. The noise brought other neighbors, including Ned's father. The horse nipped and kicked at them when they tried to get close enough to drag Mason from under its hooves.

Now Ned's father and mother joined them. "Mason's in dreadful pain," Delia Milburn cried. "Can't someone get close enough to pull him away from that animal? I'll get a tablecloth to cover its head."

Mason's screams muted to moans. He looked crumpled, his legs bent grotesquely under him. He sobbed, begging for help, for the horse to get away.

"Ben," Amanda said and turned to face the man, "you had such a way with the horse just now, can't you get it away, so . . ."

Even in the dusk, she caught the strangest look on Ben Blue's face. Then she knew. It could not be possible, but Sarah had said he was a man who could talk to horses. And he stood there with his feet spread and his arms crossed over his chest, watching the horse as the horse watched him. Ben Blue looked calm and—vindicated.

"Ben, like I said, he's a curse, that man," Sarah was saying. "But you can't just let him die!"

"I'm going for my gun to shoot the horse!" Ned's father yelled. "It's gone plumb crazy!"

Amanda admitted she had wanted Mason to suffer, but not

like this. Still it was what he had done to Matt, too, trodden
him down when he was hurt, kept others away. And she had
seen Mason yank the reins before the horse went wild. His
horses probably hated him as much as she did, that was all.
What she had thought a moment ago about Ben Blue—it
could not be. It was just that a high-spirited horse had been
spooked somehow.

"Ben," she said, touching his other elbow, "if you won't
save the man, won't you at least save the horse?"

His eyes met hers: kind eyes, but old eyes, ones which
had suffered pain and seen things best left unasked and unsaid.

He lifted his hands almost in Amanda's face in a shooing
motion. She thought a first he was going to shove her away.
The horse turned and galloped toward town, just as Mr.
Milburn came back carrying his rifle. Amanda felt icy
cold, though sweat poured from her. As others bent to tend
to the injured man, she turned to the crowd that had grown
during the ten minutes of chaos.

"Someone fetch the doctor," she called to them. "And
Mason's wife."

Later, she was relieved when they carried Mason home on
a wagon instead of bringing him into her house to be tended.
Her legs felt so much like soft dough that she could barely
walk, but the doctor had said both of Mason's were so badly
broken he might never walk again.

That night, Matt knew someone was wounded. And someone had to die. But he was not afraid. Battle was like that.
He knew it now.

Take care of your guns, boys.

He wanted to take care of Amanda, too. Lincoln had told
him to. The president, his friend, said take care of Amanda
and Christmas.

Lying safe in the dark, soft log, he was glad when he got
free of his bonds. One wrist, then the other. He sat up to un-
tie his feet. Not a prisoner anymore. Going home. Free. Take
care of Amanda.

Quiet, so quiet. He leaned over to pull on his shoes. He
went into the next room where the woman slept. He'd heard
her crying herself to sleep earlier. Good night, Mother. War
was hard on women.

He put a hand for one moment on the railing at the bottom of her bed. How he had wanted to leap over that other railing. To kill the enemy shouting on the horse. But that man had fallen in battle. The noise of battle went on now, but Matt would end it.

He walked quietly out into the hall. The door did not squeak, so the officers would never know. He went by the room with the hiding place, down the stairs. Took his rifle from the tree with hats, where it waited in the brass jar. Then went out the back of the tent, across someone's garden, down the hill.

Running now. We'll fight till we run, ha, ha! Fan out and hide, men. Fire on command. Don't straggle or you'll lose the regiment.

But he had to find Lincoln. He had to be at Lincoln's trial. A friend's a friend, Matt.

Smoke. Noise. Lost. Around trees, running. Sliding down toward the stream. Running from Rebs. Wanting to run clear home to the warm, wise woman. Lost in the trees, in the stream.

Leaning down, crawling in the tree trunk, so tired now. Wet here in the rain. Lincoln, are you here on the ice? Where is the Christmas tree? Take good care of Amanda. He had promised.

The log where he hid was so wet and so heavy and dark, but he was safe here.

Safe forever.

Amanda woke at first light. Then it hit her. Today she must take Matt to the asylum, or she would be defying the court order that Mason had arranged. She would be betraying the people of Lockwood. But hadn't they betrayed her?

Then she remembered about Mason's accident yesterday. No one had blamed anyone—a horse gone mad, run off. No one would have believed it if she'd told them about Ben Blue, and she never would. She could not believe it herself.

Aching all over, she shoved her disheveled hair back and sat up. Her eyes felt gritty; she had sobbed herself to sleep. Time and again last night, she had tried to tell herself that the so-called Moral Treatment Methods of mental medicine would help Matt at the asylum. That those two doctors she had not trusted would work hard to heal him. That she had just wandered mistakenly into an overcrowded ward for women beyond help that day of her visit.

Yesterday, Reverend Mannerly had tried to tell her that admitting Matt was the only way. Still, she could not bear to leave her husband there.

And even though Lincoln had only been gone three days and might not even be in Savannah yet, she must write soon to give him the news about Ben Blue and Mason and assure him that Matt was settled. And then she must continue to convince herself.

As she got out of bed, she heard a distant knocking from the back of the house. Surely Sarah could not be thumping bread dough that loud, this early. Someone at the back door? She'd best go see. But first, she padded barefoot in to look at Matt.

She stared, unbelieving. His bed was empty, his bonds and bedclothes lay there, almost undisturbed. And he was gone—just gone. How could someone have come in to get him without waking her? Or could he have freed himself?

Grabbing a wrapper, she tore down the hall, still bare-footed, downstairs, before she realized she should probably check the attic. He had gone up there more than once, look-ing for Lincoln, even though during his last months here Lincoln had stayed in Aunt Louise's old room. But even with Matt, old habits died hard.

She was halfway down the hall, heading for the kitchen, when Sarah emerged from it and ran toward her.

"Sarah, Matt's missing! Did someone get him up? Of all days, I can't believe it! We've got to go out and find him."

"Amanda . . ."

"What? What is it?"

"Some men at the back door from the carding mill. They done found Mr. Matt."

"Oh, thank God. You know, Sarah, it makes you wonder if he understood—if he really understood what that vile, snide Mason Rutland was yelling at us yesterday. As if he wanted to escape the asylum, and now I've got to take him there . . ."

"Amanda," Sarah said, taking both of her shoulders in a firm grip and turning her into the back parlor. She made her sit down in the chair by the side window. "Listen to me now.

They had to pull him from the canal basin, probably 'bout where he and Mr. Blake went through the ice last winter."

"Again? At least the water's warm now. Sarah?"

And then, as much as she wanted to just keep talking, keep pretending, she knew. Through all the emotional upheaval of the last days, the last months and years, she knew that it was over, for Matt, for her. But despite it all, she loved him and did not want it to be over. She wanted the past back, she wanted him back.

Somewhere, very close, in this room, a woman began to scream and scream.

Lincoln jolted and sat straight up in bed, his heart pounding. He strained to listen. Had a sound awakened him? Exhausted, he felt as if he'd never been asleep. Early dawn silvered the unfamiliar room. Disappointment crushed him to realize he wasn't in his bedroom at Amanda's house.

Then he remembered. He was at his friend's in Savannah. And he knew why he was especially restless. This was August 1, the day Amanda must take Matt back to the lunatic asylum in Newburgh.

He pictured the sprawling white edifice again, like a massive mausoleum where Matt would be interred for years to leave Amanda living, but dead to her husband—and to the rebel at heart who loved her. He hated himself for deserting both her and Matt now, but he had had to leave or more disaster would have followed to defeat them all.

He sniffed hard and got up to pace the small guest room in his nightshirt. He stubbed a toe on a corner of a stacked packing box. He cursed, hopped about, then calmed down to light a lamp.

All the lies he'd told Amanda lay heavy on his heart this morning, he admitted to himself. True, he had come to Savannah to stay with the friend whose address he had given her, but this was not his hometown or his real destination. And his friend, Hilton Hamilton, a fellow Engineer Corps officer, and his family were moving to a house outside the city in a few days, so Amanda would soon not even have the correct address of where to write him.

As much as he hated himself for it, perhaps it was for the best, he thought as he began to pace again. Where he was going, what he had to do, he did not want her to know or share his grief or danger, and she would try to if she knew the truth—that is, if the lies he'd told her did not make her hate him too much.

He jumped at the knock on his door and opened it to look out.

"Saw your light on under the door, Linc," Hilton Hamilton said, his voice low. "Y'all never used to be an early riser in the old days." They had been friends since they'd gone to college here before the war. "Can't sleep?"

"I'm afraid not. You're up early."

"A habit I never shook after the war. Some coffee, the newspaper, maybe a walk before the others arise. Now, there's so much to do with changing residences. Come on down with me."

Glad for someone to talk to, something to do to cut through this pall of gloom that had settled over him, Lincoln agreed and joined Hilton downstairs as soon as he was dressed.

The two men were quite matched in size and build; though Hilton had hair as light as Lincoln's was black, they were both blue-eyed. College friends had joked that they were "almost" identical twins that their proud mother had called by the "almost" rhyming names of Hilton and Lincoln, but they called each other Hilt and Linc.

They sat in the kitchen, amid the stacked boxes, while the portly black cook poured them coffee and beat batter, then lumbered out back to get some eggs. Some things reminded Lincoln of Lockwood House again, and he fell to brooding. He even missed sparring with Sarah, and Hilt's two daughters reminded him as much of Mandy as they did his own Lindy, though he'd never tell Hilt that.

He stared down into his dark coffee to realize that he didn't even feel good about being in Savannah anymore, a city he had once loved. It had been Sherman's prize at the end of his brutal swathe through Georgia, his infamous March to the Sea that had actually begun in Lincoln's area of eastern Mississippi. In December of '64, Sherman had dared to offer Savannah, newly captured when the battlements built by the elite Engineer Corps could not keep him out, as a "Christmas gift" to Abraham Lincoln. Lincoln's thoughts spun back to last Christmas and Amanda again.

"I said, Linc, y'all real welcome to stay with us and try to find work here, though with the burning of the business, I can't offer financial help. Blast it, man, I'm not sure I'd return home at all, because those old boys in blue running Mississippi with their carpetbag cronies are going to be looking for a Judas scapegoat. I'm telling you, since your state balked at even President Johnson's ideas for Reconstruction, Congress turned real radical and punitive. Now, y'all don't want to get caught up in that. Keep your other name from up north and find work—and a new life—here."

"I can't live that way, Hilt, and Median needs me. Besides, someone would recognize me sooner or later," he said and shrugged. "I even saw a man in little Lockwood I knew briefly when he worked with the Reconstruction supply officers in Median—one Samuel Wainwright."

Hilton shook his head and took another swallow of coffee. "The war's changed things, changed all of us, whether we want to admit it or not. Any of us," he said, lowering his voice although they were alone, "however much we used to fancy ourselves old-style, gallant southern gentlemen to the core, would have beaten that thieving carpetbagger bloody the way y'all did, Linc."

"But I didn't kill him, and, as soon as I get some more money, I have to go home to prove that and rebuild Median. I can't live with myself if I don't. I've promised myself and others."

"Gallantry, again, honor. I swear, it ruined us in the war, Linc. It's a fact that the so-called victors weren't burdened with it, but were practical to the bone. Devil take him, Sherman didn't have the vaguest notion about gallantry or honor."

Lincoln pictured again the etching of "Satan" Sherman that used to hang in Amanda's parlor to balance the one of "Honest Abe." He saw her again, running in all disheveled that night he met her, when Matt had been lost and found. He saw Matt smiling at him, nodding as if he understood his deepest fears and needs, when he obviously understood nothing at all.

"No, Hilt, I've known a few Yankees with honor, and the sort that goes deeper than kindliness or hospitality, clear down to character and integrity," he said. "Now let's take that walk through the city. I've got to learn to say good-bye to her too, eventually."

He noticed the quizzical look on his friend's face, and because he could not bear to explain about Amanda yet, he plunged on. "But I might take you all up on your offer of a place to stay while I look for a job here to get the rest of the money I need to go home. But eventually, I've got to face things back there, so I can face myself again."

"You know Susan and the girls would be happy to have y'all stay as long as you want. Linc," he added and reached out to grasp his wrist on the table, "I want you to stay here as long as you can. Give the Yanks in charge in Mississippi time to forget you or at least cool off a spell."

Lincoln shook his head and stood. "It's already been over two years."

Hilton said nothing more, but scraped his chair away from the table. When the cook came back in with a basket of eggs, Lincoln thanked her for the coffee; both the woman and Hilton looked surprised at that.

The men took their hats, Hilton loaned him a walking stick, and they went out to stride the streets of that genteel but faded survivor, old Savannah.

Amanda had calling hours in the parlor for Matt the next day and the funeral service in the Methodist Church on August 3. Flanked by her friends, she greeted people, moved and spoke. But she felt so alone. She had once belonged to a big, vital, influential family. She had once had a brilliant, loving husband and so much hope for their future with their own family. And now . . .

Now she looked out over the congregation as she rose from the service to go to the cemetery in the carriage behind the undertaker's crepe-swagged, horse-drawn hearse. In the wooden pews, Pru sat with Ned and his parents; Eliza with Rufus; Sarah and Mandy with Ben. They all were here to support her, yet she still felt so alone.

At least, she thought, no one had dared whisper the word "suicide" in her hearing; people must think a man in Matt's condition could not contemplate such a thing, was not at all responsible for his actions. Still, Amanda wondered and agonized. Matt had seemed aware of certain things.

At the well-tended town cemetery, Reverend Mannerly read the familiar words of comfort, which steadied her somewhat: "In my Father's house are many mansions, and I go to prepare a place for you."

She tried to picture Matt in a heavenly mansion. Now that he was no longer bound by earthly sorrows and had passed from work to rewards, what would he do in heaven in his new body? At least he would no longer have his mental weakness there. In heaven, he could not plead cases for those in need, for who could be in need in heaven? He would not have to search for evidence and witnesses for trials, because there everyone's trials were over. Perhaps his beautiful deep voice could ring out in praise, singing with the angel choruses.

"Ashes to ashes, dust to dust," the minister intoned and scattered Lockwood's rich soil on the lid of the oak coffin. It made, she thought, such a hollow sound, as if Matt, lying inside, had flown away already. She bent to place some heavy-headed roses, pink, ruby, and white, atop the polished lid. And then she turned away from the Lockwood monument and the individual stones clustered there—and from what had been and would not be again.

Amanda felt better back at the house, overseeing the table of food for friends in the dining room, while people stood about with heaped plates and remembered happy times with Matt. She tried to cling to everything they said; she tried to shut out the fact that with Pru's moving out and no hope from Matt's pension, that however hard she worked she might have to forfeit Lockwood House too.

"I don't know what Sam and I would have done years ago if Matt hadn't gathered all those character witnesses and found a handwriting expert for us when we could have lost the canal boat in that lawsuit," Pru said.

"Matthew was my most clever student, bar none. He always reminded me of Abraham Lincoln," Eliza announced with a wistful look as Rufus patted her arm.

Amanda's thoughts drifted to the other Lincoln she and Matt had known and admired. Surely he would be grieved to hear that Matt had died. With Matt's condition it was strange, but they really were quite good friends. How she wished he could be here now, but she said, "I can't thank all of you enough for being here with me this afternoon."

Ben Blue spoke up for the first time today. "I'm sure real

sorry I didn't know him—and that I came at such a bad time, ma'am."

Amanda went over by the window where Ben stood, looking very uncomfortable. She saw she had him to herself for the first time. Since he had arrived, things had been busy and confused, and Sarah or Mandy was always nearby when Ben came calling from the room he rented uptown above Will Roscoe's livery stables. But right now, Sarah had gone to the kitchen to bring in more cider and coffee, and everyone could hear Mandy was in the parlor playing her latest piano pieces.

"Actually," Amanda said to Ben, keeping her voice low, "I think you came at a very good time. I believe you came just in time, as a matter of fact, to bring justice for both Matt's and Sarah's sufferings."

Ben looked down at his plate. "Naw," he said. "Miz Wynne, I didn't do nothing, really. But I'm glad I got that horse to run off before that old gent'man over there," —he nodded toward Ned's father, Edward Milburn— "shot him dead. A real good thing that fine animal never been seen again, 'cause some folks here'bouts might try to take it out on him, when it was pure accident, that's all."

Amanda nodded. Of course it was. It had to be. If Sarah had not said all that silly stuff about him talking to horses—if she had not seen him and Mason's horse nuzzling each other—she would never have thought a thing was strange about the accident. And she knew that when she wrote Lincoln about everything, she'd sound like a fool if she so much as mentioned her suspicions to him.

"But I'll tell you one thing," Ben said, as she was about to walk off to see to her other guests, "Mr. Matt dying in the prime of his life makes a man think. Think real hard, 'bout what matters."

"That's right, it does. And how blessed you are to have Sarah and Mandy to love you after all you've been through."

It frightened her how Ben shook his head, but she dared not push harder. She told him to get some more of that squash bread he liked. Perhaps, she thought as she circulated among her guests to be certain that each had enough to eat, something good could come from this tragedy after all.

* * *

That night, even after Amanda had gone upstairs to bed and Sarah had put Mandy in and returned to the veranda, Ben stayed to talk. They sat on the steps, listening to the creak of crickets, watching the blink of lightning bug lanterns across the velvet lawn. Ned had walked Pru home an hour ago, and still Ben lingered. Sarah's stomach began to knot tighter than it had even when she had to tell Amanda that Mr. Matt was drowned. She sensed—she feared—she was going to either gain or lose Ben Blue this night.

"You got something important to tell me, Ben?" she finally forced herself to ask.

"Been really wishing we could have some time alone in the dark, though I got no reason to deserve it," he admitted.

Still, she noted he didn't make a move her way and just kept leaning real easy like back against the porch pillar.

"You could deserve it 'cause I love you after everything. And 'cause we promised each other our love was forever no matter what."

"You told me yesterday you can't leave Miz Wynne, and I gotta go somewhere there's lots of horseflesh."

"I know, but after all I owe her, after what she been through, I couldn't leave her yet. And I s'pose you're telling me you got to be pushing on right now."

"Did I say such, girl? Don't go putting words in my mouth."

"Like you put thoughts in horses' heads?"

"And don't go changing the subject neither."

"It's all right, Ben. I seen you do it before, and I know you took on Mason Rutland for both me and Mr. Matt. But what I can't reckon is why you never did the like to Napoleon or Mr. White."

" 'Cause they both would of blamed me, maybe sold me away or worse. Or done worse to you."

"Good glory, what worse could they have done to me?"

"You hated it? When the master gave you to Napoleon, even though some of the girls were real willing and liked him fine?"

"Why you dare ask me that?" she said and hit his arm with her balled fist. "I done told you time and again, I hated that man—both him and our so-called master—and what they done to me, to all of us! That's a big part of the reason I run!"

Then she remembered she might wake Amanda, sleeping up above, and whispered again, "You know it was always you I wanted and loved, and if you don't, you go on talk to your horses and leave me and Mandy alone for good!"

"She's a fine young un, Sarah, smart too."

" 'Course she is. But not smart enough to figure out why the man her mama loves don't love her."

"I'm coming to, but maybe you just shouldn't a told her I was her daddy."

"I don't care if that polecat traitor put the seed in me, he *not* her daddy. The man I love and gonna spend the rest of my life with gonna be her daddy. It it not gonna be you, that's your say-so. I'll just tell her the truth someday, and you can go on your way, Ben Blue."

She had raised her voice again. "Maybe if we gonna argue, we better walk on out back," she said and got to her feet. Ben jumped right up too, and they walked the lane around the side of the house.

"They ever have horses in the carriage house while you been here?" he asked, daring to take her hand after the exchange.

"Nary a one."

"Sarah, I always did admire your backbone. And your ideas 'bout freedom, even 'fore the rest of us dared think that way."

"Still, backbone and freedom can be mighty lonesome sometimes—without folks to really share them with."

"A family, you mean."

"Sure, and a special man. But I'm telling you, if I can't find one worth it, I'll just stay Amanda's friend and Mandy's mama and do real fine."

He reached for her to turn her to him. "I know you gonna do real fine, Sarah, always, and I want to be 'round to see it. Starting here and now."

"It's not just me we're talking 'bout here, Ben Blue. It's Mandy too."

"I'm asking for the whole package—mare and filly too," he said. She saw his teeth glow white in the pale, skittering moonlight. "Us all—those who know 'bout not being free— lost a lot during those bad times, but we still got fam'ly, when we can find it and is smart enough to keep it."

It seemed to Sarah the fireflies grew bright enough to

match the stars playing hide-and-seek with the clouds overhead. It seemed that lights spun all around them. She tried
to keep from crying, to keep her feet rooted to the ground.

"Any other man talked 'bout Mandy and me like we was
horses or breeding stock, I'd box his ears," she said, but her
voice trembled to give her away.

"For now, we'll stay here in Lockwood, if you'll have me,
Sarah Murry. Least long enough for Miz Wynne to get all
settled, 'cause I admire her too. Though I sure will feel
funny living in this big house like she said we could if we
let her give us that church wedding. Say, you think she'd
make us some of that fine squash bread for it?"

"If that don't beat all," Sarah said, through smiles and
tears. "I'll bet no woman ever been proposed to with talk of
horses and food like this."

"You know, girl," he said and pulled her into his warm
embrace where his mouth was so close to her ear it shot
shivers up and down that backbone of hers that he thought
was so sturdy, "I think, even with Mr. Matt being buried today, life goes on."

She nodded; her cheek felt so good against his warm
shoulder. "Let's tell Mandy 'bout everything together in the
morning," she said.

"That's good, real good. You know, I was just remembering the times down south we spent in the sweet straw in the
stables together."

"Mm. And if anyone came in, your horses would let us
know in time to stop our funning and hide."

"Oh, yes."

"Why you be remembering that right now, Ben Blue?" she
asked, her voice teasing. " 'Sides, like I said, no horses in
this carriage house, and there's precious little straw."

"But no master and no others to keep us apart no more
neither."

Together they pulled open the carriage house door. It
squeaked in protest, but they tiptoed into the blackness, and
he pulled her hard against him.

Amanda had lain in bed and listened to Sarah and Ben's
fervent voices under her window, though she could not tell
what they said. She prayed that they would solve their differences. Finally, the sounds drifted away. Once or twice she

caught herself straining to hear Matt in the next room, where now there was only more silence.

In her head she composed several letters to Lincoln, but all of them became too long, too impassioned. She recalled their early arguments. The memory of their voices merged with the strident tones of Ben and Sarah now floating in the windows of Matt's room at the side of the house. Later, Amanda was sure she heard the distinctive creak of the carriage house door.

Well, she thought, there were no horses to be stolen, and if there were, Ben Blue would tell them to stop and get back in their stalls. Still, it was just a freak accident that had happened to Mason with that horse of his. As she drifted off in exhaustion again, she thought of riding that wild, runaway horse of his clear to Savannah to see Lincoln.

Chapter Eleven

No-Knead Coffee Rolls

Mix ½ cup shortening, ¼ cup sugar, 1 teaspoon salt.

Heat 1 cup of milk, then pour it over previous mixture.

Add 2 crumbled yeast cakes.

Beat 3 eggs and add to mixture.

Add 4 cups flour to mixture.

Beat entire mixture until smooth. (Can add chopped citron or fruit now, if desired.)

Let rise in greased bowl till double.

Divide in 3 and roll oblong.

Brush each with melted butter.

Sprinkle with as much cinnamon and sugar as desired.

Roll oblong like jelly roll.

Place each in the shape of a ring in greased pie plate or tin.

Cut 1″ deep with scissors at 1″ intervals.

Let rise again till double.

Bake 15 minutes at 350 degrees.

Frost after it is cool with mixture of ⅓ cup melted butter, 2 cups powdered sugar, enough milk or cream for good consistency.

Amanda smelled smoke. Too late she realized she had left a pumpkin pie in the back of the deep brick oven and put the coffee rolls right in front of it. She ran for the oven. Acrid smoke poured out; the sight and stench reminded her of that night when Matt had nearly burned the house down, but now she was the one endangering everything.

"Drat, drat!" she cried and burned her fingers right through her hotpad as she rescued the pie. She banged it onto the tabletop and fanned the smoke with her apron before closing the oven door on the rolls again.

"Oh, no," Sarah said as she came in, sniffing hard. She instantly saw what had happened. "You been daydreaming again?"

"No," Amanda said testily. "I just get too busy and my brain goes—somewhere."

"Mm-mn," Sarah said, staring down at the black-edged pie. "Guess we can knock off the crust that shows and turn it into a pudding. You sure you all right?"

"Yes, and the coffee rolls are fine. Oh, Sarah, I don't know what's the matter with me! Sometimes it seems I'm living in the past just the way Aunt Louise used to, the way Eliza says not to."

Sarah squeezed Amanda's arm, then bent to work on the damaged pie as Amanda walked to the window to press her forehead against the cool glass there.

"I know how you feeling," Sarah said, tapping away at the blackened crust. "The past has a way of hanging on, even if we don't want it to, 'least till we face up to what we really want for the future."

Amanda nodded, but the words barely penetrated her melancholy. In the year and four months since Matt had died, she had struggled to put the past behind her and to hold the present together. In mid-November of 1868, it seemed to her that she had no future, other than living through the happiness of her friends. She was part of their families; she shared their joy. Yet she felt alone and incomplete.

Pru and Ned had married, as had Sarah and Ben. Both women were in a family way and would deliver late spring. Rufus Quinn had taken a one-year job on a lake vessel, offered him by one of the new, wealthy, and influential seasonal residents of Lockwood. Vowing that the wages would give him money for a nest egg for a little place for him and Eliza, he had gone off in a blaze of nostalgic glory. Privately he had told Amanda he was hoping that "absence would make Eliza's heart grow fonder" and that if he didn't win her upon his return, he was giving up on her. But Amanda thought he might have lost the stubborn old lady already by allowing himself to be seduced by the sea again.

With land taxes, Amanda barely managed to keep Lockwood House by taking in short-term boarders, even strangers—something she had once vowed never to do—and by working even harder at her home bakery business. Because she adamantly refused to take room and board money for Ben, Mandy, and Sarah, who still helped her manage the place, she barely broke even.

Ben, however, who worked in Roscoe's livery stable uptown, provided mounts and carriages *gratis* if she or any boarders needed them. Better yet, Will Roscoe gave her a dollar a week—exactly what Lincoln had paid her for use of the work shed—to board extra horses in the carriage house under Ben's watchful eye. Yet Amanda sensed that Ben was getting itchy feet and wanted to move on, back to Kentucky. He had refused the permanently crippled Mason Rutland's offer that he take care of Mason's breeding stables. Sarah said it was the only time Ben had ever turned down a chance to get cozy with good horseflesh.

Since Matt had passed on, Amanda had received only one letter from Lincoln, which arrived a month after he left. Well, Amanda, she chided herself even now, as she had hundreds of times, why would he want to remain a correspondent for life once he was back among his friends in Savannah? She was certain the letter she had sent hadn't reached him, for his letter showed no awareness that Matt was dead.

He had explained in the one letter, postmarked from Savannah, that he would not be residing at the address which he had given her earlier and that he was uncertain how he could be reached. He intended to spend his time, money, and efforts rebuilding his hometown. He thanked her again for her hospitality, kindness, and encouragement. She had given him hope for the future and taught her that northerners were just like those he had loved at home . . .

"Those he had loved—at home," she whispered to herself and gazed out toward the path down to his work shed. How desperately she missed him yet. In a way very separate from her treasured feelings for Matt, how she still loved—yes, loved—Lincoln Blake.

"If you got yourself together," Sarah's voice interrupted her agonizing, "Mr. Wainwright from Cleveland who building that fancy house here to see you. I told him wait please in the parlor and the mistress of the house be right with him."

"*The* Mr. Wainwright, who hired Rufus?" Amanda said, untying her soiled apron. "Why didn't you tell me?"

" 'Cause you was in no state to talk to him till you calmed down."

"He surely can't want to stay here while they build his place, as his business and family are in Cleveland. I tell you, Sarah," she said, "it's been years since we had a caller of his stature. Give us a few minutes and bring some rolls and coffee in, will you?"

Mr. Samuel Wainwright had been the first big fish snagged by the campaign to attract Clevelanders to Lockwood's little pond of a town. And he had lured a few others to begin to revive the area. He was the man, Amanda recalled now, who had addressed the crowd on Independence Day, one of the last happy times she and Matt and Lincoln had been together.

Her questions about why he was here were quickly answered. It seemed the imposing, silver-haired Mr. Wainwright always drove directly to his point. "So, you'll have a room for both my stonemason and my landscaper," he summarized their arrangement. "Allow me to pay you ahead for the first month, and we'll judge the length of their stay as we go after that. I must tell you, the stonemason is French and always fusses about his food, so I thought, if there was anywhere in these parts he could abide, it would be your table here."

"Thank you for the compliment. I was just recalling, sir, you said in your speech to the town last year that you had served down south after the war."

"Yes, here and there. I guess my commanding officers thought if I could run a shipping company before the war, I could help run Reconstruction, but it was a bear of a job. Resistance and resentment from the former Confederates, even though they were desperate for help. Stiff-necked pride abounds yet in the deep South."

"You weren't in Savannah, were you?"

"No, wouldn't have minded being assigned to a port city. I was run aground, as we say, Mrs. Wynne, in the heart of Dixie, stationed in several small towns in eastern Mississippi."

"Oh. My housekeeper, Sarah, is from Natchez."

"Natchez, at least, is west, on the river. Lockwood's the only place charming enough I've ever seen that wasn't on big water. No, I was stuck in places like Median, and—by the by, that reminds me of something that Fourth of July you mentioned, which I had simply put out of my mind. That Confederate major with you that day—I actually thought I recognized him, but knew it couldn't be."

Amanda sat up straighter. No, it couldn't be, but Freeman had ended up knowing Matt, and she'd heard of stranger things. As she recalled it, Lincoln had said he did not know Mr. Wainwright when she asked. Still, he had turned around and listened so intently to his speech.

"He went back to his home in Savannah," she said. "His name was Lincoln Blake."

"Lincoln, exactly," he said and snapped his fingers. "But not Blake."

"Perhaps you have him confused with someone else. Lincoln Blake from Savannah."

"Ah, Savannah," he said, "the place you asked about. Are you still in contact with the man?"

"No. But you think you knew him?"

"Not well. Knew of him, more like, as he was quite notorious. I came in just before it all happened and was there during the fruitless search for him. You're a lucky lady, Mrs. Wynne, to have housed him here and had no trouble with him, though I'm sure he didn't want to draw attention to himself. With a first name like that, the rank of major, that face—even though I saw him last with a beard—it just triggered my recollections about him."

"Please, what do you know? Why was he notorious?"

"He's a criminal on the run, ma'am, a murderer."

When she gasped, he went on, as if to comfort her, "Maybe the government's caught him by now, who knows. But," he said, lowering his voice and leaning forward with one elbow on his knee, "in his hometown of Median, Mississippi, he beat to death a congressional advisor, one Justin Barr, who was helping to oversee Reconstruction there. Then he just disappeared. Of course, he'd grown up around there, knew all the hills—and rocks to hide under."

"That can't be the same man. Not a murderer, not from Mississippi."

She could not, would not, believe it. Yet somehow, she knew it was all true. From the start Sarah had noted he had a deep southern accent, was from Mississippi. And he was on the run; Amanda had sensed that. But *not* a murderer, not the man who had helped Matt and held her . . .

"No!" she said, louder than she intended, as Sarah came in with a tray.

"You not want coffee and rolls now, Amanda?" Sarah asked, but when she saw her face, she set the tray down. "You give her some bad news, sir?" she asked their visitor.

"Inadvertently, I'm afraid I did. Sorry, Mrs. Wynne, but the man's name was Lincoln *Garner,* not Blake, though I'm not surprised, under the circumstances, he used an alias. Come to think of it, Blake was the name of his dead wife's people back in Median. Now, if you should hear from him again, you really must tell the authorities where he is hiding now. Since there's no sheriff here, just let my friend Mason Rutland know and he can telegraph me or pass it on. I only regret I didn't figure it out myself that day I saw him and couldn't place him and then was so busy. Mrs. Wynne? You're not going to swoon?"

Amanda stood. "No, I'm fine. Thank you for your business and your information, Mr. Wainwright. But I—I am certain I will not be hearing from him again."

"I really must be going," he said, "however delicious those pastries smell." As she escorted him out and watched him walk away, even as Sarah pounced on her with questions, the man's words—some of them—kept rolling *clackety-clack,* like a train, through Amanda's mind: *I really must be going . . . a murderer . . . Lincoln Garner . . . on the run . . . he is hiding . . . beat to death . . . in Median, Mississippi.*

"Amanda, that man take leave of his senses?" Sarah's voice broke into her thoughts at last. "That not *our* Lincoln he talking 'bout!" They sank together on the worn carpeting of the stairs.

"He was evidently never *our* Lincoln, Sarah," she said and shook her head, staring down into her lap. She gripped her hands so tightly together that her fingers turned white as bread dough. "It all fits, but I can't believe it. Do you know anything about Median, Mississippi?"

"No, but Ben might. With horses and all, he been 'round a lot more."

"You might know it was Mississippi, just like you said from the first, Sarah. The state that produced Jefferson Davis, the most reactionary of the secession states. The state with that terrible postwar black code, the population that was almost half slaves when they were freed. Who knows but Lincoln Garner wasn't a big slaveowner, just like you first suspected!"

"Think about it, about him, Amanda. No matter what I once said, I don't believe no more that—"

"No wonder Lincoln came here, a little, out-of-the way town far, far from his home. No wonder he's disappeared again. And I let Matt out with him all the time."

"And yourself. But you don't think he done that, what all Mr. Wainwright said?"

"I don't know. It can't be, but . . . Oh, Sarah, he lied to me about—about everything! His name, his home—that he didn't know Samuel Wainwright—everything!"

"Maybe not everything," Sarah said. "That man had a good heart in him, Christmas showed that, the way he treated Mandy and Matt—and you."

By its chain around her neck, Amanda tugged out the gold

locket from the collar of her dress. She almost always wore it, though it didn't always show. The raven locks of his beard—the beard that had no doubt helped to disguise him before she shaved it off—were still there. But the mistletoe had mostly crumbled to dust, for she had taken to kissing it good night for a while, more fool she. She gripped the locket tightly in her hand.

"I guess," Amanda whispered, as the tears she had fought fell at last, "I'll have to put this away. I feel—betrayed. I guess, now, I'll really have to put everything away."

After that, Amanda dreaded the approaching holidays. Last year she had slogged through without Matt and Lincoln, but it seemed that now she had lost all enthusiasm for it. Even her memories of happier times failed to rally her. Thanksgiving—what was there to be thankful for? And Christmas coming after that: she would never be able to stomach Christmas. She probably, she told herself, hated the whole idea of Christmas much more than Lincoln Garner, alias Blake, could ever have hated it—if that too was not a lie from him to gain more sympathy for himself. Sometimes, she thought, though liars and traitors they both were, he almost made Mason Rutland look good by comparison.

And so, defiantly, as if it mattered or would hurt Lincoln, she got out the portrait of General Sherman and put it back up by the hearth in the parlor that the Johnny Reb had rebuilt for her. And when Ben Blue, standing on the very spot in the parlor where she'd first seen Lincoln told her what he knew about Median, Mississippi, she felt fiercely glad at his words.

"Median a little town at the railway crossroads General Sherman done 'bout wiped off the map," Ben told her. "Ain't never laid eyes on it myself, but heard tell 'bout it in camp. The Yank army wrecked rails and burned buildings for it being a Reb army depot, you know—warehouses of supplies, arms, and such."

"A real nest of Rebels in their illegal, immoral War of Rebellion," Amanda pronounced her verdict, staring out the window at the barren trees.

"I 'spose. Guess the Rebs had a hospital there, and took over the church for ordnance and all, so that had to go too. Hear tell Sherman's boys burned miles of railroad ties and

heated the rails and twisted them around tree trunks—
'Sherman's neckties,' folks called them. I 'spose civilian
property might of gone up in flames too."

"It was a necessity for the northern victory. People should
know what risks they're taking if they are going to aid and
abet the enemy," she said, but her voice wavered and her
stomach cramped.

For Lincoln's words kept creeping into her anger, her
righteous pleasure in revenge that she had tried so hard to let
go of over the months she'd know Lincoln Blake-Garner. He
had told her that civilians did suffer, that Sherman's men left
little or nothing, that she had no idea what it was like. Those
faces of his wife and daughter which used to grace the
locket that she'd put away in the bottom of a storage trunk
under her bed appeared to her once again, then faded.

Why hadn't Lincoln at least shared the truth about Median
with her? Did he think she would tell him his town deserved
it? And, wasn't that what she had just said to Ben? Did Lincoln think she would learn of his crime and turn him in?
That she was not to be trusted—still his enemy? Yes, yes,
perhaps, because that's what she felt, or at least wanted to
feel right now. She wanted to hate him so she wouldn't keep
loving him.

"Amanda, I say something wrong?" Ben asked as she
jumped up and fled the room. "Thought you wanted to hear
all 'bout it," he called after her as she ran upstairs.

"Yes," she called down over the banister to him, without
stopping or looking back. "Yes, but not right now."

Lincoln hunched low behind the blackberry brambles and
watched the single light go out in what had been the stables
of the old Blake homestead a mile due east of Median.
Somehow, Sherman's incendiaries had spared this building
in their march out of town, though the house, barn, and outbuildings had gone up. Now, the once sturdy stable stood dilapidated with broken windows, its rough roof crudely
patched with tree limbs. He spotted places where the winter
wind would blow right through and rain pour in. First
chance he got, he'd shore up the walls. The structure's
crudeness made Lincoln recall the rugged manger Amanda
had used in the Christmas pageant.

This was his best guess as to where to find the woman he

sought, if she still lived here. His heart thundered in his chest; he sweated with exertion and anxiety. Since he had been back in Mississippi, he had moved at night. Now, at the only place where he had family—his dead wife's family—he was scared enough to turn and run away again.

Would they be glad to see him, after the grief and shame he'd no doubt brought them since he fled? Would it be to their advantage to turn him in, or if they sheltered him even for this one night, could they be implicated? He could only hope they would stand by him when they heard he was going to surrender himself tomorrow. At any rate, he had to see them first.

He ducked when he heard distant footsteps on the path to the outhouse. At least Sherman had not burned that either, for such places were luxury to the boys in blue after months of open-ditch latrines. After the occupation troops left the area, some townspeople had pulled down their outhouses to get wood to have at least a lean-to over their heads.

That winter the huge Yankee army had stripped the area in and around Median of woodpiles, fences, brush, even trees for their own fires. Then so much had gone up in punitive flames, including lumber and sawmills in this once rich timber region, that after the war wood was priced like gold. Lincoln could see that, after more than two years, things must still be the same. And to think of all that fine firewood, cookwood, and construction lumber in Lockwood—if only he could bring some of it here!

Yes, there was someone on the path. A woman walking along, head down.

Though it was dark, he sensed it was who he sought, Garnet, his wife's younger sister. Garnet had adored Melanie, and before she'd wed Chadwick Ellis, had a schoolgirl's crush on her older brother-in-law. When Lincoln tried to call out her name, his voice snagged in his throat.

"Gar—Garnet!"

"Who is it? I'll scream for my man!"

"It's Lincoln."

"Wha—can't be!"

"Garny, it's me."

He used her family's childhood sobriquet to reassure her. When she said nothing else, he stood and shuffled out from behind the bushes, holding his hands slightly up.

She whispered, "Lincoln? We thought we'd never see you again! Lincoln!"

She ran right to him and hugged him hard. Tears burned his eyes at the welcome, at the feel of a woman in his arms. How he had wished once that he could come home to Melanie like this—and how it pained him now to remember Amanda in his embrace.

"Thank God, you're safe," she cried. "Thank God!"

"But still not really safe, I take it," he said and set her back by her elbows. It was a moonless night; they had to lean close to see each other. She looked older, thinner, almost gaunt, this once laughing, lighthearted belle of the Blake family. Melanie had been more serious, always a bit calmer and wiser.

"No, you're hardly safe," she admitted, "though I guess the Yank soldier boys have given up looking for you around these parts by now. But there's a murder warrant still out." The way she elongated her words surprised him, for it had been so long since he'd heard a Median drawl. He'd learned to talk faster during his months away.

"How is Chad? The boys?"

"Making do. Lincoln, if you came in at night, maybe you can't tell, but things are still powerful bad down here, despite the so-called handouts, the Yank charity." Her voice was bitter, her face dour. "Still, too many of them like to make us eat crow—like that man you tangled with. He might have been the worst of them, but there are others just as bad."

"I hit Justin Barr, Garny, more than once, but I didn't kill him. And I've come back to clear myself so I can live here, help here. If it's the last thing I do," he vowed, regretful of the way he'd just put that, "I'm going to prove I didn't murder that bastard, even if he richly deserved it."

"They won't let you go free," she whispered, wide-eyed. "General Timmons is still in charge, and he's never forgotten—"

"I know, I know. But I have to try. I'm going to get a lawyer and turn myself in. I'm done running."

"Where all you been?"

"Up north, then—"

"Up *north*? Are you crazy? Among the enemy after everything?"

"Sh. I thought it was best. And I've spent longer than I

meant to in Savannah. Listen, Tate Boyd came back and stayed around, didn't he?"

"Yes. He and Chad are 'bout the only ones who returned in one piece, though he's starving with the rest of us. No work for lawyers any more than builders or cotton brokers. But you do recall he was just fresh out of the university before war broke out and never tried a case? He's wet behind the ears, Lincoln, so you'd better send for someone from Jackson or even Natchez—"

"I trust Tate, just like I do his brother. Tate knows me, knows this area, the people. He'd believe in me. And I've brought back money for him to hire on help if he needs it. And money for you and Chad, Garny, here." He dug in his haversack and pressed a leather pouch of coins into her hands.

"It's so heavy. You mean," she said, awed, "it's not those worthless Confederate greenbacks or even Yank paper?"

"Solid money, but you'll have to parcel it out, maybe buy things out of town, so folks don't know you have it. Most of it's to be saved for rebuilding here, after my trial. And I want you to bury this other sack for me so they don't take it when I turn myself in tomorrow. It's money for my defense and seed money for rebuilding here too."

"Tomorrow? But that won't give us time. Oh, Lincoln, forgive me for standing out here just jabbering. I wished I'd readied up the house and had some decent food here for you. But come in, come in. Miss Maud's here, though she's asleep, and Chad will be thrilled. Just wait till you see how Joshua and James have grown!"

"No, don't wake the boys, or they might tell someone I've been here if they're questioned. It was you I needed to see, maybe just to know you've forgiven me . . ."

"You haven't still been living with that, have you? That Melanie blamed you for—for things? Or that I did, however much I loved her and Lindy too?"

He hugged her again, and she hugged him back. It was what he had needed to hear, had prayed to hear, just that she still cared and understood. For that made it easier for him to believe what Garnet had told him after the war—that on her deathbed, Melanie too had forgiven him.

"I'll bring you something out to eat," she said and pulled away. "I'll bring Chad, and he'll make you come inside."

"Don't bring much if you don't have it," he whispered after her. "Tomorrow, I'll let the Yankees—I mean, our country's government—start feeding me. And I'm just hoping the fact that I came back shows them that I really knew I could be cleared, or else I would have gone on running."

"Yes. I'll be right back with Chad!"

He leaned against a live oak while he waited for her to get Chad. His brother-in-law, Chadwick Ellis, had once been a well-to-do cotton broker, but rather than build their own place, he and Garnet had lived here at the old homestead with Melanie's widowed mother, Miss Maud.

The night breeze was cool. He stared up to see it shift the ghost-gray Spanish moss dangling like lacy scarves from leaves and limbs. That sight and the sounds of night made him recall distant days when he had come calling on Melanie at the big farmhouse. He saw again their wedding reception in the side yard here after the marriage in town. He remembered how Lindy had loved to visit the farm with its porch swing and horses to ride.

Gone, all gone. But he was determined not to be. He was going to fight to survive, recover, rebuild from the ashes—and maybe then, someday, go back to Lockwood and call on Amanda and tell her he had faced it all, done it all, at least partly because he loved her.

"Chad, look, here he is!" Garnet's voice, once again girlish and giddy, interrupted his agonizing. "He's come back, and you've got to convince him not to give himself up to those devils in town tomorrow!"

Although after Mr. Wainwright's visit Amanda had been distracted thinking about Lincoln, now she became consumed by concern for him. Again and again she tried to reconcile what Mr. Wainwright had told her about Lincoln with what she "knew" about Lincoln. More than once he'd asked her not to judge him or other southerners by what she had heard or read or thought she knew. She had lived with him and trusted him. Matt, who seemed to have a sixth sense about Lincoln, trusted and loved him too. Lincoln had won over Mandy, Sarah, and Eliza. People in town had come to admire and trust him—a Confederate soldier who sometimes still wore his uniform among them.

And now she deeply resented that Mr. Wainwright had

told his story about Lincoln to others in town. It had even made the weekly *Lockwood Legend*. People gossiped and gushed over the scanty tidbits, bombarding Amanda with questions so that she hated to go out. Everyone from the Wainwrights' imported French stonemason, Jacques Chantal, to Dottie Rutland harped on it one way or the other.

"So, *madame*," Jacques said with a shift of his sleek eyebrows at the dinner table one day, "I am in the very house where the Rebel murderer lived?"

"In this country a man, even in the formerly rebellious South, is not guilty until proven so," Amanda retorted, surprising even herself.

"So, you did think the man was not—what I mean—ah, *dangereux*?"

"He was a southern gentleman in all respects, sir, well mannered and unwilling to gossip about others not around to defend themselves."

"Ah, *touché madame*," he said, but his knowing little grin annoyed her.

And she now understood how Lincoln could have come to blows with someone who taunted him. Yes, that was probably what had happened, for he had killed—or was supposed to have killed—a so-called "carpetbagger," a northerner who went down south to tell the former Confederates how to do things and, she'd heard, took great advantage of their helpless situation. Who could abide a carpetbagger's holier-than-thou attitude of snide, pious censure? She'd seen that attitude here in Lockwood; she just knew that was how it went in Lincoln's Median, which had seemed a mythical place to her at first, but now, all too often, took on similarities to Lockwood in her mind.

"Really, Amanda," Dottie Rutland said at the November sewing circle meeting, "no wonder you kept mum about that Reb visitor of yours. Either you didn't know—and I'm willing to give you the benefit of the doubt, even if Mason says that's not how you operate—or you decided to keep it a big, dark secret from all of us, just like you did your hiding slaves earlier. Imagine, living for nine months with someone who did all sorts of underhanded, violent, immoral things! Ooh," she added and seemed to shudder with a sudden chill.

"You ought to know, Dottie," Amanda clipped out and jabbed her needle into the quilt they were doing on a big frame that twelve women crowded around. She had agreed to come today only because Pru had argued that these were her friends, who only wanted what was best for her. Now Amanda stood abruptly, scraping her chair back. "I have deeply regretted Mason's permanently injured legs, but I suppose it at least makes it easier for you to know where he is and who he's with after all these years of his—his free-wheeling nature. Excuse me, ladies."

"Well, I never . . ." she heard Effie Roscoe say.

Dottie gulped air like a beached fish and was in the throes of a coughing jag.

Pru's mother-in-law Delia's pronouncement—"What Amanda said is sad but true, and we all know it!"—was the last thing she heard before the parsonage door banged shut behind her. When Pru followed her out, Amanda said she was fine and sent her back inside.

Amanda marched directly home and, for the first time since Lincoln left, fetched the key from under the sugar jar in the kitchen and unlocked his work shed. Cobwebs laced the ceiling; caterpillars had built cocoons in the corners; dust sat a finger deep on Lincoln's stacked wood and perfectly placed tools.

She sneezed, went in, closed the door, and leaned back against it, wishing desperately that some miracle could conjure him up so they could settle everything between them. Late-afternoon sun danced in the window as it had when she had come out here to be with him and brought him the oatmeal cookies. She could see his clear blue eyes light now as he tossed the sack in his hands and thanked her for them. The enchantment of that time reached out to ensnare her again.

It was the day she caught him making the sled for Mandy. He had told her the child was not to know her benefactor, because "a gift is only a gift if the giver doesn't get the glory." A private man, Lincoln Garner. She had been so certain he was trustworthy, and a man like that did not commit murder. He had been not a destroyer but a creator trying to rebuild his own life and helping to rebuild hers in the end.

"In the end" the words snagged in her mind. She would not let it end between them the way it had. She had to know he was all right. She had to make inquiries about him, locate him, let him know she believed that he was innocent. Just as she had misjudged the South, she had misjudged him at first to think he was prejudiced and bigoted. Freeman and Sarah and Mandy had been witnesses and given evidence that eventually proved him innocent of those charges. He must be innocent of murder too. If necessary, she would help him prove that.

She moved swiftly now, gathering the tools he'd left behind. They were dusty and cold and soon grew heavy in her arms. She found his leather work apron, put it around her neck, and tied it at her waist. She stuffed tools in the pockets. He should have taken these with him; a builder needed tools. Fierce determination flowed through her. She felt better than she had in months, better than anytime in the endless week since Samuel Wainwright had told her the story about Lincoln. That's what it must be, a story, a myth, like others she had believed in once, like Santa Claus at Christmas.

Burdened by the weight of the apron, she swayed and leaned as she walked, hurrying up to the house and in the back door. Sarah was feeding Ben an early dinner; he must be going out with a carriage. She nodded to them and walked right through the kitchen. Turning into the parlor, she took Sherman's picture down from the wall again and put it facedown on the table. Eliza, sitting on the settee across the room with a book open on her lap, startled her when she spoke.

"Changed your mind about him again, and I don't mean Sherman."

Amanda was amazed that Eliza did not look one whit surprised; she sensed a scolding coming. But she was beyond letting anything or anyone stand in her way.

"Yes. I've got to find out where Lincoln is and offer my support, even if from a distance. Besides, I want him to have these tools."

"You could get good money for those if worse comes to worse. I told you the same thing about Matthew's law books you donated to the Oberlin library."

"I admire your practicality, Eliza, but that's what Matt would have wanted. Avid reader that you are, I know you understood my decision."

"Yes, I did," she admitted.

"And this is what I want," Amanda declared, lifting the

heavy apron over her head and laying it carefully on the floor. She went to the desk and opened the drawer and pulled out a pen. "I'm going to write to the postmaster in Savannah about tracing Lincoln from his original address there, and I'm going to write to the Blake family in Median, Mississippi—his in-laws. I'm going to find him, send money, or whatever I can to help him hire a good lawyer if he insists on facing up to his charges. I only hope they haven't captured him and put him on trial already, though I think Mr. Wainwright would have known that."

"You're going to send Lincoln *what* money? You told me just yesterday you're barely scraping by, so—"

"I'll find a way, even if I have to sell things off from the house. Eliza, I know the letters I wrote about getting Matt help never came through in time, and the ones Sarah and I sent looking for Ben didn't turn him up—but these have to find Lincoln!'

"I'm proud of you, Amanda."

"I thought you were going to lecture me more."

"No, I should be lecturing myself for letting Rufus go to the lakes again like that, and at his age, with his health."

Amanda stopped rifling through the desk for paper. She walked over and sank down on the settee next to Eliza, who closed the book with a snap. Amanda saw she'd been reading the Shelley poems she had shared with Rufus a year ago at Christmas.

"I think," Amanda said, "you're finally realizing how much Rufus really means to you."

Eliza shook her white head, looking down at the book. "I've long known that. But watching you and Lincoln struggle to stay apart when you cared so deeply for each other as well as Matt, watching Lincoln leave, hearing what people have been saying about him—and still you've decided to stick by him. It's all made me think even more about Rufus and me and the years that have slipped away from us. And he would never have gone this time, if I'd just said yes to his proposal. I have some money put by, so it wasn't his relatively destitute situation. I didn't need him to go off like that to prove to me that he wasn't drinking or could hold a job. The problem was something lacking in me to keep me from surrendering to his devotion after all these years. Sorry to ramble so about myself, dear girl, when you're caught up in your dilemma."

"You know, Eliza, I used to get angry with you, and I thought we were so different. But now I see we are entirely too much alike."

"Two peas in a pod, if from different generations," Eliza declared, and got slowly to her feet. As Amanda stood, Eliza put one arm around her shoulders. "Amanda, I've never had a child and always wanted one, one I could admire and love—and leave something of myself to. And in you, dear girl . . . well, let me just say, anything I can do to help you with your inquiries about Lincoln—or to help you get through these coming holidays, since Rufus won't return until the lakes ice over in January, you just let me know."

On December 1, before dawn, Lincoln Blake washed and shaved carefully at the pump on the old Blake farm. Always, when he shaved, he thought of Amanda, but today he tried to push her from his mind. Today he was turning himself in to be tried for a crime he did not commit. He donned his Confederate uniform, which Garnet brushed off for him. He wished he'd had it hanging on that old dress mannequin in Amanda's attic, for it showed its age and tight packing. Just before Lincoln set out, Chad loaned him his sword so he could make a formal military surrender.

Insisting that they stay behind so the authorities would not know he had spent the night with them, Lincoln began the last leg of his lonely march to Median. Or into what had once been Median, he thought. In all the months he had been gone, little had been done to rebuild the once charming antebellum town of two hundred souls. Tents and crude sheds erected from castoffs lined the town square where once had stood the Baptist Church, the Female College, several fine homes, stores, and the two big edifices he had designed and helped build—the county courthouse and Sweet Springs Hotel. Median had been a very new town when the war hit—like many of her sons Lincoln knew, too young to die.

Even from this distance as his eyes scanned it all, he wiped away a tear with his gloved hand. The sawmills on the outskirts had not been rebuilt, nor the bayonet factory, nor the gasworks. Two railway lines from opposite directions now passed through, though rails had once sprouted in many directions near the depot that was now a hulk of limestone base and burned shell. At least the jail had not been rebuilt either.

As he had in the dark last evening on his way out to Garnet's, on the very edge of town, he averted his eyes from the place where once stood on a shady knoll the handsome house he had built, the home where he had brought Melanie as his bride. Two partly burned live oaks stood there yet, like stiff, silent sentinels over what had been. Other than that, the property did not look like what he remembered anyway, but he could not bear to behold it vacant and overgrown—absolutely as empty as he felt. Not only were the memories of his losses painful, but Justin Barr's actions and murder had defiled what should have been its hallowed ground.

Where Melanie's flower bed behind the house had once been so carefully tended, Lincoln had found the bastard Barr rutting with the willing but simple Wembly girl, Polly. Lincoln had sent her home, and for reasons beyond Polly's sullied purity, he had hit the Yankee carpetbagger more than once on the site that Sherman had already debauched with fire. Later, someone finished Barr, and his lifeblood stained the property Lincoln no longer wanted.

He knew no one else could buy the place in these tough times; it had probably lapsed into government hands with its taxes unpaid while he was gone. Even if he could clear his name and start over in Median, it would not be on this piece of land. Eyes straight ahead, he quickened his march into town.

As he came down Front Street, several people he recognized gaped at him. "That can't be you, Major Garner!" and old woman he recognized called. "Ain't seen y'all since just after the war. Where y'all been?"

"It's not where I've been but where I'm going, Mrs. Raleigh. I'm looking for personal peace and justice now," he said and tipped his hat to her. Flapping her apron, she ran off shouting for her husband, Seth.

By the time Lincoln actually got into the heart of town, he saw that there were three clapboard buildings where there had been only large tents when he had fled. Two stood side by side, clearly labeled with big painted signs: GOVERNMENT HEADQUARTERS, a two-story structure which swarmed with

blue uniforms like a hive; and GOVERNMENT SUPPLIES DISTRI-
BUTION CENTER, where evidently the Yankees still doled out
food. On the spot of the old post office stood a smaller edifice where the tent for the Government Pardoning Center
had been. There, Union officers had gloated as each former
Confederate stepped forward to take the oath of allegiance to
the government in order to become eligible for food and
freedom—at least, he thought now from the distance of time,
that's how Median men had looked at it. Lincoln could not
tell how that building was being used today, but Garnet had
mentioned that it was just as well he hadn't written them, as
civilian postal services were still next to nonexistent anyway.

He saw that the crowd behind him had grown; he either
tipped his hat to or saluted citizens he recognized. Several
men had to swing their bodies along on crutches to keep up.
Though not in uniform, some stood at attention and saluted
him back. Children shouted and dogs barked to blend with
the buzz of the adults. As he got closer to his destination,
soldiers in blue stopped to stare or join the press of people.
Finally, a stocky, burly sergeant with huge side whiskers
stepped up to challenge Lincoln's progress. A pistol glinted
in the early-morning sun as the man straddled his path.

"Halt right there! State your name and business!"

"My name is Major Lincoln Garner, and my business is
with General Chester Timmons. I believe he'll see me."

"Lincoln Garner," the man said, obviously recognizing the
name. "Well, I'll be danged. Corporal," he yelled over his
shoulder, "go on and tell the general that his favorite fugitive just showed up alone and out of nowhere."

No, Lincoln thought as he stood there amid the hubbub of
his fellow citizens, he was not alone and out of nowhere. He
was out of Lockwood and Savannah, with friends he carried
with him in his heart. And out of once busy, proud Median
with friends, who had known him since he was a boy hunting crawdads in the creek. He had in-laws here in town and
things worth fighting for.

But mostly, he was not alone because he felt that he had
been accepted, even admired—yes, loved—by Amanda
Wynne, who could by all rights have hated and mistrusted
him. And by Matt. Strange, but he almost felt Matt's trusting
presence with him too. How wonderful it would have been

to be able to bring the real Matt he had never known back here with him to defend him, his own Yankee lawyer to take on the occupying army's own.

"Tommy," Lincoln called to a boy he recognized who stood gawking in the crowd, "I'm going to be needing a lawyer, and I'd be much obliged if you'd ask Tate Boyd to drop by and see me later."

"Why, sure enough, Major Garner. Drop by where?"

"I believe I'm going to be in whatever place is jail around here, until I get some things settled."

The crowd hushed and stared behind Lincoln, so he slowly turned. Slope-shouldered and taller than he remembered him, General Chester "Hardtack" Timmons, who had served under Sherman, glared at him, but could not suppress a thin smile.

"To what do I owe this honor, sir?" the general inquired, his cold gray eyes widening with excitement when he recognized Lincoln. He came closer, hand on his sword hilt as Lincoln drew, then tendered his sword, hilt first. "Sergeant Swaggart informs me you are under arrest."

"Only because I am here to give myself up," Lincoln declared, speaking loudly enough that everyone could hear. "I have heard that some in authority wrongly believe I killed Justin Barr before I left town two years ago. I admit to striking him, but he was alive and cursing me like the very devil when I walked away from him."

"I knew I'd get you sooner or later," Timmons gloated, gripping Lincoln's sword, as if he heeded nothing Lincoln had just said. "I promised myself, President Johnson, and Justin's widow."

"Then perhaps we can work together to find the real murderer, at least as well as you've evidently worked together with the townspeople to rebuild Median," Lincoln said, before he could yank the words back. He had meant to be calm and conciliatory, not to take this tack again with the occupiers of Median. But bitterness against Timmons, Sherman, the war—everything—racked him anew.

"This man is under arrest for the battery and brutal murder of a government appointee—and friend of General Ord, Commander of this Fourth Military District!" Timmons shouted. "The rest of you, disperse!"

As Sergeant Swaggart escorted Lincoln toward the building, he muttered behind him, "The old man's been waiting for you when he could have retired. If you don't swing by the neck first, you'll be swinging a mallet at stones down in the Dry Tortugas for the rest of your life, Reb, I'd bet my war medal on it!"

Amanda had never felt so pent up, so impatient. It had only been a week since she'd sent her letters to Savannah and Median, but she had been struck with the sudden feeling that Lincoln had been gone too long to be safe. The intuition that something was wrong that had not been wrong before haunted her.

She sat, trying to keep her mind on the task at hand, at the first of the three weekly rehearsals for this year's Peace on Earth pageant, feeling anything but peaceful. It was December 1, not a cold day, yet she couldn't wait for this to be over so she could get inside.

"All right, shepherd boys wait over here after the Christmas Eve scene ends!" she shouted and shooed them into place. "Angels, come on, stop fighting with each other and just listen to Mrs. Tuttle's words so you know your entry line! The only one of you we need right now is the angel who appears to Joseph. *Sh!* Listen now!"

And through it all, Eliza read on, her sharp voice suddenly piercing to Amanda's ears: " 'And the angel of the Lord appeared to Joseph in a dream, saying arise and take the young child and his mother and flee into Egypt, and be thou there until I bring thee word: For Herod will seek the young child to destroy him ... ' "

For some reason those words chilled her. She hoped she was not coming down with a cold. Shaking her head, she recalled the winter she had nursed both Matt and Lincoln, the winter of the blizzard when she too took ill. With many memories of Christmas looming before her, she dreaded how the shiny treasures of her heart and mind and soul would seem tarnished now. But you could never go back and cling to Christmases past; she'd learned that the hard way. One had to forge ahead somehow—

"Mrs. Wynne," a wise man was saying to her, "I said, I sure wish we could get us a couple of camels from some city zoo instead of just these sheep and cows."

"Impossible!" she said, then regretted her abruptness.

Here they were, basing this entire pageant on words from the Bible, which also said, "With God, all things are possible." Was she losing hope, her very faith in the future? But however she argued with herself and tried to be cheerful, the word "impossible" stayed with her.

That night she huddled up in bed and could not sleep. She felt right on the verge of something important, something powerful, something maybe impossible. So many people and things paraded through her exhausted mind as she slipped off into slumber. Wise men, Rufus, Lincoln, angels, Matt, Eliza, shepherds, Ben and Sarah, King Herod, Mason, even Aunt Louise.

And then, she thought she saw again the manger scene shudder and topple, rushing toward her. People screamed and fled, but she was not afraid. For Matt stood there in radiant garb, his face glowing. His deep, clarion voice that she had always loved rolled toward her and wrapped warmly around her as he reached out to touch her hand.

"Be not afraid," he said, "for I bring you tidings of great joy. But you must arise and go into Mississippi, to Median, and be you there until I bring you word, for King Herod will seek Lincoln to destroy him. And, lo, I will be with you."

She tried to cling to Matt, to ask him what he meant, but he lifted up and away, though his words rang yet in her ears like church chimes. It was so good to see him again, looking like the old Matt, making sense—but was he really? She heard herself groan and sat up in bed, shaking her head.

But the dream felt so real! So real. A message from Matt, from a real guardian angel, from God? She didn't believe things could happen quite like that, but could it be? Or had she herself just worried so much that she had brought that vision on herself? But for Matt to look and sound so real . . . and to tell her Lincoln was in danger of being destroyed . . .

Her feet hit the floor. She lit a lamp. She pulled her small humped traveling trunk out from under the bed and opened it. On the bottom of it sprawled Lincoln's locket. She grabbed it, put it around her neck. Oblivious to the cold room, she began to pack.

Chapter
Twelve

※

Rolled Molasses Cookies

Cream 1½ cup brown sugar, ½ cup granulated sugar, 1 cup shortening.

Mix in with creamed mixture, 2 eggs, 1 cup sour milk,* 1 cup molasses (dark molasses preferred).

Sift 2 teaspoons baking soda, 1 teaspoon ginger, 1 teaspoon salt, 1 teaspoon baking powder, 1 teaspoon cinnamon, 7½ cups flour.

Stir all together well.

Roll part of dough out on floured board with floured rolling pin. Dough may be rolled thin or thick, depending on size of cookie desired.

Cut in circles or shapes—good for Christmas cookie cutters.

Bake at 375 degrees for approximately 8 minutes, depending on width. Cookie is done when center springs back to touch.

* Sour milk can be made by adding 1 tablespoon vinegar to one cup regular milk.

*

Amanda had eaten breakfast and laid the table before day-light crept in the windows. She looked up from frying bacon as Sarah entered in the middle of a big yawn. Looking wide-eyed around the kitchen, Sarah jerked instantly awake.

"Good glory, Amanda. You all right? Couldn't sleep?"

"No, and might not again for a while. I'm going south to-day to find out what happened to Lincoln."

"You what? Going today, just like that? And alone?"

"I'll need Ben to take me to the depot in Sandusky at first light. Sarah, I have to do this. Letters just aren't enough any-more. You and I know that takes a lot of time and sometimes doesn't work."

"But you get sick on trains. I'm going with you."

"No, you're not," she said, lifting the heavy iron skillet off the stove. "Not back into Mississippi now, and not when you're carrying a baby. You've got Mandy and Ben and re-sponsibilities here, my friend, including caring for the house and the guests while I'm away, if you will do that for me. Sarah, I must do this, and with your help here, I can."

"I understand, and I'm willing. But Miz'sippi? Thought Lincoln done left for Savannah, and that letter you got—"

"I know, but I have this—this feeling he's gone to Me-dian."

"I'll go get Ben up, tell Mandy to come down here and say a proper good-bye too," she said and started away.

"And Sarah, please ask Ben if he'll carry my trunk down—the small one, but it's heavy. I've jammed in Aunt Louise's gowns to give away and baked goods, a sack of flour and sugar to make more. I fear I'm forced to leave Lincoln's heavy tools here until I'm sure of where he is. But I intend at least to go bearing gifts of peace for the people of Median—in case they're still a bit hostile to a northerner who might need their help."

Sarah turned and stood across the table from Amanda, her hands clutching the back of a chair. "They'll learn to love you, Amanda—like he does."

"Lincoln?"

"That's what I said."

Amanda came around the table. "Sarah, I must tell you something else. I had a dream that Matt told me to go south, that Lincoln's life is in danger and someone is trying to kill him. I suppose the dream is just my own fears speaking up, but it was so real. And the warning could come true if he's gone back to clear his name of a murder charge."

Sarah listened, frowning. "Thanks to you, Ben, and Mandy, I believe in dreams *being* true and *coming* true," she declared with a decisive nod. They hugged each other before Sarah hurried upstairs.

But Sarah sent someone besides Ben down. In her blue wool wrapper, her white hair in its long night braid, Eliza appeared bleary-eyed while Ben was eating and Amanda was standing over the table, stuffing even more packets of molasses cookies in her carpetbag. In the years they had lived in the same house, Amanda had never seen Eliza look more like an avenging fury.

"You can't mean it!" she insisted.

"Good morning. I take it you've talked to Sarah. Yes, I mean it."

"Besides the impropriety of appearances, what you plan is downright dangerous."

Amanda faced Eliza across the table. Ben kept looking from one to the other, his mouth half open, a spoonful of oatmeal lifted in the air. "Appearances be damned, Eliza," Amanda said. "This is the right thing for me to do."

"But you've heard how prideful and proper southerners are. For a single woman, albeit a widow, to just arrive on their doorstep—well. And, I take it, your only contact there is Lincoln's dead wife's family. How will they react to hearing you are a woman who took Lincoln in for months and now that your husband is deceased you have come alone to see how he is?"

"If they're worth anything, they will react by being grateful that someone took him in when he was down and out. Eliza, I can't help what they think or what you think. I'm going! Besides, I'm not sure how prideful and proper southerners can afford to be after the war, though I know what we've read about Mississippi. But they're people too, just like us, only in more dire straits. That's one thing Lincoln was trying to impress upon me."

She sat down at the table next to Ben, who finally remembered to eat. She took a sip of her now cold coffee. Then she choked on the next swallow as Eliza declared, "I just needed to know if you'd thought it all through. I am going with you and will be packed directly. And money—we'll need money. I have some put away upstairs."

Amanda jumped up to chase Eliza down the hall. "Are you sure? I'll be fine. I don't expect you to do this. Eliza . . ." But the old woman just kept going at a better clip than Amanda had seen from her since she chased truants through town with a stick twenty years ago.

Amanda stood at the bottom of the stairs, her hand on the banister, gazing up. After all that, the house seemed so silent. Dawn dusted through the narrow windows beside the front door. She felt as if the familiar rooms clung to her; they meant her past, her memories, her security. The people who had climbed these stairs and walked these halls whispered to her like the wind outside. But she must leave this place and those people behind now. And yes, although she would gladly go by herself and risk everything, it would be good to have Eliza along. But it had seemed to her in the dream that Matt had meant she must go alone except for the fact that he would be with her.

She shook her head at the foolishness of the thought, then jumped when someone knocked on the front door. Peering out, she saw Ned Milburn and hurried to open the door.

"Ned, is anything wrong? Pru's fine?"

"Fine, but there's some bad news, Amanda. I was uptown to see Dr. Mills for medicine, because Mother's got another of her sick headaches. Seems they've took Captain Quinn off his ship at Port Clinton and brought him back here by wagon late last night. He's took real sick with pneumonia."

"Oh, no!" She glanced up the stairs, knowing this would terrify Eliza and change everything. Then she realized, as goose bumps pebbled her skin to make her shudder, that now, because of this—this coincidental catastrophe—she would indeed go south alone as she had first intended.

"I'll tell Eliza, Ned. Is Rufus at the doctor's?"

"No. Guess they took him up to his room."

"That cold place? Listen, Ned, if he can be moved, please tell them they can bring him here so Eliza can help nurse him."

Amanda thanked Ned and climbed the stairs to knock on Eliza's door. The older woman opened it at once, dressed for travel, though her portmanteau was open on her unmade bed, with garments strewn about.

"Eliza, you'll have to stay here. I just—"

"I told you, Amanda, I'm going. You will need me, you'll see."

"Ned Milburn just told me Rufus has been brought back with pneumonia, and he needs you more. I think, at least, you're going to want to finally climb those stairs to his room. The doctor's with him, but—"

"Oh," she cried, wavering on her feet. "Oh!"

Amanda went to her and took her hand to help her to her reading chair. "Are *you* going to be all right, Eliza?"

"Yes. Yes, I must go to him. But you—"

"Don't worry about me. I'm only sorry I must leave you now. But you understand—we both understand."

"Yes," Eliza said and jumped to her feet. "Thank God I hadn't gone, that word came in time. Here, my dear," she said as she buttoned up her cape and grabbed her hat. To Amanda's amazement, she whipped up her skirt and untied a linen envelope from the inner springs of her crinoline, then loosed a second one. "Money. Take it with you and tie it where it can't be seen."

"I have money from the baking, so—"

"Do it, Amanda. And for once, don't argue."

They hugged and kissed cheeks. Eliza hurried out the door before Amanda could remember to tell her to bring Rufus here. She followed her downstairs and called out the front door to her. Eliza nodded, waved, and rushed off.

Ben appeared from the kitchen; Sarah, as yet unaware of what had just happened, brought Mandy downstairs. "Ben,"

Amanda said, "is everything all set? I have to tell all of you where Eliza's gone, and then I'm ready to go."

Trembling, Eliza Tuttle climbed the stairs to Rufus's room. She knocked firmly and went in when Dr. Mills called out, "Yes." Looking a bit surprised, he nodded to her, then went back to bending over Rufus, listening to his heart through his stethoscope and tapping here and there on Rufus's chest with his other hand. A small lamp on the rickety-looking bedside table threw wan light, and the new day crept in through parted curtains at the single window. At least, Eliza noted, Rufus was bundled in blankets, but it was cold in here and he was as pale as his shirt.

"I thought Amanda would be with you," Dr. Mills whispered when he finished his examination.

"She's been called away. But we can take him to Lockwood House when he's able," Eliza whispered back. At her voice, Rufus slitted his eyes open.

"Now, I'll die happy at least," he wheezed and went into a convulsion of coughing that shook him and the narrow bed.

Eliza took his hand; he squeezed hers weakly. "How bad?" she mouthed to Dr. Mills when Rufus seemed to sleep again, almost instantly, though they could hear and feel every rasping breath he drew.

"Not good," he mouthed back. Then he spoke in a quiet voice, "Do you think you can get that coal grate lit, though there's not much coal? I don't think we ought to take him back outside again just now."

Glad to be given any task to help, she knelt on the dusty floor and got her hands smudged with the coal. But the match caught, and she puffed on the flame to make it spread. Such a meager amount of fuel here, but then Rufus had not planned to be back for weeks. And such a meager amount of time he might have left, she told herself and shuddered.

She wiped coal dust off on her handkerchief and sat next to the bed, holding Rufus's hand while the doctor prepared a mustard plaster for his chest. Then she, who had been too proper even to come up here before, helped take off Rufus's shirt, apply the sealing ointment to his skin, then bundle him up again.

Amanda had been right this morning to say, "Appearances

be damned!" Eliza thought. Only, now was it too late for her and this man she loved—had loved almost as long as she could remember? Louise Lockwood had died; Matthew had died; and her own mother had always said that death of people you knew came in threes. But if she could help it, the third was not going to be Rufus Quinn!

In the carriage, bundled against the cold, Amanda wiped away tears of parting. What was that Shakespeare quote Eliza had acted out at charades? Oh yes, "Parting is such sweet sorrow." Only this was not charades, but real life: her friends, her home, her past and future. Why did it seem she never had a chance to cry from joy anymore? Maybe someday she would again. And if she could just help Lincoln— see him, be with him, and know he cared deeply too—as she did for him—that would be joy.

Without closing her eyes or bowing her head, she prayed that Rufus would recover; she had made Sarah and Ben promise to take meals over to him and, as soon as possible, to transport him to Lockwood House. Now, with her goods crowded in around her feet, Amanda gazed out at her home as Ben spoke to the horse and the carriage jerked into motion. As they rolled down the lane, the big white facade of the house shrank; its windows reflected the red rising sun; its pillared veranda blurred and faded. The familiar neighborhood, Church Street, the town square, where in an upstairs room Rufus was no doubt fighting for his life—all went by. She regretted leaving the old man and Eliza now, but Lincoln might be fighting for his life too.

The rutted, snow-speckled road outside of town took them past the cemetery. She squinted through the window at the neat rows of tombstones and monuments rotating by. Her family and Matt lay there in silent sleep. Surely Matt had not really come to her in that dream—and yet it had been so real. Lincoln seemed somehow unreal to her now, but she would find him, help him—if he wanted anything to do with her.

They went past the neat white wooden fences that enclosed the rolling acreage of Mason Rutland's new horse farm. Amanda saw no steeds along the rails; if she had, she might have asked Ben to stop and tell them to run away to freedom, something Mason himself would never do again.

She could just hear Dottie and the sewing circle when they heard what she had done. But she could honestly say that none of that mattered and nothing now could hold her back.

At the depot, she felt awed by buying a ticket to Median, Mississippi, as if she were headed for the outer reaches of China. The fact that the stationmaster raised his eyebrows and read from his timetable all the stops she'd pass through from Columbus and points south staggered her. She had committed herself to nearly four days on a chugging, rocking train, when the brief trip to Cleveland with Matt and Lincoln had roiled her stomach. At least her evening rests in Lexington and Memphis would allow her time to recover a bit. Still, if she could have arrived sooner by traveling all night the way Lincoln had once ridden the rails, she would have done it.

"Sure you all right, Amanda?" Ben asked. "Not too late to turn back."

"You wouldn't say that if you'd known him, Ben. I wish you had. Perhaps you will be able to meet him when this is all over, somehow."

"Now you just sit inside here out of that wind till that train comes," he said, scooting her luggage closer to a wooden bench. He seemed more nervous than she.

"Ben, however long I'm gone, I'm so glad you and Sarah will care for the house."

"Sure will. You got no worries 'bout anything here. You know, I still have to pinch myself sometimes that Sarah and me living in a big house now, stead of just workin' for the folks that do."

"Ben, I know you want a house of your own. It's good for a family man to work for that. You've been a wonderful father to Mandy since you married Sarah. She needed that, Ben. Mandy, I mean."

" 'Course, she did. Never saw a better young'un."

Amanda nodded. Sarah and Ben did not know she had guessed that Mandy was the child of that other man. Amanda had figured it out when she compared how Ben had acted toward Mandy before and after that long talk he and Sarah had the night after Matt's funeral. Indeed, something good had come from that tragedy. The three of them were a family now, and that was what mattered. Somehow, Amanda thought, the process was like mixing and baking something sweet and wholesome from a lot of different ingredients that would be flat or too tart or sweet if they stayed separate.

"I'm so glad we found you, Ben," she told him, "and now I have to go find Lincoln." When she heard a muted train whistle, she rose and went to look out the window. She gazed across the tracks toward the ravine where Lincoln had gone that time to try to locate Ben through his hobo friends. She had told Ben about that, so perhaps he already knew what a good man Lincoln truly was. A man who cared that deeply for someone he had never met—a former slave from Mississippi—could not murder anyone.

"Good-bye, Ben," she said, turning back from the window. She pressed his extended hand in both of hers. "Keep working on learning to read and write, because I'm going to send the three of you letters or maybe even a telegram."

She bit her lower lip and lifted her carpetbag and bandbox as Ben hefted her trunk to his shoulder. He carried it back to the luggage car for her, then stood under her window, hat in hand in the stiff wind while she settled in her seat. And so, of all the family and friends and people she had known and loved in Lockwood, Ben Blue alone waved to her as the train chugged away.

"Tate Boyd!" Lincoln cried and stood to shake the man's hand right through the bars before Sergeant Swaggart unlocked his cell door. "I'm so glad to see you!"

"Since you're gonna have a military trial, Major," Swaggart said, launching a stream of tobacco juice in the general vicinity of the spittoon over by his desk, "I'm telling you to get a military lawyer with experience. Hear tell Mr. Boyd here's a virgin in the courts, wasting his time in the infantry of the War of Rebellion, and on the wrong side."

"I take it you mean the War for Independence, Sergeant?" Lincoln replied, while Tate stood glancing nervously from one man to the other. The sergeant's keys jingled as he unlocked the cell door. "Just because he was on the losing side doesn't mean he was on the wrong side."

"Hello, Lincoln," Tate interrupted and pulled him back by his elbow into the cell. The sergeant, cursing under his breath, slammed the door behind him and walked away as its clang reverberated. "The first think I'd like—to do, as your council," Tate said, lowering his voice, "is ask you to get along with anyone tied—to the opposition. Someone who might testify that you—have a touchy temper."

"I know, I *do* know," Lincoln said and sat on his cot. "But Lem Swaggart's the one with a bad temper. And we've already argued about his desk out there. It's mine."

"What?"

"It was in my library at home. The vultures must have looted it right in front of Melanie and Lindy the night they burned the place."

"They'd already gone out to—stay with her sister Garnet," Tate explained. "I'm pretty sure that's what I heard. I'm sorry about the desk, Lincoln, but—sorry about much more too. We'd best get to the business at hand."

Lincoln motioned Tate to sit on the narrow cot with him, as it was that or stand. The thing Lincoln hated most about this little cell in the line of three at the back of government headquarters was that it was very dim. It had no window and they seldom brought a lamp closer than "Swaggart's" desk, not that he had anything to read or do. He'd only been in here for two days now, but what he would not give for a window to look out. The cracks and chinks between the uncaulked boards of this quickly, shoddily erected building gave his only squinted glimpse of December daylight.

Tate Boyd sat with his long knees almost under his chin, even as Lincoln did. His clothes looked well worn, right on the edge of being tattered; when he stretched out his long legs, Lincoln saw that the sole of one shoe flopped partly loose. He was a man who at last had grown into his big features, a rugged but pleasant-looking fellow who had been a rather homely lad.

As adults, Tate and his older brother, Jess, who had been Lincoln's best boyhood friend, were still as red-haired and freckled as they had been years ago when Tate had tried to tag along with the older boys. Jess had gone into the lucrative wholesale cotton brokerage business with Chad Ellis, and, slowly, Lincoln's and Jess's paths diverged. When Lincoln had gone away to college and Jess had not, Hilt Hamilton had somehow replaced Jess in his regard. A few years later, just before the war, Tate had gone to Richmond to law school. Who knows, but he and Tate would not have more in common now that he and Jess, even under other circumstances than these dire ones.

"I try to get along with my captors," Lincoln told Tate, his voice quiet now, "but both Swaggart and Timmons set my teeth on edge."

"Welcome home, then, but you've got to make a—special effort, especially since you criticized the way they did things right after the war."

"Damn it, Tate. If they want to call it Reconstruction of the South, they have got to reconstruct, not just hand out charity, then rub everyone's noses in it and run this place like it was an army camp. Median knows what's best to rebuild Median, if we'd just get a chance."

"I agree. But let's just argue that after—we argue your innocence—of this charge."

Lincoln noticed that Tate, though he seemed perceptive and bright, spoke in a rather jerky, almost hesitant way. It was as if he broke his thoughts into strangely separate pieces. No doubt he was just nervous, coming in here like this for an important interview with someone—an alleged murderer—he hadn't seen in years. Unfortunately Swaggart was right about Tate's inexperience, but who else was there? Lincoln had no intention of asking some crafty outsider or a Yankee military lawyer to defend him, even if he was facing a military tribunal instead of a jury of his peers.

"How are Jess, Caroline, and little Jesse?" Lincoln asked as Tate took a piece of paper and a pencil from his inside pocket. "Let's see, the boy must be about twelve now. I know Caroline lost most of her family during the war."

"She did—a father and—two brothers, besides cousins, when—her mother was already gone," Tate said. "At least Jess came back, but with part of a leg gone and a bullet fragment in his back. I'm afraid he wasn't much support for a while. But she came through, took over when—Jess just wasn't himself, before I got back and could pitch in some. Someday I'm—going to find me a wife as good as Caroline and have a son as fine as Jesse. Yes, the boy's good too, under the circumstances. But, Lincoln, the point is, you've seen Median. It—all our lives—are still in shambles."

"I've come home partly to change that, Tate. If you can just help me here, I'm going to lead the fight to rebuild Median. I hope to repair or rebuild a sawmill with some capital I've earned, start to construct houses and buildings again, ones that will leave this ramshackle hulk in their dust." He gestured impatiently around his cell. "Together, we can lure some investors, renew the mills and the small farm economy, if not the big outlying plantations that needed slave labor. I've seen such a rebirth begin to happen in another small town I knew."

Tate looked astounded, then he hit his knee with his fist. "Then we'd better get busy, as they—told me I could only stay an hour today. But I'll be back tomorrow, maybe bring a friend of yours. Jess really wants to—help us, Lincoln, do anything he can."

"I can use all the help I can get, Tate. But I've brought back money for your fees too; don't think this is *gratis*."

"This town has to hang—together *gratis,* or we're all doomed," Tate muttered, with a swift sidelong glance at Swaggart, who sat twenty feet away, rustling through paperwork. "One more blasted Yank outsider, carpetbagger, government aide—or gawker—anyone who interferes, and we're about going to explode. Now, I'm going to ask you to—think back and tell me everything you can remember about every time—you and Justin Barr ever crossed swords or words, especially the day you hit him."

"All right," Lincoln said and leaned his elbows on his splayed knees as if to study the dirty floor. "Justin Barr's the last person who ever walked the earth I'd like to be dredging up memories of, but here goes."

"By golly, we're almost in Mississippi now," the man across from Amanda on the train told his gentleman companion before he shook his newspaper into submission and went back to reading it. "The place is a pitiful ruin, but it's hardly our fault."

At that, Amanda opened her eyes and looked out, hoping to see the state line. Surely there would be some sign or marker. It was, she thought, counting the days, Friday, December 4. As wretched as she felt, she thought it a significant moment. During the years of the war, though she knew better, she had sometimes pictured the southern states as armed camps with fences or walls down their state lines guarded by gray-clad Rebels with guns in their hands and bayonets in their teeth. Lincoln, of course, had shattered that myth forever for her. But now she was going to ride right into the very heart of Dixie.

She gazed out across fields at bare-boned trees and occasional dirt roads. Except for the lack of snow, it could have been parts of Ohio. At that realization, she felt both relieved and disappointed.

But when they pulled into the first dilapidated Mississippi town on the Mobile and Ohio rail line, she saw differences. At the depot, the people looked ragged and old-fashioned, even to her small-town eyes. Few looked robust, let alone well-fed. Even though the war had ended two years ago, some white and some black people seemed to be just sitting with a pile of belongings at the depot. What were they waiting for? Where were they going?

As the train pulled out again, chugging farther south, she saw people, instead of mules or horses, pulling carts. The only horse she noticed was a swaybacked nag. A woman walked beside it with the reins in her hands. Could there be that great a shortage of beasts of burden? Of men?

A man she had met yesterday who hailed from Jackson, Mississippi, had told her that one third of his state's men had not returned from the war, but that left many, didn't it? But then, where were they? Where were the big, pillared plantation houses, even if they had been damaged? Had those vast, empty stretches of untilled soil once been rich cotton or cane fields? Had no one planted winter wheat so it would be ready to be harvested soon?

Despite how queasy she still felt from her motion sickness—for she'd dared put little in her stomach until they stopped each night—she kept her eyes open. Median was almost halfway down the state, so she had a long way to go. And she wanted to know all she could about "how things really were," as Lincoln used to put it. She recalled again his farewell note to her: "Good things can come from the South, Amanda." He had been referring to mistletoe, but he had meant so much more. Not things, but people.

Several southerners had been especially kind to her on the journey. A woman and her daughter had invited her to join them for dinner at the hotel in Memphis and at the depot today a gentleman who was a Mississippian had told her some things about his home of Jackson. When she questioned him vaguely about problems since the war, he assured her that, even if a southerner had assaulted or killed a northerner in these raucous Reconstruction times, the "most" he could get under military rule was ten to fifteen years "incarcerated in the fine capital of Jackson, which that so-and-so Sherman could only half destroy."

Yes, the people themselves were what must matter to her here in Mississippi, Lincoln most of all, she told herself. Through her cape and gown of dark blue serge, she pressed Lincoln's locket into the valley between her breasts, where it hung hidden but heavy next to her heart.

On his second visit, Tate brought his brother, Jess, though Swaggart, claiming only one visitor was allowed per day, made them both stand outside the cell. Soldiers had turned away others in town who wanted to welcome Lincoln home. Now Lincoln and Jess shook hands, then clasped each other's shoulders through the bars.

"Let's pretend we haven't changed, when everything really has," Lincoln said, his voice choked with emotion at the reunion.

"I don't know if I'm up for diving naked into the old swimming hole on these crutches," Jess told him and lifted one to display it with its sort of rocking chair foot on the bottom. Lincoln had been trying not to notice Jess's left leg missing from the knee down.

"Tate thought up these when he got back," Jess said. "This way, it don't get caught on rutted ground. If I fall down, I have a devil of a time getting up. Guess I should have got myself some university learning like Tate and you, Lincoln, maybe been in the Engineering Corps behind the battlements. Sorry. Didn't mean that like it sounded. Leastways, I got my wife and child," he added, then looked sheepish at his second slipup.

Lincoln only nodded. Silence stretched between them until Tate said, "I wasn't with the engineers, and I—came back in one piece, Jess. But the point is, Jess has—something to say before the sergeant sends him away, right, brother? Jess . . ."

"I'm going to help Tate gather evidence, find witnesses, whatever it takes to get you out of this unfair charge, Lincoln. I'm going to be, if you'll forgive the bad joke, Tate's legs about town in case he gets tied up somewhere. It's real important to me to see you walk free, for old time's sake and for all you been to Median. And, Lord knows, I got the time, with the cotton industry wrecked, like everything else."

They clasped hands again. "You were once almost a brother to me, too, Jess," Lincoln said. "I can't thank you enough."

"Anything Caroline and I can do—anything!" Jess said, to make Lincoln instantly forgive him for his careless words earlier. Maybe Lincoln should blame himself for claiming they could be just like they once were. He was going to have to watch his own quick tongue, with friend and foe alike, if he wanted people on his side to help clear his name.

"All right," Tate whispered when Jess went off with his rolling gait on his crutches, "your favorite sergeant—says I can't join you today because there were two of us, so I'll make this quick right where I am. Let's go back to your comments step by step that night you happened to come upon Justin Barr on the site of your burned house where— someone murdered the man."

The first burned house Amanda saw was just outside Median. Then another, and another. She saw no outbuildings or fences here, and fields seemed to stretch endlessly, stripped even of stubble. This area was like nothing she had seen before, especially coming as she did from a flat or gently rolling region of the country. Hills and bluffs of some size surrounded Median, especially ahead to the southeast. Forests looked thick, so at least Sherman had not burned them. Where she had half expected to see some palm trees she saw only trees like the ones at home, bare-limbed now in winter, and a few pines on the heights. The train slowed and the bell *ding-dinged* as they came into what must be the depot.

She sat bolt upright, clasping her reticule and bandbox, with her carpetbag beside her on the seat and her claim ticket for her trunk in her hand. "MEDIAN" the depot sign read, through there was no building—hardly any buildings anywhere in sight except for a few distant clapboard ones set amid what looked like a tent city. Could the occupying army still be here?

When she descended the iron, then wooden steps onto a crushed stone surface, people in the street began to gather and gawk at her—the only passenger disembarking here. Her heart pounded, her legs shook; she began to tremble so hard that the cord around her bandbox rattled and the locket shuddered against her breastbone. The stationmaster took her luggage ticket and sent a black man for her trunk, but she dared think nothing of that. After all, Ben Blue had loaded it four endless days ago. And she knew that to get along here she was going to have to keep calm about the fact that she might now have to mingle with—live among—people who had once had slaves.

"Who all you visiting, missus?" the elderly stationmaster inquired. "They coming to fetch you? Thought I'd know about anyone arriving here."

"I'm new here." She had intended to ask him for a suggestion of a place to stay, but she knew better now that she'd glanced around. The way things looked—despite what she'd heard about old-time southern hospitality—she might be sleeping under the stars tonight. "I'm looking for the Blake family," she added.

"You mean Garnet Blake Ellis or her mother, Miss Maud? They're the only Blakes left around these parts. Miss Maud up in years and don't get out much anymore, but they live a piece yonder out of town."

"I, yes—that must be them. Oh, thank you for carrying the trunk," she said to the black man and gave him three pennies, which she'd learned was the going rate for porterage. "And would there be," she asked the stationmaster uncertainly, scanning the small, curious crowd she was drawing, "a place to leave my trunk until I'm settled?"

"I'll tote it for you, ma'am, anywhere you want to go!" a gangly red-haired boy called out and stepped forward from the crowd. He was probably twelve or thirteen, much older than Mandy, though he still seemed more a child than a youth to Amanda. "I'm real strong and can lift real good, my daddy says!"

She couldn't picture herself taking the trunk and the boy out of town to call unexpectedly on the Blakes, but she didn't seem to have much choice. Besides, it was mid-afternoon, and the sun would set all too soon. She had no illusions anymore that being in the South meant more hours of sun, as she had once imagined.

"Where'd you all hail from, ma'am?" the stationmaster asked. "Don't like to pry, or course, but you don't sound like you're from these parts."

"Actually, I'm from a bit up north," she said.

"And see," someone back in the crowd yelled, "even got herself a carpetbag! Think sneakin', slimy Congress gonna be sendin' female ones now to bedevil us, Alvah?"

A hundred things raced through Amanda's mind, however weak she still felt from her train ride. She could tell them the truth and ask for information about Lincoln. but what if he had come back in secret until he could clear himself? She must not tip his hand for him. Or she could hire this boy to carry her trunk out to the Blake homestead. But what if, as Eliza had warned, they would not take her in and she had to spend the night out there somewhere?

"She looks peaked and pale as milk," a woman's voice said.

"You remember what milk looks like, do you, Doris?"

Someone laughed. Amanda put her hand out to touch the boy's shoulder to steady herself. He was all elbows and legs, ears and freckles; she liked him instantly, for he seemed her only ally here.

"If she's from 'a bit up north,' as she puts it," the station-master said, rocking back on his heels with his thumbs in his lapels, "She might as well join her own kind. Jesse, you just go on and tote that trunk for her over to government head-quarters, and maybe they'll take care of her right proper 'fore some of us wonders what a lone Yank woman doing here moving in on us all."

"Sure, Mr. Wembly, 'cause I been wanting to catch a glimpse of my daddy's old friend they got locked up there. I was fishing the morning he marched down the street and give himself up, and my daddy's gonna help Uncle Tate get him off that murder charge, wait and see!"

Amanda no longer heard or saw the taunting crowd. "Someone is locked up on a murder charge?" she asked, staring at the boy.

"Our hero, LIncoln Garner," he boasted with a nod.

At that, Amanda did not know whether to cheer to cry.

"Go on, young Jesse," Mr. Wembly said and patted his other skinny shoulder. The boy hefted her trunk with a grunt and led her away.

People continued to stare, though some turned their backs, and a few nodded. Only one man doffed his hat to her. People at least cleared a path for them as if her skirts or her shadow might contaminate them. But no one said another word as she followed the boy, feeling silent sabres in her back. Still, she thought, squaring her shoulders and lifting her chin, as horrified as she was by what she had just heard about Lincoln, without moving ten feet from the train or spending ten minutes here, she knew where to find him at last.

In her four-day vigil, Eliza had sat at Rufus's bedside for such long hours that she kept nodding off to sleep, then jerking awake. Time dragged, then blurred. She had slept on an old servant's bed Ben had brought over from the attic of Lockwood House. Dr. Mills had come and gone, refusing to move his patient even to a warmer place because he was so weak. Sarah and Ben had been back and forth with baskets of food which Rufus had been too ill to eat, and she could barely stomach, though she forced herself to. He had shivered with chills and raged with fever and coughed his insides out. Now, the doctor said, he had done all he could for him. And so Eliza still watched and waited, feared and hoped.

"Mm," he groaned and squeezed her hand. His eyes opened, then closed. "Still here, my Liza?"

She bent close. He had used his teasing, childhood name for her. Was he delirious again?

"Rufus, I'm here. I won't leave you. Ever again."

"Meaning," he said and coughed, "yes?"

"Your brain is well, I see. Let's get your body better first. But yes, Rufus, yes!"

He nodded slightly; she thought the stiff corners of his mouth might have lifted in a grin before they fell slack again. Yet he watched her from half-closed lids.

"Rufus, will you take a bit of broth for me? Sarah brought it not long ago, and I'm sure it's still warm."

She bustled about, grateful to be able to do something. She had already cleaned this room, folded his things away, and stood for hours at the window looking out over the old river locks through the trees. As she carefully spooned broth between his lips, she recited, "When the leaves are on the trees, I cannot see the river locks. When autumnal blasts undress their limbs, I glimpse again my happiest days."

"Of—what could have been," he added in a whisper and managed to lift a hand to stay hers from the next spoonful.

"Yes, but sitting here, waiting for you really to come back to me, I realized I've lived my life all wrong. It was wrong of me, Rufus, to keep looking back at what I thought were my happiest days, with my family, with you in the beginning."

"What could have been."

"But you see, my dearest, I should have been looking ahead, making the future even better, that is what I did wrong. Like Amanda learned that Christmas, you can't go back, can't even look back for long, not if it harms the present or the future. I've—well, sometimes I've buried myself in books and business and righteous anger, at you, at others. So right now—Rufus, today is December fourth, I am vowing to you, to myself too, that we need to put the past away and plan. Plan to make this Christmas, this year the best. Plan to be together for the rest of our days, if you'll just get better, and still want to marry me . . ."

"Still?" he said. Twin tears squeezed out from the corners of his eyes. "Always. And you just gave me all I'll ever want to build on—to hold to . . ."

"Then hold to me and hold to life, Rufus! Please!"

She thought he nodded before he slept again. Terrified as she was every time he went off so quickly, she put her head to his chest to hear and feel his heart. Yes, beating. Yes, beating yet for life and her.

Lincoln lay on his back on his cot, his hands linked under his head. He stared up at the bare board ceiling, recalling two years ago this month when Amanda had waged her war about Christmas. He had known what she was doing, seen how stubborn she was. And yet, he could not resist her kindnesses, her smiles, her plans. Before he knew it, he was in over his head with Christmas and love for her. How clear those memories were if he but let them back to wash over him in warm waves. In the years to come, would she always seem this vital and real and close?

He wondered how all the others he knew in Lockwood were this day: Matt—though he could still be at the asylum—Sarah, Mandy, Pru, Ned, Rufus, and Eliza, even Will Roscoe and Henry Hanks, who had said they admired his skill with wood and building. It felt as if a big fist clenched his chest with longing for what had been, however dedicated he felt about his future here.

He heard a ruckus of some kind at the front door and tried to ignore it. Arguments and minor altercations were still common between officers and townspeople. He heard Swaggart's feet, which had been propped on his desk, hit the floor. Again, Lincoln tried to shut out the voices, just as he'd tried to shut out how determined General Timmons was to see him hang or be sent for the rest of his life to the Dry Tortugas, a hard-labor military prison camp sixty-five miles off the southeast coast of Florida. You might know Justin Barr had been a friend of Timmons and the general had known Barr's wife. Barr's wife, Lincoln thought, should have kept a better eye on the man, because he had a real eye for the ladies, although no good southern woman—at least one in her right mind—would give a pompous, abusing bastard carpetbagger like him the time of day.

Then, suddenly, the words, the distant voices sliced through his thoughts.

"No visitors, ma'am! He's had one over his quota for the day already!"

"Can't I see him either, Sergeant?" A boy's voice. A boy and a woman, wanting to see him. But who? Who? Garnet had already tried and been turned away this morning.

He strained to listen.

"No, you can't, son."

"But I'm Jesse Boyd, and my uncle's his lawyer."

"I don't give a hang who you are!"

"Please, officer," the woman said, her voice so quiet now that Lincoln could barely catch the words or tenor. But a chill raced up his spine, and hair prickled on the back of his neck. It couldn't be, but that voice was clipped and sure. It was no sweet southern drawl.

"You see," she went on, "I am a northerner, just like yourself. And I'm here because I used to know your prisoner, Major Garner, when he resided as an upstanding resident of Ohio after the war."

Lincoln bounded up and gripped the bars of his cell. Here—she was here! Or was he dreaming instead of trapped in this nightmare?

"So, you'd be willing to testify to his actions, ma'am?"

"I'd be happy to help Major Garner, be a character witness for him. What was your name again?"

"Sergeant Swaggart, ma'am. Lemuel Swaggart of the great state of Pennsylvania."

"Oh, not far at all from Ohio, though I've never been there! I'm sure it's as lovely as my state, though. Now, here, I have something for you in this carpetbag, Sergeant—home-baked molasses cookies, and I really hope you would not mind if I just took some in to your prisoner too. Here, Jesse," she said, "some for you and your uncle too."

"You brought those clear down here from Ohio?" Sergeant Swaggart demanded.

But Lincoln could stand it no longer. He didn't want her to see him like this, but he had to see her. How she had found him, what she knew of him now—nothing mattered but gazing on her, touching her.

"Amanda? Amand-aaa!"

"Lincoln! Please, Sergeant, I know you'll bend your rules for a fellow northerner who's come a long way . . ."

She appeared at the door and sprinted in, with Swaggart and a boy right behind her. Lincoln could not tear his eyes from her. She looked so good, even if she did seem pale. Yet there was an aura, a glow about her as if she radiated light. She dropped her things and held out her hands to him. Lincoln did not care who was looking or what they thought as he reached his arms through the bars to hug her.

"Jumping Jehoshaphat!" the boy cried.

"Guess you did know him up north!" Swaggart said. He yanked Lincoln's wrists away and pulled her back.

Reality hit Lincoln; fearful that she'd get too embroiled in his mess, he let her go. They stood, like chastened children, eyes wide, lower lips drooping, still staring at each other. Amanda broke the spell by swiping tears away with the back of her soiled glove. And then, slowly, she tugged a gold chain around her neck and pulled out from her collar the locket he had left for her. At that, such joy and hope surged through him he could almost have torn down the bars between them.

"Now, lemme me get this straight," Swaggart said. "How well *did* you two know each other up north?"

"Major Garner was my husband's best friend—a friend of my family," Amanda said, her voice shaky. "When we didn't hear from him, we wondered how he was, that's all. And now, I arrive to find this outrage being perpetrated on a good man. My entire town would testify to that, sir, if you want character references."

"Your 'friend of the family' beat and murdered a man," Sergeant Swaggart insisted. "And why didn't your husband come?"

"I didn't kill Justin Barr, and a trial decides it, Sergeant!" Lincoln interrupted so Amanda would not have to explain about Matt's condition. He lowered his voice. "Amanda, you should not have come. Who's with you? Not Matt?"

"I didn't think you knew. Matt died over a year ago. He drowned in the canal basin before they could take him away."

"Your husband was supposed to be under arrest before he died?" Swaggart demanded.

"Please, Sergeant, may I have a moment to speak with Major Garner?" she pleaded. "And then I'll be happy to give you a signed statement or whatever you need."

Swaggart frowned but pulled the boy away. As he did, Lincoln took a good look at the lad for the first time. It was Jess Boyd's son, all right. How much he had grown in the two years Lincoln had been away! He forced himself to reason instead of just react. He had to be sure.

"Jesse, your daddy told me he and your mamma would do anything they could to help me," Lincoln called after him. "Would you run and tell them there's a friend of mine here who will need a place to stay, folks to take care of her until she can go back home soon?"

"Sure," Jesse called over his shoulder, as Swaggart finally steered him away and out the door.

"And no passing anything in the cell to him, ma'am!" Swaggart yelled back in. "Nothing till I look it over!"

Amanda wrapped her fingers around Lincoln's on the bars. "That man you recognized in Lockwood—Samuel Wainwright—told me," she said. Afraid Swaggart would come right back, they spoke low and fast.

"Amanda. I'm so sorry about Matt. I had no idea, though I sometimes sensed something—"

"Yes. Lincoln, I have so much to tell you. But I'm here to help, to see you through this."

"You can't. You'll have to go back home. Amanda, there's

so much involved here. Listen to me now. My lawyer is the boy's uncle, Tate Boyd, who lives with the boy's parents. Jess Boyd was a friend of mine, so he and his wife, Caroline, will help you until you can go. You can't stay here long!"

"I guess I can, Lincoln Blake-Garner! I can testify to your good and helpful nature—"

"And my honesty? My passion for you that made me leave? And get dragged through the mud? The prosecution will put the worst possible slant on it, on us."

"All right, now," Swaggart bellowed as he came back in and shouldered Amanda away from the bars, "let's see that so-called bag of goodies you were going to give the major here, ma'am."

Amanda did not like the wink he gave her. She stood for a moment, confused. Yes, she had some of those molasses cookies here somewhere. And what had Swaggart done with those she gave him?

"Oh, here, I dropped them," she said and bent to retrieve the paper packet.

Swaggart rustled it open, plunged his big fist in, and fished one out. He downed it in one gulp. "My job, see, ma'am, is to guard the prisoner, and that means testing his food, least the home-baked variety, don't it now, Major? Delicious goodies, lucky son of a gun," he said with a snide laugh and thrust them between the bars at Lincoln. Feeling like a caged animal at feeding time, Lincoln took them.

"Come on, then, Mrs. Wynne, you said it was, I think," Swaggart said and offered her his arm. Instead, she bent to retrieve her scattered luggage, filling her arms with that, evidently to avoid touching the man.

Despite Lincoln's shock at seeing her and his fear that she would be involved or hurt, pride coursed through him that she had come, that she bested Swaggart like this.

"I hope you won't mind, Sergeant," she said, "if I send the boy back for my trunk and call upon you at a later time. After a lengthy train trip, I am exhausted."

"Ah, sure, no, I understand," Swaggart said. "But we are gonna need you to talk to our lawyer about a statement and all."

"Of course. You see," she said with a glance back at Lincoln, "my husband was a lawyer, so I understand about the important preliminaries of a trial as well as proper, lawful procedure during. Lincoln, I'm sure the sergeant will let me call on you tomorrow," she added as Swaggart scrambled to take her carpetbag and bandbox from her and escorted her outside.

Still, Lincoln felt ecstatic that she was here; he felt he had drunk a whole bottle of bourbon and could dance across the clouds on it.

But a sobering thought thudded him back to earth. Surely she could not intend to really help with the investigation. To be planning to sit through the trial. To put them both through a wrenching, permanent farewell if the government could manage to imprison him for life or hang him. He gripped his hands hard together, then realized he had crunched the cookies that he held.

He sank down on his cot and opened the packet Swaggart had already plundered. Broken, crumbled cookies, and a few whole ones lay within. But a sweet, rich smell wafted out to him; in his mouth burst the taste of home and hope. And of Amanda's love.

Chapter
Thirteen

Sugar Cream Pie

Prepare one piece 8″ piecrust, unbaked.

Combine ½ cup light brown sugar, ½ cup granulated sugar, ⅓ cup flour.

Stir in 2 cups light cream (as for coffee), 1 teaspoon vanilla.

Pour into unbaked pieshell.

Sprinkle 2 handsful brown sugar evenly over top.

Dot with chips of butter.

Sprinkle with dash of cinnamon (optional).

Bake at 400 degrees 30 to 40 minutes, until lightly browned.

(Filling will thicken as it cools.)

"Why, come right on in. Y'all look just like a wilted flower from your train ride my boy told me of, Miz Wynne," Caroline Boyd called to Amanda. She motioned her toward the odd-looking house to which Jesse had led her, down a little lane not far from the center of town.

Most of the place was dug out of a gentle hillside; above ground stood only waist-high stone blocks supporting a flat, bent, dented tin roof patched with limbs and brush. A single, tall, forlorn-looking chimney stood watch over the huddled house. With a jolt, Amanda realized this must be the cellar of a home that had burned. She ducked her head to go down wooden steps, put her carpetbag and bandbox on the floor, and sat on the three-legged milking stool her petite hostess offered. It looked to be the best piece of furniture in the place.

Jesse followed with her trunk, placed it on the edge of the cold stone hearth, then stood staring. On the way over, he had explained to her that his father and uncle were not here right now. But his mother would be glad to meet her, and she could stay in "a corner" of their place. He had evidently told his mother who Amanda was and what Lincoln had said, for Mrs. Boyd's initial inquiries were polite ones about her trip. As the woman poured her a cup of water from a dented pewter pitcher, Amanda studied her and realized that, if she herself looked like a wilted flower, Caroline Boyd was a faded one.

Despite the woman's red hair and green eyes, color and vitality seemed drained from her. Amanda could only guess she was in her late twenties, for she appeared older than her years. Her eyes loomed large in a delicate, porcelain-perfect face that looked as if it might crack if she smiled. She had no doubt been a beauty, but seemed drab and listless now. Even the tiny sprigged flowers of her calico gown under her brown shawl had paled to gray; her once fine womanly form had shrunk so that the dress hung on her, even when belted with woven vines. In this young mother and wife, Amanda saw the southern women Lincoln had tried to describe when she had dared to say things were not good in Lockwood.

"I can't thank you enough for your hospitality, Mrs. Boyd. I assure you, I intend to pay my way. I keep a boardinghouse at home, you see, and I wish to board here, not live free on your kindness to a stranger."

"I declare, I won't have you paying one mite, nor will my husband or brother-in-law. 'Be not forgetful to entertain strangers: for thereby some have entertained angels unawares,' " Caroline recited with a distant look in her eyes. "My mother was quite a reader of the Book, and she'd turn over in her grave, God rest her dear soul, if I took money from a guest."

"But guests are invited, and I have not been," Amanda protested gently, accepting the water. "And though I assure you I'm no angel, I like that Bible verse." She recalled how Sarah and Lincoln had suddenly showed up at her house on that same day that seemed so long ago, but she did not share that memory with Mrs. Boyd.

"Now, my boy," Caroline said to Jesse, her face stern but her voice soft as a wisp of wind, "you march yourself right on out to the well and wash up. I won't abide you coming in here so dirty from your ramblings and mudlarking about."

Jesse looked as if he'd argue but, scuffing and shuffling his way out, did as he was told. While Caroline peeled and cored a mottled apple, Amanda subtly surveyed the room. Black stains on the unlit hearth suggested the household had once smoked meats down here. Her nostrils flared at the damp, smoky smell that lingered.

She admired how Caroline tried to keep up standards by fussing over her son's cleanliness and looking so immaculate herself in this cellar. As for keeping house here, she did more than what could be expected. Amanda recalled how she had struggled to dust Lockwood House and fretted at the constant renewal of dirt and grime. But, she thought, at least she had a home and furniture to be cleaned.

Here, the packed dirt floor had been swept, evidently with the crude, homemade broom by the hearth. Water-spotted tent canvas, with thin sections where smudges had been scrubbed, hung on ropes in all four corners to create private nooks. Amanda supposed when it was very cold they closed the door and lit the small kerosene lamp on the table, though some light sifted through chinks between the unmortared stone blocks. For now, the windowless place was illuminated only through the open door.

She wondered how many people were living here and regretted she had to impose on them. From what she had seen so far, she deduced she was looking at some of the best accommodations Median now had to offer.

"I hope this apple will tide you over, as you're probably wondering about supper," Caroline said. "It will just depend on if my husband and brother-in-law—that's Jess, whom we named the boy after, and Tate—bring back rabbit or some squirrel. We like to take as little as possible from that government distribution center. We've even gone to coon and possum stew sometimes."

At that, Amanda could hardly swallow the apple, and not because it was mushy. These people were living like pioneers, just as Aunt Louise and her parents had told her about in the "good old days" in Ohio. But these days in Mississippi were neither old nor good.

"My husband, I'm afraid," Caroline went on, perching on the rough half-log bench beside the narrow table, "returned from the great conflict without part of one leg, and it—it—everything changed his outlook on life, of course. But he even goes out of town with Tate, who does the hunting in the hills. Now that my husband's on special crutches, he walks here and there every day, keeps regular hours as if he still had the cotton brokerage office uptown. Since my brother-in-law's been back, things have been better."

She bit off her last comment as if she'd said something amiss. The woman had the disconcerting habit of not looking at Amanda when she spoke to her, but Amanda guessed she was just ashamed to admit all this.

"As soon as I see what they've shot," Caroline Boyd continued, "and know if we need a cook fire tonight, I'll warm some wash water for you. I am regretful there is no soap right now. I've just been boiling clothes, though now my husband said best to save what good wood we have for the dregs of winter."

Amanda was more determined than ever to pay her way here. Not that she'd seen any place to buy food or necessities uptown; it made the closure of some of Lockwood's stores and mercantile establishments seem like nothing. Worse, most trees in Median, even bushes and fences, had gone with the buildings. Amanda pictured all that brush and wood just there for the taking in the ravine behind her house, the wood that Lincoln had gathered for their hearths and her stove his first few days with them.

"You know, I think that long train ride had lulled my brain," Amanda told her hostess. She hit her hands on her knees and stood. "I don't mean to be just sitting here like a bump on a log when I have a contribution for supper tonight. I brought some bread and other baked goods, even some flour and sugar. That's why my trunk's so heavy, small as it is, but I hope your son will forgive me when he tastes some of this."

"But surely you intended that for Lincoln," Caroline protested quietly.

"I intend it for anyone who is helping Lincoln disprove this unfair murder accusation, and I gather that is your entire family."

"Oh, yes, more than anything, we don't want him to suffer for that. Why, it's common knowledge that every true-blue resident of Median wished that dastardly man—Justin Barr—dead, just like we did General Sherman . . ." She turned away, biting her lip, tears in her green eyes.

Amanda hurried toward her, then stopped before she touched her shoulders. She must not think she could comfort this stranger the way she had Pru, Eliza—certainly not Sarah. This once proud southern housewife was being more or less forced to take in a northern guest who appeared to be, at least by comparison, well-heeled and well fed. How it must hurt to be able to offer only a corner of the cellar that was, of cruel necessity, home sweet home.

"Lincoln told me how hard things were here," Amanda said, her voice a mere whisper. "I'm so sorry."

"I am much obliged for your concern." Caroline sniffed

once as she stooped over to lift five mismatched, chipped porcelain plates from under a piece of canvas on the floor—and one dented silver tureen so tarnished it was black. She put them on the bare table as she spoke, her back still to Amanda.

"Believe me, Miz Wynne, it doesn't do a speck of good to regret losses, like the town, right down to this cellar that Sherman's vandals raided of its goods we had stored for winter before they burned the fine home above it when I begged them not to." Her words tumbled out in a rush. "Doesn't help to regret how the conflict changed my man either."

"I do understand that. My husband came back from the war without his wits. He was totally addled and later he accidentally drowned."

Caroline spun around to face her. Tears matted her thick auburn lashes. At last she looked directly into Amanda's eyes. She said only, "Oh, no!" though for one moment, Amanda thought she could actually hear her real thoughts: Well now, I'm not obliged to be one speck regretful for what happened to any of you Yankee vandals!

But Caroline added, "If I didn't have my son healthy and happy—yes, happy, despite it all—and my diary to tell my troubles to, I declare I do not know what would have become of m—"

"Mama, is this clean enough?" the boy interrupted, jumping down the steps, holding up his palms for his mother to see.

"For now," Caroline said, not looking at either him or Amanda.

"Clean enough to try some more of my baking," Amanda said, "so you can tell me what you like."

"If it's anything like those cookies the sergeant took away from me, bet it's grand," Jesse admitted with a gap-toothed grin.

"And that reminds me, my boy," Caroline said, as Amanda stooped to unlock her trunk with Jesse hanging over her shoulder, "you are not to be anywhere near those Yank soldiers, no matter what."

"Aw, Mama, I wasn't. It was only—"

"I'm afraid it's my fault he ended up at government headquarters, Mrs. Boyd. He was good enough to carry my trunk for me, and that's were the stationmaster said we should go."

"Forgive my saying it, Miz Wynne, you being a northerner and all," Caroline said, glaring at her fidgeting son, "but that's a hard, fast rule in my house. My brother-in-law might be dealing with their ilk to defend Lincoln, and my husband wants to help too, but the Boyds don't mingle with northern soldiers."

Amanda opened her mouth, then closed it. She had almost asked if they weren't all simply *American* soldiers since what Caroline called "the great conflict" was over now. But she saw the woman's face stiffen and caught the sudden sharp tone to her soft-as-silk voice. Despite the veil of hospitality and propriety donned here, Amanda realized Caroline Boyd had cloaked herself in hatred. For her, the big conflict, and maybe a passel of little ones too, would not, could not be over yet.

For one moment Amanda was tempted to insist that the South deserved to suffer: they started the war, their women urged the rebels on, and they all held on so long that they forced the catastrophes that befell them. But she shoved down her bitter feelings and found she could not judge quite so harshly now. So Amanda thought as she dug out two packets of bread, some cookies, and her sack of flour, she would begin waging hand-to-hand combat for woman-to-woman peace with this offering.

"Oh, Mama, look!" Jesse shouted and snatched the cookie Amanda extended to him after she put the other things on the table.

When Caroline looked at her son, Amanda glimpsed hunger of a different sort in her watery green eyes. But she only turned back to arranging the plates on the bare tabletop that Amanda now saw was an old warped door.

"We are deeply obliged for the food, Miz Wynne. The Yanks giveth and the Yanks taketh away. Thanks to your very own food distribution center, my menfolk will be delighted to see such bounty on my poor table once again."

The woman's tone and words cut Amanda to the bone. Only then did she realize she had overstepped—perhaps more than once—in this short time. Arriving with her apparent largesse of money and food as if to flaunt it in their faces was not what she had intended. But she could not get the words out to explain and apologize. They both avoided each other's eyes; Amanda was grateful when Caroline showed her to her triangular space behind the hanging canvas to the left of the door.

When the crude curtain shut her off, Amanda sank weak-kneed, onto the cornshucks on the floor and put her head in her hands. Her back against the dank stone wall, she cried silently for all she had found in Median and for ever thinking that her hometown was in dire straits. Median seemed to her the dark underside of Lockwood, the nightmare just one step beyond the bad dream when the town fell apart. But in the face of it all, she vowed, somehow, to help Lincoln and make a difference for being here.

Amanda did not even unpack what little she had; there was no place to put things, and she knew better than to offer Caroline an old gown from the trunk right now. But she could, she thought, find the well where Jesse had washed and get the tears and train soot off her face.

When she stepped out from behind her curtain, she found the room empty. Nor did she see anyone outside, so perhaps they had gone to meet the men. Behind the house, Amanda found the well with the metal-enclosed pump over it. At least Sherman's men had left this much, she thought bitterly, then shook her head. It would not take her long living here to hate the hero of Ohio just the way the southerners did. She pumped water, washed her hands and face, cupped her hands to drink more, then leaned there, looking around in the deepening dusk.

All seemed barren, cold, and dark. But she must not let that stop her from the main reason she was here. Tomorrow, she must give Sergeant Swaggart her statement and try to see Lincoln. More important, she must covertly gather statements from everyone she could, to begin to ferret out who had really killed Justin Barr. Caroline had said every citizen of Median hated him, so that hardly narrowed the field.

Also Amanda hoped to meet Lincoln's wife's kin, though she knew she must step especially carefully with them. Perhaps they could contribute some information to help him. But mostly she needed to survey the scene of the murder in case she could discover any evidence, even though the crime had happened over two years ago. Matt had said that was sometimes possible; she intended, literally, to leave no stone unturned. She was going to help clear Lincoln's name whether his lawyer, Tate Boyd, knew it or not and whether he wanted her help or not.

She located the brush lean-to erected where a sturdy outhouse had once probably stood; gratefully she used its primitive facilities. On her way back to the house, she heard men's voices and walked faster, then slowed her stride. She told herself she must not rush, must not push with these people, even though time was of the essence. When she came to the end of the house, she heard words rise from the mingled voices:

"Of course, you all were right to take her in, Caro, especially since I told Lincoln we'd help. You could hardly put her out with Melanie's sister. What is she to him really, do you suppose? Why is she *really* here if he didn't even know she was coming?"

Caroline's words did not carry to Amanda.

"Just so she doesn't get in our—your way, right, Tate?" the same male voice asked.

"Anything she can tell us might be of—help, Jess. A Yank character witness can't hurt—with a military judge who may be a bosom chum to Hardtack Timmons. Unless they can use her forwardness—against Lincoln too."

Amanda put her hand to the stone house to steady herself. Her forwardness? Coming down here unescorted, they meant; yes, she had realized what people might think. But how could any of her actions be used against Lincoln in a murder trial? As for herself, she was not here to chase him like some fast woman—to save him only to seduce or claim him for herself. Was she? She leaned harder against the unyielding stone.

Head down, she stared into the gathering darkness. She had to admit that she loved Lincoln and wanted him badly, as badly as she'd ever wanted anyone in her life. And though she had come to help, she feared for the first time that she might harm him. No. No, she would not let that happen.

Lifting her head, she strode out around the corner calling, "Mrs. Boyd, I hear voices. Are your menfolk home?"

"So you see, Mrs. Wynne, Lincoln admits to—striking the victim more than once, and at—the murder site," Tate Boyd explained to her after dinner. The five of them had partaken of squirrel and mashed turnips—and Amanda's baked items she felt both good and bad about when the men devoured them and Caroline picked at them and smiled her brittle smile.

The Boyds had sent young Jesse to bed in his corner, though Amanda wondered if he couldn't hear all the adults said. Or maybe the boy was used to this and could sleep through anything. Jesse's father, called simply Jess, instead of Jesse, looked nervous that his brother, Tate, was telling Amanda all of this. Caroline seemed distraught at the idea of "tangling with Yank soldiers again." In the dim light of the single candle, she kept jumping up to fetch one thing after the next and trying to draw the conversation this way and that with side issues Tate did not follow.

Jesse's parents obviously thought that Amanda, another Yankee invader of their land, and a woman, no less, had no right to know these things. But it was getting on a good footing with Lincoln's lawyer, Tate, that mattered most to Amanda, and she gave him her full attention.

"So the first problem is," Tate summarized, ticking it off on his fingers, "Lincoln had motive and opportunity to murder the man."

"But with no witnesses, that's all circumstantial," Amanda said. "Besides, Mrs. Boyd tells me many people hated Justin Barr."

Both men's heads snapped around to stare at Caroline. "I know it's men's affairs. That's all I told her of it," she said, her tone suddenly defiant.

"And," Amanda continued, "the fact that Lincoln admits motive and opportunity, yet came back to see justice done . . ."

"I can tell, as you—say, Mrs. Wynne, that your husband was indeed a—fine lawyer," Tate told her. "How I'd like to have a wife someday that could share an appreciation for my—work with me and well as a domestic haven, when we can—all rebuild Median someday."

Tate went on to explain how Justin Barr had been not only pompous and arrogant but "well connected to the powers-that-be."

"So," he concluded, touching his middle finger, "the second problem we—are dealing with is prejudice and resentment, subtle and otherwise by victorious former Federal career officers who—need a scapegoat. And when Lincoln was briefly back here after the war, he criticized and stood up to them. Even since he's been back, he's goaded them once or twice."

"Perhaps I can help you there," Amanda said, "by reminding him he does not need their hostility, even if their goodwill is beyond salvaging."

"My advice," Jess Boyd said, clearing his throat, "and I'm speaking now not as Tate's aide, but as Lincoln's best friend from the time we were tadpoles chasing tadpoles, is for you all to keep clean out of everything, Miz Wynne. Lord only knows, even your sincere efforts at assistance could well backfire."

"He just means—" Tate put in.

"I know what he means," Amanda said quietly. "I'm sure it is well-meaning advice best well taken. But I've already promised to give Sergeant Swaggart a character reference for Lincoln, so people are going to know he worked for and lived with my family up north."

Caroline leaned closer to the table. "Even if you all wondered how Lincoln was getting on, you should not have come," she declared. "It is most, even for these times, untoward and unseemly."

"It's untoward and unseemly that Lincoln should be imprisoned for a murder he did not commit—I know he didn't!" Amanda exploded and hit the table with her fist. It bounced and rattled on its tree trunk stand before she calmed herself. She was grateful that Jess and his family still cared deeply for his old friend after all these years. And she told herself again, she *was* an outsider and a Yankee to boot. Nor had she meant to make an enemy of her hostess, who glared at her before looking away again.

"I just can't see how," Amanda added quietly, "in the end, the truth can hurt him."

"In the end," Tate said. "Yes, I was coming to that. I take it you don't understand the—dire consequences if I should lose this case, Mrs. Wynne."

"I realize an innocent man could go to prison in Mississippi for ten to fifteen years."

Tate shook his head and looked down at his hands, now

gripped before him on the table. Amanda tried to read Jess's and Caroline's faces. In the flicker of the single candle, Caroline's features looked carved from old ivory; Jess glowered at shadows across the room.

"Please tell me the whole truth, Mr. Boyd," she whispered to Tate.

"The third problem," he said, "the one that—is keeping me as seriously concerned as the first two, is—that because General Timmons and his commander, General Ord want to make Lincoln a scapegoat, they have been pulling strings, since long before Lincoln even turned himself in."

"And?"

"If he's convicted," Tate said, looking crestfallen, "they hope to take his life. They intend—to hang him, though they'd actually need the president to—sign the execution order. At the very least they intend to have him sent to hard labor to the island military prison off the coast of Florida called the Dry Tortugas for the rest—of his life."

"No! Oh, no. But, even if he did do it, which he did not, even if it was the generals' friend who died," she insisted, "they can't do that! I talked to a man on the train who said that so close to the war, during this so-called Reconstruction, an assault and battery not proved to be murder would mean a decade of prison, probably in the state capital at Jackson! Take his life? Imprisoned for life? It isn't fair!"

Those last three words hung in the air, seeming to reverberate and echo. Staring down, Tate shook his head; Jess still glared away; at last, Caroline's gaze challenged Amanda's. No one spoke at first, but she felt their condemnation for daring to say such an obviously stupid thing as *it isn't fair!* to those who still lived among the ashes. But what terrified her more than anything was that she knew from her previous futile battles with the government over Matt's dilemma that fairness would have little to do with Lincoln's trial and sentencing.

Tate cleared his throat and said, "I'll do all I can to prove his innocence."

Caroline leaned toward the table again. "You see, Miz Wynne, this whole thing is the realm of the men, like the war was. I realize now it's best to let the men care for such things. They have their public arena, and we have ours—our proper, private, domestic one."

Amanda gaped at her; she held her tongue, though she wanted to berate all of them. Tate Boyd should make a ringing declaration that he would see to it that Lincoln walked free! How dare Lincoln's boyhood chum imply she should stay out of this. And Caroline—did she really think that the men of the world did things so well on their own if they had controlled the "realm" of the war?

Amanda really looked at Caroline instead of Tate for the first time in an hour. The woman clutched a leather book to her breasts, and it was not a Bible. She had fetched an old-fashioned quill pen and soapstone inkwell—all this, no doubt, for the diary she had mentioned on equal ground with her son. Amanda noted too that the woman had brought a towel and a plate of water. Off and on, she had been cleaning both her quill tip and her hands while the others spoke.

"I thank you all for your advice as well as your kind hospitality," Amanda managed to choke out. "I will be heedful during my stay here with you, but I must do what I can, for the sake of the friendship Lincoln tendered both me and my deceased husband. My entire town owes him a debt, for he helped begin to rebuild our community as I'm sure he will yours when his honor is untarnished once again, thanks to the excellent defense I'm sure Mr. Boyd will present in court."

Feeling she had made an overly flowery closing statement before judge and jury, she excused herself and went to bed. She heard the men step outside and their voices move away. She lay flat on her back on cornshucks on the dirt floor; every time she shifted, they crunched and rustled. But she could still hear the scratch of Caroline's busy pen and the occasional swish of her wash water. Amanda shuddered to think what was going into that diary about the new "untoward and unseemly" Yankee visitor who had been forced on her and hers.

As exhausted as Amanda was, she could not sleep, even after the men came in and Jess told Caroline to come to bed. More shuffling, shifting of cornshucks, sighs. A throat cleared; a few whispers. Whatever had she gotten herself into, Amanda wondered, staring up into the darkness of the cellar. But more important, what was Lincoln facing in this desperate bid to clear himself and take his life back into his own hands?

She had at first felt relieved to see how informed his lawyer was; however, he admitted to being "untried" himself in the courtroom, a play on words Matt might once have made. And young Tate Boyd seemed sincere and very concerned about his client. Granted, he seemed a bit shy, but then so had Matt been in the early days of his career, and he won several cases of consequence then. Just as Matt had become another stronger, surer person when he so much as scented a courtroom, Tate would too. He would, hopefully, speak loudly, and not hesitate so much so that it sounded as if he were unsure of himself or were making things up as he went along. If not, the judge and jury might think him a rural bumbler. He was just nervous now and, of course, trying to keep his voice down so his nephew could sleep, something she regretted she had not done very well when the panic of Lincoln's plight hit her.

She thought how close Lincoln lay in his dark prison cell while she had this cellar. Separated and trapped, both of them, again. How many nights she had lain, awake like this, staring up at the ceiling of her bedroom while he slept in the attic just above. Would they ever have the time or place to be together—perhaps to share a marital bed? A warm and wonderful place, a home of their own, even as rude as this one in Median, where, when she lay on her back and stared straight up, she would feel and see him hovering or shifting or thrusting over her in the union of their love.

She drew her legs tightly together and tried to roll quietly onto her side, pulling up an old gown of her aunt's for a coverlet, for Caroline had offered no blanket. She wondered how her friends were doing at home, snuggled in their warm beds now. Pru and Ned, happily wed, expecting their first child. Sarah, Ben, Mandy, and their baby to come, a family. Especially, her thoughts went out to Eliza and poor, ill Rufus. She prayed that he would live and they could find some way to live together as happily as—as she wished she and Lincoln could someday.

Again, the chill crept up her legs and she fumbled in the open trunk to pull out more gowns for covers. She almost fancied she could smell the lilac scent Aunt Louise had favored, as if she were here with her, keeping her warm, comforting her. Amanda realized she must find a way to give

Caroline some of the gowns or their material at least, if she would take them, an early Christmas gift, she would tell her.

Amanda jerked alert again. Yes, Christmas! How could she have forgotten about Christmas down here? Concerned only about Lincoln's dilemma, she must make it matter again, for both of them.

By now, it was probably long past midnight, so this was December 5 already. She dared not let herself consider that, if things went even more wrong, it might be Lincoln Garner's last Christmas on this earth or, if they sent him away, his last in the newly reunited states. No, that could not happen; she would not let that happen. Yet, just in case, she must find a way to make Christmas mean something good and hopeful for him, just as she had done that Christmas she came to love him. And how she had hated the idea of Christmas without him last year and this. If anything happened to him, she would never be able to face Christmas again, never!

But did Lincoln love her as she did him? He had admitted his passion for her more than once, including today. That was not love, but even so, she could not lose him; he could not die! Yet she had once been convinced of the same with Matt, and he was gone forever. Now Lincoln lay in bondage in the stubborn South. How Amanda wished that she could spirit him up north to freedom, hidden by her love and captured in her arms.

The next morning, Amanda saw Caroline nearly jump out of her skin when a soldier appeared at the door while she was sweeping. But he wanted Amanda and informed her that she was expected tomorrow at government headquarters at ten in the morning to give a "formal deposition about the prisoner." And, he said, if Amanda wished in the future to visit the prisoner, she must make application at least twenty-four hours ahead. However, she could not be promised the interview would be granted, as the prisoner was to have only one visitor per day, and his lawyer was seeing him this morning.

That shook Amanda. As Lincoln's trial approached, wouldn't Tate be with him almost every day? Tomorrow at least she would see him when she went to give her statement and would discuss that unjust rule with his captors.

After their visitor left, both women, for their own reasons, sat silent at the table until Caroline went back to her cleaning. Amanda intended to visit the Blakes today, but her hostess had said it just wasn't done to go "calling" before noon. Now Amanda got the glimmer of an idea to get Caroline Boyd at least to accept food from her without feeling it was charity.

Though Amanda had not noticed it last evening in the dim light, she sat up straight as she saw it now: an old oven door was cut into the brick of the smoke-blackened, broad hearth chimney. Though she herself had never been without a modern oven with its own match-lit firebox beneath it, she'd heard her mother and Aunt Louise tell how wood could be burned directly in a brick oven to heat it. When it was swept out, the retained heat radiated from the bricks to do the baking.

Amanda absolutely refused to let her baked goods and ingredients go to waste because of these obstinate southerners. If not starved for sustenance, surely they were ravenous for the deep comfort and joy wholesome baked food could bring, especially at holiday time.

"Caroline, besides my boardinghouse, I had a little bakery business at home or I couldn't have kept a roof over my head. And, though I don't know how I'll get the ingredients here once the few things I brought run out, I'd like to barter some baked goods for the use of your oven, beginning right now."

"My oven? As there's not a thing to put in it, I've never even opened it. It surely doesn't get enough heat from the wood we burn on the hearth. Our slave girl Bess did the cooking but, like most of them, she took off long ago when Sherman came through, and I haven't baked a thing. Truth is, I never had before, and I suppose there's some art to it. I might have learned the feminine ornaments at the Female Seminary in Jackson—you know, French, piano, singing, drawing—but I never did really learn to bake as such. It's been a struggle, but I do what I can with what we have, just roasted or in the pot."

All through that tumble of words, Amanda's mind raced. She realized for the first time how lonely Caroline must be for the society of another woman's company. After all, in the short time she—a Yankee outsider—had been here, Caroline had revealed much about herself in a frenzy of talk. The poor woman seemed a self-exiled prisoner in this place, when the men went out and about each day. Surely, she knew other ladies and had friends round about to visit, though she had told Amanda she almost never left the grounds. She had boasted they had once owned spacious property here, but they could barely pay taxes for this plot of ground now—even with the court records burned and their lot lines in dispute. Was Caroline staying about the place to be certain they lost no more here, or was she afraid of something beyond her own lot lines?

But what bothered Amanda even more was that she realized she had intentionally not asked whether they had once kept slaves. Lincoln had said he did not, and that had been all that mattered to her then. Here she had tried to shut slavery out of her mind. She fought the anger that stirred in her at herself and at this glimpse into Caroline Boyd's previous life. Why, that kitchen girl Bess she mentioned so casually who had run off was another Sarah! At least, Amanda tried to tell herself, slavery, how ever wrong, was ended, and she must not hate this woman, however misguided she was then or now.

"Miz Wynne, please don't look peeved. I'm not saying no about the oven, you understand, if you want to clean it out, but most folks here'bouts don't have a pittance for such luxuries as pies or such anymore, unless you are meaning to sell to the soldiers, and I declare, you know how I feel about them."

"I'd rather give goodwill away than sell things right now, Mrs. Boyd. And I intend to barter for ingredients. As for the old oven not heating from the hearth, I know a more direct way, if you'd just let me borrow your son so we could go out and gather some wood."

"For good wood, you'd have to go way up in the hills, but Jesse knows where to find brush. We keep our woodpile hidden outside so no one else disturbs it. But as for borrowing my son or using my oven, Miz Wynne, be my guest."

Despite feeling more disillusioned about Caroline Boyd, Amanda felt better about the prospects of the day. She set to scrubbing the cobwebs, mice droppings, and grime from the narrow, deep old oven. While the bricks were drying, she and Jesse scouted the closest hillsides for scrub wood. If they both carried an armful back, she would give Caroline the extra.

"Why aren't you in school, Jesse? It's not Christmas vacation yet, is it?"

"No, but see, the Female College got all burned up. Both boys and girls had classes at the college. Mostly, till a new school gets built, we're all learning at home, I guess."

"So your parents are instructing you?"

"Sure, though we got no real books around but my uncle's four lawbooks, and they's not too int'resting."

"Your uncle only has four lawbooks?" she asked, picturing the rows of volumes Matt had owned, the shelves of Mason Rutland's library. The knot in her stomach tightened every time she thought of Tate defending Lincoln.

"Then there's my mother's diary," the boy added, "but I'd get skinned if I read that. 'Sides, she hides it every day, but I know where it is."

"I guess if Lincoln Garner could only get freed, he could build a new school here," Amanda said, bringing the conversation back to the center of her thoughts.

"Guess so. Mostly he did the courthouse, and the hotel, and his house. You know, Miz Wynne, at the Sweet Springs Hotel, they served sugar pie there and some of us—now mind, this was when I was just a boy—used to take some right off the back window sills when it was cooling. Once they saw us, and then did we catch it! Glad they don't send folks to prison for taking pies!"

"You know," she said, smiling at his innocent humor, "I was going to trade your mother for some of those old apples for a pie, but if you favor a sort of sugar pie, I know one you'd love. The only thing is, we'd need to find and trade for some eggs, butter, and milk."

"Trade what?" he asked. "We never got anything to trade."

"Trade some of the things I brought in my trunk. You did see that's a magic trunk, didn't you? Kind of like Santa Claus opening his pack early for Christmas?"

"Aw, I don't believe in Santa Claus, especially not with the war and all. If there's a Santa, he doesn't come to Median, Mississippi, anymore."

"Maybe he will someday," she said. She wanted to hug the boy, but her arms were full of scrubby brush and he probably wouldn't let her anyway. So she said only, "Actually, Jesse, my trunk, small as it looks, was so heavy because I brought sugar and flour and a few baking tins as well as the bread and cookies with me. But we'd need the other things too."

"Old Lady Cresswell has two chickens and a goat," he told her, big-eyed, his freckled face eager. "Would goat milk and butter do? Sure enough, I would fancy a sugar pie like back before the war when we had a real town and all."

She regarded the boy's expression. Even the mention of Santa had hurt him, but he looked excited now. He recalled those precious days before disaster struck. She saw herself in him, looking back on the flush days in Lockwood before the canals closed. Yet this boy had been through so much more. At least he still clung to remnants of his childhood; the war and the problems of his parents had not taken that away. Amanda knew now how this child could be what kept Caroline going through her pain and grief of all that was lost. For the first time in months, she longed for her own child to rear and love—a child with Lincoln Garner.

"Miz Wynne, you all right? You kind of look like you was gonna cry."

"I'm fine, Jesse. You know, I've never used goat's milk, but let's try it. I just wish your mother understood that I'm very grateful for how kind she's being to me. My helping to put food on the table is just my thank you to her."

"I could tell her for you, if you want."

"Let's hope in time, I can show her."

By late morning, Amanda had bartered one of Aunt Louise's old taffeta gowns for six eggs, a block of butter, and a tin of thick goat's milk. Her goat, Mrs. Cresswell told her, was the only milk-giving beast within a two-mile walk out of town, where someone had a cow. The old lady wanted to know all about why she was here and wanted to explain all about how Lincoln oversaw the building of the courthouse, which her husband had roofed, but Amanda soon made her excuses and hurried back to the Boyds'.

She built the fire in the oven. In Caroline's tureen she mixed dough for four bottom piecrusts from her flour and the butter. She rolled out the dough using a tin cup and fitted and fluted the crusts in the tins she'd brought. She raked out the ashes, then popped in the pie crusts. As they baked, she pulled them out much too often in the dim light of the cellar to be sure they didn't burn.

Meanwhile, at the hearth, she mixed, stirred, and boiled the filling of what would make two Sugar Cream Pies. Then, to stretch the meager ingredients she had, she mixed enough slightly different filling for two Butterscotch Pies. The two recipes were similar but cream pie lovers could tell the difference: her father had liked the Sugar Cream, her mother the Butterscotch.

All the while, Jesse hung about, watching her every move, sampling the brown sugar, and getting underfoot until Caroline stopped dusting long enough to make him sit in the door light to recite his sums and subtractions. He sounded so proud at each right answer that Amanda's heart went out to him again. And she was proud of the four piecrusts she produced from the oven and into which she poured the rich, sweet fillings.

"I'm bartering one of these for the use of your oven today, Mrs. Boyd," Amanda said.

"I—oh, yes, they smell delicious. I'm so glad you can use the oven."

"And, I must admit, I intend to give one to Sergeant Swaggart this afternoon, though I'm starting to hope he chokes on it."

At that Caroline's eyes seemed to smile, but her face did not. "To get in to see Lincoln sooner, you mean?"

"I doubt if that will work, but I will apply to see him tomorrow and make the point that the one-visitor rule should not include Lincoln's lawyer's necessary visits. Would you like to go with me to visit Lincoln? If you think I could benefit from chaperoning . . ."

"Oh, I didn't mean to criticize or imply—no, I told you I never go near those government people, not even to visit Lincoln. Jess and Tate visit Lincoln. Besides, I'd be likely to put poison in any pie to a Union soldier, pardon me for putting it that way."

"I understand, but they are not really Union soldiers anymore, you know, no matter what their uniforms look like. No more than Lincoln, your husband, or Tate is a Confederate soldier anymore. But as for my giving Sergeant Swaggart a pie, I'm hoping to catch more flies with sugar than vinegar, if you know what I mean, Mrs. Boyd. For Lincoln's sake."

"Yes. Yes, I do know what you mean. Unfortunately, we women are sometimes forced to be kind instead of cruel because of those we love." For one moment, Amanda sensed Caroline would share a heartfelt revelation, but she only turned to her son. "Jesse, all that fidgeting is driving me to distraction! You can go on out now."

"But can I go out to the Blakes' with Miz Wynne after dinner?" he pleaded.

"If you do not go near the government headquarters with her, then, I suppose."

"Now where can I cool these pies so a boy won't run off with them?" Amanda asked, and Jesse giggled on his way out the door.

"I take it," his mother said, "my son's been telling you about old times around here. My, they were grand!"

"And could be again someday—with a few changes," Amanda said.

"Doesn't do to hold out hope in times like these," Caroline protested, but her voice was still wistful as she stood leaning on her broom in the doorway. "Still," she admitted with a shake of her head, "if someone would have told me last week we'd have fresh baked sugar pie for supper . . . I am regretful, Miz Wynne, that I snapped at you yesterday about the baked goods and about your coming to Median. It wasn't my place."

"But this is your place," Amanda said, coming closer, "and I'm grateful you took me in. I don't mean to flaunt the fact that where I'm from is better off right now than her , really. I know we were on different sides in the war, but I'd like us to be on the same side now. For Lincoln, for Median. And I wish, if you could, you would call me Amanda, even if that's untoward and unseemly too."

"Now, don't you go tossing all that back in my face— Amanda."

"I won't mention it again."

"Won't you call me Caroline then?"

"I would be very pleased to, Caroline."

"Best I tell you one thing more. Even if I've not been the best of hostesses, don't go getting your hopes up about being friends with Lincoln's family. That's his wife's family, you know, his mother-in-law and sister-in-law and brother-in-law out there."

"He said his wife wrote him once she could not forgive him for being away when their daughter died—but that she recanted later on her deathbed."

"So you *were* very close to him," Caroline said, and her eyes narrowed a bit. She tilted her head back against the door frame and stared upward, gripping the broom in both hands. "Good heavens, we've all done or said things we didn't mean, things we regretted. But Garnet Blake Ellis and her family might be mighty protective of Lincoln, that's all I'm saying."

"I can't thank you enough for warning me."

"I just don't want that precious pie to be thrown back in your face, like I might have done yesterday and am heartily regretful for it."

"Let's not mention any part of our rough beginning again. There's a time just to put things aside and go on."

Her hands still gripping the top of the broom, her chin on her hands, Caroline nodded. "I used to think so," she whispered, so quietly Amanda had to read the words on her lips.

Caroline quickly leaned her broom in the door and went out to the pump. Though Amanda could not see her from the door where she watched Jesse coming back for dinner with his Uncle Tate and his father, she knew by the screech of the old pump handle that Caroline was washing her hands, again and again and again.

Chapter Fourteen

❄

Butterscotch Pie

Prepare and bake one-piece piecrust. Let cool.
Stir 2 egg yolks with 1 heaping tablespoon of flour.
Add gradually, 1 cup of milk.
Fry 1 tablespoon of butter in skillet until ready to brown.
Add 1 cup brown sugar and 4 tablespoons milk.
Boil about 5 minutes, stirring constantly.
Add other ingredients and stir until thick.
Pour in pie shell and let set.

❄

"Mrs. Wynne, you must admit this deposition you just gave us is rather one-sided," Colonel McKitrick told her, as he peered over his spectacles and straightened his papers by turning and tapping them repeatedly on the table.

"I am only one person with one opinion, sir," Amanda said. "I should hope I would not give you something two-sided or two-faced. And I, as well as my fellow citizens of Lockwood, even though we knew he had been a Confederate, thought highly of Major Garner."

"What your fellow citizens thought is hearsay, ma'am. You've been spouting legal language at me, so I'm sure you understand that even if Lincoln Garner, alias Blake, is up for sainthood in Lockwood, it is inadmissible in court without the individuals here to testify."

A new thought hit Amanda. Would it be inadmissible if she telegraphed home to ask for written, signed affidavits? Unfortunately, Mason Rutland was the only one in town who could properly witness them, but it might be worth a try. She planned to telegraph home anyway, so she could pass that idea on to Eliza and Sarah, as well as letting them know she had arrived safely.

"I'm sure you're right about that, sir," she said. "And I do appreciate your kindness in all this. I just didn't want you to look on Major Garner as some flaming, never-say-die Confederate, as we dyed-in-the-wool northern Ohio Yankees did not see him that way at all."

"Point well taken, ma'am," he said and scribbled down something else.

Amanda had tried to remain calm and polite with Colonel McKitrick, partly because she had learned he would be assisting the prosecuting attorney when he arrived from Washington. However, the news that "the enemy" prosecutor was being sent from the nation's capital was beginning to breach Amanda's tenuous composure. The military tribunal which would conduct the trial—the judge and a three-man jury—would be military men from somewhere else. Obviously, as Tate had warned her, General Timmons and his commander were pulling some very high governmental strings. Didn't that indeed indicate that someone high up was intending to make a show case out of this? And probably not in favor of someone who supposedly killed a congressional advisor with Washington connections in the Rebel state of stubborn Mississippi during the volatile Reconstruction period.

In Colonel McKitrick's questioning of her today, she had been deeply disturbed by his carefully couched implications about her relationship with Lincoln. At least the man had let up when she told him that Lincoln had left before her husband died and that she had fought to keep from committing Matt to the asylum. She thought the colonel even sympathized with her battle with the government to clear Matt's name and get him a pension, for he said he had briefly been assigned to the Pension Department in Washington and admitted that he regretted the unjust tarnishing of Matt's reputation.

Now, as the colonel escorted her down the stairs and outside, she steeled herself to be as polite as possible to that "Swaggering Swaggart," as she had come to think of him. Colonel McKitrick doffed his hat to her as he bid her goodbye.

Amanda had been disappointed this morning to be taken to the side entrance and upstairs and not through the downstairs common room where the jail cells were located. They had meant it that she would not be seeing Lincoln if she did not ask a whole day ahead. So she intended to get on the books right now for every day Tate Boyd wasn't visiting him—and to discuss the unfairness of that with Swaggart.

She waved to Jesse, who was waiting faithfully for her across the street, then headed for the front door of government headquarters. More bad luck! Swaggart sat on the bench outside with the door closed, as if he'd been expecting her and had no intention of even allowing her a glimpse of Lincoln.

She gripped the handle of the twig basket Caroline had loaned her to carry the pies. "Good morning, Sergeant," she called and tried to put a pleasant look on her face. At least he had the good manners to stand, she thought, then scolded herself for being turned against these soldiers by the attitude of others.

"Morning, Mrs. Wynne," he said and touched his hat brim. "What all you got in there this time?"

"A butterscotch-flavored pie for you and one for Major Garner."

"You wouldn't be trying to bribe me for access to the prisoner now, would you?"

"No. It was you who told me that you had to taste anything I sent in to him, and I know your word is law around here."

"Wouldn't be smuggling in a key picker or a little derringer in there?" he asked as he peered in at the pies, then with her help, lifted two of the three out.

"Most certainly not! An innocent man who gives himself up wants to go through with a fair trial, not run from it. Cut into both pies if you think I've hidden something within, but please, Sergeant, will you give one to him if I can't do it myself?"

"Sure, sure," he said, sounding gruff but looking quite sheepish. Did she dare hope, if she was careful here, she might have an ally, however covert, in Sergeant Swaggart?

"I'm also here," she told him, "to sign up to visit the major tomorrow and whatever days are free. Especially Christmas Eve, and—"

"Whoa, now, ma'am. First of all, can't do that so far ahead, and second, his trial's being moved up to start late next week, probably on the sixteenth or seventeenth. Guess the brass wants to have this all over and done with by the holidays."

"Oh. So soon."

"Yes, ma'am. And that means his lawyer will be visiting him most every day, so there goes the single visitor rule—"

"Which you must admit is hardly justifiable, considering the charges and the rush to crucify the man!"

"Crucify! Look, lady, I can't help rules!"

"I realize that," she backtracked quickly, "but I thought you had some power over the rules that governed the jail. I agree that Major Garner's lawyer should meet with him every day, maybe more than once. But don't you agree that at least an additional visit should be allowed, one that is just from family or friends to keep his spirits up? How would you feel if you were on trial for your life and knew it could be your last Christmas, Sergeant Swaggart? I know you have sway around here. Couldn't you give me permission to see him at least tomorrow, or convince your superiors? You can hardly count that first haphazard visit the day I arrived, and I stayed away yesterday, as you required."

"Sure, sure, I know," he said, shifting the pies up and down in his hands as if he were weighing them as well as her words. "All right, late tomorrow morning—if his lawyer's not with him. After that, can't promise a thing."

"Thank you, Sergeant. I just sensed you would be impartial and fair."

She had sensed nothing of the kind, of course, she told herself, as she started toward the small building that served as the post office, for she had been told that was where she'd find the telegraph machine and its military operator. With Jesse following her at a distance, like a shadow, she gave the man her message, which he scratched out on paper with a pencil. She paid in advance for the number of words, then stood watching him as he *tap-tapped* them into his apparatus.

TO: SARAH BLUE AND ELIZA TUTTLE, LOCKWOOD, OHIO
ARR. SAFE. PRAY RUFUS WELL. L. MURDER TRIAL NEXT WEEK.
SEND STATEMENTS OF HIS GOOD CHARACTER FROM TOWNFOLK,
IF POSS., WITNESSED BY S. WAINWRIGHT, NOT M. RUTLAND. ME-
DIAN IN BAD SHAPE, ESP. SAD THIS TIME YEAR. IF CAN, SEND
CRATE FLOUR, SUGAR. SEND L'S TOOLS. I'LL PAY YOU FREIGHT
LATER.
SIGNED: A.L.W.

"I'll pay later," the words stayed with her to match her steps as she and Jesse started out of town to the east at a good clip, on their way to visit Lincoln's in-laws. If Lincoln was not cleared, she would indeed pay later, for the closer she got to losing him, the more she knew she loved him.

* * *

"So this was where Lincoln built his house," Amanda repeated Jesse's words as they stopped by an overgrown, weedy yard just beyond the outskirts of town. Two stunted-looking oaks, drooping gray-green moss, stood, but little else remained.

"They had one of the best houses around," Jesse told her. "And he had his workshop out back. It was real first-rate."

"I'm sure it was," she said, picturing that other, cruder little workshop in Lockwood where she had spent some precious minutes with him. "And this is where the murder took place, isn't it?"

"Out back where there was some gardens," the boy told her. "Want me to show you? I been here before and seen it all."

"I suppose I could come back later, but, yes, I guess I'd like to see it."

Jesse kept talking, telling her about how he'd come here with some other boys, but Amanda's thoughts drifted. It had been a smaller house than hers, but she knew it was well designed, well built. What had been the cellar was now a gaping hole filled with heavy, charred beams. Weeds had grown even there. She wanted to take the time to really look around, but not now. Yet, she stood and stared, imagining voices, lives, those faces which had once graced Lincoln's locket that she now wore. She turned away and stubbed her toe on a half-buried stone, almost spilling the last pie from the basket.

"You all right, Miz Wynne?" the boy asked, instantly at her side as they walked back to the road.

"I'm all right, Jesse. I wasn't watching my step because I was thinking about the people who used to live back there."

"Miz Garner and her girl, Lindy Rose, you mean? They tool sick and died of the cholera."

"I know."

"I was sick once too, real bad, but didn't die."

"I see you didn't. I am awfully glad about that."

"Because Mama got me some secret medicine, I guess."

"Why was it secret?"

"I wasn't supposed to tell anyone about it back then. She told me I had such a high fever I was funny in my head—having dreams or delude—delu—"

"Delusions or delirium?"

"That's it. Because right before Daddy came back home to us from the hospital up north, I thought a soldier in blue came and sat with me sometimes at night."

"A soldier in the cellar at night? You probably were delirious, Jesse, because your mother does not like soldiers, especially ones in blue."

"I sure know it."

"Where was your mother when the soldier visited?"

"She went outside somewhere, maybe to get more medicine uptown, but the stores were gone by then. It's the only time I ever been real sick or real scared, besides the time Sherman burned the town. Say, the old Blake place is right around that next big bend up yonder, and they're sure gonna like that pie."

"I really thought about not bringing it," she admitted to the boy, surprised how she told him things as if he were an older friend. Maybe she was getting like Caroline, overly anxious to talk to anyone who came her way in Median, when it was Lincoln she longed to talk to. But it simply helped to voice problems out loud, and Jesse was a good listener for a child. If he repeated to his mother what she said, all the better.

"You see," she told the boy, "I don't want folks in Median to get the idea that I'm showing I have nice things they can't have right now. But sharing baked goods is one way to be neighborly up north, so I'm going ahead with it, just as I'm going ahead with being here in Median to lend support for Lincoln Garner."

Lincoln was surprised when Sergeant Swaggart tipped a pie sideways to hand to him through the bars. " 'Sugar and spice and all things nice,' " the sergeant chanted, but his voice was not taunting. "The lady herself is coming to see you tomorrow, and she'll probably bring her whole kitchen then. Wish I had the charm to bring fair damsels rushing in from other states to feed me. But she brought me one too," he said, looking amazingly bashful for Swaggart. "Strictly a bribe, though she said it wasn't." He lumbered over to "their" desk—which Lincoln had decided not to argue about further until he was exonerated—to hack out a hunk of pie with a penknife. "Never thought I'd see a woman could bake better than my mother," he added, his voice wistful, however full his mouth was.

Lincoln had been simply staring at his pie. He was ecstatic with it. Just looking at it, touching it, lifted his spirits, far out of proportion to the gift itself. But great gifts always had value far more than they were worth, he thought.

He had to dig out pieces with his hands because they'd taken sharp things from him, but it was as delicious—more so than if he was sitting eating it at Amanda's table in Lockwood. Just a pie, but it spoke to him of thoughtfulness, of caring—of love, that he dared not discuss with her right now.

He regretted he had spoken to her of passion the other day when he should have talked of love. He had left Lockwood when he did—when she and Matt both needed him, because in very different ways, he had loved them both. If—when—he was cleared, he would send for her or go to her, but he did not want her here to see his hanging or to wave farewell if they sent him to the damned Dry Tortugas for life. No, he could not bear that.

He looked up expectantly when the front door opened. Swaggart had said she was coming tomorrow, but he could not help hoping . . .

It was old Alvah Wembly, the stationmaster, who'd been the first elder of the Baptist Church here. He'd been beyond the age for service in the war, but people had said he stood his ground like a hero, defying Sherman's men the day they burned the town. Still, they'd knocked him down and ignited the church because it had been converted to an Confederate arsenal. They'd said that the fireworks when it went up shook Median to its roots.

The gallant old gentleman had reared four sons and one daughter after his wife had died giving birth to the daughter; all four boys were lost in the war. The girl, Polly, was amply endowed in womanly form, if simple in the head. She still lived with the old man, and most people in town were quite protective of her. But since the Yankees had burned the church, Alvah Wembly, like several others in town, had not so much as spoken to a Federal soldier. So it was odd he was here now, carrying a canvas sack.

"Got some mail for you, officer, just off the train from

Washington. Didn't see the man over in the post office and thought it might be important, so I brang it in direct."

"Well, now, sir, I do appreciate the special delivery," Swaggart said as Alvah thumped the bag on the desk. Then, quickly, as Lincoln watched, Alvah coughed loudly into one hand, waved to Lincoln behind Swaggart's back with the other, and rolled a tiny white ball toward Lincoln's cell. He bent to retrieve it as the old man coughed again to cover any sounds and went back outside.

"That old coot must think there's a pardon inside for you," Swaggart said as he put his feet back up on the desk. "Like with most of your fellow townsmen, we're lower than pond scum to him, even when we're here to help rebuild this place."

"In the long run, Median and Mississippi are going to have to rebuild Median and Mississippi, Sergeant," Lincoln said, but he didn't want to start an argument now. He rolled the tiny, hard ball between thumb and finger, hoping Swaggart stayed where he was, looking away. Could it be a note from Amanda? From Tate or Jess about some new evidence they had uncovered? From Garnet or Chad, since they had asked to see him and were turned away? He had no business with Alvah Wembly.

Slowly, carefully, while Swaggart went back to eating, Lincoln unpeeled the small piece of paper from what turned out to be an agate marble. The script—not Amanda's—was tiny and written both ways on the paper so it looked like a plaid. In the dim light, he had to squint to read and decipher it:

L. G. I know the righteous deed you did, saving my Polly from that defiler of our women. Polly told me when she came in all dirty and disheveled that night. I am an old man now with a weak heart. If you will give your word to keep protecting my Polly like you done once, I will admit to killing J. B., though I want my girl's name kept clean of it. If you say you are innocent, I believe you but they will not. I will say I did it because his ilk torched the church, the town, the South. I come to you with this rather than to Tate so you can decide. Sir, you are an honorable man. Whether or not it is you who executed J. B. for his crimes against the sovereign South and southern womanhood, I will gladly lay down my life for you and Polly. If you agree, let me know through Tate and I will step forward, and ask the good Lord's forgiveness for the lie. Otherwise, I trust you to say nothing to anyone.   A. W.

Lincoln rewadded the note and stuffed it in his straw bed-ticking. Deliverance, and yet he could not accept. He had not breathed one word about Polly—not even to Tate—and had not intended to in court, even before this proud yet pitiful note from her father. Besides, who knew—if the old man confessed to the murder they might break him down on the stand or in one of their backroom inquisitions like they'd put Lincoln through at first.

And didn't Alvah Wembly know that someone in town would take care of Polly after he was gone? Or had he meant Lincoln would marry her? Surely he knew that was out of the question. Under any circumstances, Lincoln knew he could not allow the old man to plead guilty, not unless he re-ally had killed Barr, and he doubted that. The old hard-shell Baptist might be willing to die for a cause, but he would not murder for one. He would leave real vengeance to the Lord.

Still deep in thought, Lincoln sank slowly down on his cot and lifted out another handful of the sweet comfort Amanda had sent him.

As they approached the old Blake farm, Amanda and Jesse walked up an overgrown lane. Like most side roads around Median, without wagons or carriages to keep it trimmed back, it was being slowly strangled by encroaching grass and weeds. Amanda felt relieved the place had been a vegetable farm and not a big plantation, for perhaps the owners had not kept slaves.

They went across what had been a front lawn laid out with neat-edged flower beds, now trampled askew. Amanda thrilled to see a building, then realized the farmhouse itself had burned and sunk into its cellar. The standing structure was the old stables. She saw no one but before she could knock, she heard distant voices.

"Sounds like Josh and James," the boy told her. "They're much younger than me, ages 'bout three and six."

As they walked around the stables, they saw a thin woman gowned in gray, wrapped in a maroon shawl, pushing the smaller boy on a crude, one-rope swing suspended from a tree. The child straddled a round wood seat. In this lone tree growing amid stumps where once an orchard had stood, the older boy held to another rope, swooping and squealing. The scene made Amanda's eyes burn with unshed tears. How normal, how lighthearted. Life, even after tragedy, did go on.

"Hey, Miz Ellis!" Jesse yelled beside Amanda so loud she jumped. "I brought someone to see you all!"

The woman turned and shaded her eyes into the thin winter sun. She came toward them with steady strides, holding her shawl tightly to her while her boys watched. Amanda saw she looked very much like the tintype of Lincoln's dark-eyed, dark-haired wife.

"Mrs. Ellis, I'm Amanda Wynne from Ohio. I'm staying with the Boyds."

"I know who you are. People talk in town. And I received your letter, just yesterday when we were in. I'm Garnet Ellis. My husband, Chadwick, is not here just now, but my mother is inside taking a lie down."

"I heard the mail service might be slow, and that letter is obviously dated now that I'm here. Mrs. Ellis, I'm staying in Median to try to testify to Lincoln's good character."

"Mighty kind of you to take him in up north, though I told him he was crazy to go there."

"I'm sure he had his reasons. My husband greatly admired him—I guess I wrote that in the letter to you. But I had no idea about Lincoln's troubles when he lived with us. He didn't tell me, didn't even give me his real name or hometown. But he did speak of his lost wife and daughter—how deeply he loved them and how hard it was to lose them."

"That's nice of you to be concerned for my dead sister and niece, but quite unnecessary, as they have been properly mourned here. And don't you think, if Lincoln did not give you all any way to identify him or find him, he wanted you to let him be? I am sure you mean well, but I think it best you leave the premises and—for Lincoln's sake too, believe me—leave town. Go back home, Miz Wynne, to your own memories and losses."

Amanda's felt hurt by her response, but she was angry too. "Don't you see that clinging to memories and losses will do us all in? We can't keep looking back and hating and regretting. Lincoln wants to rebuild Median, and it looks to me that it sorely needs it, both the buildings and the people."

"And you think, even if he is cleared, that you can be a part of that?" Garnet demanded. "Can judge us?" Her dark eyes snapped fire. She clutched her shawl even closer around her spare, stiff form. Then came the scream.

Garnet whirled back toward her boys. Jesse had wandered over to push the younger lad and done too good a job of it. The child had somehow sailed right off his makeshift swing and sat wailing on the ground. Garnet lifted her skirts and ran, with Amanda right behind her.

"Didn't mean to hurt him!" Jesse was yelling over the lad's shrieks. "I was just pushing him a little bit!"

"My darling Josh," Garnet crooned to the child, while the other boy stood leaning over her shoulder. "Oh, look, his arm!"

Amanda put her pie basket on the grass and knelt beside the child. No bones protruded, but the arm looked bent, and the boy howled when his mother so much as touched it.

"You might know his father's gone," Garnet said, tears matting her eyelashes. "I've never set a bone, but I won't have him crippled!"

"Can't we take him in to the doctor in Median?" Amanda asked.

The woman shook her head so hard that strands of hair cascaded loose from the tight bun. "Killed in the war."

"But the army will have a doctor!" Amanda insisted. Too late, she remembered the army doctors had not helped Matt, but this boy needed medical care. "I can help you get him into town."

"The army is here to care for the army, and not—"

"Of course, they will help. Believe it or not, they are good men, just like your soldiers were. Your boy's hurt, Mrs. Ellis. If you won't take him in, I will send someone out. Yes, perhaps that's best, so we don't jostle him on the way in. I promise you I will send someone out."

To be heard over the boy's screams, they shouted at each other. But, at least, Amanda thought, as badly as this fast, first meeting had gone, they were not really shouting against each other any more.

"Come on, Jesse, we've got to hurry back to town. Oh, this is something I brought," Amanda said as she stood and took the pie out to plop it on the ground where the three of them huddled together now. "It's a sugar pie, and maybe that will help quiet him. I hope to speak with you under better circumstances, Mrs. Ellis."

"I—yes. All right," she said, wiping her son's nose with the corner of her shawl.

"Jumping Jehoshaphat, I didn't mean to do it," Jesse muttered to Amanda as they hurried back toward town. "I didn't mean to hurt Josh."

"Of course you didn't. You were just trying to help and pushed a bit too hard," she said, already out of breath and with a stitch in her side. "When we get to town, you go on back home, because your mother will be fretful if you go with me to find an army doctor. That's why I didn't send you back for him on your own."

She wondered if the boy's memories of being ill with the soldier in blue sitting at his bedside could mean Caroline had once been desperate enough to go for an army doctor and broken her own code of disdaining contact with the enemy. But she had other things to worry about right now.

Although Amanda expected her relationships with people in town to improve after she sent the army doctor—a very nice, concerned young man from Cincinnati named Dr. Fisher—out to set little Josh Ellis's broken arm, she soon found she was mistaken. Whether or not they thought she was in collusion with the soldiers she did not know, but people still walked around her, or looked away, or at most merely nodded or tipped a hat, if she dared to say good day. More than once she thought she had heard the sibilant sounds of a whispered, "strumpet" or "hussy" when several women passed by.

Especially at the Boyds', Caroline, Jess, even Tate had been upset with the day's occurrences. They sent Jesse to bed without supper and hardly spoke to Amanda at the meal, so she felt she should be sent to bed too. The next morning when everyone else had left the house, Amanda saw that, despite her explanation and apologies last night, Caroline still had not forgiven her.

"All I can say is you weren't providing much guidance for my son if he was allowed to hurt the Ellis boy like that," Caroline said, carefully washing the cracked chimney of their sole kerosene lamp. "Jesse's been through too much to be made to feel guilty for breaking a little boy's arm, and I am mortified by it all. And," she added as she squinted at each invisible streak on the glass, "the injured child is Lincoln's nephew, you know, and neither he nor the Ellises need more grief right now."

"To repeat myself, Caroline, it was an accident, pure and simple. Jesse did not mean to push the child too hard, and I certainly did not mean for it to happen. Since you let Jesse roam on his own a good deal, I assumed you felt he did not need constant watching."

"But you had him telling you all about the murder and showing you the spot, didn't you?" she demanded, still bending to her polishing. "My son's no part of any of the terrible things that happened around here."

"Is that really what this is all about? I did have him show me the place, but he said he had been there before with some boys, so I surely wasn't . . . Caroline, I *am* sorry."

"Let's not say a thing of any of it again. Only, I do believe it best that Jesse no longer be your companion about town in your amateur investigations. As I said once before, you should leave things which should be in Tate and Jess's realm alone."

"Would you keep clear of things if you could lose the man you loved?" she demanded. She was amazed she had blurted that out; she tried to repair the damage. "Caroline, as Garnet Ellis says, people in town do talk, so I hope that bit of heartfelt news I'm sharing with you will not soon be all over, however few folks it seems you see."

"I guess as hard as we try, there is nothing but bad blood between us," Caroline said, looking up at last. "I wouldn't blame you one bit if you went home."

"Are you asking me to move out?"

"Of course not. Lincoln asked that we take you in, and we're glad to do it and happy to have you here."

If there would have been a decent door on the place, Amanda would have slammed it right off its hinges as she went out. Trying to calm herself, she set off for her interview with Lincoln.

Lincoln had to admit he was as nervous as a schoolboy when Amanda came in with Sergeant Swaggart. "What, no bakery shop today?" Lincoln heard his guard tease Amanda. Lincoln had noticed how Swaggart's face lit to see her—and how the big, burly lout had trimmed his side whiskers and slicked back his dark hair. It hit him then that, should he not get out of this mess, there would be many men who would want to court Amanda.

"Pies last most individuals more than one day," she told Swaggart, who chuckled.

She may not have brought so much as a crumb, Lincoln thought, but she almost had Swaggart eating out of her hand. And he had overheard a Colonel McKitrick, who had evidently taken Amanda's statement earlier, telling Swaggart he had been impressed with her. But he dared not hope any of that would make a difference. It would be a sound defense in court and his own convincing testimony that would get him off so that he and Amanda could really be together somehow, somewhere.

"Lincoln," Amanda said, as Swaggart took his time noisily fumbling with the cell door. Lincoln's eyes locked with hers; he felt he could have soared. She made him feel so alive, strong but needy too.

"Good morning, Amanda," he managed to reply. When Swaggart opened the door and she came in, Lincoln stood as if at ease, but he felt coiled tight. He wanted so badly to sweep her into his arms, to devour her in kisses and caresses. She wore a dark-blue gown with a black pelisse, a feathered bonnet—and his locket. He had worn the only clothes he had in here, his gray uniform. He clenched his hands behind his back to keep from leaping at her. All that would do no good, not with his guard dog twenty feet away. Awkward, feeling they were on display, they stood, talking low.

"I've missed you terribly," she whispered.

"I too. It never gets easier. With you, it has never been out of sight, out of mind."

"The same for me. Lincoln, I wanted to tell you about this dream I had, about Matt," she said and explained it as best she could. It not only surprised him but gave him chills. He reached for her hands and held them tightly.

"As you say, it can't be real," he said, "but it's a lovely dream. He'll always be with us, at least here."

As he spoke, he touched her locket, pressing it to her

breast. She heaved a sigh, which pushed her firm softness against his hand. "Oh, my sweetheart," he whispered, "what are we going to do?"

She shook her head and gave a small shrug, as if unable to speak. Her eyes when she lifted them again were glazed with tears. "As least you have Median people on your side," she said. "They hate me."

"They just don't know and can't trust you right now. Amanda, think how they've suffered."

"I know. I do, but that was war."

"For some of them it's still war and will be for a while unless we can find something to heal their wounds."

"We?" she said. "You used to get very angry when I would say we and mean us—you and me."

"See? People's wounds can heal with love. But I don't think they hate you, and they won't if they really get to know you. How do you think I felt at first in Lockwood, even when you and Matt took me in?"

She nodded; her feathers bobbed and tickled his nose. He breathed in the sweet, windswept scent of her hair. Though it was not the lavender fragrance he always associated with her, he inhaled again as if he could fill himself with the very essence of her being. He wanted to shove her bonnet back, remove her pelisse and gown, to see and touch her everywhere.

"I believe but a moment ago," she whispered, "you used the word love."

"I did. I meant it. Amanda, I love you and always will, no matter what. If things were different, I would propose all sorts of things . . ."

"Honorable ones, I hope," she said, but her voice broke on the tease. "Actually, I don't care if they are honorable or not. I just want to be with you, here in this jail cell, if they'd let me, but everyone wants me to leave, Lincoln, and I can't."

"You must."

"What? You just said—"

"It's because I love you that I want you to go. Amanda, this is no good, your being dependent on the kindness of strangers when you have a home and a town where they love you. You've helped me by being here, by letting me know you cared enough to find me. By giving a statement to the authorities. If the trial comes out well—"

"It will! Tell me you know it will!"

"Of course. But we know life can deal those who don't deserve it terrible blows. I want you to go home, and I swear to you I will send for you or come to you when this is over."

"But I couldn't bear not knowing right away. Lincoln, the trial starts next week! Besides, there might be something I can do!"

He knew that tone, that set to her mouth, that look that darkened her amber eyes. He was doomed to do this her way. "Will you promise me one thing then?" he asked.

"If I can."

"If the judgment goes against me, you *will* go home. We may have a farewell, but you will not wait around to see me shackled or put on a train south or whatever. You will not be there when they take me away or—execute a severe sentence."

He saw he had gripped her upper arms as he spoke. He had pulled her to him, lifted her almost off the ground.

"Yes, I promise," she breathed, almost into his mouth.

"Hey, you two in there, don't do anything to embarrass a soldier boy, all right?"

Neither looked at Swaggart or answered him, but they stepped a bit apart. Still he clenched her hands; their eyes held.

"I love you, too, Lincoln Garner, and always will," she whispered.

And though, after that, still standing in his cell, they reminisced and even dared to plan a bit, after they had exchanged vows of their love, there was nothing else they needed to say.

Amanda emerged as if stunned into the early-afternoon sun in the heart of Median. She was surprised that Sergeant Swaggart closed the door behind himself and began to walk her home. Knowing better than to go farther toward the Boyds' in his company, she halted on the other side of the street.

"Mrs. Wynne, I have something to tell you that I reckon you will judge more bad news," he said. He had one hand on the hilt of his sword, one leg stiffly ahead of the other. He hesitated almost as if he were in pain.

"Tell me then."

"I pleaded your case about extra visitors and won."

"But that's good ne—"

"Listen, please, ma'am. Except maybe Christmas Eve where I'd penciled your name in, if he's still around then— you know what I mean—other folks in Median took all the extra visitors' spots—and it wasn't my doing. Somehow it was done through General Timmons's office."

"What? What folks?"

"Lots of people, one a day with a waiting list, not counting Tate Boyd's regular visits, like I said."

"Did Tate Boyd ask for this? Does Lincoln know?"

"Boyd, no. Lincoln, I'm gonna tell him, but he said the other day he thought you should go home."

"Yes, but surely he's not behind this. Can the townspeople hate me so much, sergeant?"

"Maybe they think it's for your own good. Maybe folks really want to see him. He's the local hero 'round here. As for these folks hating someone, they're real good at that, and you're hardly the belle of Dixie to them, you know. The only other Ohioan most of them knew when he visited here was General Sherman."

She could only nod. Despite her recent joyous moments with Lincoln, she felt betrayed, deserted, and overwhelmed. Almost defeated. She wished she had a log to crawl into on this battlefield, just the way Matt had on his.

"Now if I can do anything to help, ma'am, let me know— like buy you a train ticket, carry your trunk, protect you from these folks ... "

"Thank you, Sergeant Swaggart, but I haven't made up my mind what to do just yet. But I appreciate your being honest with me."

"And, Mrs. Wynne, I want you to know one more thing. I know—I see—how much you care for the major. His being a Reb and all, he must be a fine man to earn your love."

"Yes, believe me, he is."

"So I just wanted you to know that though he and I go at it pretty good sometimes, I got no personal grudge against him. Matter of fact, I think that Justin Barr he—or someone—killed was a real son of a bi— I mean, son of a gun. It's one thing, see, to be lording it over the vanquished, but it was not his place to be ordering around army officers like he was a general too and sending them here and there in town like errand boys—just 'cause he was in tight with the generals through connections or something!"

She stared at him, not certain what to say. His face had gone beet red, and veins stood out like cords in his bull neck, though she could tell he was trying to control himself.

"You know, Sergeant, it just goes to show you do have some things in common with these southerners. I'm yet to meet someone who liked the man."

"Hard to fathom," he said, looking sheepish now, "but heard the ladies did. 'Course not around here, where women treated him like the plague."

"Yes, like most of them are treating me right now," she said. "Thank you for your help, Sergeant. And for being fair with your prisoner."

As she headed toward the Boyds', her feeling of futility turned to fury, not against Swaggart, who at least tried to help her, but against Tate, Jess, and especially Caroline. They could have let her know about visits to Lincoln; Tate could get her in if he wished to. She would rely on the Boyds' so-called southern hospitality no more!

Perhaps she could get that old woman who lived out of town with the goat to take her in. She, at least, had wanted to talk and had not set herself up as judge and jury. Amanda knew she could hardly stay at the Boyds' if she was not to influence young Jesse, who had been her only real friend. How she wanted to confront Caroline with what the boy had told her about his dreams of the blue-coated soldier. Had Caroline been in collusion with the enemy and piously pretended otherwise? Amanda had read about plenty of female southern spies and turncoats. Had Caroline too used a Yankee doctor when her son was ill and did not have the courage to admit so to her touchy husband? She strode faster and faster toward the cellar door.

But when she saw the ruins of the place again, her anger ebbed slightly. She heard Lincoln's words of just a few minutes ago: Amanda, think how they've suffered. Caroline Boyd already lived in her own hell, one which, however much she washed it and herself, she would not get clean. And it was surely not Caroline who had gone to General

Timmons's office to demand that Median citizens be put on visitors' lists.

Amanda's shadow fell across the dirt floor as she entered. At the table, Caroline was writing in her diary, but she snapped it closed. Amanda walked to the corner and pulled back the curtain on her cubicle.

"I'm going to leave, Caroline."

"Oh, did Lincoln suggest that too? I'm sure it's for the best. I'll write to you about his trial, if you leave your Ohio address."

"That won't be necessary as I'll be boarding somewhere else nearby," she said. She heard Caroline gasp.

"Then please, stay here. My husband and Tate will blame me if you leave."

"Then tell them it is not your fault—or I'll tell them, if you like."

"But it is my fault, isn't it? You blame me?"

Amanda stopped stuffing clothing in her luggage. "Not evidently half as much as you blame yourself, Caroline. I used to blame myself for the fact that my father gave bad financial advice to my hometown and many people lost money, their stores, their livelihoods. But then I realized I am not my father, and I went on to do my best. My brothers died when I lived, and I used to think it should have been me, but I realized it should not have been me, if that's the way God wanted it. For little Jesse's sake, Caroline, don't blame yourself or let your husband blame you, or—"

"Just get out! You don't know anything about me, about us. Get out!"

Amanda managed her carpetbag and bandbox in one hand and her trunk under her other arm, now that much of the weight was gone from it.

"Good-bye, Caroline. And though you found out I was no angel, thank you for entertaining a stranger," she said.

She had to stop to get a better grip on her trunk, but she did not turn back, even when she heard the diary thud against the steps and sobs follow that.

It was the most unusual wedding Lockwood had seen, at least in recent memory. It was most certainly not a shotgun wedding, but—Eliza had to admit—one organized quicker than a blast from one.

When the invitations had gone out, strictly by word of mouth, she had included the peculiar request that, in lieu of gifts for the bridal couple, donations of clothing, toys, money, or transportable food would be taken to send to Lincoln Blake's destitute hometown of Median, Mississippi.

Much murmuring had ensued, since the corset of tight times still squeezed most people. Yet it was near Christmastime, the war had been won, and Lockwoodians remembered Lincoln's quiet strength and skills among them. Whatever hardships Amanda's father had brought to the town, people cared deeply for her. Then too, most of the town had once sat under Eliza's tutelage, and when she commanded, they still jumped. Guests came with armloads and boxes of goods.

Instead of signing their names in a wedding book, guests arriving at Lockwood House were asked, if they could, to write their impressions of Lincoln—using his real name, Garner—for his trial down south. Both the minister and their guest of honor, Samuel Wainwright, whom Ben had gone clear to Cleveland to fetch in a carriage pulled by four sleek prancers, countersigned every statement. Mason Rutland knew better than to attend, although Dottie breezed in and out, and with a donation of fancy children's clothing, no less.

The ceremony too was a bit singular, Eliza had to admit. The bridal march was the Christmas carol "O Come All Ye Faithful," played as a duet by Pru and her favorite student, Mandy. The younger pianist made a few mistakes, but ones so loud, so daring, no one could doubt she had intended them as clever embellishments. And, despite the minister's initial reluctance, he read passages from *Romeo and Juliet* as well as from the Bible.

Not wanting to waste one more day of their lives unwed, perhaps they had rushed the ceremony, Eliza thought. For during the nuptials, her Romeo, who had not yet fully recovered his strength, sat in a chair, next to his Juliet, who stood. But they held hands tightly, and she felt radiant and lovely.

And though everyone was so happy for them, and Sarah outdid herself with a table of delectables, without Amanda's genius the wedding cake came out lopsided. Eliza sensed a pall hung over the festivities, for Amanda was greatly missed and Lincoln's plight was deeply mourned.

"If I thought it would do on bit of good, I'd sit on the crates of these wedding gifts in the baggage car all the way to Median on the train and surprise her," Eliza Tuttle Quinn told her guests. "Amanda's like a daughter to me, and I miss her like the dickens."

"Mm-mn. And if that court don't free Lincoln," Sarah announced, "Ben and I gonna go down there with a pack of wild horses and raid the jail and spring him free."

"Oh, Mama, can I go too?" Mandy cried.

"Now you just come on over here on your Uncle Rufus's knee," Eliza told the child when Sarah and Pru hurried back into the kitchen. "Rufus, explain things to this girl."

"Your folks," he said to Mandy, "much as they want to, aren't going down to break anybody out of jail. I'm sure the jury will declare him innocent of all charges. An honorable man like Lincoln what's-his-real-name couldn't murder anybody—not outside of wartime, and that doesn't count."

"Why not?" Mandy asked, primly perched on Rufus's knee, while Eliza bustled from guest to guest, though she kept her ear cocked to their conversation.

"Because the rules are different in war," Rufus told her.

"But why?"

"Thunderation, Mandy, I'm just trying to explain to you why Lincoln is no murderer!"

"I already know that," the girl declared. "Someone who gives good Christmas gifts to somebody who bothered his woodcutting would never kill no one."

"Kill anyone," Eliza said, hurrying back with a cup of punch for Rufus and one for herself.

"Remember when you said I looked like Santa Claus?" Rufus asked, accepting the punch and taking a good swig of it. "Mandy, why don't you just go on and tell me what you want this year for Christmas, since it's coming up close now."

"All right. Number one, a new sister and a new brother, but Mama says there's probably not two in her belly at once. Two, to be the Virgin Mary in the pageant, but Mrs. Tuttle—I mean, Mrs. Quinn, won't let me. And three to see Mrs. Wynne again, and to have Santy Claus fetch Major Blake—I mean Garner—right out of jail up the chimney and take off with him in his sleigh."

"An excellent job of explaining things to her, my love,"

Eliza said to Rufus, as Mandy jumped off his lap and went for more food.

"I believe I'd best leave teaching the next generations to you, my dearest," Rufus said with a grin and patted her knee.

"The next generations, yes, my Rufus. No one will be better than you and I at looking ahead to a happy future," she said, and they tapped their glasses in a solemn salute. "If only it can be so for Amanda. She's given so much, deserves so much."

"At least," he said, "she and Lincoln are together now. They know how precious time is. Besides love, time together is the greatest gift of all."

He stood and took Eliza's arm, then kissed her hard while everyone clapped and cheered. That last little speech was, Eliza thought, another poem to cherish from her beloved. But for wondering how Amanda was doing, she had never been happier.

Chapter
Fifteen

❄

Garnet Ellis's
Southern Pecan Pie

Make single piecrust for 9″ pie.

Beat 3 eggs until light.

Add to eggs 1 cup granulated sugar and 1 teaspoon of brown sugar and beat again.

Add 1 cup cane syrup, ½ cup melted butter, 1 cup pecan halves, ¼ teaspoon salt, and 1 teaspoon vanilla. Stir.

Pour into unbaked 9″ pie shell.

Bake 10 minutes in hot (400 degrees) oven; lower heat to 350 degrees and finish baking until crust of filling is set.

"Amanda, though I can barely see them yet, I do believe we have guests coming down the road from town," the old woman said, as she walked into the house and produced six eggs from her apron. "Now won't that be nice?"

"How do we know they are our guests, Mrs. Cresswell?" Amanda asked, giving a last quick stir to the corn pone batter she was ready to bake in the Dutch oven on the hearth.

"No one walks by anymore. You haven't seen a soul but us for two days unless you walked back into town, have you? Only the hills out yonder and, a far piece past them, Tuscaloosa, and that's the next state."

Amanda's new hosts, the elderly Elias and Reba Cresswell, had one of the oldest homes in the area, partly built of stone. Because Sherman's incendiaries could burn only the wooden roof and the upper floor, that left them with half a house. Elias's roofing skills had served him well to weave limbs and cover them with sod to fill in where roof and windows had been.

Upon the momentous occasion of Sherman's visit, as old Elias put it, they had managed to shove a goat and several chickens in their root cellar to salvage some of their food supply. So for the last two days Amanda had been living in what was, for the Median area, the lap of luxury.

The old couple were a delight and comfort to Amanda—bright, industrious, and kind. Mrs. Cresswell talked unceasingly, and Mr. Cresswell told countless stories about the Choctaw Indians he'd known in this area before they were driven west. But Amanda, as much as they chattered, often in unison, desperately wished she and Lincoln could be together as many years as the Cresswells had been, and yet be so companionable and in love.

Now Amanda wiped her hands on the apron she'd made from one of Aunt Louise's old gowns; Mrs. Cresswell was wearing one and had been making curtains with yet another. Amanda shuffled over and peered out through the slit in the sod window. She had learned to step carefully here, for the chickens and goat were brought in at night to protect them, and they often wandered in during the day, not to mention mice skittering about in the dark. It might be a bit too much like living in a barn, and she missed young Jesse, but it beat being in town with the high-strung Caroline.

"Who's coming, Mrs. Cresswell?"

"Can't tell at this distance. Now, my Elias still has eyes sharp as any Indian's, don't you, dear?" she called to him as he came to the door to announce visitors too, only to hear his thunder had been stolen by his wife.

"Why, yes," he said, stopping to scrape mud from his boots at the door. "But I don't have that Choctaw craftiness in the forest, not at all, nor their moccasins either. The Indians would have just sneaked up on us, and I've seen these folks acoming from a far piece, long before you saw them, dear."

When they all went out to see who was coming, Amanda gasped. Garnet Ellis walked beside a man pushing a wheelbarrow, within which sat their two boys.

"Oh, it's Lincoln's family," Amanda said and strode out to meet them.

Though Garnet did not smile to see her, she no longer frowned. She introduced Amanda formally to her husband, Chadwick, a wiry, sandy-haired man with a world-weary face, and to the two boys.

"And how is Josh's arm doing?" Amanda asked as she escorted them into the yard where the Cresswells waited. The boy proudly displayed his plaster of Paris cast, and everyone fussed over it.

"The doctor was very nice and said you had offered to pay him," Garnet said. "We don't wish to be beholding to you."

"And you've come all this way to tell me that?" Amanda asked. "Mrs. Ellis, the truth is, I offered to pay Dr. Fisher, but he wouldn't take any money, so I promised him some quick bread next time I bake here. He said he only wanted to help."

"Oh, yes. He did seem—accommodating," Garnet admitted, twisting the fringe of her shawl. "But actually, we've come to tell you something else."

"Nothing's happened to Lincoln?"

"No," Garnet said, with a shake of her bonneted head. "But we were in town to trade for some potatoes with Mr. Wembly—he's the stationmaster at the depot—when a train came in from up north. And it had four crates for you, heavy ones of who knows what. So we wheeled them to Mr. Wembly's house for you."

"Oh, for me! I sent for Lincoln's tools, but that could not take four crates."

"At any rate, we thought," Chad Ellis added, as he shook Mr. Cresswell's hand in greeting, "we could escort you in to see them. And if need be, I could use our wheelbarrow to move them where you want. Truth is, we had that old wheelbarrow out in a field when Sherman's swarm came through, and it's about the only wheeled vehicle not army property or requisitioned as such in the county right now. I tell you that villain whom Lincoln is accused of killing even tried to take our stables from right over our heads, the only shelter we had!" Amanda stood amazed to see Chad clench his fists at his sides and a vein throb in his forehead. How quickly he had gone from calm and conciliatory to this.

"To pull it down for its boards to make himself an office in town," Garnet explained with a quick, staying hand on her husband's arm. "But fortunately for all of us, before Chad could confront Barr about it, General Timmons told the blighter the army had building supplies coming in by train."

Amanda noted well this tale of Justin Barr. Here were others who held a grudge against the man. But would any of that help Lincoln? He certain would not want a defense based on the fact that someone like his brother-in-law hated the deceased and had no doubt argued with him too. Maybe Chad had confronted Barr, no matter what Garnet said or believed. But how could Amanda make such inquiries without ruining these tenuous relationships?

"All that's over now, Chad," Garnet said, still touching

his arm. "We have Lincoln to worry about. And his friend Amanda."

"I appreciate your thoughtfulness," Amanda told them. "And I'd be pleased to go back into town with you."

She found herself fighting tears. She had been expecting more cruelty, and they had come to offer kindness. For some reason, she felt this heartfelt offer on their part—as citizens of Median and Lincoln's in-laws—was her first major victory in Mississippi.

The four crates took up more than half of the corrugated tin shack where Mr. Wembly lived with his adult daughter, Polly, who was not quite right in the head. When Amanda realized that, she felt very close to the Wemblys, however little she really knew them. The pretty, shapely blonde oohed and ahed over the crates as Chad pried off creaky lids with a rusted metal crowbar.

With Garnet and Chad holding up their boys, everyone peered at the wonders inside: Piles of worn and new clothes, shoes, books, sacks marked FLOUR, SUGAR, SALT, PEPPER, CIN-NAMON, NUTMEG, PENNY CANDY, Lincoln's tools, bolts of yard goods, sewing supplies, a tumble of walnuts that had come loose from a sack. One entire crate bulged with children's toys, some looking used, some nearly new. Cards, backgam-mon games, checkerboards, a chessboard. One crate was jammed with smoked hams wrapped individually in paper with potatoes around them for packing. And a thick pile of letters was marked in Eliza's precise writing: "For Amanda to use at her discretion for Lincoln Garner's trial." Those Amanda lifted out and clasped to her breast; she would scan them and give them to Tate immediately. Myriad other pack-ets of who-knows-what were stuck amid the bigger items.

"Oh, just look!" Polly squealed.

"Well, God bless us all!" Mr. Wembly declared with a grin, as he patted a ham as if to assure himself it was real.

"A whole emporium!" Chad murmured, while Garnet stood wide-eyed and speechless.

"Toys!" chorused Josh and James.

"A Christmas miracle from Lockwood, Ohio, to Median, Mississippi," Amanda concluded, wiping away tears. She was ecstatic with the gifts, for they gave her camaraderie with these people. But she knew from experience she could not expect all Median to react this way if she tried to hand this out as bounty from the North.

"Now I don't want any of you to tell people where all this came from until they are ready to hear it, even if they never know. Lincoln used to say 'a gift is only really a gift if the giver doesn't get the glory.' Besides," she went on, meeting each one's eyes in turn, "I don't need any of the Confederate faithful tossing good Yankee hams into the dirt on Main Street."

"Don't think folks facing another empty Christmas would do that," Mr. Wembly murmured.

"Then, Mr. and Mrs. Ellis, could I ask you to help me distribute these things tonight with the wheelbarrow?" Amanda asked. "I know it's not Christmas yet, but word will somehow get around Median faster than greased lightning if we don't move fast. I've learned that the few days I've been here."

At that, the adults looked sheepish, while Josh and James could not stand still. Amanda stooped down to fish out a piece of barley sugar candy for each boy, then gave Polly one too. "These are the last citizens of Median I am bribing to help me, so what do the rest of you say?"

"Yes, yes, of course!" Garnet cried.

"I may be nigh on seventy, but I can still lift, so can't I help too?" Mr. Wembly asked. "I know better'n most who lives where in this higgledy-piggledy confusion of a town we got now."

"But we will save the children's toys until Christmas Eve," Amanda added, though she gave the Ellis boys a top with its wraparound string. "Agreed? If—even if Lincoln's trial is over by then, even if we have to face the worst, the children of Median will still have a Christmas."

To celebrate their windfall, they sliced a small ham and ate on a table made from the crate lids while they planned their delivery route for the night. Amanda skimmed the letters and Chad took them to Tate. Mr. Wembly kept running out when trains came in. Since Lincoln's trial was slated to start tomorrow, visitors began to pour into town.

"A reporter from the *Vicksburg Times* and one from Jackson, too," Mr. Wembly told them when he returned this time, huffing and puffing like a locomotive himself. Then later,

"A fellow from the *New York Times,* no less, and he's going to put everything on the wire service to the whole blasted country."

Amanda stopped unpacking the crate of hams Garnet counted for her. Her stomach twisted tighter. "I'm terrified the government wretches will try to make Lincoln a symbol of the South rebelling against the Reconstructionists," she said. "It just infuriates me they would play with the life of an innocent man like that—just as they've been playing with all of yours!"

Everyone stared at her, Garnet with her mouth open in surprise. Did they think all the Yankees loved all things the government did? Amanda fumed silently.

Chad nodded and smiled at her; Garnet reached out to clasp her hand—another little victory, Amanda thought, however frightening the big defeat of losing Lincoln loomed.

Later that afternoon, Mr. Wembly came back in and announced, "The government prosecutor's here from Washington, one sour-looking fellow name of Orrin Stock. The southern circuit court judge they're bringing in to make it sound like it's fair and square—though he's a congressional appointee too—is named Benson Graff, and it's clear from the look of him he hasn't missed a meal in months."

Amanda recalled the cartoon she had seen in the Memphis newspaper about the gluttonous carpetbaggers running amok in Dixie, devouring the pathetically thin southerners. For the first time, she felt a bit defiantly southern herself.

"Are the three military men who will make up the jury here yet?" she asked Alvah Wembly. He nodded as he unwound his tattered red muffler. "All circling like vultures, Mrs. Wynne. But somehow, Tate Boyd with his fancy lawyer learning from Richmond will shoot them out of the sky, you bet your life he will."

"We're already betting Lincoln's life on it," Chad muttered.

Amidst the bounty of the gifts from her hometown to save Christmas, Amanda nodded solemnly. She has never felt more in need of a gift from heaven to save Lincoln.

The morning Lincoln's trial began, Amanda felt torn between hope and fear. How wonderful it had felt last night to deliver Lockwood's gifts to Lincoln's town, but how the prospects of the new day terrified her. How much stronger she felt to have Chad and Garnet's friendship, however tenuous, but she knew others still mistrusted, maybe detested her. And this day, when she had meant to look rested, calm, and assured should Lincoln glance her way, she felt exhausted, overwrought, and on edge.

She wore the same clothes as yesterday and had slept on the floor with the Ellises in the Wemblys' crowded, single room. Still, her dreams had been sweet, despite her learning too late that there was a ten o'clock curfew they had ignored, making their rounds from midnight until three. At least they hadn't been caught. And although they had a wheelbarrow instead of a camel, she had felt a bit like one of the Three Magi bringing their gifts to the sleeping city of Bethlehem. Even leaving food and clothes at the Boyd's house, her heart had been full. And she had saved out a ham for the Cresswells.

Amanda nodded and smiled at Lincoln as Sergeant Swaggart brought him from his cell to sit at one of the two makeshift tables at the front of the common room of government headquarters. He had evidently been watching for her from his jail cell, since he knew where to find her in the fourth row of the crowd. Still, she had to stand on tiptoe and peer around heads to see him. He wore a slightly too small, dark suit someone had obviously loaned him; Amanda was relieved that Tate had convinced him not to wear his Confederate uniform. She began to feel better about Tate being Lincoln's lawyer.

Since there was no courtroom in Median, Swaggart's desk—which Garnet whispered to Amanda had come from Lincoln's house before it burned—had been taken up front for the judge and two plank tables brought in for the defense and the prosecution. The recorder sat on a stool before a portable army camp table. Swaggart stood in full military dress next to the empty desk. The three-man jury entered and sat in chairs, front right. A single witness chair was center front, nearly under the American flag. A crude rail fence kept the observers back. In such crowded quarters, there were no seats for the crowd, not that Median had any to offer. Newspapermen, townspeople, and soldiers stood cheek by jowl.

Dr. Fisher, the military doctor from Ohio who had set Josh Ellis's arm, smiled and tipped his hat to Amanda. Armed soldiers lined the periphery of the room.

Only one thing pleased Amanda in these surroundings: she was close enough to people to hear snatches of whispers about "ham, potatoes . . . clothes . . . no idea . . . shoes for Jeb . . . thread and needles for the calico . . . but who?" Then it annoyed her to overhear, "Surely not extras from the distribution center . . . from Hardtack Timmons? No Christmas in Reconstruction. Maybe from Vicksburg . . . brought by the newspaper man? Ask Wembly . . ."

Then she panicked to catch from someone's stage whisper, "If it's bribes to accept their cockeyed verdict on Lincoln, I'll shove it all down their damned Yank throats rights in the middle of this sham of a trial!"

Perhaps, she thought, she should let people know where the bounty came from, but obviously not now. She stood, with Garnet on her right and Dr. Fisher on her left; she scanned the crowd for Caroline or even Jesse, but saw neither. How could they stay away, with Tate and Jess here fighting for Lincoln's life?

"All rise!" Swaggart bellowed, serving as bailiff as well as jailer. Someone behind Amanda snickered, but the few who were seated stood. Colonel McKitrick rose to his feet next to the stern-looking prosecuting attorney, Orrin Stock; Jess Boyd grabbed his crutches to stand with Tate and Lincoln. The corpulent Judge Graff entered up the center aisle and scraped back his chair to sit at the desk.

"Circuit Judge for the Fourth Military District, United States of American, Benson H. Graff, presiding," Swaggart shouted. "Court is now in session. You may be seated."

Although Amanda tried to remain confident, it took only the opening statements to make her knees go weak and her stomach roil. Orrin Stock proved to be a master of rhetoric. He adroitly hammered home Lincoln's being the mouthpiece of censure of the Reconstruction leaders like Barr . . . Lincoln's being the instigator of a public altercation with Barr. Forcefully gesturing, Stock stressed that the murder site was part of the multiple motive.

"And we will prove, gentlemen of the jury, that in the dark of night and the dark of his murderous heart, former Confederate Major Lincoln Garner did with dire intent and

malice aforethought willfully lure to the site of his property
and beat Justin Barr with his fists and pieces of wood. Finally, he took the life of this friend of government, this congressional appointee, this political patriarch of the plan to
bind our nation's war wounds. Battles were over and lost for
Major Garner and his ilk, but he still went on with the
slaughter! And then, knowing his heinous deed would be
dragged out into the broad light of justice, he fled the town,
the state, the still rebellious South!"

Townspeople murmured as Stock took his seat; some hissed.
Judge Graff whispered to Swaggart, who announced—looking
none too happy about it—"The presiding judge has the right to
clear this court of spectators unless there is silence and respect
at all times!"

Amanda held her breath as Tate delivered his opening remarks. "This, gentlemen of the jury, should be a case of simple assault and—battery at most, not a capital murder case,"
he began.

He paced too much; his voice seemed either too quiet or
too strident. His delivery was jerky as he stressed that the
defendant admitted his difference of opinion with the victim,
his dislike for him, even the fact that he lost his temper and
hit him because he felt he was deriding the burned home he
had shared with his dead wife and child. The accused would
testify himself what really happened that night, including
that Justin Barr made inciting comments about the defendant's wife. And since Lincoln Blake admitted he struck
Justin Barr and knocked him down before he stalked off, the
murderer could be a man or woman, weak or strong, since
Barr was in a diminished state to defend himself.

"But, I repeat," Tate said, "Lincoln Blake did—not murder the deceased. The defendant's giving himself up to the
justice system and the fact many others had—motive and opportunity after the accused left the site will—prove that Lincoln Blake did not kill Justin Barr any more than he
had—killed anyone else during the war. I point out the
first of many erroneous assumptions the prosecution is making and, no doubt, shall make: Lincoln Blake did not—
'slaughter' anyone, during the war or after."

As if silently urging Tate on, Amanda pressed her
clenched hands between her breasts. When he made a strong
point, she found herself leaning forward, waiting for him to

complete a thought, hoping it did not sound as if he were hesitant or fabricating Lincoln's defense as it occurred to him.

"As Lincoln Blake served with—distinction in the Engineering Corps," Tate went on, "he was first and foremost a builder, not a—destroyer. Before the war, during the war, he built battlements and bridges. After the war, up—north in Ohio and south in Savannah, he continued to build, not tear down. We have numerous witnessed character references that show he is trusted and admired even by northerners—though, obviously, not the ones running—this trial."

"Your honor," Orrin Stock interrupted, "I am loathe to object to this man's mere opening statement, but his comments are highly prejudicial."

"Agreed. The jury members will disregard that slight to the court. Defense council is cautioned against a repeat of same."

"We will prove," Tate continued, looking a bit more rattled, "beyond a shadow of a doubt that—this man did not kill Justin Barr. And we trust that this honorable citizen of Median, Mississippi and the United States of America will be able to receive a—fair trial here and be judged as an individual, and not as a symbol of the beaten but still—proud South."

The prosecution began to call its witnesses. The young soldier who had found the body the morning after the murder testified. To Amanda's surprise, Dr. Fisher was the next witness, for he had examined the body and found death was caused by a crushing blow to the head with a rock, although the deceased, aged forty-six years and in quite robust health, had also sustained several bruising blows to the face, head, and shoulders. Because of the state of rigor mortis on the body, Dr. Fisher judged that death had occurred between nine and midnight the previous evening.

Amanda berated herself for not thinking to speak to Dr. Fisher about any of this; she had gone out to the murder site once after she'd been there with young Jesse, but after all this time had seen nothing amiss. If only she could have done a thorough investigation of her own without upsetting people more than she already had. But once she came to know people as individuals here, where so many had hated

Barr, it became more difficult, not easier, to discover who might have committed the murder.

Next, two other soldiers, then General Timmons himself testified they had examined the murder site and found splintered, bloodied wood on the scene, wood that had once been carefully shaped and sanded—and the defendant was known to be skilled in woodworking. Amanda was annoyed that Tate did not claim hearsay, but she supposed they would just have dragged someone else up to establish that, even if Lincoln's workshop had been burned months before the murder.

After the dinner break, General Timmons, sporting rows of brass awards and regalia on his ornate uniform, continued his testimony to recount how the defendant was a "community rabble-rouser when we were trying to keep things peaceful here so we could begin to rebuild Median the way it should be done."

With each witness, Tate managed his own counter-examination and rebutted some of the most damning things, but only, it seemed, by throwing a slightly better light—the southern viewpoint—on the accusations. Amanda realized that nothing had really been refuted or thrown out.

A sinking feeling in her stomach dragged her down. She began to feel light-headed as well as heavyhearted as she studied the judge's reactions, the stony faces of the jury. Had they already made up their minds? If so, Lincoln might be doomed. Staring at the back of his dark head, she tried to send him her love. He sat square-shouldered and erect, listening intently, jotting down notes that he passed to Tate at times. But she was so afraid for him.

When court was adjourned for the day, Swaggart put Lincoln back in his cell before she could even call out a word to him. As the spectators were herded out by the tightening noose of soldiers, she had to jump up several times just to see back over the heads of people to catch a glimpse of him.

Outside, she saw Jesse standing across the street and lifted a hand to him. He smiled and waved back, but did not run over. Evidently he had orders to wait for his father and uncle but not to talk to her. Chad and Garnet joined her.

"I don't think things went that well," Garnet said with a sigh.

"I don't either," Amanda admitted, no matter how optimistic she wanted to be. "But it often feels that way when the prosecution presents its case. When they rest, our side gets its opportunity."

"I'm sure," Chad said, "putting Lincoln on the stand will eventually turn the tide, if too much damage has not already been done. And the fact he will testify that Barr made statements slandering Melanie, or some such. With God as my witness, I still could kill Barr myself if I had him here!"

"Please, Chad," Garnet pleaded, "that won't help now. Besides, there's something we wanted to tell you, Mrs. Wynne." She linked her arm companionably through Amanda's to pull her away from Chad. "I'm afraid your instincts about secrets being hard to keep in Median were correct. Elvira Gwin happened to see who delivered things outside her door last night, and she was telling people about it during the dinner break. Poor Mr. Wembly wanted to cover up for you, but his Polly blurted it out."

"Oh, no! Are they going to throw everything back at us?"

She was surprised to see Garnet smile. "Well, in a way. Come along, as we have something to show you."

Garnet and Chad escorted Amanda to the house where a young mother named Sarah Pickens was caring for the Ellis boys with her own children. Outside of the log lean-to, Amanda saw five little ones squealing and clapping over the top she'd given the boys.

"Much obliged you brought her by, Garnet," Sarah said, after introductions. Amanda still felt tense; she was certain Sarah Pickens was one of the women who had hissed "hussy!" at her a few days ago.

"I was just wond'rin' if you'd do a favor for me, Miz Wynne," Sarah asked her. "My Silas signed up for a meetin' with Lincoln Garner tomorrow, and he can't keep the appointment. We were hopin' you all could fill in for us. And I know a couple other neighbors hopin' you'll cover their days too."

"Oh. Why, yes, of course."

"Good then, Silas would have asked you himself, but since he has the only decent axe in town, he had to go with the men as soon as court was over for the day. Up on Laurel Mountain above Sweet Springs, they went," she said as she jiggled a drooling baby on her hip. "They figured with Christmas about nine days away, best cut us a town Christmas tree, like we did a couple of years before the war."

"Oh, really?" Amanda asked.

"Sure," Sarah said with a nod, shoving loose hair back under her battered-looking bonnet. When her two-year-old toddled up to cling to her skirts and cry, she gave Amanda her baby to hold. "See, Miz Wynne, some gifts come last night, like they was from Santa Claus or fell straight out of the clear blue sky and got us in the holiday mood, and—" she lowered her voice here—"we made old man Wembly admit there might be a toy or two for the little ones come Christmas Eve. 'Course that Boyd boy said something about if there's magic, it might of come out of Miz Amanda Wynne's traveling trunk."

"Did he? I'd like to think Jesse would believe in the spirit of Christmas once again," Amanda said, jiggling the baby as she had seen his mother do.

"Besides," Chad added, "some of us thought it might show the outsiders here for the trial that Median is not a beaten town. We're ready to pull together to rebuild, if we can just get Lincoln back to lead us. A tree and such might put outsiders in a more kindly mood than they look like in that courtroom right now."

"That would take a miracle!" Garnet muttered.

Despite how things had gone in court today, Amanda felt immensely better. These people were including her in their plans; she was no longer part of "the outsiders."

When eight men carried a big cut juniper tree into town and erected it on the edge of what had once been the town square, she could sense the new spirit in the air. People were not going to let this latest invasion of Median stop them from reclaiming the town—and Lincoln—as their own.

People introduced themselves to Amanda for the first time, even though she recognized many previously taut or taunting faces. She was invited to church next Sunday—with Alvah Wembly preaching—in the grove near Sweet Springs, weather willing. Tom Heston and his wife, Letitia—Tom had been the antebellum mayor—insisted she join them for a ham and potatoes supper, "not a ham quite like we used to have basted with cane sugar, but mighty fine." They ate on a plank table that then became the front door of their tiny, drafty place made from an old stone fence mortared with mud.

Amanda was exhausted but kept going on the sheer thrill of being accepted by Lincoln's friends. By a lit candle—"the last one left the mice haven't nibbled," Letitia Heston said— Amanda helped women thread red crabapples for decorations on the town tree. By someone's lantern burning precious kerosene, they draped its branches with swags of crimson, and Silas Pickens put a tin-plate star on top by climbing on Chad's shoulders. The blue-green juniper berries smelled spicy in the crisp night air.

People were mostly silent, as if awed by what they had done working together; no one sang carols as they might have back in Ohio, but Amanda was more deeply touched than if she had been home. These happenings from the heart were much better than any long-rehearsed Peace on Earth pageant back in Lockwood! And just think how thrilled Lincoln would be to see all this when he stepped out the front door of government headquarters a free man.

By this time, several soldiers, including Sergeant Swaggart, had come out to stare at the tree-trimming scene; even General Timmons, coming back from somewhere, put in a brief appearance with Judge Graff.

That brought Amanda's soaring spirits back to earth with a thud. It looked like all Lincoln's enemies were in collusion, however much this evening's happenings had meant to her. For what would it profit her if she gained the whole town, but lost Lincoln?

The next two days, that thought seemed prophetic. Events in town went better; Lincoln's trial, worse. Someone had draped cedar and holly swags outside of the post office and the government headquarters, though not the hated distribution center. People Amanda had never met came up to her at odd times—for she was staying with the Wemblys to be closer in town now—to give her tiny treasures they had been hoarding, with encouragement to use them for some Christmas baking: citron so old it was almost petrified, walnuts, even pecans, a stone jar of cane syrup, raisins, a crock of honey.

Fortunately, Amanda had offers of three ovens in old chimneys in town, because she was not about to ask to use Caroline's, the only woman in town now apparently not speaking to her. But since the trial began, Amanda had baked only three pecan pies, using Garnet's recipe. Her joy of baking for the holidays was held captive by the downward spiral of the proceedings. All her energies seemed sucked in by the trial; for the first time in her life, she could not lose herself in the creativity of baking, even for others.

She lived for her brief visits with Lincoln bequeathed to her by townspeople. When someone gave her some mistletoe—at the church service, no less—to decorate "some sort of a cake," she put it in her reticule to take to him on her next visit. Somehow, she had to boost his outlook. He too was pleased about the town's resiliency, but melancholy about the way his trial was going.

"I told you she'd be back to baking!" Sergeant Swaggart yelled to Lincoln as he escorted Amanda toward his cell across the now empty courtroom. It was Sunday afternoon, and the trial might well be over tomorrow or at least by Tuesday, Lincoln thought. These precious visits from Amanda, his time with her—everything—might be over then too.

"I'm afraid I only brought one pie, Sergeant Swaggart," Lincoln heard her tell the man, who looked about as eager to see her as he himself felt. "And since you need to taste it, you and Lincoln can share this one. I remember, Lincoln, you told me once—on the Fourth of July, I think it was—that my caramel pie was good, but you loved southern pecan better."

"Oh, I wouldn't take his favorite pie," Swaggart said as he unlocked the cell door, though Lincoln had thought for one moment he would say "his last pie." "And, whatever happens, Major," he continued, "just wanted you to know—no hard feelings, least on my part. And if it was up to me, I'd give your desk back too."

"When Lincoln is freed," Amanda put in, "perhaps you can do just that."

But when the cell door clanged closed and Swaggart walked away, Lincoln saw Amanda's bright facade shatter. Her full lower lip trembled; she could not meet his eyes and hers filled with tears.

"Here, Garnet's recipe," she told him, extending the pie. He took it, put it down on his cot, and, despite Swaggart nearby, reached for her.

She came against him with a little moan and clamped her arms around his waist. Her soft body fit against his angular one perfectly, he thought; how sweet her breasts, hips, and thighs, even through the barrier of the skirts and corset. He lowered his mouth to take hers, which she gave willingly, then with wild abandon. They knocked her bonnet back, tumbling some curls loose; they ignored the sound of Swaggart's feet at he walked away instead of toward them to stop them.

When they finally came up for air, both breathing hard, they leaned in the corner of the walls, holding tight. "I brought you some mistletoe, but I guess we don't need it," she said, with a half laugh, half sob.

"Amanda of the gracious gifts," he said, gently pushing a stray curl behind her ear, then pulling it loose again to smell it, to taste its tip in his mouth. "I'd like to give you the world for this Christmas, Amanda Lockwood Wynne, but I may not even have myself to offer soon."

"Don't say that. And you're all I want. But you testify tomorrow, don't you? As Chad says, that will turn the tide."

"Yes, tomorrow about mid-morning. Tate and I have worked hard on it. I'm hoping that his broken delivery, which is in such sharp contrast to Stock's glibness, will work for us, not against us."

"Yes, yes, it could."

"Oh, my Amanda," he said and pulled her to him again so the side of her face melded with his throat and his chin cradled her forehead. "If I can just walk free again, I'm going to take you up to show you the beauty of the hills outside of town. One thing I didn't have time to do before I surrendered myself was go up to see if my father's old hunting cabin still stands. It was a bit ramshackle when I was here two years ago—imagine a place that didn't burn. And that's where the sawmill I'm going build here in town can begin to cut wood to make planks, because I inherited about forty acres up there with the cabin and I sent money to Jackson for those taxes. Amanda, there's so much rebuilding and repair to do here."

"And I wasn't going to tell you until Christmas, but your woodworking tools came with the crates from Lockwood."

"*My* tools?"

"The ones you used up north. I will not have them rusting

away in that old work shed when you are going to need them here."

"Good," he said, his eyes misting as he hugged her hard. "Good. I swear, as soon as I get out of here, I will put them to use repairing that cabin for us."

"It sounds wonderful. The hills look beautiful from here, so green and fresh—and free."

"Yes. I've been thinking about being free, how it really feels. Sarah used to scold me for not understanding what she'd been through in slavery and what it meant to be free. Tell her, when you see her—her and Ben—I understand better now, will you?"

"Yes," she said, her lips moving against his throat where she was pressed to him, "but you can just tell her yourse—"

"And I want you to give Eliza and Rufus my very best wishes upon the great occasion of their wedding," he went on. A wedding. He dared not think about that now.

He had been doing so much thinking lately about leaving no inheritance to anyone here—not even Garnet's boys, beyond those forty acres, the little cabin, and buried coins. He had once started to built a legacy and a dynasty, but all that was gone now, unless he could start over with Amanda. Even the structures he'd designed and built here had been destroyed. But he had repaired and built a few things in Lockwood: Amanda's porch pillars, Mandy's sled, stalls in the livery stables uptown, other odd jobs.

And more important, he was sure, as Tate had tried to imply in his opening court statement, that he had tried to build bridges to people. As he had lost some of his confidence lately that the trial would go his way, he had cherished that knowledge. After Amanda had rescued him up north, he had forged ties to family and to friends like Matt, Sarah, Mandy, Eliza, Rufus, Pru and Ned, renewed bonds with Hilt Hamilton, and here at home with Chad, Garnet, Jess and Tate—that was what would last, what really mattered on the road of life. No matter what befell him, he had given people gifts of time and himself and his love. That was his real legacy to them. But what about Amanda? For she had become much more than friend or even family.

"Lincoln, don't tell me all these messages for others as if you're saying farewell," she protested, pulling back in his embrace to look up in his face. "They cannot *prove* that you killed that man. Even if you had motive and opportunity, so did many others!"

"But many others didn't tell Barr and Timmons publicly that their precious so-called Reconstruction was not going to work, not with an occupying army sitting here!"

"Sh. Swaggart."

"I know. I didn't mean to take our time with all this. I just wanted you to promise you would tell Lockwood people that I cared for them. And to tell you how much I love you. I hope to see this through to tell you myself the way I really want to—to show you—like this and more. But, Amanda, if anything happens to me, I just want you to know that I take the memories of you with me. Amanda coming out to the work shed in Lockwood, Amanda seducing me with Christmas—"

"Seducing? Lincoln Garner!"

"Amanda the day we cut down the Christmas tree near the canal, Amanda shaving my beard and feeding me those little meringue things . . ."

"Angel Gifts. Lincoln, I too look back and yet I can't bear to now. As Eliza says, we've got to look ahead."

"Yes. Yes, we will . . ."

He kissed her again. She seemed to unfurl like a flower for him, her lips letting his tongue in, her eyes opening to watch him, her ripe body seeming to curve against his again. He cherished and savored this, but it pained him too. It was what he might never have from her again and yet wanted so desperately he could have ripped down these bars and carried her off into the freedom of the hills . . .

Voices permeated his thoughts, men's voices. He set her slightly back. Swaggart, yes but another too: the prosecuting attorney's aide, Colonel McKitrick.

"I saw Mrs. Wynne come in," McKitrick was telling Swaggart at the front door. Bless the big brute, Lincoln thought, for staying across the room, looking out the single window when he and Amanda were together today.

"It's been a while, over the half hour," McKitrick said, "so I thought she'd be going."

"Guess the half hour limit just slipped me by," Swaggart told him. "You need to see her?"

"Yes, I have some good news for her."

"Good news?" Amanda said, seeming to emerge from her

dazed expression. "Lincoln, maybe it's something about you!" She gripped the bars as the men came over and Lincoln stood beside her, not touching her now.

"Sorry, ma'am, nothing about the trial," the colonel said, looking from one to the other. "Mrs. Wynne, I told you I used to work in the pension office in Washington, you may recall. When you told me your deceased husband's plight—when she was giving a deposition for you, Major Garner—I took a few extra notes. Then I wrote it up and telegraphed someone I still know there. Anyhow, to make a long story short, the national pension office has cleared the name of—" he glanced down at the paper in his hand, " 'Matthew Wynne of Lockwood, Ohio and does hereby grant to Amanda Lockwood Wynne as his widow and sole survivor seventeen dollars a month for the remainder of her natural life.' And it's retroactive from the date he was discharged, so there will be a sum of—ah, some one thousand thirty seven dollars forthcoming in the first payment."

Lincoln saw her just stare at the paper that Colonel McKitrick extended to her through the bars while Swaggart unlocked the door. Then she took it, held it to her.

"Oh, Lincoln, Matt's name cleared! Matt's name cleared and yours will be too, I just know it!"

She hugged him, hugged the blushing Swaggart, hugged Colonel McKitrick. She hugged Lincoln again, and they read through the letter together.

"I'm so happy for you, Amanda—for Matt too, even though he's gone," he told her. "And the money will help you keep Lockwood House."

"I don't suppose Matt could have even understood this, but I wish he'd known! I'm going to telegraph Eliza first thing tomorrow. It's going to be all over the headlines of the *Lockwood Ledger* next week, you wait and see!"

"I hope to get to see it. It's cheered me mightily too. We won't be afraid tomorrow, as if this is a sign."

Fortunately, it was only after Amanda finally had to leave, and Swaggart stood with McKitrick in the front door, that Lincoln overheard another sign—a portent of doom.

"I believe him that her husband was a friend of his and everything between him and Mrs. Wynne was on the up and up," Swaggart said in his best attempt at whispering. "But I don't think any of the truth he's told 'bout anything's gonna save him, do you, Colonel?"

Whatever McKitrick answered didn't matter, Lincoln thought as he sank onto his cot and the pie slid toward him. He put it on the floor and flopped flat on his back with the heels of his hands pressed over his eyes. He did not cry, but he wanted to. Amanda had been the recipient of some real blessings lately, but he didn't think he could ever be again. Her taking him in and healing him and loving him had been a blessing so big, he was not due any more in this life, so he'd best cling to memories and not hopes now.

Before court the next morning, Amanda sent her telegram to Eliza and Sarah to tell them about Matt's name being cleared and the pension. Then as she began to walk toward the Cresswells, who had come into town for the day, and Chad and Garnet, who were all waiting for her, the telegrapher called her back.

"Coincidence, ma'am, but a message is coming in for you right now! It's kinda like they passed on the wires."

"Why don't the four of you go on without me, but just save me a space?" Amanda called to them to send them ahead.

The message was, ironically, from Eliza, wishing Lincoln good luck from his friends in Ohio, the citizens of Lockwood. Amanda had a good notion to read it right out in court so Orrin Stock could object to her as he had so many times to Tate. The government attorney had turned out to be a thespian as well as an orator. His dramatic sweeping gestures, so in contrast to Tate's reserved nature, actually reminded her of the way Eliza had acted out those endless Shakespeare quotes playing charades.

How dear Eliza was to send this telegraphed message of hope. She did miss her, miss all of them. But while Lincoln needed her here, she had no intention of going home. And if Lincoln was here, however much Lockwood might always be her hometown, she wasn't just sure it would really be her home anymore. And this huge sum of money she had coming this month—only part of it would go to Lockwood House. She was thinking about investing in a sawmill here in Median.

Just as she was going into court, she glimpsed young

Jesse, watching her from across the street as he walked away from his house. She waved to him and he waved back with both hands, but he kept going. It was a good thing, Amanda thought, he wasn't headed home, for his mother would have a fit. Amanda didn't know what he'd been doing, but both hands were filthy. He would be forced to wash them before his mother would even let him in the house, poor boy.

And then Amanda stopped dead in her tracks. In her mind's eye she saw Eliza, acting out that scene from Shakespeare's tragedy *Macbeth* where Lady Macbeth washes her hands again and again and again. What was the quote, though? "What, will these hands never be clean? Here's the smell of the blood still."

She gasped. Though she might never prove it, she knew who had really killed Justin Barr!

Turning away from people still streaming in for the trial, she lifted her skirt hem and tore across the street toward the thicket of army tents.

Chapter
Sixteen

❄

Special Occasion Cake

Prepare pan (approx. 8″ x 12″ size) by greasing and flouring well.

Boil together in a saucepan for 5 minutes, 2 cups water, 2 cups brown sugar, 1 pound seedless raisins, 1 teaspoon salt, 2 tablespoons shortening, 1 teaspoon cinnamon, 1 teaspoon allspice, 1 cup crushed nuts. Cool mixture.

Add 2 cups flour, 1 teaspoon soda sifted together.

Bake at 375 degrees for 40 to 50 minutes. Test with toothpick to see if it comes out clean.

Ice with brown sugar icing.

Old-fashioned Brown Sugar Icing*

Boil in saucepan, 2 cups brown sugar (or 1 cup brown, 1 cup white sugar), ½ cup cream or canned milk, 1 tablespoon butter.

Stir constantly over low heat for 2 minutes from low boiling point.

Remove mixture from heat, place pan on cold dishrag and beat until ready to spread.

*This is a challenging icing to make because it can go "rock hard" if overboiled. It is best to remove it soft after the boiling point and let it thicken by being stirred. Better put on cake too soft rather than like taffy or butter brickle!

Amanda ran past army tents toward the center of camp where she had located Dr. Fisher the day Josh Ellis broke his arm. She had not seen the doctor in court after that first day he testified; she hoped he had not gone this morning either, even though the fact that Lincoln was to testify in an hour or so had drawn even more people. Several soldiers stopped to stare at her or called out; she did not stop to explain but hurried on.

The flaps to the medical tent were closed, so he must not be here. In dismay, she knocked on the tent pole. "Dr. Fisher! Dr. Fisher!"

To her relief, he whipped back the flap. He was bleary-eyed, unshaven, and coatless. "Mrs. Wynne. Has there been a problem at the trial?"

"Only that they want to hang the wrong person. Doctor, may I ask you a question about something that happened several years ago?"

"I've testified everything I know about the murder."

"I wanted to ask you whether Mrs. Caroline Boyd came to you for fever medicine for her son, Jesse. It would have been just after the war ended, but before her husband returned."

"No. I'm telling you, Mrs. Wynne, until you had the good sense to come for me when that other boy broke his arm, the southerners—point of honor—never asked me for a thing, even when their own were ill. A boy with a fever, though— you know, Justin Barr himself asked me for quinine tonic and paregoric pills once, and said something about a sick boy. It was during one of those spotty cholera outbreaks when I had sick soldiers to tend to. There is probably no connection."

"There is!" Amanda declared. "Excuse me, doctor, and thank you again."

He called after her, but she did not turn back. She knew enough now to confront Caroline Boyd, though several pieces of the puzzle still did not fit. And she still pitied the woman, because it must have broken her to ask Justin Barr for help—and then, probably, to pay his lecherous price for that medicine for her son.

Amanda reconsidered the shreds of evidence that must surely prove her theory: Justin Barr had an eye for the ladies, and Caroline had been attractive; a blue-coated soldier, probably some "errand boy," like Swaggart had said, had sat with the delirious Jesse while Caroline slipped out to meet Barr; after Lincoln had hit Barr, he was in a weakened condition so that even a woman—almost anyone—could have killed him. Anyone who could have lifted a rock, as Tate had put it. Tate! Even if Amanda could get Caroline to confess, would Tate allow his sister-in-law he so admired to step forward to save Lincoln?

She slowed her steps to catch her breath as she approached the sunken Boyd house. No wonder Caroline had hated and avoided soldiers after being shamed, after realizing her husband could find out she had gone to Barr, perhaps even broken her marriage vows to him. So Caroline had killed him to silence him—or for vengeance. Amanda moved slowly to the open door of the cellar; she was surprised to see smoke rising from the chimney at this time in the morning when Caroline never built a fire until evening. Amanda's shadow fell across the dirt floor as she leaned down to look in the door.

No Caroline at the table or sweeping for once. Then she saw her bent behind the table, feeding the hearth fire—with pages she was noisily ripping from her diary. Evidence? Amanda had to seize those remaining pages.

"Hello, Caroline," she called and started down the steps.

"Oh, you startled me. The trial can't be over already."

"No. Lincoln's going to testify about mid-morning today."

"So Jess and Tate said. Surely they will believe him then. That will clear his name."

"And if it doesn't?"

"It has to."

"There are big surprises in life, Caroline. For example, I'm shocked to see you burning that diary, when you told me it and your son got you through the hard times."

Amanda came down the steps and slowly walked closer around the table. She saw how few pages were left. "The hard times," Amanda went on, "like when Jesse had a fever, and you did what you had to in order to get him help."

Caroline's face cracked into a frown; her eyes darted. "I don't know what you mean. Oh, he must have told you of those nightmares he had—when he was delirious once."

"I'm sure it's all been a nightmare, especially to have to deal with Justin Barr when he offered help."

Caroline tossed the rest of the pages on the fire. Amanda scrambled to save them with feet and fingers. Caroline backed away; when Amanda stood with several singed pages, she thought the woman would toss plates at her, for she bent to the place she kept them. At least, if it came to a struggle, Amanda thought, surely she was stronger and could best her. But how she wished she had asked someone else to come! Especially when Caroline stood with not plates but with a tiny derringer pistol in her hand.

Amanda gasped and held up both palms, as if that could ward off a bullet. "Caroline, put that gun down. People will understand how it was."

"Will they? The women of this town I can't look in the eye? Tate? My boy? Jesse never did when he guessed, and then beat it out of me. Oh, yes, are you surprised? Jesse was violent when he got back and kept falling down in front of the boy and me. He beat me real regular until Tate came to live with us and made those special runged crutches for him so he could get around. You and 'people' don't know how it was, not at all! Now put the rest of those pages in the fire!"

Amanda pretended to do as she said, trying to keep them to the hearth just beyond the flames. She kept talking low to Caroline. "You know, Dr. Fisher is a nice man. He would have helped you nurse Jesse. You didn't need Justin Barr—"

"Barr told me I did. Otherwise, the tonic was only for soldiers. He said some others wanted to requisition this house, but he'd stop them if I—cooperated. After Sherman, Barr was the worst—the very worst—and I let him ... let him ..."

Amanda shuffled slowly closer until Caroline thrust the gun out stiff-armed, held with both hands. She shook visibly; the gun trembled. "I will shoot you! I will!"

"Caroline, Dr. Fisher knows I'm here," she lied, wishing it were true, "and he's going to testify that Justin Barr asked him for medicine when Jesse was ill. Caroline, please don't let Lincoln suffer for what you've done ..."

"But I didn't kill Barr! I was only glad when someone else did—probably Lincoln! If you make me tell my shame in court before the whole town, it will still come back to Lincoln. I will say I told him and he did it for me. Yes, if Dr. Fisher says anything, I'll tell them that."

Both women jumped at a voice, followed by a knock on the open door. To Amanda's chagrin, Caroline hid the gun by stepping closer and thrusting the short barrel hard against her ribs. For one moment she pictured a shot going through her there, entering her heart. They saw a soldier at the door; he stooped down to look in, but Amanda knew better than to shout for help.

"You're called to court as a witness, right now, ma'am."

"Me?" Amanda said, ready to ask him to escort her. Her lengthy deposition and the letters from Lockwood had been entered as defense exhibits and read by the jury, so neither side had planned to call her. But now she hoped ...

"No, ma'am. I mean Mrs. Boyd here, called by the defendant's lawyer."

"What?" Caroline cried, leaning against Amanda, pressing the gun in harder. "By Tate? That can't be! Even if the doctor testified, Tate wouldn't call me!"

"Orders to fetch you, ma'am. That's all I know."

Amanda froze as she heard and felt Caroline cock the pistol against her. Surely, she would not shoot anyone with a soldier here. But she was shaking so hard, who knew the thing would not just go off? Amanda realized she must be desperate too, but she dared not struggle with the woman right now. If she had killed before—and Amanda still thought she might have murdered Barr—she could again.

"Thank you, sir," Amanda answered for Caroline. "I'll accompany her, and we'll be right with you!"

"I swear I will shoot you, Amanda," she whispered. "I'm

only going to the door of that courtroom to get Jess or Tate to excuse me from this. Tate can't have called me. He said nothing of the kind. Are you and this soldier in this deceit together?"

"Caroline, hardly. I—"

"I've never forgotten you're a Yank, an Ohioan, like Sherman. You looked down on me, tried to steal my son's affections. I will shoot you if you make one wrong move. Now, let's go slowly, and keep quiet with that man nearby!"

"You're shaking too hard to walk all the way with that thing cocked, Caroline. Put it down, and I'll go with you. You don't want your son to find out—"

"Walk! Now!" Caroline ordered, and so they did.

The soldier had gone a bit ahead, obviously impatient with their slow gait, for it seemed they linked arms and merely strolled. Amanda wished the man would come closer, inquire if they were all right. She thought about feigning a swoon, but she dared not. Her only hope was being rescued in court. Yet she could not believe either that Tate had really sent for Caroline.

The soldier made a path for them to enter the crowded courtroom. Heads swiveled; Jess Boyd came on his crutches toward them as fast as he could up the narrow center aisle, looking distraught.

"I was shocked," he said to Caroline, "when he sent for you."

"But why? Why?" she demanded, poking the gun like a knife against Amanda's ribs.

"He must have found out you knew something," he whispered, wide-eyed before Amanda's presence seemed to register with him. As he frowned at her, Amanda realized that perhaps Caroline was not the culprit. Perhaps someone else close to her, someone possessive, who had a volatile temper, however debilitated he looked, had murdered Justin Barr. But right now, above all else, she had to get away from this gun in her side.

At that moment Tate's voice rang out over the buzz of the crowd, calling Caroline Boyd to the stand as a defense witness. Heads turned toward Tate, including Caroline's and Amanda's. Jess jerked around. It was Tate's voice and yet louder, clearer, surer, without hesitation. Amanda's hopes lifted that he seemed more confident. Goose bumps glided up her arms and prickled the hair on the back of her neck as Judge Graff repeated Tate's words: "The defense calls Mrs. Caroline Boyd to the stand."

Caroline cried, "I can't . . . can't," and collapsed in Jess's arms. Amanda jumped away; the derringer dangled from Caroline's limp fingers. Amanda seized it before Jess could, then closed the hammer and shoved it in her reticule. She pushed down the aisle where her friends had held a place for her, meaning to tell them what had happened, to show them the gun. But when Tate spoke again, she stood on tiptoe, ignoring their questions. Her wide gaze caught Lincoln's equally surprised one.

"Your honor!" Jess Boyd, supporting Caroline in his arms, called out to interrupt Tate. "My wife has swooned. I request a delay to speak with the defense council."

"No need," Tate replied. "With your permission, your honor, my assistant, Mr. Boyd, may look to his wife until such time as she is quite recovered. We shall go at this another way then. The defense calls the defendant, Lincoln Garner, to the stand, as previously announced."

Amanda thrilled at the transformation in Tate's demeanor. Surely he had some new evidence, for he strode the front of the courtroom instead of walked it; he gestured broadly, not jerkily.

"I thought Lincoln would be ready for this," Garnet whispered to Amanda, squeezing her arm. "But he seems shaken. Look at how he's gazing so surprised at Tate."

Amanda could only nod as the questioning began to lay background for the night of the murder. Tate seemed totally in control; Lincoln fiercely intent, if a bit hesitant.

"So you do admit you were bitter toward Justin Barr before he began to taunt you that night on your property, Lincoln?"

Amanda leaned forward. At last Tate seemed to be using subtle techniques she remembered from Matt's triumphs in court, tactics she had previously assumed all lawyers were taught: admitting there was some motive, calling the defendant by a first name so the jury came to feel they knew him as a person, even as a friend.

"Everyone I talked to in Median was bitter toward Justin Barr," Lincoln answered, clearing his throat. "Yes, I was. And when he made several disparaging remarks about the women of our town, as well as joked about renaming Median 'Chimneyville,' I lost my temper and hit him twice with my fists."

"Did he go down, Lincoln?"

"He did. Though I am one of the few fortunate Confederates who was assigned to the Engineering Crops and never killed a northern soldier, I was younger and stronger than he and I knew how to fight."

Amanda breathed more easily. Lincoln too seemed to be taking Tate's cue and speaking with assurance. "You left him conscious?" Tate inquired.

"Absolutely. Cursing me, Median, even my dead wife, whom, thank God, he had never known. He was sprawled right in the ruins of her beloved flower beds at the time. If I were the one who had killed him, I would have done it then—but I did not."

"Yet you fled the next morning?"

"I did. When I heard Barr was dead, I knew who would be railroaded into a trial."

"As indeed you have been—"

"Objection, your honor!" Orrin Stock cut in.

"The terms means that the person being charged is put on a fast track to accusation and guilt, your honor!" Tate countered, staring Stock down until he sat again. "And since no other suspects were investigated—when the town is full of them, both southerners and army men—I'd call that railroading. Why, if the eighty-some citizens of Lockwood, Ohio, who have sent character references for their former enemy, Major Lincoln Garner, had known Justin Barr, they too would qualify for suspects even though they've never been in Median!"

"Objection!" Stock shouted again, but the rest of his words were drowned out by the eruption of applause.

"Order, order!" shouted the judge, banging his gavel again and again. Then Swaggart bellowed for order, too.

Amanda had seen that courtroom ploy before, the casting of clever, indirect aspersions on accusations by homely humor. She realized now that she had greatly misjudged Tate. He was only tentative until he was under pressure; she had known others like that, who would not apply their full talents or attack a task until the very last moment. And she had known a boy once in school who had stuttered terribly and dreaded rhetoric lessons until Eliza had encouraged him to talk about George Washington, a subject he knew and loved.

"But let me go on to the next point raised earlier by the prosecutor, Mr. Orrin Stock of our country's capital," Tate proceeded, hands behind his back, pacing a bit, looking sincere and thoughtful.

"Tate's really hitting his stride!" Chad whispered. "He hasn't hesitated once, and he's much more forceful! Maybe law school in Richmond taught him to save the best for last."

Amanda did not respond, for she was transfixed. Her heart thundered in her chest. She dared to cling to hope now, to believe that some sort of revelation could save Lincoln.

"And that point Mr. Stock raised earlier, Lincoln," Tate went on, "concerns the striking of Justin Barr with some shaped and sanded wood from your workshop—a workshop that had not existed for over a year on the night of the murder. Did you strike the man with any such piece or pieces wood, splintering it over him?"

"I did not."

"Do you have any explanation for that wood—ah, prosecution exhibit B, I believe it was," Tate said and walked to the jury table where the exhibits were laid out. "I believe the larger splinters of wood can be fitted together to make— something," Tate said and turned and pressed the three largest pieces together, then lifted them over his head to display them to the entire courtroom. No one so much as breathed. Amanda gaped in recognition of what he had partially assembled.

"So," Tate said, "a rocking chair rung, only shorter. I don't know if anyone else recognizes what this is, but I do, because I made it."

"Objection, unless this is a confession! And the defense counsel was not even in town when the murder occurred!" Stock bellowed.

Amanda could see that Lincoln now grasped where his lawyer was leading. He looked stunned, evidently to realize that Tate would implicate Jess, Tate's beloved brother, Lincoln's friend who had said he wanted to help clear him.

"True, I was not in town," Tate admitted, after Judge Graff overruled Stock's objection for the first time. "But I was back here briefly after the war before I returned for good, and made—I am sorry now to say—these rungs for ... Why, even Sergeant Swaggart here, even perhaps General Timmons, can tell us what this wood found at the murder scene is from."

"Objection! Swaggart and Timmons are not testifying."

But Swaggart said loudly anyway. "That's from the bottom of Jess Boyd's crutches. Never seen ones like that anywhere else. Why, I even remember when he fell and broke one crutch to bits and had to make another. So that means he was there that night and hit Barr with the original crutch and who knows what else!"

"Objection! We are trying Lincoln Garner here! Objection!"

Tate turned and stalked the center aisle, fire in his eyes. The crowd gasped and shifted slightly toward the side walls to give him room. "I am only analyzing your previously admitted evidence, counsel. Unless you wish to cross-examine this witness, I again call Caroline Boyd to the stand."

Suddenly, Amanda realized she had seen it all before. The rush of surprise witnesses, the reexamination of exhibits, the bravado, the building crescendo from the dynamic presence in the courtroom that was not evident in daily life. The transformation of an apparently ordinary local man who became the very epitome of justice in the crucible of special circumstances. The dedication to the defendant at any cost. It could not—*could not* be—but how much Tate reminded her of Matt right now!

"I call Caroline Boyd to the stand, to be following by testimony of Jess Boyd!" Tate said when Stock stayed silent for once.

"Can't find the Boyds, your honor!" came a soldier's voice from the back of the room. "They stepped out while he tended to her, but they ain't out here."

"Go to their home, search around, soldier!" Judge Graff commanded. "This court will take a fifteen-minute recess. The witness—I mean, the defendant—may stand down."

Amanda tried to fight her way through the crowd toward Tate, but he moved away to confer with the judge and the prosecutor. She had to tell him how fine he had been—how selfless to risk his own family to help save Lincoln. Trembling, she leaned on Garnet for support. Then, she caught Lincoln's gaze, which said as clearly as if he'd shouted to her across the crowded, buzzing courtroom: "Do you believe this turn of events?" Tears in her eyes, she shook her head at first, then forced a taut, trembling smile.

Just when Swaggart shouted to bring things back to order, the same soldier who had come to fetch Caroline ran back into the room, up the aisle past Amanda so she could see clearly that he waved in his hand singed pieces of paper, torn from a small book.

"Your honor, your honor!" he cried. "They're gone somewhere but they left a confession on their table, see, here!"

Judge Graff bent over the papers with Tate and Orrin Stock hovering at his desk. He summoned the three jurors while the courtroom hummed and seethed.

"In this signed, dated confession," Judge Graff finally announced, "Jess Boyd admits to following Justin Barr the night he was killed. He saw Lincoln Garner hit him twice and—'for the honor of those raped by the North'—as he puts it here—Mr. Boyd beat Justin Barr with one of his crutches and smashed his skull in with a rock. Sergeant, the jury has agreed that the murder charge against Lincoln Garner is now reduced to simple assault and battery. The prisoner will be sentenced tomorrow morning. And, for Pete's sake, someone send out a search party after the Boyds. With his leg, they can't go far! Are there any closing comments from either side?"

"None, your honor," Stock muttered, looking shell-shocked.

"Only," Tate said, "that I deeply regret that I had to implicate those I love—to save a man all Median loves, your honor."

Amanda saw Lincoln wipe tears from his eyes. She, too, biting her lower lip, began to cry silently. For she recalled that dream she had had of Matt, which had sent her to Median. She heard his promise to be with her here and recalled how she and Lincoln had wished more than once that Matt could defend him. Looking back over her shoulder as the courtroom was emptied, she let Garnet and Chad escort her out.

Caroline was found shortly after, returning to town with her son, who had been gathering wood in the hills. All she would say was that Jess had fled, she knew not where. She was put temporarily under detainment in her house, with a soldier at her door. A warrant was issued for Jess's arrest, the surrounding hills were searched with dogs, but no trace was found, despite the fact he would not go far or fast on crutches.

The sentencing of Major Lincoln Garner in court the next morning took just long enough for Judge Graff to pronounce the verdict: "A great travesty of justice had been committed against Lincoln Garner. This court completely exonerates him from any suspicion in the murder of Justin Barr. However, since the defendant did assault and batter the same, he is guilty of those deeds in the eye of the law. Seeing that he has already served three weeks' jail time, that sentence is reduced to one year's probation, during which, it is hoped, Lincoln Garner as architect and builder will help to renew Median. This court of the Fourth Military District is now adjourned."

Whoops and cheers shook the building. Swaggart smiled and slapped Lincoln on the back before Amanda, Chad, and Garnet could fight their way through to him. Lincoln lifted Amanda off her feet and hugged her. She wrapped her arms around his neck and held tight. Still holding her, he embraced Garnet, Chad, Tate, Alvah Wembly, everyone he could reach.

When finally the crowd began to disperse, they made their way out into the cold winter sun. Lincoln stopped in the doorway and looked around outside, while those still with him waited and nodded tearily at each other. He squeezed Amanda's hand and breathed deeply of the crisp December air and smiled to see the decorated Christmas tree Amanda had described to him. Only then did he seem to return to earth.

"Tate," he said, hurrying a few steps to catch his lawyer's arm as he started away. "How are Caroline and the boy?"

"She's closed them in the house, but you know, in the long run she may be better off without Jess. I'll take care of them, beginning with getting that soldier away from her door."

"Let me know if we can help. Tate, how did you discover it was Jess? It took such courage on your part to sacrifice him for me."

"But you were my client," he said. "Jess sacrificed himself when he—murdered that man, then used me to keep close to the evidence. He betrayed both of us, Lincoln. But the thing is," he said and shook his head, "I didn't know Barr coerced Caroline or that Jess had—murdered him. I didn't know it until it just came to me somehow standing in court, when I saw for the first time how that splintered wood fitted together. Suddenly, when I knew in my heart what had really happened, I somehow felt confident, felt I knew what to say."

"You were wonderful, Tate," Amanda said and hugged him.

Managing to look both proud and humble, Tate whispered, "I feel changed inside, deeply touched somehow—inspired. This victory has given me new confidence to go on to other challenges and trials. I was never sure before that I could be a success in court, but now I know I can do important, good things in my life." Still looking dazed, he turned and walked away.

"I actually hope they don't find Jess," Lincoln muttered as the others surrounded him again.

"Doubt if they will," Alvah Wembly whispered to them, as he stepped forward. "I gave him a boost up on a northbound train to an empty boxcar where two other fellows were already huddled up for their free ride. It's the depot master's job to chase such as them off, but it's almost Christmas. And I appreciate your help, Lincoln—you know what I mean."

"We'll rebuild the church as soon as we can, Alvah," Lincoln said as the old man squeezed Lincoln's arm, nodded, and walked away.

"Jess heading up north, riding the rails," Lincoln whispered to Amanda. "Poor bastard. I can only hope he finds someone to be kind to him at Christmas, just like that other hobo refugee from Median did."

Lincoln pulled Amanda off alone around the other side of the tall town Christmas tree. Garnet and Chad waited for them by the telegraph office. As people passed, they still spoke to Lincoln and Amanda, slapped his back, greeted her, and eventually went their own ways. Several soldiers saluted Lincoln as they dispersed from duties of guarding the assembled crowd.

When they stood alone, Lincoln cleared his throat and

said, "I'm still awed by Tate's transformation. Yesterday in court, I felt inspired too, as if someone were looking after me. Amazing!"

Their eyes met and held. A shared smile danced between them. Lincoln squeezed her hands in his.

"A miracle," she whispered. "At the very least, a Christmas blessing, and we shall take it for that."

"Amanda, I don't deserve any more blessings than knowing you has given me already, but will you marry me? I'll ask you later, if you'd like, properly, more romantically, but will you? We'll have to live here for a year—maybe more, build a life here, but if you want, we can visit Lockwood in the summers over the years—or for Christmas. Besides, I told you the folks here would come to love you. Will you marry me, Amanda?"

"Yes. Yes! I would have said yes in that wretched jail cell, even if we had to live in the Dry Tortugas!"

He threw back his head and shouted a laugh to the skies. They hugged and kissed, and then he set her back. "Today's the twenty-second," he said. "I have something to do, to prepare a place to take my bride for a week before we move back here. If you have no objection, Alvah Wembly—he's the closest thing we have to a pastor right now—can marry us on the twenty-fourth at Garnet and Chad's. They can stand up for us."

"That sounds perfect. But you mean you're leaving until then? I don't want us to be apart anymore. Can't I go with you?"

"I'm going to borrow Swaggart's horse and ride up to check our cabin in the hills. Amanda, it may need repairs, and it must be a mess."

"I can go and help!"

"And leave Garnet to plan everything? I was even hoping someone would bake us a wedding cake."

"Lincoln, it will be eternity until then. Are you sure you'll be all right?"

"I'll take Chad's gun. And there's no danger these days up on Laurel Mountain."

"Laurel Mountain . . . it sounds so far from Lockwood. But, if you're there, I wouldn't want to be anywhere else."

"We'll build a small home near town as soon as we can.

But, before the house I really want to build you someday, the sawmill will have to come first."

"After what everyone here has been through, love and co-operation come first!"

He laughed again and kissed her and spun her under the Christmas tree.

Lincoln arrived at Chad and Garnet's the morning of the wedding, riding Swaggart's horse he said he had "borrowed" for a week. "I asked him to the ceremony, Dr. Fisher, and Colonel McKitrick too," he told Amanda and Garnet as they bustled around him decorating the plank table with ropes of fragrant pine and holly. When no one protested that he'd asked the soldiers, he said, "Now, that's a first step toward real Reconstruction around here!"

"I just hope the little food we have will multiply like the Lord multiplied the loaves and the fish for the Jews," Garnet muttered with a shake of her head. "These two hams had better stretch!"

"They'd better, as I know the Lord wouldn't so much as multiply one ham to feed the Jews," Amanda put in with a smile. "But even if, as Lincoln says, we're fresh out of miracles, folks will understand."

"There is a surprise or two awaiting you on Laurel Mountain," Lincoln said, teasingly grabbing at her skirts. A ball of mistletoe hung over the door, and he kept steering her over there to kiss her under it. "Oh, by the way, I see it didn't take you long to telegraph the good news—all of it—to Lockwood. A telegram came to Mr. and Mrs. Lincoln Garner." He took it from his pocket and leaned over her shoulder as she read Sarah, Pru, and Eliza's best wishes for their marriage. He linked his hands around her waist and propped his chin on her shoulder as he nuzzled her temple and ear to make her giggle in delight.

Chad came in with the cake Amanda had mixed and baked in Doris Moorhead's chimney oven. She had left it for Doris to take out and frost. As Amanda admired how good it looked, she recalled how that devil Justin Barr had infuriated Lincoln by calling Median "Chimneyville." It might be that right now, but from it would rise a new town—with its own bakery shop someday—she was sure of it.

* * *

The afternoon of Christmas Eve, people turned out in such droves for the Garner–Wynne nuptials that there was almost "no room at the inn." How perfect, Amanda thought that their vows were spoken in a stable, for she felt angels—at least one—was looking down on them. A baby cried (Sarah Pickens' fussy infant) and plain and simple people came bearing gifts.

They were hardly gold and frankincense and myrrh but might as well have been: food to share with all; little, salvaged, hoarded treasures to help set up a household; and an heirloom quilt from Garnet, Chad, and Miss Maud. The Cresswells insisted Amanda accept their Dutch oven. Alvah Wembly described more than once the big woodworking table he had made for Lincoln out of the four crates that came from Lockwood. Lem Swaggart promised "his" desk and a chair to go with it for their new house when it was built. Tom and Letitia Heston produced a bottle of fine bourbon for the wedding toast, and Elvira Gwin brought a keg of applejack so old that a jolt of it made the partaker's hair stand on end.

Everyone Amanda hoped would be here was, except of course, Caroline and young Jesse. Tate was congratulated repeatedly for the fine job he did in court, and for his integrity and the boldness to expose the real criminal, even though they all still thought Barr deserved his comeuppance. During all this, officers Swaggart, Fisher, and McKitrick mingled with the southerners who had so long detested their very presence. But not this afternoon, for the ceremony spoke of love and union, of promises to keep for a lifetime.

And when Colonel McKitrick presented Amanda with a government check for one thousand and thirty-seven dollars, she presented it to Lincoln for the sawmill with a smile and tears.

"You selling shares in a sawmill?" Elias Cresswell asked. "What about those of us got a few coins hidden in bird nests or the outhouse? They good enough to invest in this new town we're gonna build?"

"We'll need every bit we can get, Elias," Lincoln told him.

"Who's gonna work with you?" Alvah Wembly asked Lincoln as the newlyweds strolled about, greeting their guests.

"Chad will be my partner, and Elias is going to help us put on the roof—after he cleans out his bird nests, et cetera," Lincoln said with a grin. "And when young Jesse Boyd gets a few more years on him, I'd hope to train him to work it too—if Caroline will allow it."

"I can't think she'd *ever* show her face now," Doris Moorhead said. Tate had downed enough applejack he looked instantly ready to scrap over the comment.

"Caroline Boyd," Amanda spoke up, putting a staying hand on Tate's arm, "went to war too, only one to save her child and the cellar that housed him. If she doesn't show her face, it's because she's been afraid to. But if you can take in a Yankee outsider like me—an abolitionist to boot—I'm sure she'll be forgiven and accepted here."

Several nodded. The awkward moment stretched out silent and tense. But Amanda heard Doris apologize to Tate as the bridal couple began to circulate among their guests again. Amanda especially liked Garnet's mother, Miss Maud, who, stiff-backed southern matriarch though she was, said, "I agree with you about Caroline, the poor thing. Always was a bit flighty. Spilled punch all over my peach silk gown at a dance here once." It was almost like having Aunt Louise back.

And Amanda had Aunt Louise with her in another way, for she wore the last of her own gowns she had brought to Median, a velvet rose-colored one with thick lace at the neck and sleeves. To think she had once thought it out of style, Amanda mused, fluffing the leg-o'-mutton sleeves. Everything in this ramshackle, makeshift town and wedding felt just right to her, absolutely elegant, as if it had leapt full-blown from the pages of the latest *Godey's*.

After serving the wedding cake—which had to be cut into tiny pieces to feed everyone—they even had some waltzing to Christmas carols sung off-key, no less. And then, an hour before dusk, the bridal pair said their farewells, so as to make it up to the cabin before it got dark. Amanda could not believe this wonderful day was over—and that her long-awaited wedding night was soon to begin.

"You and Chad will distribute the children's gifts to-night?" Amanda whispered to Garnet.

"Yes, of course. But you said you wanted to take Jesse's to him on the way? With Caroline like she is, you all sure?"

"Yes," Lincoln said. "It's right on our way—and it's the right thing. We want her to know that the boy—her too—are still part of Median, despite what she and Jess did."

As everyone trooped out to bid them farewell, Lincoln lifted Amanda up before him on Swaggart's big horse, then mounted in the saddle behind her. A thick roll of bedding and two saddlebags bulging with supplies were tied on behind Lincoln.

"If you don't come back in a week, I'm gonna get another horse and come looking for you to serve your probation sentence," Swaggart called out to Lincoln with a loud guffaw.

"He's already begun to serve a lifetime sentence today," Seth Raleigh shouted, "and seems happy enough about it!"

People called out mingled farewells and blessings as they plodded down the lane. A light snow began to fall, though it wasn't sticking to the ground yet. The temperature was tumbling; they could see their breaths, which mingled every time they talked or kissed.

They rode through town and turned up the lane to Boyds'. Lincoln reined in the horse before the door. He lifted Amanda down slowly, sliding her against him. "We're here to give Jesse gifts, not exchange our own yet," Amanda teased. Just as Lincoln bent to kiss her, the door opened and the boy stood there.

"Oh, thought I heard a horse, and knew it wasn't Uncle Tate. Mama, it's snowing some. Come and see!"

"Your uncle will be here soon," Lincoln told Jesse as Caroline appeared, standing behind him as if she meant to hide. "We missed both of you at the wedding, but we understand how you wouldn't want to celebrate right now, losing Jess and all."

"But," Amanda added, stepping forward with the gifts in her arms, "since it's Christmas Eve, Caroline, we hope you'll let Jesse celebrate just a little. Here—a book on George Washington's life and a checkerboard. No checkers, but I'll bet you and your Uncle Tate can make some."

Amanda stood with the gifts in her outstretched arms. "Jumping Jehoshaphat!" Jesse whispered under his breath. But he hesitated and turned back toward his mother. Amanda thought the lines in Caroline's face looked softer now.

"We are much obliged," Caroline said, her voice breaking so she had to clear her throat. "Go ahead, son, and don't forget your manners. Amanda, I'm so sorry I acted crazy the other day. And Lincoln, about what Jess did . . ."

"It's all right, Caroline," Lincoln said. "You just remember, there's a new year coming soon—for all of Median."

"I'm glad my boy has a book to practice his reading in, and that ham was mighty fine—Jess's last dinner at home . . ." She turned away. But Jesse took the gifts with a wide grin.

"Don't thank us for those things," Amanda told the boy and ruffled his red hair. "Let's just say they're from Santa's magic trunk."

He thanked them anyway and went to show his mother, calling out, chattering to her as he shut the door behind him.

"A good enough beginning," Amanda said, not budging for a moment.

"I'll send a message to Jess through the hobos later if she wants. Who knows but when the army is finally gone if he can't return," he mused aloud as he lifted Amanda back up on the horse.

"I hate to say it, but maybe she'll be better without Jess after everything."

"Yes. Tate admires her too. But I don't envy them trying to live together with Jess somehow between them."

They did not speak again as they left the town and took the lane past the stream and grove called Sweet Springs and the curving path up the side of Laurel Mountain. It was enough for Amanda to sit before him, sheltered in his arms as the wind sang carols in the pines and snow sifted down to seal them together. The higher they went the darker it got, the thicker the trees, the deeper the snow, the more silent the scene, but she was not afraid. The horse had been here so recently that it seemed to know its way.

"There!" Lincoln said at last and pointed at the little, one-room cabin on a rise framed by snow-etched trees.

She looked, remembered, and rejoiced. For once, outside the little workshed in Lockwood, she had caught a mind's-eye glimpse of that cabin. But she didn't tell him now, for words caught in her throat at this precious place and the blessings that had brought her to it.

He carried her over the threshold, stopping to kiss her under the mistletoe he'd hung above the door. They unloaded quickly, and he bedded down the horse in a windbreak behind the cabin; he built a fire with wood he had previously laid on the simple stone hearth over which he'd draped swags of evergreen with cones. It was the most wonderful job of Christmas decorating she had ever seen.

He'd made a bed of fresh pine boughs under blankets. Proudly, she flapped their new quilt over the bed. A crooked table with a crock full of orange-red bittersweet on it, two chairs, one window overlooking the valley below, that was all, but it was enough and more to break her heart with its beauty. For anywhere with Lincoln was a place of glad and golden hours like these.

"Are you hungry?" she asked as the flames flared and they stood side-by-side to warm their hands.

"With that wedding feast? No, Amanda, for once I'm not hungry for anything but you."

They came together in a firm embrace that turned fierce, then frenzied. When a log rolled and sparks flew like fireworks, they jumped apart and laughed like children as she shook out her skirt and he kicked the log and embers back in place.

"Our first home," she told him and returned to his arms.

"I've always felt at home with you," he whispered in her ear.

Somewhere from snowy clouds above, she heard the angels sing.

Author's Note

My description of fictional Lockwood, Ohio, was inspired by a real boom-and-bust canal town I dearly love, Milan, Ohio. Although Milan is mostly known as being the birthplace of Thomas A. Edison (in a house which can be visited and in which my great-great-grandfather, Henry Loher, was also born), it is a lovely place to visit to just soak in the small-town, historical ambience.

Median, Mississippi, is loosely based on the town of Meridien, Mississippi, which Sherman's army burned before it began its famous (or infamous, from the southern point of view) March to the Sea.

The recipes included in this book are ones which have been in my or my husband's families for years, with two exceptions: the apple cake is from Carla Noll, a former fellow teacher; and the pecan pie is from our southern-born-and-bred friend and now our neighbor, Mattie Chappel.

Like Amanda, I love to bake, especially at holiday time, and I hope you do too. It is a joyously busy time of the year, but one in which we must save enough time for sharing our God-given gifts—especially time and love—with people around us. For, besides heaven's angels, there can be earth-bound ones too.

KAREN HARPER